Boogiepop

BOOGIEPOP OMNIBUS 1-3

Follow Seven Seas Entertainment online at sevenseasentertainment.com.

TRANSLATION: Andrew Cunningham
ADAPTATION: Patrick King
COVER DESIGN: KC Fabellon
CHAPTER TITLE DESIGN: Nicky Lim
INTERIOR LAYOUT & DESIGN: Clay Gardner
DIGITAL MANAGER: CK Russell
LIGHT NOVEL EDITOR: Nibedita Sen
EDITOR-IN-CHIEF: Adam Arnold
PUBLISHER: Jason DeAngelis

ISBN: 978-1-626929-17-3
Printed in Canada
First Printing: October 2018
10 9 8 7 6 5 4 3 2 1

"Apparently the Boogiepop stories were being kept secret from the boys. A myth only the girls knew."
– Suema Kazuko

"I think he loved her more than I did."
– Tanaka Shiro

"An alien. He took her with him back into space."
– Kimura Akio
"So, all it ultimately amounts to is nothing?"
– Niitoki Kei

"Why can't we pick who we fall in love with? It would be so much easier..."
– Kamikishiro Naoko
"Which is it? Which is the truth?"
– Echoes

Boogiepop and others

written by
Kouhei Kadono

illustrated by
Kouji Ogata

english translation by
Andrew Cunningham

Prelude

OPENING THE SHOJI SCREEN, the boy took a step onto the tatami of the darkened tea room.

"........."

Wordlessly, he stared into the center of the room. Cushions and low tables were scattered everywhere.

Only a small amount of light managed to pierce the decorative screen above the door and enter the room, making it difficult to see anything clearly. But he could see the scene easily enough.

In the center of the room was a girl. One look and he knew she was dead.

She was upside-down, thick white cotton socks on slender legs thrust into the air like the arms of a cheerleader at a pep rally. Her shoulders were limp on the floor, her head twisted around so it faced the same direction as her body. There was no blood anywhere.

Her long black hair seemed to flow across the tatami, and her vacant eyes just seemed to stare back at the boy.

"........."

The boy took a slow step backwards.

As he did, something hot slid downwards from above, just grazing the tip of his nose.

Startled, he glanced upward towards the ceiling.

He froze.

"You saw me," said the killer hanging from the ceiling. It wore a girl's shape, but was a creature of indeterminate gender. "Now that you have seen me, I cannot allow you to live." Its voice was somewhere between laughing and singing.

A moment later, the boy felt his body flung aside, as the creature lunged down towards him.

"—Gah!"

For some reason, the boy felt oddly happy.

* * *

...The actual events probably form a very simple story. From a distance, they appear to be quite confusing; to have no clear threads connecting them whatsoever, but the reality is that this is undoubtedly a much more straightforward, commonplace tale.

But from our individual standpoints, none of us were quite able to see the whole picture. All of the people who somehow had a part in this story were unable to see beyond their own unique role.

My name is Niitoki Kei.

I'm in my second year at Shinyo Academy, although I'm so small that I'm often mistaken for a junior high school student, or worse, some elementary school kid. Despite all this, I'm the president of the student discipline committee.

"Kei's like a big sister. She might look like a kid, but there's just something reliable about her," my friends always tell me, half-mockingly.

I don't consider myself to be a particularly serious person, but everyone around me seems to think that I am. They're always asking me for some type of advice or help, and I've got a major sort of glitch where I can't ever seem to tell them no.

"Can you, Kei?"

"Niitoki, please!"

Someone says these words to me and I just can't settle down.

But this has basically nothing to do with me being on the discipline committee.

Our school is only an average, mid-level sort of place, but like many other high schools, it considers guidance to be the teacher's job, and the discipline committee is just there for decoration. It's sad, really. There are a number of students who have run away from home or gone missing this year, but none of the teachers care enough to put forth any effort into finding them, and all the headmaster does is whine about how much of a headache they are, and how poorly they reflect upon the school. Whatever.

All this negligent attitude does is irritate the hell out of me. My tiny little sense of right and wrong is next to useless. It's not like they'll ever listen to me.

If anything of any significance had happened to us, we wouldn't have been able to do a damn thing about it.

As it was, we knew nothing.

See, all the people close to me, myself included, had no way of knowing each other's problems or just what we were fighting.

We simply had to guess blindly and just act on our gut.

The man who came from the sky, the woman made from his design—the twisted, strange events they brought about must have begun around that time.

Right as my heart had been broken.

Chapter One
Romantic Warrior

Takeda Keiji
third year, class F

1.

THE STORY OF BOOGIEPOP is one that weighs heavily upon me. It's a subject that I still haven't finished sorting out my feelings about.

He's no longer around, but I'm not really sure if I'm supposed to feel relieved about that fact or not.

He was...unusual, to say the least.

I'd never met anyone as strange as him in the seventeen years that I've been alive, and I doubt I ever will again.

After all, he was a transforming superhero.

That sort of thing is only fun if they're on TV. If you're standing right next to one, it causes nothing but trouble. And, in my case, it wasn't exactly somebody else's problem.

I never once saw him smile.

He always looked grim, and would look at me and say depressing things like, "Takeda-kun, this world is filled with flaws." This, with *the exact same pretty face* that always made my head reel.

But Boogiepop is gone now.

I'll never know whether or not everything he told me was a lie.

* * *

One Sunday, with the middle of fall fast approaching, I was standing in front of the station, waiting for my girlfriend, Miyashita Touka. We were supposed to meet at eleven, but it was already three o'clock, and she had yet to appear.

Did I mention she was a year younger than me? Apparently, her family was pretty strict, and for some stupid reason, I was expressly forbidden from even attempting to call her house. All I could ever do was simply wait for her to get in contact with me. So, once again, I was forced to stand there fretting while I patiently tried to wait for her to show.

"Hey, Takeda-senpai!" someone called out.

I turned around to find Saotome standing there. He was my kouhai, on the same committee as I was. There were three other students with him, two of them girls.

"What's this, a double date?" I said, aware that I was coming off as old-fashioned.

"Something like that. You waiting for yours?" Saotome gave off pretty much the same impression whether in uniform or out. Wherever he was, he seemed to blend in. "You do realize that dating's against school rules, right?"

"Look who's talking."

"Oh, you're on the discipline committee as well?" the guy next to Saotome asked.

Oh, yeah, sorry, I thought...but I couldn't say that to a kouhai, so I just shrugged.

"Then I guess we've got nothing to worry about," he said, putting his arm around the shoulders of the girl next to him.

Guess they were together. Go figure.

"Yeah, I don't give a damn either, but the teachers are a different matter. Better keep an eye out so they don't catch you," I grumbled.

They all gave knowing laughs, then nodded and took their leave. As they walked off, I heard one of the girls say, "Guess who's been dumped!"

All I could think was, *Mind your own damn business!*

I mean, it's not that I actually like being on the discipline committee. It's just that someone had to take the job and that someone ended up being me.

That day, Touka never did show.

(Have I really been dumped? Surely there would have been some sort of warning, right?)

I waited despondently until five, unable to let things go.

I knew I had to, though.

I dragged myself away, feeling like the world had cast me aside. I was the only person in my class not going to college. Heck, everyone else was off studying for entrance exams. It's no wonder I felt so left out.

Then it happened.

Staggering towards me was the kind of guy who would stand out in any crowd.

He was a skinny young man, with roughly cropped hair that stood on end. He wore a badly torn, dirty white shirt that was just flung over his body. The shirt was unbuttoned, leaving his bare chest exposed. The bottoms of his pants legs trailed along the ground as his bare, shoeless feet shuffled across the pavement.

There was a serious looking wound on his head, and half his face was covered in blood. Though mostly dried, the blood stuck to his hair in clumps. One look at him, and I knew he was a mess, yet I couldn't avert my gaze.

His eyes were unfocused, and he was moaning aloud. This was not some new fashion, but clearly a bona fide, genuinely crazy psychopath. Probably on drugs.

(Yeesh, there are actually guys like this showing up in our town now, too...?)

Spooked, I averted my course, giving him a wide berth. Everyone else was doing the same, so there was a sort of air pocket forming around him.

He tottered along in the center for a few moments.

Then, suddenly, he collapsed to the ground.

Before anyone could react, he began to sob quietly.

"Enhhh...enhhhhh..." he sniveled. "Unngghhhhh."

Great, slobby tears rolled down his cheeks, heedless of his surroundings.

A circle of people—myself among them—formed around him, watching. None of us dared move towards him.

It was the strangest thing that I'd ever seen.

It was bizarre, like something out of a surreal Eastern European movie.

But there was one person who did approach him.

He was shorter than me and dressed in a long, black cape with a collar that wrapped around him like a great coat, and a black hat like a shrunken pipe or a top hat without a brim. The hat was a size too big for his head, and half covered his eyes.

On the hat and cape bits of metal gleamed, like rivets or some sort of badge, sewn along the hem. It gave off the impression of armor.

To match his all-black outfit, he wore black lipstick. His face was so white; it was like the ink painted on top of a glossy Noh mask.

Clearly, this was another crazy person on the loose.

The cloaked figure leaned his black hat over to the side, and whispered in the psycho's ear.

The psycho stared up at the cloaked figure with empty eyes.

"......"

The man nodded and the psycho stopped crying.

There was a slight stir from the crowd around them. It seemed that some form of silent communication had been established.

The cloaked figure's face snapped up and glared around at us. It was clear that he was seething with anger.

"Do you think to do nothing when you see a fellow human crying?!" he suddenly shouted, loud and angry, in a clear, boyish soprano voice. "Is this what the advancement of civilization has lead to?! Urban life weeding out and killing the weak?! It's appalling!"

The crowd concluded that he was simply another loony and avoided eye contact, quickly dispersing. I started to follow suit, but he spun towards me, catching my eye. It was then that I finally got a clear look at his face.

Words can't begin to do justice to the shock I felt at that moment.

Perhaps the best example I can give is to describe it like one of those nopperabou ghost stories—you expect a faceless ghost, but instead, the ghost looks just like *you*. At first you just don't get it, but then you do, and it totally freaks you out.

I stared at him, eyes wide open and mouth agape.

But for him, I seemed to be little more than another face in the crowd, and he soon shifted his glare to the man next to me.

Two policemen came rushing up. At last, someone had reported the psycho.

"That him?"

"Get up!"

The policemen roughly tried to yank the man to his feet. He made no attempt to resist.

"No need to be so violent. He's afraid," the black-hatted figure said, not fazed by the idea of lecturing policemen either.

"What are you? His family?"

"Just passing by," the figure replied softly. "Don't twist his arm like that!"

"Step aside!" the policeman shouted, as another tried to shove the cloaked figure away.

But the cloaked figure bent his body like a dancer, and evaded the policeman's sweaty arm.

"Wah!" the policeman cried, overbalancing and falling to his knees.

It was like some kind of kung fu, or maybe tai chi. All I know is that the cloaked figure's motions came off as being extremely graceful and fluid.

"This is what happens when you resort to violence," the cloaked figure spat.

"And that's what I call interfering with a police officer!" the cop bellowed, springing to his feet.

"Try performing your duty before you accuse me of interfering with it. It is your job to save people who are in trouble, not to trample them beneath your feet," the cloaked figure said, as if delivering a speech.

Meanwhile, the police had forgotten about the psycho, who had begun aimlessly tottering off down the street again with surprising speed.

The policemen turned hurriedly to give chase, shouting, "Hey, you! Stop right there!"

The cloaked figure in the black hat spun around, his cape fluttering, and dashed away.

"Ah! Wait!" The policemen clearly couldn't decide which quarry to chase.

The cloaked figure moved like the wind, and vanished just as quickly around the next corner.

I was left standing there, stunned.

I was not stunned because of the cloaked figure's bizarre behavior. Well, maybe I was, but much more shocking was having the image of his face burned into my eyes. The hat was low on his face and partially concealed it, but there was no mistaking those big, almond shaped eyes...they belonged to the girl that I had been waiting for all day—Miyashita Touka!

And thus ended my first encounter with the mysterious cloaked figure—Boogiepop.

2.

THE NEXT DAY, I went to school earlier than usual.

The school I go to, Shinyo Academy, has that *something* a lot of other schools don't. Every student has an ID card, and every time we go in or out of the building, we have to slide it through a gate checker, like one of those ticket readers at the train station. They call it the Campus Advanced Information Administration System (or CAIAS, for short). Supposedly it helps the staff keep track of the exact number of students that attend, since the student population has started to decline as of late.

But in actuality, it doesn't really change anything. Despite the grand design, this year, there have already been several students who have run away from home, or worse, simply vanished. The system they're so proud of is really powerless when it comes to stopping students from doing whatever they like once they're off school grounds. It's what free will is all about.

Anyway, our school is up in the mountains, so we have to walk up long, steep, green roads just to get there. On this particular morning, there was hardly anybody out on the road. The sports teams had long since started morning practice, but the rest of the student body had not yet started to arrive.

"Yoohoo! *Keiji*!!" came a cheerful girl's voice from behind.

I turned around to find a girl from my class, Kamikishiro Naoko, walking towards me.

This girl had a habit of over-pronouncing people's names, like she was sight-reading a word in some other language. Plus, she was always chirpy.

"Now, now. Why so gloomy on such a *beautiful* morning?" she said, running to catch up, and thumping me hard on the back.

Both Kamikishiro and I were breaking the school rules against dating. You could say that it gave us a certain connection; a certain ease to our interaction. A sort of sympathy that we couldn't expect to get from friends of the same gender. We always joked around together, but today I was hardly in the mood.

"You're early," I said curtly. "Not going for your usual dramatic entrance?"

Kamikishiro was almost compulsively late and she always insisted that it was due to low blood pressure. If a teacher tried to chew her out for it, she would apologize dramatically—and quite flirtatiously, I might add, which generally left the male teachers flustered, but always seemed to do the trick, getting her off the hook. A powerful technique, indeed.

"Yeah, well, had some stuff to take care of today. But spill already! How was your date yesterday?"

"F-forget about it."

"You have a fight or something?" she asked, peering closely at my face with interest. She had a tendency to express her emotions a bit too obviously. She was very pretty, but had an open, loud laugh. This seemed to make some people think badly of her, no matter how good a person she was at heart.

"A fight? I wish we could have," I sighed.

"Wait, what? That sounds serious!"

"Whatever."

Another student passed us on a bicycle, so we fell quiet.

As always, there was a committee member posted at the gates, like a train station guard, making sure the cards went through the gate check smoothly.

"Oh, Takeda-senpai, you're early," said today's guard, Niitoki Kei. She was the discipline committee president. Despite the ominous title, she was a tiny, cute girl with a childish face.

"D-ditto," I said, waving. We'd been on the health board together last year as well, so we had seen each other regularly for two years.

"Mornin', *Kei*!" said Kamikishiro. Although they were friends already, Niitoki had ignored Kamikishiro's dates on several occasions, and this had brought them even closer together.

"My, my, are you two *together* now?" Niitoki said, eyes wide.

"That's scary, coming from you," Kamikishiro laughed.

"I didn't mean it that way, really. Even if it were true, my lips are sealed."

"Trying to earn a favor, eh? Looks expensive."

"It is," the committee president laughed.

If she knew that Kamikishiro had both a second and first year student in her saddle, I doubt she could have been so blasé about it. She was pretty serious, and she would probably get so angry that steam would shoot out of her ears.

We put our cards through the gate check and went inside.

"Senpai, don't forget the meeting today!" she said as I waved in acknowledgement.

Kamikishiro giggled. "She's so cute."

"Who?"

"*Kei*. You know she's got a crush on you, right? Puppy love..."

"You're one to talk."

Every relationship she had ended up like a war zone. I'm amazed she could still joke about it.

"So what was it? *Fuji-chan* dump you?" Who knows why Kamikishiro always called Touka by a different reading of the kanji in her name, but here she was doing it again.

"She stood me up."

"I can see why you got chest pains, then! Ah ha ha!!"

I suspected that she, too, stood up many a man.

"What are girls thinking when they do that?" I asked. "It sure as hell isn't about their boyfriend."

"That's not an easy thing to answer. Hmm... It all depends, really. I know that it's not always because they don't want to see you, though. You know, stuff just sort of comes up."

"So what if they stand you up and dress like a man?"

"Hunh? What are you talking about?! What's that supposed to mean?" Kamikishiro's eyes widened.

Understandably. I didn't know the answer either.

"Never mind. Must have been seeing things."

"I don't really get it...but you've got a lot of time on your hands, so you really ought to start taking love more seriously, ya hear?" she said in a sing-song voice.

"What?" I replied, scowling, and she burst into song.

Life is brief, young maiden, fall in love;
before the crimson bloom fades from your lips,
before the tides of passion cool within your hips,
for those of you who know no tomorrow.

"You're in a good mood. You in love *again*?"

"Kinda. Tee hee hee."

"For crying out loud, how many is this now?"

Before we hit the halls, we smoothly shifted to a more standoffish attitude. We weren't going out, but it was never a good idea to start any rumors.

I let my feet carry me to Touka's class.

Once there, it wasn't like I could actually talk to her, so I wasn't exactly sure why I was going—I just couldn't seem to help myself.

Touka's room was year two, class C, and it was still empty.

Feeling suddenly tired, I flopped down on a chair inside.

Once again, the cloaked figure's words ran through my mind: *Do you think to do nothing when you see a fellow human crying?!*

I paused for a moment.

Was that *really* Touka?

A twin brother, perhaps…?

No, she'd never mentioned one before.

I heard someone coming, so I quickly got up and left the room.

I stood as inconspicuously as I could in the covered passage, a few yards away from the room, and kept watch. The more I watched, the more pathetic I felt.

(Aw, hell…)

Touka was about the twentieth student to arrive.

She was the same as always. There was no sign of any strange hat.

But for some reason, she had an enormous Spalding bag in addition to her usual school bag. The sort that people generally keep sneakers or gym clothes in.

Then she noticed me.

She shot me a quizzical, innocent glance.

I found myself grinning and nodding.

She smiled softly and nodded back.

Nothing different than usual.

She didn't seem at all bothered about having stood me up either.

So as not to get noticed, we hardly ever spoke to each other at school. But words weren't necessary. We had worked out our own sort of sign language that only the two of us knew.

So I made one of those signs, putting my index finger up. This sign meant back of the garden after school.

She made the same gesture, showing consent.

Yeah, it was just like nothing had happened.

Feeling like I was surrounded by a heavy smoke cloud, I drifted back to my own classroom.

Kamikishiro wasn't there yet. Probably still 'taking care of stuff.' Same as me.

* * *

The discipline committee meeting was during lunch.

"Ehem. I expect that all of you have noticed, but this year, discipline has become rather slack. There are now four girls, students here, who appear to have run away."

They called it a meeting, but we hardly ever spoke at all. The teacher in charge always droned on and on at us the whole time.

Frankly, we may have been called the discipline committee, but not one of us was operating under the illusion we could actually control anybody. Most of us were, like me, breaking those rules ourselves.

The boy I met in town yesterday, Saotome, was the secretary. He took minutes in a notebook. Despite double dating on the side, he melted right into the atmosphere here, like a model committee member.

"If any of you happen to hear about anything like that, then please, come running to me. One of their friends might be able to get in touch with them."

We made no response. We never did. The teacher never seemed to notice.

"Incidentally, the infamous Kirima Nagi failed to arrive this morning. Make sure to keep an eye on her, hear? No telling what that girl's plotting in the shadows."

He glanced sharply around the room.

We remained silent.

The only sound was the scritching of Saotome's pen, jotting down absurdly complete minutes.

Suddenly, the PA system crackled to life.

"...Miyashita Touka, second year, class C. Please, return to the infirmary at once. Miyashita Touka, second year, class C..."

I jerked in my seat, and it made a screeching sound on the floor.

"Mm? Something the matter?" The teacher glared at me balefully.

"I, uh, feel dizzy," I said to excuse my actions, but in fact my head was reeling.

"Are you okay, senpai?" the president asked. "You look pale."

"Third year? You go on back to class."

Seniors had exams to study for and didn't really play a major role on the committee. Heck, they didn't even need to come the meetings in the first place. Of course, I wasn't taking exams, but the teacher hadn't bothered to remember that, apparently.

"Okay."

I stood up, and the president followed suit.

"Sensei, I'll take him to the infirmary."

The teacher made a face, but then simply ordered her to hurry back.

"...That okay?" I asked Niitoki.

"Are *you* okay?" she whispered back.

I said nothing else, but rushed to the infirmary.

There was no one there.

I let out a huge sigh of relief.

The announcement had asked Touka to "return," so she must have been there before, but gone out again.

(No, she was supposed to go home, but she must still be on campus. Her card hasn't been swiped through the gate...)

Thinking furiously, I slumped down on the bench beside me.

"...You're worried about her?" Niitoki asked.

"Yeah, a little."

I looked up, and she spoke quickly, stiffly, "I thought as much. I'm in the same class as her."

I gaped at her, but she kept talking.

"She's been a little off recently. Like she can't sit still. Glaring outside during class. The teacher yells at her about it a lot. I thought she might be having trouble with you or something."

I had no answer.

"I like you too, you know. But—"

"........."

"But it looks like you like her more than me."

She was glaring at me now.

I couldn't think of any way to respond.

"I'm going back now," she snapped, and bolted out of the infirmary.

Needless to say, I was out of it for pretty much the rest of the day.

* * *

After class, I went to the place where we had agreed to meet, but Touka wasn't there.

Sunlight barely filtered down to the deserted rear of the building, so it was quite dark around me.

I threw my bag on the ground, shoved my hands in my pockets, and leaned against the wall.

I couldn't figure out what to do next, so I stared aimlessly up at the sky.

The edge of the school roof made a clear straight line cutting the sky in half.

But there was a shadow jutting over that line.

I gasped in shock.

It was the silhouette of a person. A person with a flat, pipe-like protrusion on their head, wrapped in what seemed like a cape.

At that moment, I knew it was him. It was the mysterious cloaked figure.

When he saw me, he spun around and pulled away.

I yelled towards him, "W-wait!"

Right beside me, there was an old fire escape. It was connected to windows on each floor and went all the way to the roof.

I vaulted the locked gate at the bottom and raced up the stairs to the roof—in clear violation of school policy.

When I hit the roof, I yelled, "Miyashita! That you?!"

The cloaked figure slowly emerged from the shadows. He stared directly at me again.

"You...know Miyashita Touka?" he said in Touka's voice. It was a little deeper, more male sounding, but if you listened for it, it was clearly hers. "I see. We met yesterday, didn't we? I have done you wrong. I ignored you, and for that...I apologize."

I rushed over to him and grabbed him by the shoulders.

"What the hell are you talking about?!"

Suddenly, my body was flying through the air, and then came crashing down upon the concrete with a hard thud.

"——?!"

Had he swept my legs out from under me? The pain raced through my entire body before I figured it out.

"What... What's going on?" I cried.

"I should state clearly that I am not Miyashita Touka. Currently, I am Boogiepop," the cloaked figure whispered.

"C-currently?"

So, Miyashita had been herself this morning? Is that what he meant?

"I'm sure you've heard the idea before. Simply put, it resembles the concept of the split personality. Understand me so far?" this "Boogiepop" continued.

"S-split—?"

"None of you have noticed yet, but danger is hovering over this school...and all mankind. That is why I have emerged."

I couldn't quite decide if I really should be referring to Boogiepop as "he" or not, but I could tell from his expression that he was deadly serious.

3.

THAT EVENING, I called Touka's house directly.

"Miyashita speaking," her mother answered.

In my most serious voice, I said, "Hello. This is Takeda from the Shinyo Academy discipline committee. Is Touka present?"

When she heard the words "discipline committee," Touka's mother made a little gasping sound into the receiver.

"H-has Touka done anything...? But we haven't seen *that* since she started high school..."

That?

"I'd like to speak to her directly, if possible."

"O-of course! Just a moment," she said in a much too respectful tone for some high school kid. Any other mother would have just said, "Hang on a sec," or something equally trite. She must have been distressed.

"Touka speaking," said Touka, in her usual voice.

"Hi, it's Takeda."

"Yes?" she said flatly. Presumably her mother was hovering near by.

Apparently, the Miyashita residence still didn't have any other extensions.

"Did you go somewhere this Sunday?"

"Not really," she said, knocking the receiver twice. I took this to mean the same as two fingers held up in our sign language. It meant, *Sorry, not right now.*

Obviously, I already knew that, but I had to ask anyway.

"Hey."

"Yes?"

"You ever heard of Boogiepop?"

"Eh?" she said blankly. I'd caught her completely off guard. "What's that?" She wasn't acting. She really didn't know.

"Never mind. It's not important. I just really wanted to hear your voice, is all. Sorry."

"Thank you," she said, very politely as if for her mother's benefit. I translated it as a sign of pleasure.

So, it looked like she didn't hate me after all.

"Then I'll see you tomorrow at school."

"Sounds good."

I hung up first, and silence overcame me.

I crossed my arms and tried to think. That Boogiepop guy had been right. Touka had completely forgotten about our date the day before, as well as our promise to meet after school today.

* * *

"She doesn't know," he had said, standing on the school roof, in the light of the setting sun. "If something threatens to erode her foothold of ignorance, she instantly ceases to know that as well. To erase the anomaly caused by not meeting you yesterday, she will have deleted all memories of the date from her mind."

"Deleted?" I said, still reeling, barely keeping up. "You mean, she's forgotten that we were supposed to meet?"

"Precisely. But this is assuredly not because she doesn't take you seriously. Quite the reverse. I imagine she loves you quite a lot. Which is exactly why she needs to forget so thoroughly."

"How so?"

"So that she doesn't feel guilty. She doesn't want to even think about you being mad at her. But *that* is something beyond her control," he said from her very own lips.

"What exactly *are* you? How long have you been...possessing her?"

"Possessing? Can't say I like that choice of words. It's not like I chose to appear."

"Then why do you?!"

"Because danger is upon us," he said, gazing at me levelly.

I flinched. His gaze held daggers.

"I am automatic. When I detect adversity approaching, I float up out of Miyashita Touka. That's why I am Boogiepop—phantasmal, like bubbles."

"Adversity? What kind of...?"

"There is a devil nesting in this school."

I know that sounds absolutely nuts coming from me, but when he said it, the look in his eyes was unmistakable—he was completely serious.

The setting sun sent long shadows across the roof. Boogiepop's black clothes made him look half invisible and he virtually faded into the darkness.

"It's hidden among you now, but it poses a very real threat. It has barely begun to stir, but once it does, it will mean the end of the world."

His words were the ravings of a lunatic, but if you actually looked at him and heard his voice, they were horribly convincing.

"Are... Aren't you the same thing?" I asked, resisting him with everything I had. For me, this man taking up residence in Touka's body was pretty much the same as the end of the world.

Touka's other personality replied calmly, "I'm aware of that, which is why I never come out for long. This is also automatic. The rest of the time, I live peacefully as Miyashita Touka, gazing at you with ardor."

"Ardor? Hey...!"

There was something antiquated about his manner of speaking. He even called me "kimi," like a scholar from the Meiji era.

"My time today will shortly end. There is little meaning in my keeping watch like this, once school is over. Everyone has already gone home."

"...So this dangerous being you've been going on about is one of the students?" I found myself asking.

Boogiepop nodded, "Most likely."

"What is it, exactly?"

"It is better if you don't know."

"Why?"

"Because it is too dangerous. If you know more, something might happen to you. I would prefer to keep Miyashita Touka's lover out of harm's way."

I know I'm repeating myself, but he really does keep saying this with her face and her voice.

"If it's that dangerous, I think I should know. That body doesn't belong to you alone, you know." Even as I spoke, part of me was arguing that I shouldn't take this guy seriously. Clearly, this was all just a paranoid delusion, caused by some bizarre psychological disease, brought about by an instability in Touka's mind—yet the creature before me was Touka and not Touka at the same time. I couldn't think otherwise.

Boogiepop sighed. "All right, but don't tell anyone else."

"Right," I replied, swallowing hard. I steeled myself for anything.

But his words were too simple, and caught me by surprise.

"It's a man-eater."

* * *

After I called Touka's house, I slumped dejectedly on my bed.

My head was a mess.

A split personality?

The school—no, the entire *world* was in danger?

What the hell?!

As delusions went, it was pretty damn delusional. It was like one of those crazy school-bound RPGs.

(But I don't want to exactly go and drag Touka off to some psych ward...)

Boogiepop had said Touka forgets everything. So, in a

worst-case scenario, even if we went to a hospital and had a doctor look at her, Boogiepop might never even appear. That would make her seem like the sane one, while whoever took her would come off looking like a complete idiot.

On the way home from school, I had bought a paperback called *The Scream Inside—Multiple Personality Disorder*, so I decided to delve into it then. I'd just grabbed the easiest looking one, but to my surprise, there had been an entire section in the bookstore on psychological disorders. Surely, the world was crazy enough already without all these diseases, I thought.

The writer wrote in a very conversational tone, so it was readable enough, but the sentences were filled with difficult words that left my head spinning. I did catch the phrase, "This disease is exceedingly rare—if not almost unheard of—in Japan."

As far as I could tell, multiple personality disorder generally arises when someone is trapped in an oppressive situation and unable to cope with reality, shifting their emotions onto another personality in an attempt to create a new life. "The human psyche is open to the possibilities of both good and evil. In my opinion, multiple personality disorder occurs when one of these possibilities, suppressed by societal pressures, declares independence and begins to fight to exist. Regardless of how diseased the result or how destructive it is on the host body and those around it, the possibility makes no distinction between good or evil." There was a lot of stuff like this where I kind of understood what I was reading, but at the same time, didn't. Apparently in Japan, the basis for this type of action usually didn't have a clear form, which meant that the vast majority of incidents would result in schizophrenia rather than multiple personality disorder. To me, it's like talking about the difference between "God" and "The Universe."

The author's name was Kirima Seiichi. There wasn't an author's profile attached to the book, so I had no way of telling who he was or what his credentials were. But somehow, what I'd read just felt right.

(Then what sort of possibility was Boogiepop? What had suppressed him?)

I flopped back onto bed and stared at the ceiling.

Do you think to do nothing when you see a fellow human crying?!

Those words rang through my head again. For some reason, I just couldn't stop thinking about them.

* * *

"...So that's what it said. What do you think?" I asked Boogiepop. It was the next day after school, and we were both on the roof again.

"A suppressed possibility? Hmm... Not a bad explanation, I suppose."

Miyashita had not been in class, so I'd swung by the roof on the off chance he was around. It seemed as though he took over the moment classes ended.

"However, in my case, I am not one of Miyashita Touka's other possibilities."

"Then what are you?"

"Good question. This world's...?" he said quite naturally.

For a moment, I couldn't grasp his meaning. It felt as though he hadn't finished his sentence, but, instead, had just let it trail off. *This world's...?* This world's *what*?

Ignoring my blank look, he forged on, "I have no autonomy. I have no idea what Miyashita Touka might be thinking. She may well have some possibility, some hidden desire that produced me. But that has nothing to do with me. I have no dreams. I have only my duty. I am here only to carry out my purpose."

"To save mankind?"

"Yes."

"Why you?"

"I do not know. I would like to," Boogiepop sighed, staring up at the sky above.

Not looking at me, he continued, "So you wish to 'cure' me, then?"

I jumped. Of course, part of me did want to. Miyashita Touka was my girlfriend. But I also felt it wasn't something that I *had* to do.

"Mm, no... I dunno."

I wasn't making a guarded answer to keep an eye on his reaction; I was genuinely not sure any more. It didn't seem like his presence was hurting anyone. Touka herself remained blissfully unaware.

(Only thing it actually interferes with is our dates.)

"I admit it would be better if I did not exist. If only there were no need for me..."

His profile was exactly like that of the girl I loved, and it looked somehow forlorn, so without thinking, I blurted out, "It must be hard for you..."

Not exactly the way you react to the ravings of a delusional multiple personality, I admit.

"Well, I'm hardly ever here, so..."

I'd thought he might be angered by my awkward attempt at sympathy, but he responded quietly. Not crazy at all.

The two of us looked up at the sky. It was cloudy. This time, there was no beautiful sunset...only darkness. There was a chill in the air, and it seemed as though a cold rain might start to fall at any second. It was the kind of day that dampens your spirit.

"Can I ask you something?"

"What's that?"

"The first time I saw you, what did you say to that homeless guy?"

"Nothing important."

"How did you make him stop crying?"

"I just gave him the encouragement he needed. Every person needs help when they're suffering."

"He needed help? How did you know?"

"He was crying. You could tell he was suffering just by looking at him," he said plainly, like it was the most obvious thing in the world.

"But—but..." I sputtered, then sighed. "The rest of us ordinary people can't understand that way of thinking." Even as I said it, I felt pathetic.

"You're a good man," Boogiepop suddenly said.

"Huh?"

"I think I know what Miyashita Touka sees in you."

"Please don't say things like that with her face. When I meet her tomorrow, I won't know what to do..." I said, realizing that this meant I had completely accepted Boogiepop as an independent existence.

Boogiepop made a strange expression. Beneath the low brim of his hat, his left eye narrowed and the right side of his mouth twisted upwards. It was a very asymmetrical expression that Touka herself would never make.

"Don't worry. I am me, and she is herself."

Later, I wondered if that expression was a strained sort of grin, but at the time, it baffled me. It was a sort of grin that seemed both sarcastic and somewhat diabolical at the same time.

I never did see him smile, though.

4

AFTER THAT, it became routine to join Boogiepop on the roof every day as he "kept watch."

"I'm not really part of my class anymore," I complained to him.

"You aren't taking exams?"

"No, my father knows someone who owns a design firm, so I've been working there part time. He said that I had good sense and that I shouldn't bother with college. That I'd be better off just starting to work for him directly."

"The boss' favorite craftsman, then."

Touka had once said, "Are you sure? Sounds risky to me..." but Boogiepop sounded impressed.

Happily, I enthused, "Exactly, a craftsman. That's what a designer is, really. We make what we've been asked to make."

"Seems like you've got both feet on the ground," Boogiepop said, sounding almost jealous. He lived half in some unearthly realm that only he could see.

"But Miyashita thinks it sounds dangerous."

"She would. I don't know her all that well, but there are far more girls who shun romantic men than there are those who are attracted to them."

"Really? I mean, romantic?" It was an embarrassing word.

"I have no such hopes, but I believe humans need some sort of dream. Am I wrong?" Boogiepop always looked especially serious when he said things like this.

"I dunno," I muttered.

"When you have no dream, when you can't imagine a future, that means something in this world is flawed. Unfortunately, it is not I who will battle that flaw, but you and Miyashita Touka," the self-described defender of the world said, staring into the distance.

Based only on his words, and on his outfit, it was impossible to think of him as anything, but a clown. After all, he had a woman's face, but he talked like a man.

But if he was a clown, then I wanted to be a clown, too.

* * *

Being with him, talking with him, I could see no traces of Touka anywhere. What had happened to her to make him appear?

"When did you first come out?" I asked, one day.

"About five years ago. Miyashita's parents were fighting, considering divorce. Her uncertain feelings at the time may have produced a stubborn creature like me. But I, myself, was far too busy fighting a killer that was stalking the streets to really pay much attention."

I had a hunch which killer he was talking about. Five years ago, a serial killer had murdered five girls, and hung himself when it seemed they were about to catch him. It was a very well-known story, so it made sense for it to be incorporated into his delusion.

"Miyashita's mother sounded like she knew about you..." I trailed off.

"Mm, she's seen me a few times. We're talking back in Junior High, after all. Miyashita Touka was not exactly free to move around. She even caught me climbing out the window once."

"Must have been surprised."

"She was hysterical, which caused me no end of trouble. She locked me in the house, so I had to knock the woman out to make my escape. Danger was approaching, after all."

"Seriously?" No wonder her mother was freaked. It also explained why the Miyashita household didn't let her have a phone in her room.

"After that, I suspect Miyashita Touka was dragged off to a psychologist, but I can only speculate. I never appeared."

"She didn't show any...unusual signs?"

Since the condition was almost unheard of in Japan, the doctor probably didn't believe a word of it.

"Probably not. I imagine they had their doubts about the mother, though. After all, her parents were having marital problems at the time. But apparently, the whole fuss caused her father to blame himself and make amends. Things settled down after that."

"Hmmm..." This reminded me of something from the book I'd read. Not a multiple personality case, but a manic-depressive girl. At school, she never spoke a word to anyone, but she was always bright and happy at home. Her parents and grandparents were apathetic and cold, and she desperately tried to brighten up the gloomy atmosphere. Unfortunately, the stress was too much for her, and its effects started to manifest externally. Her behavior grew stranger and stranger, until finally she was taken to a doctor and the truth came out. She was treated, her family repented, and the house became a much more peaceful place. This sort of "peace making" psychological disorder is apparently referred to as "the Trickster."

For some reason, it sounded a lot like Boogiepop to me.

"So," I said, and explained all this to him.

He made that strange expression again. "Miyashita Touka may well see it that way."

"But you're still here, even though that situation is over. Why? You never come out at home any more, right?"

"Right."

"Then why?"

"I can't explain it. I simply have my duty to fulfill."

"You'll just disappear when this 'danger' is over?"

"Yes. I will be a little sad to go this time, though. I won't be able to see you again."

This surprised me.

"You won't...?"

"Right. Miyashita Touka will be here, of course. I imagine you prefer her." His shoulders slumped a little.

I couldn't think of anything to say, so I remained silent.

The two of us stared quietly up at the evening sky.

Boogiepop began to whistle. The tune was fast and bright, his breathing skillfully alternating fast and slow, but it was a whistle, so it sounded rather sad somehow.

I remembered that Touka couldn't whistle.

(A suppressed possibility...?)

Even as her boyfriend, I suppose I was suppressing some part of her.

This thought weighed heavily on me.

He finished whistling, and I applauded. "You're good. What song is that?"

"Overture to the first act of 'Die Meistersinger von Nurnberg.'"

"Of what?"

"The most flamboyant piece the noisy, romantic, old composer known as Wagner ever wrote."

"Classical? Hunh. Thought it was rock..."

"You'd have preferred 'Atom Heart Mother'? I tend to like the old music," he said, narrowing one eye.

All of our twilight ramblings passed in this fashion.

5

ONE DAY, Kamikishiro was gone. She just stopped coming to school.

I didn't know much, but it seemed that she had run away.

"You're kidding?" I said as I heard the news.

"Really! The teacher told us. She hasn't come home," one of the girls in class said calmly.

"Why? Why would she run away?"

"I don't know. That girl hardly ever talked to us. I bet she thought her pretty face would let her get by in Tokyo or something," the girl snorted.

The girls in class were much less expressive than Kamikishiro, who was always laughing and joking.

"B-but...she had good grades. She looked like she was ready to pass the entrance exam for the college that she wanted to go to, right?"

"You sure know a lot about her."

"What, did you have a thing for her, Takeda-kun?"

"It's not like that. Still..." I started to say.

The leader of the girls in class, Sasaki, said quietly, "I think I know how she felt. She just...wanted to escape."

"Escape? From what?" I asked, surprised. Kamikishiro had

two boyfriends, one a first year, in the other a second year. I wondered if she was escaping them.

But Sasaki meant something else. "You wouldn't understand, Takeda-kun."

"Why not?"

"Because you don't have exams. How could you possibly understand the pressure?"

I had no defense against that argument.

"Right, you can't understand."

"Yeah, yeah."

The other girls joined in, almost accusatory.

The other students weren't watching us directly, but they weren't not watching, either. They just sort of sat around us, flipping through their vocabulary flashcards.

"I'd run away if I could. But I can't. We're not as irresponsible as Kamikishiro," Sasaki said very coldly.

Everyone nodded.

Not one of them appeared to be the least bit worried about her.

"*...When you see a fellow human crying*," I heard Boogiepop's voice whisper in my ear.

The teacher arrived. We stopped talking and went back to our seats.

I was barely able to sit through class.

The guy in front of me was studying something else. Everyone was only in class for their transcripts; all of them were certain that their test scores were far more important than learning itself.

Even the teachers agreed, so they just lectured tediously, never calling on anyone, never asking if there were any questions.

Why the hell were we even here?

What had happened to Kamikishiro? Had her cheery exterior been a lie? There had been I thought it was, but I hadn't expected her to be the sort of girl to just up and run away.

For those of you who know no tomorrow.

But even so, I was just like the people around me. I knew nothing.

I hadn't even known that Touka was possessed by this Boogiepop guy.

I didn't listen to the teacher for the rest of class, and I sure as hell didn't take any notes. For all my complaints, I was even less serious about this than the people taking exams. Without any purpose, I just sat there stewing.

* * *

That day, Boogiepop wasn't waiting on the roof.

"…………"

I waited for him a while, but eventually the sun set, and I had to give up and go home.

* * *

When I climbed up to the roof the next day, Boogiepop was waiting for me, but this time in a girl's school uniform; no strange costume.

"Hey," he said, raising his hand. This gesture is how I knew it was him. Otherwise, I would have taken him for Touka.

"No costume?"

"Don't need it any more. So she didn't bring it with her."

He had explained once before that Touka would unconsciously carry it around with her, but I hadn't ever thought anything of it until now.

"What do you mean?"

"The danger is over," he said flatly.

"Eh?"

"Everything's finished, Takeda-kun."

"W-wait! That's so..."

"That's all there is to it. That's the way I'm made. When the danger is gone, I disappear. Like bubbles."

"The danger...weren't you going to save the world? It hasn't been saved at all!"

"But my job is finished. What you mean by 'save' is not my job," he said, shaking his head quietly.

"But you said you were going to fight the devil that lives in this school!"

"I did. I'm not the one that killed it, though..."

My mouth flapped wordlessly. I couldn't think of anything else to say. "But...but...that's..."

"Thank you, Takeda-kun," Boogiepop suddenly bowed his

head. "I enjoyed my time with you. Until now, I had never done anything, but fight. You're the first person I could really call a friend. Perhaps you only spent time with me because I'm part of Miyashita Touka, but I had fun. I mean it."

"........."

I suddenly realized just how much I liked him.

I'd liked him since we first met in town.

And not because he had Touka's face.

Everything I wanted to say but couldn't express...he could and would at the drop of a hat. That's why I liked him so much.

"Don't go."

"Eh?"

"Don't go anywhere. You're about the only friend I have. I'd really like to keep meeting you," I hung my head, almost whispering. I may have been crying.

Boogiepop made that face again.

"That's not true, Takeda-kun."

"It is!"

"You simply aren't connecting with the world around you right now."

I stopped breathing.

"Miyashita Touka's worried about you, too. Don't let yourself think you're the only one who's worried."

"But... But what about you? If you just vanished without anyone the wiser, wouldn't that make you sad?"

"You're the wiser, aren't you?"

"But I'm..."

"I'm afraid you and Miyashita Touka have your job to do, just as I have my duty. You two have to make your own world. You don't have time to waste belittling yourself," Boogiepop said curtly.

There was nothing left for me to say. I hung my head and stuttered, "B-but..."

When I looked up...there was nobody there.

Startled, I raced across the roof.

But there was no sign of him anywhere.

Just like the first time I saw him, he'd vanished in the wind.

* * *

When I came down the fire escape, I found Miyashita waiting for me at the bottom.

I could tell instantly that it wasn't him. When she looked at me, she smiled.

"You're late, Takeda-senpai!" she said, in a tumbling voice.

"Eh..."

"You told me to wait here? And then you show up late, you big meany."

I was taken aback. Then, it hit me.

She doesn't know anything.

She doesn't even notice that she doesn't know. Her memories are automatically corrected.

That explained it.

She had automatically created a reason for her to be here.

"Ah, uh... S-sorry. I bumped into a friend."

"On the roof? Were you called out by the school thugs?"

"Does our school even have any?"

"Good point," she laughed.

Suddenly, I felt a great affection for her. "You got cram school today?"

"Yeah, at five."

"I'll walk you to the station."

She looked surprised. "Leave school together?"

"Hey, I'm on the discipline committee."

"You sure?"

"The gate guards are all my kouhai. They'll let us by."

I didn't let her squirm out of it, but we didn't hold hands or anything.

Niitoki was watching the gate. For some reason, the school's problem child, Kirima Nagi, fresh off from suspension the previous Friday, was standing next to her.

She was slim and tall, and all the guys said she was as pretty as a model, but she looked a little harsh to me.

She was the polar opposite of Niitoki, and I was surprised to see them acting so friendly towards one another. When they stood next to each other, they looked like sisters with years between them, or perhaps a mother and child who were closer in age.

"Oh, senpai," Niitoki said, smiling despite seeing her classmate Touka standing next to me.

"Hey," I grunted.

"Hmm. So, you're Miyashita Touka," said Kirima Nagi abruptly, suddenly standing right in front of her.

"Y-yes..."

"I'm Kirima. Nice to meet you," she said, thrusting out her hand. She sounded more like a man.

"Hey!" I said, butting in, but Touka bobbed her head and took the offered hand.

Kirima Nagi made a wry smile that reminded me of Boogiepop, and walked on by.

While we were still stunned, Niitoki said, "Come on now, senpai, Miyashita-san. Run your cards through."

We did as we were told and exited the school.

The road was covered in fallen leaves.

"These maple leaves look so beautiful when they're falling, but once they've fallen, they're just a mess," Touka said, walking carefully to avoid getting them stuck to her shoes.

"Mm, but they're still lovely when they fall."

"That your opinion as a designer?"

"Not really."

"I'm jealous of you, you know," Touka pouted as she suddenly started stomping through the leaves.

"H-hey..."

"I've got to take a quiz on idioms today. I hate it." The leaves squelched beneath her feet as if she were tap dancing.

"You say that, but—"

"But I'm still going to college," she interrupted, still keeping her face turned away from mine, slopping through the leaves. "No matter what you say."

"What I say?" I couldn't remember saying anything against it.

"You went and decided what you were going to do all by yourself. You're all confident now. Like you're snickering at the rest of us."

"That's what..." I was about to say, *Everyone else was doing,* but she looked up at me seriously, and I bit my tongue.

"That was pretty stressful, you know. I thought it was going to eat me alive. But I'm over that now. Finished with it."

She looked up.

I was surprised.

She looked just like Boogiepop.

"To tell you the truth, senpai, I remember standing you up that Sunday."

"Eh?"

"But I wanted to mess with your mind a bit. Sorry," she said, and bowed her head.

Her movements were Touka's. There was no hint of Boogiepop.

(It can't be...)

Her anxiety had called out Boogiepop?

Was that the 'devil in the school'?

Does that mean—that I had defeated it?

She had told me of her worries through Boogiepop, and she no longer needed to be afraid. The "danger" had passed.

I stopped in my tracks. My eyes were wide. Touka was staring at her shoes. "They're all dirty now," she said.

She giggled then, sheepishly.

Boogiepop had said he had no dreams. He never laughed.

"Eh heh heh."

I looked at Touka's pretty, cheerful smile, and thought, Boogiepop can't do *that.*

It's our job to laugh.

Interlude

Backing the story up a little...

SOMEWHERE BETWEEN DAY AND NIGHT, in a dim, gloomy room, a girl lay on her side, without a stitch of clothing on her. She wasn't moving.

The Manticore stood next to her.

The room was silent.

Slowly, elegantly, it stooped over the fallen girl.

It brushed aside the girl's hair, and kissed her on the forehead.

It moved down to her nose, then her chin, neck, chest, stomach, and abdomen, licking each of them, leaving a thin blue trail. Everywhere its saliva touched changed color.

When it had licked the girl all over, the Manticore moved its mouth away.

The girl's body began to change.

All over the surface of her skin, snap, snap, thin cracks tore open.

"............"

The Manticore watched in silence.

At last, the girl's body crumbled inwards, like a mud sculpture left in the sun.

A purple smoke rose into the air.

The Manticore sucked the smoke into its mouth.

The smoke rose and rose, but the Manticore never stopped breathing it in, like a fish tank with the plug removed, sucking it all away. Its throat moved, swallowing it down.

When it had swallowed the last puff, the Manticore ran its tongue over its beautiful, lipstick red lips.

A drop of liquid slipped from the corner of its mouth and rolled off its chin. This drop of liquefied smoke was the color of blood and flesh.

There was no other trace of the girl, or of the smoke.

Oh ho ho!

Oh ho ho!

Oh ho ho ho ho ho...!

In the darkness, the Manticore laughed.

Her name was ancient Persian, and it meant "Man-Eater."

That delicate laugh bloomed like a morning rose, triumphantly extolling its evil.

Chapter Two

The Return of the Fire Witch

Suema Kazuko

second year, class D

1.

RECENTLY, a strange rumor, or rather, a bit of a ghost story, has been spreading among the girls of the second year classes.

It's something about the mysterious Boogiepop.

Boogiepop is short, wears a black cape, and has a tall hat that's sort of like the one Maetel wore in *Galaxy Express 999*, only narrower. He's an assassin, and he can kill people instantly, without pain. He always does so when you are at your most beautiful, before you start to wither away, before you grow old and ugly.

Nobody knows where he's from, but most people seem to agree that he has something to do with the string of missing high school girls in the area.

Everyone wants to believe that the runaways were killed by an assassin that wanders in the shadows, fleeting like the morning mist, instead of running off to Tokyo or some other grim reality.

Reality is always rather dreary. When people vanish from it, it's natural to want to connect them to some sort of fantasy, to some other world.

One day, shortly after summer vacation, I was eating my lunch when the girl in front of me, Kinoshita Kyoko, looked up from her crossword puzzle and asked, "Hey, Suema, what was the actual case that inspired *The Village of Eight Graves*?"

"The Tsuyama Thirty," I said, without a second's thought.

"Hunh, Tsuyama Thirty—hey, it fits. Thanks."

Everyone eating with us was staring at me. "How did you *know* that?"

"You are *obsessed*."

"Don't be stupid, *everyone* knows that."

"We don't! Nobody does!"

"There was a book on it out last month," I replied, in a knowing manner as if to brush them off.

"*We* didn't *read* it! Why would we?"

"You're a little scary, Kazuko."

Everyone cackled.

"What kind of person can murder someone?" Kyoko asked, suddenly looking up from her crossword again.

"What kind? All kinds."

"I mean, like, who in this class seems likely to?" she said, lowering her voice.

"Oooh, do tell, do tell!" Everyone leaned closer.

"Uhhh, someone a little stiff, like they're off in their own little world and are kinda stubborn when it comes to stuff?" Even as I said it, I knew I might as well be saying her name.

"So...Kirima Nagi?" Yep, first name out; the most notorious student in our class. She was skipping today, apparently; no sign of her all morning.

"Hmm, well, she's not normal, that's for sure."

"Not normal? The Fire Witch is six kinds of crazy!"

"She's skipped two days since the new term started. Wonder if she'll even bother coming tomorrow..."

"She might as well not. Even when she does come, she causes trouble the moment she steps through the gates and gets herself sent right back home."

"Kya ha ha! Sounds like her!"

"So far as killing goes, I hear she actually *is*."

"How so?"

"You know, one slip and you miss your period..."

"Ah!"

"Then she gets herself suspended before anyone notices and takes care of it..."

"I believe it!"

There was no evidence at all, but that didn't stop them from talking.

Everyone was laughing, though, so I laughed with them.

I didn't hate her like they did.

Sure, she was trouble. But there was something about the way that she looked at people that was pretty cool; the way she didn't seem to care whether you were older or even a teacher, but just looked straight at you.

"She's got no parents, right?"

"Yeah, like, they live abroad or something? You heard she was the top scorer on the entrance exam, right? But she wasn't the speaker at the entrance ceremony. Know why?"

"Why?"

"Her guardian's name isn't Kirima."

"She's illegitimate?"

"Yeah. She just gets money and lives by herself in some apartment."

"No way..."

"So, she can do whatever she wants. Bring a different guy home every day, or like Suema says, 'Start killing.' She could have a mountain of bodies at her place, and no one would ever know."

"In the freezer?"

"All frozen up."

"Thaws them out and cooks them!"

"Ew, gross!"

Everyone laughed again.

I went along with them.

We laughed a bit too loud and Yurihara-san, who was sitting nearby, looked up from her study guide and glared at us. She was the best student in the class...and in the running for top of the school. I'd heard she'd taken practice tests at her cram school, and outscored students from the best schools in town three times running. She was also beautiful...and a little stuck up—meaning that she had no friends in our class. Even though she might've felt a little out of our league, she somehow knew that all it took was a cold glance to quiet us down.

"Maybe Nagi is Boogiepop?" Kyoko said.

"Ew, no. Boogiepop's a beautiful boy."

At the time, that was my first encounter with that name, so I felt myself compelled to ask about it.

"You don't know? But he's a killer!"

"It's not like I know everything."

They filled me in, but I'm into criminal psychology, and this was just some school horror story. God, it was beyond absurd. They made it out to be less of a serial killer and more like some crazed monster.

"Hmm... That's kinda scary." Everyone was watching, so I had to pretend to be alarmed.

"Kind of a turn-on, huh? Wonder how he kills them?" With that, they all started babbling away, swooning over this fantasy man of theirs.

Did he strangle them? Run them through with a knife? They kept suggesting rather time-consuming methods of killing, and I started to get irritated.

"Can we get your expert opinion?" Kyoko asked teasingly, suddenly turning to me.

"Sure...poison gas."

"Ew, like Sarin?" They all said at once.

"Nah, hydrocyanic acid gas. It's colorless and invisible, but very poisonous, and it kills you instantly. You can spray it on someone, and it vanishes quickly, leaving no evidence. The body isn't even dirty. Smells like peaches."

"Hunh...?" Everyone was staring at me, slightly creeped out.

Oops, I thought.

I'd done it again. I knew full well this kind of knowledge wouldn't interest them.

At this point, the class lady killer, Kimura-kun, came over and said, "What's up?" Everyone replied, "Nothing..." Apparently the Boogiepop stories were being kept secret from the boys.

A myth only the girls knew. It seemed I was the last one in class to hear about it.

I always am.

"........."

That depressed me a little, so I only half listened to their conversation, nodding when it seemed appropriate.

My interest in criminal and abnormal psychology stems from a personal experience I had.

Five years ago, in seventh grade, I was almost killed.

There was a serial killer hiding in our town, and he killed himself just when the police were about to catch him.

The killer took sexual pleasure in killing, which is freaky enough, but among the notes that he left behind was one with my address and a detailed account of the route that I took to school.

Had he not killed himself, it turns out that I would've been his next victim.

The police investigated my family to see if they had any connection to the killer, just to be certain. Of course, we'd never even seen him before. My parents tried to keep it a secret from me, but I found out when the police started questioning me directly.

I would be lying if I said it wasn't a shock.

But more powerful than the shock was the unreal feeling that it gave me.

My life had been in the hands of someone with no connection to me at all. I just couldn't wrap my head around the idea, which is exactly how I got interested in that sort of thing to begin with.

I never told my friends why.

I knew they would look at me differently if I did. "The psycho liked her," they would say, which is more than a good enough reason to put me on the bullied list. It was a bit too harsh of a truth to laugh off.

But just being interested in that sort of thing was enough to make me different, and the class tends to treat me like Doctor Murder, but it's a far cry from being bullied.

* * *

After lunch, we all went off to our fifth period classrooms.

Even though I was in the science program, my next class was Modern Japanese, a subject that automatically got on my nerves. Our school let you choose between science and humanities concentrations in your second year, but even so, we had to complete one course from the other program during our second year. An absurd requirement, if you ask me.

A friend from another class who was also forced to take Japanese walked across the covered walkway with me. Usually, there were three of us, but Niitoki-san was at a meeting for the discipline committee today.

As we walked, the PA came and said, "...Miyashita Touka, second year, class C. Please, return to the infirmary at once. Miyashita Touka, second year, class C..."

"Hunh, wonder where Touka went?" the girl next to me asked. She was in the same class.

"She was in the infirmary?"

"Yeah, she got sick at the start of fourth bell..."

"Faking it?"

"Mm... She *is* dating a senior..."

"Skipping out for a date?"

"Maybe. But dating *is* against the rules, so don't tell Niitoki-san," she said, putting her finger in front of her lips.

I grimaced back at her. "I would never."

"They're probably on the roof or something now..." she said, glancing out the window. Suddenly, she let out a piercing shriek.

Startled, I asked, "Wh-what?"

"Th-th-th-there!" She pointed out the window, her finger trembling.

"What?"

"Boogiepop! On the roof!"

"Eh?" I stuck my head out the window.

But there was nothing.

"Nothing there."

"There was! I saw it! It moved away!"

"You sure it wasn't somebody else? Miyashita-san?"

"I don't think so! It had a black hat on! Like a pipe!" she said, still in a panic.

Clearly, she was seeing things, but nobody believes that when it happens to them. Reverse psychology was more effective. If I pretended to believe her, she would start listening to me.

"Okay. Let's go see," I said, and she spun to stare at me in horror.

"Hunh?"

"If Boogiepop is real, then I want to see him."

"No! Don't! It's dangerous!"

"Don't worry. Go ahead, I'll meet you in class."

I headed for the roof.

I ran up almost all of the stairs, and I was pretty out of breath by the time that I reached the door.

But the door to the roof was locked. Oh, right; they had belatedly sealed it off after someone had thrown themself off.

I peered out the window. I could see most of the roof, but there was nobody there.

When I got down the stairs, she was waiting for me, looking worried.

"Wha-what happened?"

"Nothing there."

"Really?"

"Yep. I looked everywhere."

"Hunh. I guess I must have imagined it..." she said, relieved.

"I guess," I replied, surprised to find myself disappointed. As we headed to class, it occurred to me that there was a fire escape at the back of the roof, and if someone had gone down that, I wouldn't have been able to see them. But it was too late to go check now.

Nothing like that happened again, and our peaceful, safe lives dragged on.

2.

"SAY, SUEMA, what are murderers thinking?" Kyoko suddenly asked me, one day late in fall, as we were on our way home from school.

"Eh, why?"

The two of us were walking along the bank of the river. Kyoko and I were the only two members of our circle of friends that walked to school, so we always went home together. Most students take the bus to school. Hardly anyone walks, so there was no one but us on the street.

"Oh, no reason," Kyoko dried up.

"You're always asking me stuff like that recently. What's up?"

"Oh, nothing. Never mind."

But there had to be a reason for it.

"Tell me."

"You see..." Kyoko whispered very quietly.

"Yeah?"

"She's suspended now, right?"

"Hunh? Oh, you mean Kirima-san?"

Two weeks ago, she'd been suspended for smoking on school grounds. She was due back the next day, though.

"Do you think...she would really kill someone?"

"Hah?" I doubted my own ears. Sure, she was the odd girl out, but Nagi was still our classmate. She hardly deserved to be called a murderer.

"What are you talking about?"

"You said it yourself—when was it? We were eating lunch..."

That had been a long time ago. I had completely forgotten.

"Uh, did I? I might have..."

"Do you really think so?" Kyoko was creepily serious.

"Even if I did say that, it was just an example," I hastily explained.

Kyoko's expression didn't change. "The girl is *scary.*"

"Well, I'll grant that she's not easy to get to know..."

"She did something to this girl I know. She hasn't been the same since," her voice trembled. She meant it. She wasn't kidding.

"Something? What?"

"Threatened her, I think."

"For money?"

Kyoko shook her head. "No, not money. She's rich, you know."

"Yeah. She has her own apartment. Then what?"

Kyoko didn't answer.

Like anyone on earth would, I told her that I could keep a secret, but she still didn't say anything, so I asked, "Does it have anything to do with why Kirima got suspended?"

"I don't know..."

"You don't know?"

"I feel like she got herself suspended *because of* it..." Kyoko said, but I didn't follow.

Come to think of it, Nagi had not been suspended for smoking, but for having a cigarette in her lips.

And the place she'd been caught—the teacher's restroom. It would have been extremely strange if she had *not* been caught.

A female teacher had found her, and Nagi had glared at her so fiercely that the she fled and got a male teacher, making quite a fuss.

She made no excuses. Or apologies.

She never did.

I had never once heard her say "sorry" during all the times the teachers had yelled at her.

One time, a teacher scolded her for staring out the window, and Nagi had curtly quipped, "You're boring." However, her grades were too good for the teachers to take any drastic measures.

Still, she skipped a lot.

We're not just talking leaving a bell early, either. No, she would drop the whole day; never even come to school...for three days running! Yet when she came back, she knew everything that we had covered while she was gone, and she could answer any question that the teachers threw at her.

Nobody knew what she did when she wasn't in school and no one ever had the guts to ask.

She was enigmatic and more than a little scary, so somewhere along the line her nickname became "The Fire Witch." Word had it that this was because she knew some form of black magic, like the "Karma Dance," which sounded plausible enough.

Even so, it was hard to imagine that she had intentionally gotten herself suspended. Suspensions went on your permanent transcript.

"That's going a bit overboard," I told Kyoko, but she didn't answer.

She stared up into the air, muttering, "She's gonna kill me..."

This I could not ignore. "Why? What for?"

Suddenly, Kyoko's entire body shuddered once, then froze. "Eeeeee!"

I followed her line of sight.

There was a girl standing on the road a short distance from us. She had been sitting on the bank, and stood up when we approached.

She wore an old, worn leather jacket and thick leather pants. There were metallic guards on her knees and elbows, like what bikers wear. Her slightly wavy hair was bound in a bandanna, and beneath her eyebrows, her eyes were less glittering than gleaming. She glared at us...at Kyoko.

"I've been waiting for you, Kinoshita Kyoko," she said, in her distinctive manly voice.

It was the suspended Kirima Nagi, in the flesh.

"No! Ahhh!" Kyoko screamed.

She fled behind me, shoving me towards Nagi.

Reeling, I almost smacked right into Nagi as she ran towards us.

But Nagi slid by me without so much as a glance in my direction and took off after Kyoko.

"W-wait!" I yelled as I hurriedly gave chase, but Nagi was fast. Looking closely, she was wearing big black boots. I thought they were rubber at first, but I was wrong. These were steel-toed work boots, the kind that construction workers wear. The kind that can't be crushed, even if several tons fall on them. Kick someone with these, and they might as well die.

This was clearly not a fashion statement. It was a level beyond biker wear or air sneakers.

The bag on her back was strapped to her body, and didn't budge as she ran. It was like...

(...like she was dressed for combat?!)

No normal high school girl would ever dress like that. Not even a gang member.

She looked more like a hitman.

"H-help me!" Kyoko yelled.

Nagi snarled back, "You call for help, and you'll have to talk to the cops!"

That shut Kyoko up. She stopped in her tracks.

That was enough for Nagi; she closed the distance between them, and tackled her mercilessly from behind. Both girls hit the ground, sliding down the river bank.

Wheezing, I caught up to them to find Nagi twisting Kyoko's arm behind her. It looked just like a hold from something I'd seen on TV, like judo or kung fu. Kyoko couldn't move a muscle. We clearly hadn't learned this sort of wrestling at school.

"Ow! Ow! Ow! Let go!"

"Want me to go ahead and break it? Even you'll take some time to heal then, eh, Manticore?!"

I have no idea what she meant by that.

"No, don't! I'll never do it again, I swear!" Kyoko shrieked.

"Stop that, Kirima-san!" I cried, jumping on her, but she kicked me away.

She spoke to Kyoko again, "It's not just me. Echoes is looking for you too! Keep pretending and you'll lose an arm! And then, you won't have any hope of winning!"

What on earth was she talking about?

"I swear! I swear to God I'll never do drugs again! Please don't! Please!" Kyoko sobbed. Drugs?

"I know you killed Kusatsu Akiko! Don't lie to me!" Nagi roared.

I thought my heart was gonna stop.

Kusatsu Akiko—?

That was the name of a first year girl who had gone missing.

"I didn't! I didn't! It wasn't me, I swear! She just gave me the drugs!"

There was an unpleasant popping sound from Kyoko's arm.

Kyoko's eyes rolled up in her head.

"...Damn, you're normal!" Nagi snarled and let go.

Kyoko rolled down the bank.

"Kyoko!" I shouted, racing over to her and putting my arms around her.

"Don't worry. I stopped before the joint was destroyed. It'll hurt for a few days and then be fine," Nagi said.

Kyoko was trembling.

"What's going on?!" I screamed.

"You should ask Kinoshita herself, Suema-san," Nagi replied, her voice completely serene.

Kyoko's teeth were chattering. She'd been scared half to death. Understandably; so had I.

"This is going too far!"

"But it's better than getting arrested, right, Kinoshita?" Nagi said. Kyoko stiffened. "I hope you learn from this. Next time, you'll know better than to do stupid shit just because your friends do it."

She turned to leave.

"Wait!" I yelled.

Nagi looked at me, and said, "Suema-san, maybe it's time to let go of what happened five years ago. Get too hung up on something like that and *it'll come back to haunt you.*"

Her gruff voice matched her boyish face perfectly. But that wasn't the problem.

"H-how did—?"

How did she know I'd nearly been murdered five years ago?!

"H-hold on a minute..." I tried to stop her, but the Fire Witch stalked away without another word.

3.

I HAD TO SWEAR to keep it a secret before Kyoko would tell me anything.

"We...we were at the same Junior High," she said. "We were all on the table tennis team. Even in Junior High, we hung out together. Kusatsu was one of us, but a year younger. She was team captain when we were third years, so we sort of stopped thinking of her that way.

"So, three months ago, Kusatsu called to say she had something good, and that everyone should hook up with her.

"It was a weird sort of drug.

"No, not uppers; I think it was something else. It was a sort of bluish, see-through liquid. You took a sniff of it, and it was like your head opened up, like you became transparent, like every corner of your body was washed clean.

"Glue? No...I don't know, but it didn't have that strong of a smell.

"Kusatsu didn't tell us much, but she said some pharmaceutical company had created it as a test product. Yeah, it was probably bullshit. But, hey, it was free, so we all tried it out...

"Right. She never charged us anything.

"She was never exactly a generous person, so I'm not sure why...

"And a little while later, people from our group started running away.

"No, I don't know where they went! They didn't tell anyone. They just, you know, vanished. Yeah, girls from other schools too.

"And then, Kusatsu vanished. By this point, the rest of us were starting to wonder if it had something to do with the drugs. We didn't know where she got it, but maybe it was something nobody was supposed to know about it and they were taking us out. Then suddenly one of us announced that she wasn't gonna have anything to do with us anymore.

"This made us nervous. We had to know why.

"She said Kirima Nagi had threatened her. Somehow, she had found out about the drugs, and she had told her to never touch them again...

"Not just the one, though. She hit every girl...in order. I was the last one.

"Started two weeks ago, right after she was suspended. That's why I said she had intentionally gotten herself suspended—so she would have a good reason for not coming to school, and so that she could move freely.

"No! I'm never touching drugs again!

"Hunh? No way! Why would I know Kirima Nagi?! I've always avoided her up to now.

"Please, don't tell anyone, Suema! Keep it a secret! I probably should never have told you either. But I had to. I just had to!

"Keeping quiet was just too frightening...it was crushing me..." She trailed off.

I held Kyoko, comforting her until she stopped crying. Then we killed some time in a booth at *First Kitchen*, so that her face could return to normal before I took her back home.

It was night by then, and as I walked through the darkened streets, I thought things over.

Her fragmented story suggested that she had only seen a small part of what was really going on. I couldn't guess much from what she'd told me, but it sounded like she hadn't been one of the ringleaders of this group of ex-table tennis team players. More like she did whatever the much less stable girls told her to; just a third wheel, hanging on to the cool kids.

She wasn't even a victim. She was just in the wrong place at the wrong time.

Nagi had said Kusatsu Akiko had been killed...

And she knew about my past.

But...how?

Who was she?

Should I tell the school...or the police?

(But I promised Kyoko...)

If word got out that Kyoko had done drugs, that would be it for her—she'd be finished. It wouldn't end at suspension, either; she'd be expelled as an example to the other students. I didn't want to do that to her.

It was very dark outside.

The streetlight above me had clearly not been changed in years, and it was flickering madly.

"............"

I stopped walking.

I opened my bag under the unsteady light, and thanks to my bad habit of carrying far too much stuff around with me all of the time, I had the class directory with me. It listed not only phone numbers, but also addresses.

I looked up the address of the person three names before my own.

Somewhat surprisingly, Kirima Nagi, like me, lived close to school. I could walk there.

(Okay, let's do it!)

I snapped my bag closed and walked as fast as I could in that direction.

But why did I have to meet her?

Kyoko, who was actually part of it, was running away as fast as she could. That was the more natural reaction. Anyone normal would do the same.

I was clearly a third party; I had nothing to do with anything.

But I didn't *like* that.

Five years ago, things had all happened without me knowing about them. I only found out when everything was finished. My own will played no part in the matter.

If there was danger, I wanted to see it.

That's why I had chased after Boogiepop, even though there was clearly no such thing. It was all the same to me. I didn't care what it was...I just wanted to confront something.

(No more blissful ignorance for me.)

Kirima Nagi might really be a witch. I hoped she was.

* * *

"...Uh?"

I was standing on the right street, but there were no apartment buildings, only houses.

I checked the address again and again, but I was clearly in the right place.

But I couldn't find any house with the name "Kirima" on the gate. Checking the directory again, I noticed that it had "Taniguchi" written in very small characters next to it. She must live there.

(...must be that guardian with the different name.)

There *was* a house with "Taniguchi" on the gate, and the numbers seemed to match.

It was a really normal-looking home, a ready-built house like any other. A little on the wealthy side, but normally so.

Unable to connect it with Nagi's bizarre appearance during our earlier encounter, I hesitated, debating for a long time before I pushed the buzzer.

When I finally did, it made a half-hearted, ultra normal ding-dong sound.

"Who is it?" the voice from the intercom said, surprising me. It wasn't Nagi's voice, but rather that of a boy.

"Um, is, uh... Is Kirima-san...?" I stuttered, all flustered.

"You're Nagi's friend?" the voice said quite cheerfully.

A moment later, the door swung open. The cheery boy stood in the doorway. He was taller than either Nagi or me, but younger, probably in Junior High. And that smile—it was friendly and warm.

"Come on in. But Nagi's not home yet, I'm afraid."

"O-oh, um..."

"Come in and wait. She should be back soon."

He led me to the guest room.

The inside was normal too.

There was even a set of little dolls in the shape of the zodiac signs sitting on top of the cabinet.

"Here," the boy said, putting a cup of tea and a plate of cookies in front of me.

"Uh, thanks." It was really good. I know nothing about tea, but I'm pretty sure this was what they called good tea.

"Gosh, I don't think I've ever met a friend of Nagi's before," the boy said airily.

"Y-you are...?" I asked.

"Her brother," he replied. They looked *nothing* alike.

"Um, I'd heard Kirima-san lived alone, so..."

"Yeah, I got here about six months ago. I lived abroad with my parents until last spring, but I've got entrance tests for high school next year, so I thought that I ought to get used to Japan first."

"Your parents..."

Nagi had parents after all. But why was their name Taniguchi?

At this point, we heard a voice call out, "I'm home," from the entrance. It was Nagi.

"In here," her brother said as he stood up and went to meet her.

"You brought *another* girl home?" Nagi said.

Her brother laughed. "This one's yours. She's been waiting for you."

I nearly yelped when Nagi came in.

She had changed into her school uniform, like she'd just come home from school.

"Oh, it's you," Nagi said quietly as I stood there speechless. "Let's go upstairs."

Following her lead, we went upstairs to her bedroom.

The polar opposite of downstairs, her room was free of decoration; nothing but computers and books. One bed, two desks. One was for studying, apparently, since the surface was empty.

The other desk was for her computer—or, should I say, computers. It was kind of hard to tell just how many she had. There were multiple boxy computer towers and an assortment of other machines attached to them. She had three different monitors, all lined up next to each other. At first, I assumed two of them might've been televisions, but the screen savers were a dead giveaway. Worse, the pile of machinery spilled out onto the floor, filling nearly half of the ten-mat room. It felt less like a girl's bedroom and more like some mad hacker's secret lair. Much to my surprise, there were no signs of any black magic books at all. All the books that lined Nagi's shelves were merely an assortment of reference books and difficult looking hardcover tomes. Still, Nagi's collection of computer software boxes looked to have her book collection beat.

Nagi pulled the chair out from the study desk, and offered it to me. "Sit."

"Okay," I said, and did.

"Surprised?" Nagi grinned.

"Hm?"

"By Masaki. Everyone thinks I live alone."

"Um, yeah. I didn't know you had a brother."

"He's not my brother. We're not related," Nagi replied, shaking her head. "He's my mom's second husband's son from a previous marriage. He's a good kid, but a bit too good at manipulating me. Gonna grow up to be a real Don Juan. Sad."

"So, that's why his name's...?"

"Right, my mom's husband's name. I kept the old one."

"Hmm... Why?"

"'Cause I've got a father complex," Nagi replied. I couldn't tell if she was joking.

"Your father is...?"

"I thought you'd know. Kirima Seiichi. Wrote a lot of books."

"Ehhhh?!" I interrupted rather loudly. "You're kidding!"

"Nope."

"But...the writer, Kirima Seiichi?!"

Of course, I knew him. I'd learned most of what I knew about criminal psychology or depth psychology from his books. *The Scream Inside—Multiple Personality Disorder*, or *When a Man Kills a Man*, or *Where the Killer's Mind Changes*, or *A Nightmare of Boredom*, or *The Proliferation of "Dunno,"* or *VS Imaginator*, and so on. He'd written far more summaries, essays and commentaries than novels. In fact, I'd never read any of his actual novels, just his scientific writings. He called himself a modern day enlightenment thinker, which is kind of hokey, but he did write an incredible number of books.

"That's my dad. He's dead now, though."

"Yeah, I knew that...but really? No, I mean really, *really*?"

"Why would I lie?"

"I know... But still..."

"You didn't think I had a strange name?"

"Never occurred to me. Wonder why not?"

Even as I asked, I knew the answer. I had unconsciously convinced myself that Kirima Seiichi or any other writer was hardly likely to live near me. Perhaps I wanted the people that I admired so much to live in some higher realm of existence than I did.

"Basically, I'm living off of the inheritance. Can't really beat it, either. Pays for school."

"Really? But your mother..."

"She wasn't married to him anymore. I got everything. She tossed her half away on her own. She was already a Taniguchi, and she didn't want anything to do with Kirima. That took care of taxes, so I pay rent here."

There I was, just some normal girl from a typical middle-class nuclear family, just sitting and listening to the Fire Witch herself talking about her atypical life! Her whole situation just felt sort of unreal to me. It's no wonder that she acts the way she does. She'd hardly even been brought up in anything close to a proper environment.

Even so, there was something that I had to ask. "Um, so..."

"What? The reason?"

"Yeah. Why'd you save Kyoko?"

"My, my. You call that saving?" Nagi looked pleased.

"She told me everything. She got on some weird drug. You saved all of the girls from that, right?"

"Maybe I did, maybe I didn't."

"Why? How'd you find out? What did you do about it?" I was relentless.

Nagi simply stared back at me.

I felt my heart beating. She was certainly pretty. I felt like she might actually say, *I used magic.*

What she actually said was, "My father died when I was ten."

"R-right," I stuttered, feeling like I should make some response. She carried on as if she didn't care whether I was listening or not.

"My mother had already left us when he died, so there were only the two of us in the house. He never drank and he never chased after women. All he did was work. One day, I came home from school and found him lying on the floor. I called an ambulance, but all I could do was wait next to him as he spit up blood.

"He asked me, 'Nagi, what do you think about being normal?'

"I didn't know what he meant, so I shook my head.

"He said, 'Normal means you leave everything as it is and nothing ever changes. If you don't like that, you've got to do things that *aren't* normal. That's why I—'

"Those were his last words. He passed out and never woke up again. The cause of death was gastric perforation leading to dissolution of the internal organs. Disgusting way to die. I even heard that when the doctor cut his stomach open during the surgery, the smell was so bad that veteran nurses just started puking all over the floor.

"So what? I don't know. I just kind of gave up living normal after that."

She stopped.

When I said nothing in response, she added, "It's a messiah complex."

"R-really?"

From her face alone, you would think her a demure beauty. I found myself staring at her delicate lips, somehow unable to meet her eyes.

"I'm a psycho, all right. Got all the childhood trauma anyone could want, right here."

She said disturbing things so easily. Still, she didn't look like a monomaniac to me.

"But that's—" I started to say, but Nagi turned towards the computer behind her, cutting me off. She logged into one of the computers, loaded up some program, and hit a few keys.

A list popped up on one screen. It rolled upwards from the bottom of the screen. It appeared to be a list of people's names with numbers after them.

"Here," she said, pointing at the screen.

It read: "2-D-33 Suema Kazuko 8:25 AM-3:40 PM"

"That's..." I said, realizing that it was my very own attendance record.

"I'm logged into the school's network. You can get a basic outline of a student's movements with this. I noticed Kinoshita's group was suddenly getting worse, so I checked it out. Hit the drug story."

I was horrified. "Isn't this illegal?"

"Course it is," she said readily.

My mouth moved, but nothing came out.

"I have to do this," she said quietly. "Schools are kind of isolated from the rest of society. It's a strange environment where the police can't do jack. Something violent happens, whether it's caused by a student or a teacher, and the first thing that they do is try to cover it up. Even if someone dies, they'll take a cue from the times, and claim that it was a suicide caused by bullying, find some students who look like bullies, and just expel them for it...and that may well end up being enough, half the time."

"T-true, but..."

"I know it's wrong, but someone's got to do it. We sure as hell can't expect the teachers to."

"That's not what I mean, but..."

But who was this girl, who would intentionally get herself suspended to do any of this?

A messiah complex—

That was a creepy type of megalomania, in which you believed yourself to be some sort of savior.

In Kirima Seiichi's books, there was a case where a middle-aged man believed himself to be Batman, put on a costume, and attacked an acquitted murder suspect. He wound up being killed himself, and the killer walked a second time, pleading self-defense. If the suspect had truly been innocent, the whole thing was a tragedy based on absurd principles, but if he had been guilty, then it was a tragedy in which justice had been utterly defeated by evil. Either way, it was a sad tale to recount.

And that was how Kirima Nagi saw herself.

Certainly, Kirima Seiichi spent most of his time analyzing sinister phenomena in the underbelly of the human mind, putting out books and articles on the distortions of reality that made people commit crimes, so if you wanted to, you could certainly make a case for him having a messiah complex as well.

That his daughter—a daughter who had diagnosed herself as having a father complex, no less—was the same, was not particularly odd, but—

As I sat there in silence, Kirima thrust a phone at me. Not one on the house's line, but one undoubtedly taken out in her name and paid for out of her own pocket.

"Call."

"Er... *Who*?" I asked, my eyes widening.

Much to my surprise, Nagi replied, "Your house, of course. Tell them you're bringing a friend home for dinner, and that they should make extra."

4.

THE NEXT DAY, Nagi came to school, off her suspension. Kyoko avoided her, and despite chasing us down the day before, Nagi acted as if she didn't even know us. Right from the start of first period, she was slumped over her desk, sleeping soundly. The teachers said nothing, apparently letting sleeping dogs lie.

Nagi stood up to go to the bathroom once during break, and I slid out after her without letting Kyoko see me.

"Um, Kirima-san," I said.

"*Mm*?" She looked back remotely, clearly still half asleep. "Oh, you again. Sorry, but I'm gonna be up all night tonight, so I need to get some sleep while I still can. Talk to you later, okay?" Her business finished, she returned to class and went straight back to sleep.

"......"

I was itching to talk with her more about yesterday, but any attempts that I tried to make were clearly going to be thwarted.

I had ended up taking Nagi home for dinner the night before.

Why? Because she said, "Your folks probably get excessively worried when their daughter comes home late, with what happened before and all. Tell them that you met me, and that you invited me over, since my parents are off on holiday."

Since she was right, I did as I was told.

Her non-blood relative brother said, "Come again," as we left the Taniguchi house. It was pitch black, the sun having long since set.

We set off on foot, with Nagi silently following after me.

Unable to stand the silence, I asked a foolish question. "Don't you ever show your soft side, Kirima-san?"

"Sure. I'm careful not to be too hardcore. I can play a normal girl,." Her voice went up an octave as she said this, and she forced the corners of her mouth upwards into a dubious looking smile. She was a pretty girl, so it didn't look all that unnatural.

"Well, good," I said, laughing. But what I'd asked her wasn't what I'd really wanted to know.

As I squirmed, she said, "You're smart, aren't you?"

"I suppose..." I wasn't sure how to take this, coming from the girl who was the top scorer on the entrance exams and the top student in the school, as far as make-up test were concerned.

"I think so. That's why I explained to you what I did, you know?"

"Yeah. I won't tell anyone." I meant it. After all, no one would believe me.

She shook her head. "That's not what I mean. About Kirima Seiichi."

"Hm? What about him?"

"You've been studying from his books, yet his daughter is doing this kind of stupid shit all the time. In other words, get out while you still can." Her shoulders slumped.

I stopped in my tracks and just looked at her. "Why do you say things like that?"

"Why? That mess five years ago has nothing to do with you. Let go of it. It'll come back to haunt you. It'll warp your personality—just like it has mine!"

"Why?"

"Why..." Nagi looked slightly irritated. "Do you really want to end up like me?"

Her eyes glared at me, her face that of the Fire Witch. But I didn't pull back. I wasn't afraid any more. I glared right back into those eyes.

"How did you know that I was almost killed five years ago? I never told anyone."

Nagi stiffened. She'd made a mistake. "Um, I—that is..."

"You've barely spoken to anyone in class, so you must have assumed that Doctor Murder's past was public knowledge. But nobody knows. Just the people who were a part of it. Just my parents and the police."

Nagi turned her head to the side to avert her gaze.

"Oh my god."

Nagi remained silent.

"So it was you," I said. "*You saved me.*"

They'd told us the killer hung himself. But that explanation had never sat all that well with me.

She had taken him out. Just like she had saved Kyoko.

"It... It's not important. It was a long time ago," she said, sullen.

"It's pretty dang important to me! I've been over this hundreds of times. Why am I still alive? I'm only alive because the killer went and killed himself? Yeah, that makes me feel real good, knowing that. That means that the only way that good things happen is if you just sit and wait for bad things to self-destruct. What kind of explanation is that?! It sucks! And you know what else sucks? That there's nothing we can do to make the world a better place."

Yes.

That was it.

Justice might well prevail in the end, but ordinary people like me had no guarantee of surviving that long. We might get killed on the whim of some serial killer first.

But knowing that there were some people fighting for us—that would make things a lot easier to bear. If we knew these people had saved us, we'd feel much more alive than if we only survived because the bad guy just up and killed himself.

"That wasn't me," Nagi said coldly.

"Liar."

"That was Boogiepop. Ultimately."

Suddenly presented with the name of a fictional character, an urban legend, I was put off my stride. "*Hunh*?" I said, dazed.

"Never mind. The point is, you have nothing to feel responsible for," she said roughly. Her tone seemed to imply that she had been joking a moment before, evading my question.

"But I..."

"Please, I don't want to talk about it," she said, and bit her lower lip.

And so we walked on, without my having said the most crucial thing.

* * *

As third period began, Nagi was still asleep.

I found myself staring vacantly at the curve of her back.

She looked so isolated, so lonely.

I imagined saying so much to her. Stuff like, *Kirima-san, all I wanted to do was thank you. Thank you for saving me. If you can't repay the person who saved your life, then there's something wrong with the world. Right?*

Sadly, I couldn't imagine how she would respond.

Her body twisted on her desk. As she did this, she moaned aloud.

The teacher finally lost it and shouted, "Kirima!"

Nagi's head rose slowly from her desk. "Wha—?"

"What did I just say? On second thought, prove this formula!" The teacher slapped the blackboard behind me. His handwriting wasn't legible at the best of times, and having it rubbed away in places didn't help matters. All this made it next to impossible to read the whole equation if you hadn't taken notes during his lecture.

Nagi narrowed her eyes, staring at the board for a moment,

and said, "a<b, ab>c. When c is a rational number, x=24, y=17/3, z=7." Then she flopped back on her desk.

The teacher's face turned beet red. She was right.

We all giggled, but Nagi ignored us and went right back to sleep.

It was just another typical school day.

Her oddball behavior might be her way of preparing for her next fight, but to the casual onlooker, she just seemed insolent.

She stirred in her sleep again, moaning. The moan sounded oddly girlish, and I stifled a laugh.

After all, the Fire Witch had finished her suspension, and was back among us.

Interlude

ECHOES WANDERED THE TOWN. The clothes he'd procured a week before were now mere rags, and the police had nearly arrested him as a suspicious character, even though all he'd really done was just walk down the street. He'd been saved by some mysterious boy in a black hat, and managed to escape without hurting a soul. On the way here from the mountains, he had already been forced to seriously injure six people.

He knew the Manticore was near.

But human towns were built too close together, and the people living in them all seemed to congregate together. He had no idea how to find the Manticore here.

"............"

As the sky grew darker, he found himself in a back alley, and once more, he collapsed on the ground.

This time, there were no people around. The alley smelled of rancid water.

"............"

He looked up at the evening sky, but he couldn't see the stars here. In the mountains, he had been able to see them even in broad daylight.

But he couldn't cry any longer. The boy in the black hat had told him, "You're chasing something. Cry when you have found it."

This was true.

He could not rest here.

He had to stop the Manticore's slaughter. The Manticore was made from him. It was his child.

She had the power of communication that even he lacked, not to mention the powers that let him blend in with this planet's ecological system. This "transformation power" in particular could do untold damage to the environmental balance of this planet's primarily human civilization and prevent him from carrying out his main objective.

His objective—

He had to fulfill it. That was why he had been created. But the Manticore's existence was a hindrance to his objective, to his decision.

He had to make a decision, one way or the other.

That decision had to be rigorously balanced. Like him, the Manticore was alien to this planet and should not exist here. He had to dispose of her.

"............"

He staggered to his feet.

There was a scream. A young women had come into the alley and caught sight of him.

He waved his hands trying to show that he meant no harm. But he didn't need to.

"What are you doing here?" the woman asked, coming

towards him. It had not been a scream of terror, but simply surprise. "Oh no, you're hurt! How did this happen?"

On closer inspection, the woman was still a girl.

Without any reluctance, she wiped the blood from the wound on his head with an expensive looking designer handkerchief. The wound itself had long since healed, and he felt no pain from it, but the blood was still there, dried to his skin.

"H-hurt..." he said, trying to explain that it did not need tending. But there were few words in her speech for him to return and he could not produce a phrase with meaning.

"What should I do? Call the police?"

"P-police..." was all he could say.

But somehow the girl understood what he meant from this.

"No police, hunh? Okay. Where's your house? Nearby?"

He picked some words from her speech, forcing a sentence. "No—hou-house." When he spoke to people, he could only return words they had spoken, so as to not provide them with information beyond the limits of their understanding.

"Homeless? Looks like you're in some kind of trouble."

He nodded. He waved his hands, telling her to back away from him.

She patted him gently on the shoulder. Body language for "calm down."

"No way, José. I leave you here and I won't be able to sleep at night."

Somehow, she seemed to understand what he wanted to say, even though he could not speak directly.

"*Hmm*, let me see... For the moment, let's put you in school. There's a card reader at the gate to get in, but I think I know a back way in."

"Sch-school..."

"Yeah, I live in an apartment building, but there are prying eyes everywhere. See? You aren't the only one with problems," she said jokingly, and grabbed his arm, pulling him forcibly to his feet. Then she dragged him after her.

He didn't know what else to do, so he followed her.

Who was she? he thought, and almost instantly she answered, "Me? My name's Kamikishiro. Kamikishiro Naoko. I'm a senior at Shinyo Academy. You?"

"*Ah... Oooh...*" He couldn't answer. He was not allowed to provide humans with information about himself.

"You can't talk?"

"Can't...ta-talk."

"You're talking now. *Hmm*... They call you *Echoes*? Strange name. Almost like it was made for me to call you by."

Kamikishiro giggled. She had not yet noticed that she was understanding things that he had not said.

She smiled at him. "Don't worry. I know this kooky girl named Nagi. Anytime there's trouble, we talk to her and she usually takes care of it. Assuming you aren't a bad guy, Echoes," she finished with a wink.

She pulled out a cell phone, thumb flying over the keys, dialing this Nagi person with a practiced motion.

Chapter Three
No One Lives Forever

Saotome Masami
first year, class D

1.

FIRST YEAR STUDENT Saotome Masami first fell in love when he was fifteen. Until that point, he had never opened his heart to anyone and simply remained a "nice guy" to the people around him. Needless to say, this was a major turning point in his life.

* * *

"Saotome-kun, you free Sunday?" asked his classmate Kusatsu Akiko, shortly after the start of the second term as they were performing their after-school cleaning duties.

"No plans to speak of."

"See, Sachiko has some free movie tickets, and she said we should all go together." Akiko had dark skin and high cheekbones. She looked at Masami, waiting for an answer.

"We?" Masami asked, leaning on his broom. This lowered his face to her line of sight. He was tall, with a face that had just enough charm to get him compared to pop idols. But it was always a different person every time, never fixing on one resemblance.

"You know Sakamoto-kun from class F? He made a pass at Sachiko and got the tickets, but she's a little nervous about going it alone."

"So, you need a discipline committee member as an escort? I know Sakamoto pretty well, and I don't want to be a drag."

"Oh, you don't need to—well, maybe you do," Kusatsu Akiko said, smiling weakly at him. She was pretty forthright with everyone else but Masami, but she couldn't contradict him directly, because she was in love. Masami was well aware of this, and privately, he was annoyed by it. Until now.

But today, he simply smiled back at her, instead.

"But if you just want me to tag along, fine. Not like I've got anything better to do. If we run into the guidance teacher on patrol, I can probably talk us out of trouble."

Kusatsu Akiko's face brightened. "Really? Well, the truth is, Sachiko's secretly pleased that Sakamoto-kun asked her, so I don't think you'll need to intervene."

"Whatever."

They both laughed.

You could never call Kusatsu Akiko a good-looking girl, but when she smiled next to the far more evenly-featured Masami, she gleamed like a still image from a soap opera.

* * *

When the four of them met at the station, they appeared to be a very close-knit group. They ran into Masami's senpai on the discipline committee, Takeda Keiji, and he took one look at them and asked if they were "double dating." There was clearly a hint of romance in the air.

The movie was a big Hollywood action movie, part three in a series, neither harming anyone nor doing anyone any good. The only part that Masami enjoyed was a bit where a minor villain was shot in the chest and knocked over backwards. His arms were flung out to the sides, and he slid backwards like a figure skater. In Masami's eyes, he looked light and free.

They left the theater, and a passing group of teenagers glared at them murderously. Walking quickly, faces grim, they all carried bags with large square lumps inside.

"Cram school?" asked Noguchi Sachiko, this evening's instigator. "I hope we never end up like that."

"Yeah," Kusatsu Akiko nodded. Masami remembered her letting it slip that she couldn't go to college, because her father's company was about to go bankrupt.

"That's a long time from now. We ought to enjoy ourselves while we can," Sakamoto Jun said, trying to distract Noguchi Sachiko.

"Yeah, just forget about it. Just live your life. Not like you can live forever," Masami said breezily.

"Oh look, it's Yurihara from our school," Noguchi Sachiko said, pointing.

Yurihara Minako, second year, class D. She was one of the best students in the school and legend had it that she consistently beat out the best students at other cram schools on their practice tests. But she didn't look at all like the brainy type. Heck, she didn't even wear glasses. Instead, she had long straight hair with the kind of shine that no amount of treatment could ever give. It matched her slender face, giving the impression of a Heian era princess.

Yurihara Minako passed by them as they whispered, walking at a slower pace than the other students, and vanished into the cram school.

"She's so relaxed. You can just see the aura of her genius."

"You know she was scouted by some prep schools, right?" Sakamoto said with a knowledgeable expression.

"Really? They can do that?"

From the fuss that they made, you would never have thought that they were talking about a senpai.

All the while, Masami remained quiet, smiling to himself. He didn't even glance at Yurihara Minako.

They had promised not to let their eyes meet in public.

"Anyone up for karaoke? There's a place near here with a great track list," Kusatsu Akiko said brightly. She was in a good mood, now that she was out with her beloved Masami.

In the karaoke box, Masami sang easy pop songs, ones that had been all the rage up until recently, but had passed their peak, and everyone was starting to get sick of them now. He almost always sang that sort of song at karaoke. He preferred an American band called The Doors, which had broken up ages ago (long before he was even born) when the lead singer died of a drug overdose. But he never told anybody. The Doors weren't in a lot of karaoke machines, but he never sang them even if they were.

He had a good voice, but since everyone was a little tired of his selections, they never really seemed all that interested.

He always applauded other people's performances, never forgetting to keep up appearances. He never stuck out, was occasionally a little scorned, but he never made anyone jealous, and no one ever realized that he was keeping them at a distance.

He bought drinks for everybody. He took them directly from the tray when the waiter brought them and even passed them around himself.

He put Kusatsu Akiko's drink in her hands. Nobody saw him drop a small tablet, about five millimeters across, into her cup before he handed it over. Yurihara Minako had "synthesized" the tablet, and as promised, it quickly dissolved into the diet cola. Kusatsu Akiko never noticed a thing.

2.

THE FIRST GIRL that Saotome Masami fell in love with was a second year student, Kirima Nagi. He told her this in May. She rejected him quite harshly.

"Sorry, but I don't have the time," was all she said.

"Is... is it because I'm younger?"

"No, not really... You're normal, right? Me? I'm nothing but trouble. Thanks, but sorry."

"O-okay." He was far less hurt by this than he'd expected. Quite the opposite; he found himself rather relieved to be brushed off coldly.

It was two months before he identified the source of those feelings.

* * *

"Hey, Saotome, you take Kusatsu home. I'll take care of Noguchi," Sakamoto whispered in Masami's ear as their time in the karaoke box ran low.

"Sure. Good luck," Masami whispered back.

As the four of them left the shop, Kusatsu Akiko suddenly proclaimed, "I...I don't feel so good." Her face was white as a sheet.

"That's too bad. I'd better take you home," Masami said, putting his arm around her shoulders.

"Uh, hang on! Saotome-kun!" Noguchi Sachiko cried, all flustered. She was about to be left alone with Sakamoto.

"You two have fun. Don't worry, I'll look after her."

"Er, but..."

"You heard the man. Let him go," Sakamoto said, cajoling. As the men had planned, they split off into two pairs. Noguchi Sachiko was steamrolled under Sakamoto's promises that he wouldn't "try anything."

Afterwards, he did get her to a hotel, where they had relations, but Noguchi Sachiko's parents found out and her old-fashioned father stormed the school, tracked Sakamoto down, and cursed him out in front of everyone. But in all the fuss, the two of them never had a moment to notice the events that followed. They had completely forgotten they were ever with Saotome Masami that night.

"Bye!"

"Yeah," Masami replied, as the four became two.

"I feel sick..." Kusatsu Akiko's voice grew gradually weaker in Masami's arms.

Masami never spoke a word. He simply hauled her along as if she were a piece of luggage. The silence was deafening.

Kusatsu Akiko was in no condition to be insulted. Her face was well beyond pale; you could see the blood vessels under her skin.

Not caring, Masami dragged her into the backroads. All they did was leave the lights and noise of the main drag for a narrow back road, but it was as silent as a graveyard, seemingly light years from the bustle of the city.

Before them was a giant parking garage that had failed in its bid to reopen and had thus been abandoned. The land was intended to become an office building, but the owner had been unable to find any clients, and had had no other choice but to make it into a parking garage. As luck would have it, the owner had then gone bankrupt, and it was now just another of the country's forgotten bad debts.

Masami slipped between the railings of the surrounding fence, holding Akiko under his arm. She said nothing. She had already stopped breathing.

He dragged her up to the seventh floor of the parking lot. This far up, there was no chance of them being disturbed by thrill seekers.

Leaving Kusatsu Akiko on the ground, Masami stuck his face outside. It was pitch black all around them. Even if a normal human on the ground had been looking upwards, they could never have seen him.

He looked at his watch. It was a digital watch with a backlit screen. Unlike radial watches, it had the advantage of not making a sound.

The time confirmed, he nodded to himself.

Staring into the blackness below him, he waved his hands.

There was a small noise from far below him, like someone pushing a tack into a board.

Within an instant, a human shape appeared in the air in front of Masami.

It was a girl.

The shape slid past Masami, entering the parking lot. It landed right at the top of its arc; there was no sound as its feet touched the floor.

The girl had jumped all the way to the seventh floor.

She turned towards Masami. She had long, bountiful black hair plastered to her head and a cram school bag in her hand.

It was Yurihara Minako.

"Were you successful?" she asked.

Masami nodded. "Over there," he said, pointing to Kusatsu Akiko's corpse, which lay on its side, no longer moving.

"That one? The other girl was better," Yurihara said, frowning. Agitation could not be farther from her mind.

"Not really. This girl has friends all over. Lots of friends from Junior High," Masami replied, voice devoid of warmth.

"Does she? Then fine. You know more than I do, Saotome-kun." Yurihara handed her bag to Masami. He took it like an obedient little hotel bellboy whose only job was to serve.

Yurihara stooped down in front of Kusatsu Akiko.

"*Mmm*... Seems like a waste not to eat her *now*," she said, her beautiful face contorting.

"Yeah, but if we use her, you'll be able to assimilate four or five more in no time," Masami chuckled. "For now, we wait, Manticore."

"Human society makes it hard to move." Yurihara the Manticore said, sighing. She lowered her face next to Kusatsu Akiko's.

Her long hair started to get in the way, so she held it back with her fingers, and kissed the corpse tenderly.

Her tongue pried the body's mouth open, forcing a gaseous form of the essence manufactured inside her body into Kusatsu Akiko.

Watching this monstrous, sinister spectacle unfolding in the darkness, Masami was entranced. As if he felt sexual pleasure, his face was even more ecstatic than at the moment of ejaculation.

For thirty long seconds, Yurihara kept her lips pressed to the corpse's.

Finally, she pulled away, wiping her mouth with the back of

her hand. Her lips were bright red, but not from lipstick—the color did not rub off on her hands.

The color of her skin was so sleek she appeared to be wearing makeup, but this was also her natural state. When she had copied the real Yurihara Minako, she had copied the makeup as well.

"She should be revitalized momentarily," Yurihara said, with a satisfied smile.

"Hmm..." Masami said doubtfully. To make sure, he kicked the corpse lightly. Its fingers twitched. "Good."

Bit by bit, the entire body began shaking violently, as if it were lying on top of a high voltage electric fence.

Then the torso shot upwards, as if on a spring.

The eyes and mouth popped open, and a blue liquid, neither tears nor saliva, came pouring out of them.

"Woah! Can't let that touch me," Masami said, backing away from the sweet scent wafting off of the volatile liquid.

"Yes. For humans, it will work like a drug. It would not do for you to become addicted as well, Saotome-kun." Yurihara placed herself between Masami and Kusatsu Akiko. "Look here, woman," she ordered.

The no longer dead Kusatsu Akiko did as she was told, slowly rolling her head towards Yurihara. The flow of liquid had stopped.

"I have given you power. Power to corrupt humans. Use this power to supply me with more humans."

In normal society, Yurihara's words were unthinkable, but the previously dead girl nodded.

"Corrupt them well. When they suddenly vanish, we want

the humans around them to assume that this was the logical next stage of their recent poor behavior. Including yourself."

Behind her, Masami nodded proudly, like a parent whose son had just correctly answered a question on visitor's day.

Yurihara whispered, "You have no memories of what happened here. You went bad of your own free will..."

3.

FIVE MINUTES LATER, Masami was walking along the street, once again supporting Kusatsu Akiko.

"*Mm...mm*?" Her fainting spell ended, and her eyes opened. "Wh-where are we?"

"Ah, good. You're awake," Masami said, stepping away from her.

"*Eh*? I was asleep? Oh no! Why didn't you wake me?" Kusatsu Akiko asked, quite flustered.

"I shook you several times."

"Oh no! I'm sorry! I wonder what...*uhhh*..." She tried to figure out the last thing she remembered, but she couldn't remember a thing. Obviously, it never occurred to her that she had died and was now merely functioning as a puppet, thanks to the stimulus of the drug.

"You're pretty heavy, you know that? It was hard work carrying you," Masami said sternly.

Kusatsu Akiko turned bright red, but for some reason, she wasn't that hurt by his words.

They parted ways in front of the station.

"See you at school tomorrow."

"Yeah...don't tell anyone about tonight. Especially..." she started to say a name, but trailed off.

She felt like there was a boy who she really didn't want to see her in an embarrassing moment like this, but for the life of her, she couldn't remember his name or what he looked like.

"Especially who?" Masami asked, with a knowing smile.

"*Mm*... Never mind," Kusatsu Akiko's love had vanished with her memories.

"I had fun today," Masami said kindly.

But she simply replied, "Oh?" as if she didn't care at all, and turned her back.

She felt like there was a big, gaping hole in her heart, but she had no way of telling that her will and spirit were swiftly vanishing.

Masami paused to watch Kusatsu Akiko venture into the station, then swiftly turned on his heel and walked back into the city.

Yurihara was waiting at the Tristan coffee shop. She was seated in a booth towards the back.

"It went well?" she asked. She was wearing glasses and had her hair in a sauvage style. Masami knew that Yurihara could control her hair at will, but these quick hairstyle changes always took a moment to get used to.

"Yeah, her emotions are already fading," Masami replied. He sat down and ordered lemon tea and marron cake to soothe his sweet tooth. "Without knowing what she's doing, she'll make all of her friends try a drug that even she doesn't remember getting. Like a sleepwalker in the night, she'll regurgitate the fluid made by the cells in her body. She won't even try to figure out where it comes from. Her brain is shrinking, and she can't be bothered to make decisions on her own."

They looked at each other and giggled.

From the side, they looked like any peaceful, harmless young couple. But Saotome had already sacrificed the lives of three girls to Yurihara—the monstrous man-eater known as the Manticore.

They had met two months before, just before summer vacation.

Masami was a member of the tea ceremony club, largely because it never did anything. He had heard that it was a good idea to have been a member of a club in high school when it came time to apply for universities or jobs. Yurihara Minako was a member, as well. Much like Masami, she hardly ever bothered to show up for the club's infrequent meetings.

One day, it suddenly started to rain in the evening, despite blue skies all afternoon. The whims of summer. Masami had not planned to go to the club meeting, but since he had no umbrella, he thought he might as well kill some time in the tea room. He turned around at the shoe boxes at the entrance to school and went back inside.

The tea ceremony club didn't have a room of their own; they simply borrowed a room that was usually used for student guidance, as it was the only Japanese style room in the school. The faculty sponsor was the assistant principal, Komiya, and he was much too busy to ever show his face at meetings.

That day, the room was deathly silent and there was no sign of any other students.

Next to the door was the tea ceremony club attendance book. If your name was written in this, it appeared that you had attended the meeting. Even if you rarely came, as long as your name showed up in the book, you were treated like an active member and could stay on the rosters.

Masami opened the book, and was about to write the date and his name, when he realized there was already an entry for that date. Someone else was already here.

Yurihara Minako.

"……?"

Even if she had gone to the bathroom, it was strange that she hadn't left her bag. Before now, Masami had never even had the slightest interest in Yurihara Minako. She had a reputation for brains and beauty, but had never mattered to him in the slightest. And, like many a man before him, he had always been baffled by the idea of beauty.

He had already lost his virginity in Junior High to a girl with a face covered in zits, who was widely reputed as being rather ugly. Their relationship was kept secret, but less because he was embarrassed and more because he just didn't want to listen to everyone else's shocked commentaries on the subject. He didn't think anything at all about dating an ugly girl. In fact, after she started dating him, her pimples vanished and actually she became quite pretty. She soon left him for another boyfriend. But Masami wasn't particularly upset. He had never actually loved her to begin with; he simply used her to relieve his sexual appetites. Instead, she ended up crying and apologizing, even though it had been her idea to break up in the first place.

Masami no longer remembered that girl's name and he couldn't remember Yurihara Minako's face all that clearly, either. He knew she was supposed to be good looking and that she had good grades, but that was about it.

"Senpai, you here?" he asked, taking off his slippers and stepping onto the tatami in his socks.

He opened the shoji leading into the inner room. It was less of a room than a storage area for tables and cushions.

The moment he opened it, his eyebrows leapt upwards.

In the storage area, Yurihara Minako was upside-down against a pile of cushions, face twisted around so that it faced the same direction as her torso. Her head was on backwards. Her neck was broken with her spine clearly severed. Her eyes were open and empty.

She wasn't moving...at all.

She was dead.

The first thought that flashed through Masami's mind was relief that he had not written his name in the attendance book. He didn't want to get mixed up in something like this.

He took a step backwards.

This saved his life.

A hand with razor-sharp claws passed through the air just in front of his face.

Some hidden killer had attacked him.

(*What*—?!)

He looked up.

There was a naked girl clinging to the ceiling, hands and feet thrust in the cracks between the wood paneling. He thought it was a woman, but only assumed this because he couldn't see any male genitalia between its legs. Later, he was to learn that there was no genitalia there at all.

The girl grinned. "You saw me," she whispered. "Now that you have seen me, I cannot allow you to live," she continued as if she were sharing a joke. If there had not already been a corpse lying beneath her, he would not have taken her seriously.

Masami was stunned. He simply stared blankly up at her, immobile.

If he had been a girl, he would have heard the legends. He would have thought, *It's Boogiepop!*

She moved like the wind. She kicked Masami in the chest, sending him flying into the opposite wall before he knew what had happened.

"—*Gah*!" He yelled as his back slammed into the wall. He moaned in pain, "*Unh...*" and was about to pass out, but he knew deep down that he couldn't let himself succumb to his body's frailties.

She laughed softly as she approached. There were traces of mud and leaves on her body. The mountains behind the school ran deep. She had probably ventured through them and come out at the school.

She looked like a majestic wild animal; she had a strange beauty about her—a strange fearlessness he had never seen anywhere else, an established aloofness found only in things that were beyond human understanding.

Masami simply stared up at her.

"Nice timing. I had just thought that it would be better to copy a male than a female. I shall take your shape," she said, reaching out towards Masami.

As if freed from possession, he blinked and said, "Wha-what?" He frowned, "C-copy?"

"Yes. I shall become you and blend into human society. No one will ever be able to find me."

"*Hunh.*" His face scrunched up—but not because he felt despair at the sight of his approaching demise. No; the next thing he said was, "In that case, it would be far more effective to keep me alive." He sounded a little put out by this.

The girl frowned. "Why...?"

"Oh, it's just that you'll just have a much easier time as a stuck up teacher's pet with no friends at all, like our little Yurihara Minako here. If you try to take my place, people will notice the difference. I've strived to maintain at least mid-level popularity here. People know me."

He sounded deeply disappointed by this—because he was.

He wanted to be killed by something much more powerful than him. Even with Kirima Nagi, he had not really wanted to date her; he had wanted her to kill him.

Such was his nature. And for the first time, he understood this truth about himself clearly.

He didn't know why exactly. There was obviously nothing

out of the ordinary happening at home and he had no childhood trauma to contend with, like Suema Kazuko had almost encountered. But there it was, clear as day.

A deep search for something kind of reason, would have revealed it as a reaction against his life style—a way for him to fight against his deliberate pretense of mundanity. But that was far too shallow a reason to satisfy a psychiatrist. People like Masami, who had a fetish for indirect suicide, were not particularly unusual.

"......?" The naked killer looked down at him, baffled. Until now, everyone who had ever seen her had felt nothing but hatred and fear—but this boy showed no signs of either. "Why are you so quiet? You do not struggle...you do not beg?" she found herself asking.

"That's because I love you," Masami answered, honestly and quite sincerely.

"*Hunh*?" For the first time in her life, the girl was dumbfounded.

* * *

"You were right, Saotome-kun. Yurihara Minako's form fits my needs well. Nobody thinks it strange if I don't talk to them in class. She was always like that, apparently," the Manticore said, in the dimly lit coffee shop. Her face so perfectly matched Yurihara's that for all intents and purposes she *was* Yurihara Minako, as the former owner of that name had long since been erased from the face of the earth.

"I thought so."

"The classes at school resemble some sort of game, but this studying for exams is utterly pointless. I just have to read the explanation and I can understand anything."

"You're much smarter than most of us humans, then."

"Even Yurihara Minako's parents haven't noticed the difference. They communicate with her so cautiously. Are all humans like that?"

"Mostly. But be careful. There are a few egoists who think other people are a part of themselves. My parents, for example."

"Shall I kill them for you?" Yurihara suggested airily.

"Not yet. It's still too early," Masami replied just as evenly.

"True. We must be cautious until we control the world," she giggled.

"Exactly," Masami grinned back.

At this point, the waitress brought the lemon tea and cake Masami had ordered. She overheard them talking about "controlling the world," but just assumed that they were talking about some sort of new video game.

She did, however, think that the couple was far too horny, and that they should get a room before they started making out right there in the restaurant.

They can't even be out of high school yet, but they're acting like newlyweds. They're all over each other! she thought. She was still reeling from a harsh break up, so she slapped the bill on the table a bit roughly and left.

Masami carried on, "Should we make ourselves any new slaves beyond Kusatsu Akiko?"

"Yes—if possible, I'd like two or three more. Too many, and

we might get noticed, though... But at some point, we'll need them on a larger scale. Better to test the process out now."

Their plan was simple: remake human society with themselves at the center. Yurihara certainly had the power to make that a reality. She could become any human she wanted and could make any human do her bidding.

The idea was Masami's. He offered to cooperate with her, but when she told him of her powers, he found himself rubbing his hands together with glee.

"We can use that," he said eagerly.

When she heard his plan, it sounded quite reasonable, so she agreed. All she'd thought about before now was her own survival. She'd never actually thought about the rest of the world. And more importantly, she had always been alone. She'd been cloned as an "experiment" and had no family of her own. The only person who had ever told her "I love you" was Saotome Masami, whom normal society would classify as a crazed lunatic.

"But there must be agents from the 'institution' pursuing me. What should we do about them?"

"At the moment, all we can do is hope that they don't find you. Give it a little more time, and we'll be able to fight back."

"And demolish anyone who wishes to 'erase' me as a 'failure'?"

"Exactly! You're no failure. You're going to be the new ruler of the world," Masami said forcefully.

Yurihara rested her hand on top of his. "Saotome-kun, you are my prince." The man-eating monster stroked the hand of her Mephistopheles, while sweetly whispering, "I love you."

It may have been twisted, but they were unmistakably in love.

4.

As they had planned, Kusatsu Akiko gradually began to come to school less and less often. Her family was falling apart, and was behind on her tuition payments, so nobody thought this at all unnatural.

She got her friends hooked, and Yurihara and Masami took them. The first one they nabbed was Suzumiya Takako, second year, class F.

It was easy to take her. She and her friends always gathered in seclusion, and all that Yurihara and Masami had to do was follow them as they left and simply take them down.

Unfortunately, they were unable to alter them in the way that they had Kusatsu Akiko. They died, but they did not return.

"It seems it requires a very delicate balance."

"Good thing we decided to experiment first," they said, whispering in the darkness.

They had been killing high school girls from Shinyo Academy and other local schools, one after another. To cover this up, they laid down a few red herrings to throw off the authorities.

Once the precedent had been established, the rest of their work went smoothly. There were no signs of fuss at school. At Shinyo Academy, there had been a special meeting and a resulting morning lecture, but that was all. Missing person reports had probably been filed with the police, but they were buried in a mountain of missing girls totally unrelated to them at all, and swiftly forgotten about.

"The students that ran away were all slackers to begin with," the guidance teacher told Saotome at the discipline committee meeting.

This generalization was so insensitive to the students' individual circumstances that the committee president, Niitoki Kei, stiffened her tiny body and turned her cute, childish face downwards to hide her steaming glare.

But Masami was taking minutes, so he wrote the gist of the comment down in his notebook. "Disturbance in behavior precedes disappearance." As he wrote these words, he was expressionless.

He never let even a faint smile steal across his lips.

Everything was going exactly according to plan.

Still, he was left expressionless. Nothing the teachers said and nothing happening around him could change this. He had killed five people without so much as remorse, and here he was, still acting like an ordinary student.

But when the teacher stated that, "Incidentally, the infamous Kirima Nagi failed to arrive this morning. Make sure to keep an eye on her, hear? No telling what that girl's plotting in the shadows," Masami's cold heart skipped a beat. He didn't show it, but even now that he had the Manticore, hers was one of the few names that could affect him.

* * *

Kusatsu Akiko's behavior became strange a month after she had been altered.

Even when she came to school, she seemed particularly out of it.

When people spoke to her, she barely seemed to notice, much less reply.

(*...Uh-oh.*)

Masami figured that Kusatsu Akiko had begun to break down much faster than expected.

They couldn't leave her like this. She was clearly evidence. If she collapsed somewhere and was taken to a hospital, they would surely discover her condition, and the "institution" that made the Manticore would soon find out.

So Yurihara was forced to eat Kusatsu Akiko, and the first stage of their experiment ended. Unfortunately, they had still not managed to recruit a second subject with any real success, and it was putting considerable strain on both Masami and Yurihara's relationship.

"Damn it! Why doesn't it *work*?!" Yurihara yelled, growing ever more high strung.

"It's nothing to worry about. We will have many more opportunities."

"I know that, but..." Yurihara said, and then looked up at Masami. "I'm sorry. I'll get it right next time."

"We should wait a while," Masami replied calmly.

"Why? I can do it now!" Yurihara said almost shrieking, her voice clearly echoing through the empty parking garage.

"That's not the problem. We're reaching the limit of what we can do in the school. We have to look for more prey elsewhere. But we need to prepare. Not only for more experiments, but for your food supply as well. We've taken care of both of them at the same time so far, but you need other forms of nourishment, don't you?" he said gently, his tone showing a marked contrast to the horrific meaning behind his words. He rested his hand on her shoulder.

"All right, we shall do as you say." Yurihara nodded obediently.

* * *

The day after Kusatsu Akiko vanished, Masami got involved in something a little out of the ordinary.

During break, he was on his way back from returning a slide ruler he'd borrowed from the teacher's room, when a female teacher came flying around the corner, extremely flustered.

"Y-you! You're on the discipline committee, aren't you?!" she asked, her face brightening the moment she saw Masami.

"Yes, Saotome, 1-D," Masami replied.

"Thank god you're here! Please keep watch! Don't let her get away!" she shouted, and continued on down the hall.

"......?" Masami looked puzzled, and walked in the direction that she had come from. It was the staff bathroom.

Since it had been a female teacher, he poked his head through the door. He had no particular enthusiasm for ladies restrooms, but he didn't hesitate at all in his actions. He simply walked straight inside.

But once inside, he was badly shocked.

"Oh, it's you, Saotome-kun," said Kirima Nagi, in the flesh, standing smack dab in the middle of the white room, nodding at him.

"S-senpai, what's going...?" He didn't need to finish. The moment he asked, he noticed the unlit cigarette in her hand. "That's...!"

"Yeah, well, you know how it is," she said, making no effort to hide it.

"They caught you, didn't they? But why? And in a place like *this*?"

"Whatever," Nagi gave him a half grin. It made quite an impact. It was this sort of impression that had made him fall in love with her in the first place.

"Senpai, um..." he tried to talk further.

She cut him off. "Sorry again about that other thing. I still think it's better for you this way."

"Oh, no, that's..."

"Oh, hey, you were 1-D, weren't you?"

"Yeah..."

"Were you friends with Kusatsu Akiko?"

Masami thought his heart was going to leap out of his mouth.

"Er, n-not really..." he mumbled.

Nagi glared at him. "You knew her?"

"I went out with her once."

"On a date?"

"No! I mean, *uh*, it was like..." he said, scrambling to form a coherent sentence.

Nagi looked at his face, and grinned again. "Not what I'm asking. You notice her acting weird lately?"

"Well, yeah, I guess so."

"How long?"

"Maybe...two or three weeks?"

"Matches up..." Nagi whispered to herself.

Masami felt a shiver run down his spine, but he didn't let it show.

"Matches what?"

"Mm? Oh, never mind," Nagi said evasively.

"Something happen to Kusatsu? If there's anything I can do to help, senpai..." he pressed.

"Nah, it's nothing important."

"Of course it's important. I mean, *this* is deliberate, isn't it?" he said, taking the cigarette out of Nagi's hand.

"Hey, Saotome-kun," Nagi said, troubled.

"It's something big enough that you're deliberately getting yourself suspended, isn't it? Let me tell the teachers."

"They won't do anything! Teachers are nothing but wage slaves," she said coldly.

Masami couldn't argue with that. He had suggested it precisely because he had the same opinion. If they left things up to the teachers, everything would be forgotten in no time.

"Then..." he persisted.

Nagi took his hand and held it tightly.

"Thanks, but no. You're normal, and you shouldn't have anything to do with this."

"But..." he said as three male teachers came stomping into the ladies room.

"You again!" they shouted at Nagi.

Nagi was unaffected.

"*Um...*" Masami tried talking to them, but they didn't even look at him. One of them took the cigarette out of his hand, and said, "This is evidence!" thrusting it out towards Nagi.

She said nothing.

She was hauled off to the guidance office like a wanted criminal.

Masami followed after her, looking worried, but one of the teachers told him to go back to his room, so he simply watched them leave.

There was nobody else around, and the color in his face slowly faded.

"............"

From down the hall, he heard the office door slam open. All Masami could do was turn and walk away. There was no emotion left on his face.

"............"

Nagi's choice of words kept echoing through his mind. She had said, "Matches up." All he could think was that it matched up to the first girl who had "run away," Suzumiya Takako.

Nagi knew something.

Something too close for comfort.

"…………"

His mask cracked for just a second, letting out a glimpse of his true face underneath.

His eyes were withered, inhuman, like a man who has just wandered in the desert for a week with no water and let sand creep into every pore on his body.

5.

"KIRIMA NAGI? Why would she?!" cried out Yurihara when she heard Masami's story. They were in the pool changing rooms, where thankfully nobody ever dared to come during winter.

"I don't know. But she's clearly caught wind of something."

Masami told Yurihara about Nagi six days into her suspension. During that period, he was stalking the girls that they had planned next to entrap and kill. It quickly became obvious that Nagi was taking them down one after the other—all of Kusatsu Akiko's Junior High school friends. Today, he'd seen her attack Kinoshita Kyoko, and make her promise never to take drugs again.

In the shadows of the school, it was clear that she was playing out some sort of hero fantasy of her own.

"Why?! We did everything right!" Yurihara cried out hysterically.

"Yes, we did. Which is why she hasn't caught wind of us yet," he said quietly. But inside, he knew just how precarious of a position that they were in. If they had been just a little bit late in disposing of Kusatsu Akiko, Nagi would most certainly have deduced what was wrong with her. It had been a very close shave.

"We can't kill anyone else from Shinyo Academy. We don't want her suspecting that you're a student here."

"Why don't we just kill her?" Yurihara suggested.

"Not yet. I don't know how much she knows or how she found out. We need to know that, at least."

"She needs to die! We won't leave any evidence behind! And she's crazy—nobody'll notice when she vanishes."

It was obvious that they were in the same class. Yurihara knew Nagi all too well.

"But her current parents are very rich. And she's got several hundred million yen in the bank. She disappears, and I guarantee you that it won't be put down as a runaway. When money gets involved, there's no telling who'll come out of the woodwork. That's how human society works."

Yurihara remained silent. She looked at the floor, bit her lip, and then whispered petulantly, "...Is that the *only* reason?"

"*Eh*?"

"Is that the only reason you won't kill Kirima Nagi? There's another reason, *isn't* there?"

"What are you talking about?"

"Saotome-kun, don't lie to me. You're in love with her, aren't you?"

Masami looked away.

"Wh-why do you think that?"

"Am I wrong? I'm right, aren't I?" she asked as she looked up and glared at him.

"I..." Masami started to say, when suddenly...

"—what are you doing in here, Echoes?" a cheery girl's voice asked, as the door to the changing room swung open.

From the stripes on her uniform, it was clear that she was third year. And a bright and sunny girl at that.

"Uh, oops? My mistake, sorry!" she said, scratching her head.

"*Ah*! D-don't—!" Masami yelled, pretending that the girl had caught them in the middle of a romantic moment. It was okay, though. She hadn't overheard them.

"Sorry! Sorry! You two have fun now!" she commented, smiling. She was clearly blushing from embarrassment as she started to duck back out the door.

But at that moment, Yurihara's body shot forward like a bullet. She let out a hiss like a king cobra, and sank her teeth into the back of the third year girl's neck.

There was a sharp cracking sound.

"W-wha?!" cried Masami, trying to get between them, but he was already too late. She had bitten through the girl's spine, killing her instantly. It was over before the girl even realized what was happening to her.

"What the hell were you thinking?! I just told you not to kill at school!" Masami yelled, turning on Yurihara.

But when he saw her face, his manner changed.

She was as white as a sheet and shivering violently. "H-how... how is *he* here?" she whimpered with her latest victim's blood splattered across her mouth.

"What do you mean?"

"Him! Echoes! He's here!"

"Who—or—what is Echoes?"

"My 'original'! The over-evolved man!" She hugged her hands to her chest, but that didn't stop her shaking.

"C-calm down! You can explain later. First, we have to get rid of this body!" Masami yelled, glancing down at the girl's corpse. Looking closely, he recognized her face. "She's...Kamikishiro Naoko?"

She was one of Nagi's few precious friends. That was how he knew her. Nagi had taken a year off in Junior High due to illness, but she had been in the same class as Kamikishiro at the time.

(Why is Nagi's friend...? Is this just a coincidence? No, it can't be...)

He felt the last piece fall into place. Just as they had disposed of Kusatsu Akiko in the nick of time, once again Fate had given them a desperately needed chance.

"Don't worry, Manticore. The advantage is on our side." He smiled, and gently put his arms around her trembling shoulders.

"*Eh*?" she questioned as she looked up, and was greeted with a warm and knowing nod and a luminous smile.

* * *

They carried Kamikishiro Naoko's body to a secret room in the basement. Yurihara leaned over the corpse and began disposing of the evidence.

As he watched, Masami grinned.

(I'll make sure you live through this. I promise. Whatever happens to me...it'll be worth it.)

A single line of a song ran through Saotome Masami's mind.

For some reason, it was not a song by his beloved group The Doors. He had forgotten the exact name of it; it was just a song that he had overheard somewhere and barely remembered. He couldn't even remember the whole line; just a snippet echoing through his mind like a broken record.

It was a song by a band that wasn't anywhere near as famous as The Doors; they were a freak band called Oingo Boingo that were famous for their weirded-out tunes. The name of the song was "No One Lives Forever."

The poppy, cheery tune didn't match the sinister name, nor the blood-ridden lyrics. Masami began singing under his breath.

"...No one, no one, no one, no one, no one no

one no one no one no one no one no one no one no one no one
no one no one no one no one no one no one no one no one no
one no one no one no one no one no one no one no one no one
no one no one no one no one no one no one no one no one no
one no one no one no one no one no one no one no one no one
no one no one no one no one no one no one no one no one no
one no one no one no one no one no one no one no one no one
no one no one no one no one no one no one no one no one no
one no one no one no one no one no one no one no one no one..."

His smile continued till the rest of the phrase, "lives forever," came back to him. The smile contained more than the radiance of one prepared to sacrifice his life for the object of his affections—there was a hint of evil and of deeply personal pleasure to it, too.

In front of him came a sound like wind whistling through a crack in the wall as the man-eater consumed the girl.

Boogiepop

and others

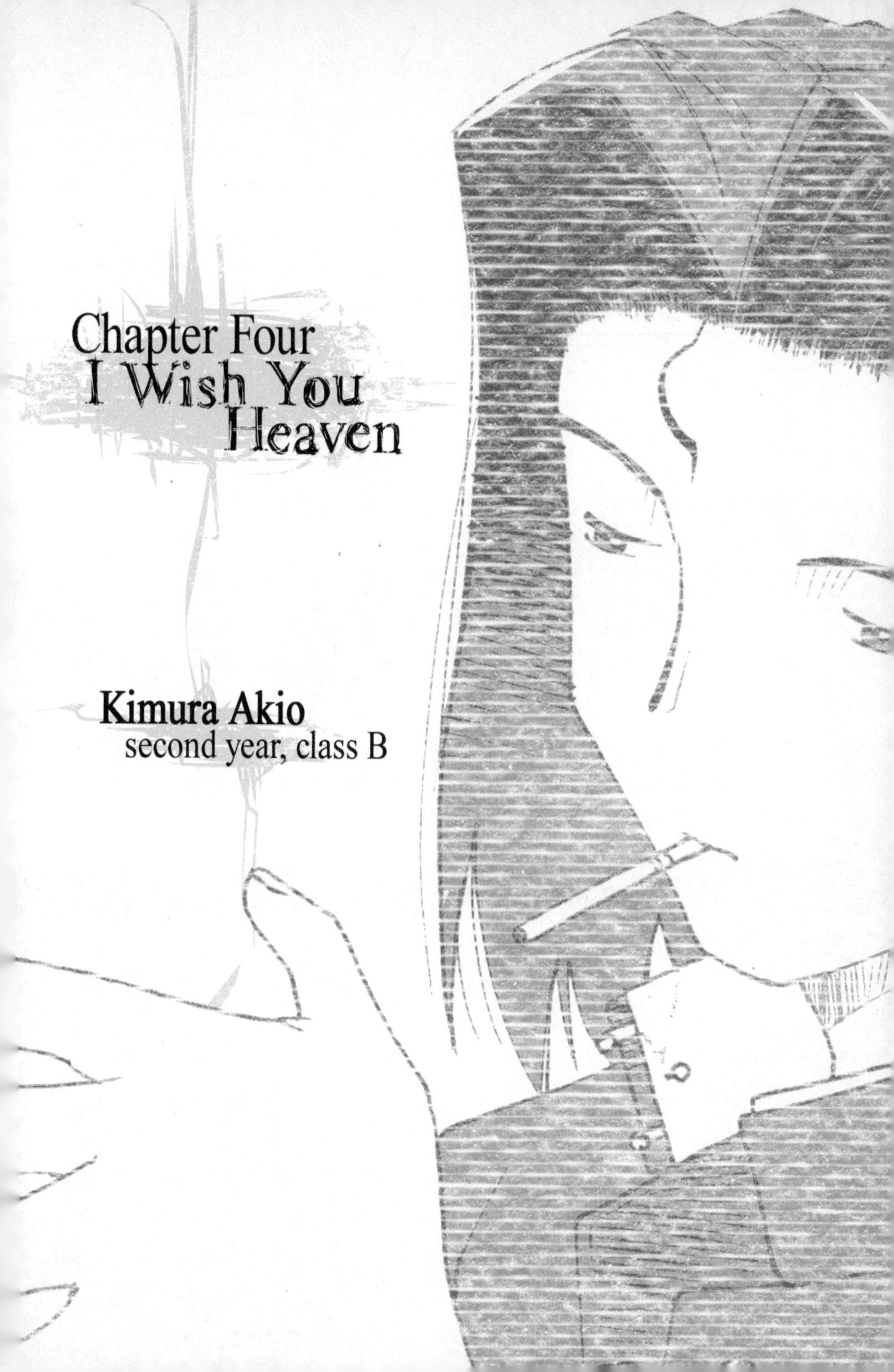

Chapter Four
I Wish You Heaven

Kimura Akio
second year, class B

1.

"Kamikishiro Naoko is dead. You should forget about her," was all that was written in the letter. It looked like a computer print out.

"What?" I picked up the envelope and studied it for a moment, but all it had listed on it was my name, "Kimura Akio" and home address. There was no return address at all, and judging from the stamp, it had been posted in the same town where I attended high school.

At first, I thought it must be a prank by one of my old classmates. My little fling with Kamikishiro Naoko had kinda become public knowledge after it ended.

But it seemed a bit late for that. Two full years had passed since I'd last seen her, and this kind of prank seemed a little irrelevant now.

Still, she vanished abruptly during my second year, and I still don't know why she disappeared. I doubt anybody knows. Had anybody *ever* really known what had gone on in her head?

* * *

Kamikishiro Naoko and I first hooked up in a pretty strange kinda way.

This all took place not too long after the spring term had begun.

I was smoking a Caster Mild around the back of the school one day at lunch, when a boy and a girl showed up. Luckily for me, I was hiding behind a tree, so they didn't see me.

There was kind of a long, meaningful silence, so I took that opportunity to hide even better, hoping to get an eyeful.

But they barely even looked at each other, they just sort of stood there, fidgeting.

(*Ah ha...*)

Just as I got it figured out, the girl opened her mouth.

"Did you...read the letter?" she said, clasping her hands.

"*Mm*," he said evasively.

The whole thing was kinda old fashioned, and I was just about to lose interest, when the boy suddenly looked around nervously and asked, "You are alone...right?"

"*Hunh*?" she blinked. And so did I. Most people usually come alone at moments like this. Though, of course, there are always some losers that need their friends to goad them on.

"So you're not gonna beat me up or anything?" he asked, relieved.

What, was this kid afraid of girls or something?

Then I finally noticed.

His slippers were blue, and hers were yellow. Our school was set up so that each grade had a different color. I was wearing green ones. The boy was a first year, and the girl was third year.

"No, nothing like that!" she exclaimed. The moment that I knew she was my senpai, she started looking extremely grown up… and hot. I'm pretty picky when it comes to girls, but I could tell she had on makeup that subtly made her eyes look bigger. But it was natural makeup, so that the teachers would never notice. It was also obvious that she worked pretty hard at making herself always look cheerful.

But the other one, this first year kid, looked like a child. He was a baby-faced pretty boy, yet kinda ordinary—but hey, some girls are into that.

"Then what is it?" he asked the older girl vacantly.

"You know…" she said, turning red and staring at her feet. Her expression clearly showed that it wasn't anything but what it was.

(*Hunh…?*)

I knew how the kid felt, though. He couldn't figure out *why*. Why was this pretty senior asking a kid like *him* out? It was natural to be dubious instead of happy.

Course now I'm in college, I know loads of girls who have boyfriends younger than them. But that just doesn't happen in high school. Up to high school, you're in a sort of unmistakable feudal system. A girl could date a college guy or a Junior High kid or anyone she wanted to outside of school—but there was an unwritten rule that a girl could only date boys her year or older on the inside.

"Um…Kamikishiro-san?" he asked, very troubled. This is where I learned her name.

"What?" she replied, looking at him with a mixture of anxiety and expectation. Men find this kind of look hard to say no to.

But he was looking away and didn't see it.

"I'm sorry! I just can't do this!" he sort of shrieked as he turned and ran away.

"*Ah*...!" Kamikishiro almost chased after him, but stopped herself. Her shoulders slumped.

From behind, I could see her head hanging down and a little sideways. Somehow, this angle made her all the more beautiful, like some sort of female Don Quixote, fighting the invisible school rules. Gotta say, it impressed the shit out of me.

While I was off feeling all impressed, she suddenly rolled her head around like an old man getting out of the bath.

"Not again," she said exhaustedly, and then spun round and looked right at me.

I didn't have time to hide. Our eyes met.

"Enjoy the show? *Ah ha ha*!" she laughed, and strolled over to me. She'd known I was there the whole time.

"*Uh*, n-no. I-I didn't mean to watch," I said, scrambling.

She reached out her hand, and said, "My fee," as she pulled a Caster Mild out of my pocket. "Damn, I've been dying for a hit of nicotine all day."

She stuck the cigarette between her lips and looked at me expectantly. I hurriedly lit it.

"Pretty smooth," she said with a smirk. She let out a big puff of smoke. Her manner was the polar opposite from a moment before.

But looking at her profile, I could make out the tear tracks.

"You were serious," I said, expecting her to deny it and move on.

But instead, she just nodded and said, "You bet I was." She slumped into a crouch and continued, "Serious as I've ever been." She hugged her knees to her chest and buried her face in her skirt.

"Why can't we pick who we fall in love with? It would be so much easier..." she said forlornly.

"Well, yeah, true—but frankly, I think you're better off getting rejected by a guy like that," I said in a very honest tone.

She looked up. Her tears had made her eyeliner run a bit. Unexpectedly, she said, "...Don't."

"What?"

"Don't be nice to me. I don't want to fall for you, too."

"*What*?!" I yelped, completely off balance now. She stood up, no longer crying, and smiled. "Just kidding. But you're a good guy. So, what's your name?"

"Kimura, 2-B."

"I'm Kamikishiro, 3-F. You planning on going to class this afternoon?"

"Not really." I had Modern Japanese and Political Science left, but I was planning on skipping them.

"Then I'll buy you a MOS Burger. You know, pay you back for cheering me up. C'mon, I know a way out the back," she winked naughtily.

And that's basically how we got started.

That's pretty much what we were like the whole time. We were never really "in love," as such. We might have looked like we were from the outside or something, but she never really fell for me. At least, I don't think she did. That was two years ago.

2.

EVENTUALLY, Kamikishiro did convince that first year kid—his name was Tanaka Shiro—to go out with her. When she attacked, no one could stop her.

One time, I just had to tell her, "I just don't know what you see in him." She often called me up and asked me to hang out with her.

Yeah, you could call it a date. We'd watch movies, eat out, shoot pool and bet money on the game. We'd also do other stuff too—but you know how it is.

"Well, you see...he's an archer."

"An archer? On the archery team?"

If I remember it correctly, we were on one of those slow moving ferris wheels at an amusement park. It was like a picture postcard of those cheesy high school dates that you see in manga.

"Yeah. First time I saw him, he was still in Junior High and was in some contest. You ever seen one? They all line up and shoot. The first one to miss loses. It was pretty damn cool. He did pretty well, but eventually lost. But his eyes...when he stared at that tiny little target so far away there was this glitter in them. Gave me goosebumps. And then, he'd let the arrow fly...and swoosh!"

"Sounds kinda shallow..." I said, somewhat disgusted. All that had nothing whatsoever to do with Tanaka himself, or with his personality. Of *course* he'd be reluctant.

"I'd much rather play around with someone like you, *Kimu*-kun. You're more fun. And I got no plans to take up archery myself. But I can't shake the feeling that kid is meant for bigger things."

"And I'm not, you mean? *Ouch*," I grimaced. The words 'someone like you' made things crystal clear. Nothing I could do when she put it that way.

"Yep. You're like me that way. I'm a mess. And, frankly, so are you, *Kimu*-kun."

"Can't deny that," I said, chuckling. It was true. If it wasn't, then why would I be dating a girl who I knew full well had another guy on the side? Still, I was falling for her pretty hard by this point. Yet I never even considered trying to get her to break things off with Tanaka. It wasn't just a mess—it was a freaking train wreck just waiting to happen. And on top of that, she was hardly the only girl I was seeing. Yeah, we were exactly the same.

"I'll be honest. *Shiro*-kun doesn't get me at all," she said, sighing bitterly. "He tries not to hurt me, but he always talks kinda standoffish, and that just hurts me more. He just doesn't get that at all."

"*Hunh*. Can't say I do either."

"I'm just getting in his way. I don't think he really needs to be in love yet."

Sometimes, I found her nearly impossible to understand.

It's easy to do the typical guy thing and just bitch that girls are all complicated and stuff, but her level of complexity was clearly at a notch or two above the other girls her age. I'm pretty sure most of them wouldn't have been able to follow her, either. As it was, the only friends that I knew she had were me and some girl in her class called Kirima Nagi. That girl was even weirder than Kamikishiro, so I guess that's why they got along. Truthfully, Kirima was better looking than Kamikishiro, but I always did like Kamikishiro better. Even now.

"But do the two of us need it? I guess so. Feels like I'm kinda incomplete on my own, you know?"

"That's it exactly! See, we're the same," she said, gave me a tiny smile, leaned forward, and put her lips on mine.

It was no big deal. It was not exactly the first time we'd kissed.

"...you do that with Tanaka?" I asked curtly.

"Hell, no," she grinned, denying it instantly.

She was always at her most attractive when she wasn't outright trying to be sexy or to act cute. I never figured out why.

* * *

I was pretty sure that the letter was a prank, but something about it just kept bugging me. I decided to skip class and head over to the town where I'd gone to high school. Call it a hunch, but whoever had sent the letter probably lived there.

My family still lives there, but I didn't swing by; I just headed straight for Shinyo Academy. I didn't think any of the current students were behind it, but my legs took me in that direction anyway.

"Ah! Akio! Over here!" someone called as I waited for the bus to arrive.

I turned around and found a girl who'd been in my same class during my first and third years—Miyashita Touka. The first thing that I noticed was the huge Spalding bag over her shoulder.

"Hey, what's up?" I replied.

"What're you doing back here? It's not even New Year's yet!" Miyashita is a cute girl, but I'd never made a pass at her—which is probably why we're still friends.

"Yeah, no reason in particular. You?"

"You didn't hear? I failed exams. I'm a ronin. On my way to cram school as we speak."

"Oh, right."

"Yep. Guess you forgot all about us when you moved up, huh?"

"You sound bitter. Fighting with that designer boyfriend of yours?" I asked, knowing that she'd been dating an older boy in that line of work since her second year.

"Do not even talk to me about *him*. He never even calls!" she said, pouting.

"He's probably trying not to disrupt your studies."

"*Nah*, he studies more than me. He's trying to get some sort of award. Makes me sick."

"Hmmm..."

"What about you? Got a college girl yet?"

I made a face. "Nope."

"Aw, that third year girl still dragging you back?"

"She was a third year then. She'd be twenty now."

"You're... You're counting her birthdays? She dumped you and vanished! Give up on her already!"

"It's none of your business," I spat.

She looked pissed, but she grabbed my hand.

"W-what?"

"Come with me. *We* are having *tea*."

Still pissed, she dragged me into a nearby café by the name of Tristan.

"What about cram school?"

"Screw it. I'm gonna fail again this year anyway," she said recklessly.

She plunked herself down in a booth and shouted at the counter, "Two American coffees!" She then turned on me to tell me exactly what I already knew, "You're an *idiot.*"

"I know," I replied petulantly.

"No, you don't! You think you're some sort of hero, don't you? What with that mess two years ago," Miyashita announced. She'd always been like this, sort of self-righteous and inclined to stick her nose into everything.

"I do not. That was just..."

"It wasn't you, was it? Her lover. You didn't even know who it was you were taking the fall for, did you?"

"........."

Two years ago, after Kamikishiro had vanished, they found a blanket, pillow and electric heater in a storage room near the gym, where nobody ever went. It was obvious somebody had snuck into the school and had been living there. At first, they thought it was a drifter, but then they found an accessory that had belonged to Kamikishiro (according to one of the girls in her class), and it turned into a student body scandal.

I don't know what kind of people Kamikishiro's parents were, but their daughter had disappeared and the school suspected her involvement in illicit activities, yet the parents made no protest at all to the accusations. In her continued absence, the school made preparations to forcibly expel her. At which point, a certain male student announced that he'd been her lover, and all hell broke loose after that.

"She didn't bring any outsiders into the school. Don't expel her," he'd said.

The teachers didn't even pretend to believe him. But the students made a huge fuss about it and just to calm things down, the school suspended the boy and relented on Kamikishiro's punishment.

But Kamikishiro never did show up again. Her name was even kicked off the rosters at graduation, due to a lack of credits.

It all amounted to nothing in the end. There was never really anything to the story. As a result of the commotion, the boy got his comeuppance, though. He received a series of Dear John letters from all of his many girlfriends, telling him that he was a loser and that they were dumping his sorry ass.

"...No, I knew who Kamikishiro was seeing," I told Miyashita with a faint smile.

"Liar."

"No, really."

"Then, who? Who'd she drop you for?"

"An alien. He took her with him back into space."

No sooner were the words out of my mouth than a slap echoed through the café. Miyashita had belted me one across the face.

"Get a grip on yourself! Be a man, and just move on!" she said, furious.

Wasn't like she had any special feelings for me, mind you. She was just that kind of girl.

"S-sorry," I said, rubbing my cheek sheepishly.

But I hadn't been joking. That was exactly what Kamikishiro had said to me.

3.

"KIMU-KUN, do you think human existence is justified?" Kamikishiro asked, out of the blue one day.

"Nope," I said, instantly. I was getting used to her non sequiturs.

"Dang, neither do I," she sighed.

We were lying next to each other on the bank of the river that ran along the road leading up to school. Since most of the students took the bus, people hardly ever walked along this road. It was already dark out, and we could see stars above us.

"Humans just aren't that great. However much our civilization advances, we can't seem to do anything to make ourselves happier," I said, obviously, trying to impress her with something profound.

"Yeah...maybe," she replied. She seemed kinda serious.

"Why do you ask?"

"I just met this guy, but..."

"You in love again? What about Tanaka?" I asked, surprised.

"Yeah. Yeah, I am, but let's put that aside for a moment," she said, sitting up. She gazed at the wavering reflection of the city lights on the moving water of the river. "He's from outer space."

She looked serious. She had to be joking, but she didn't seem to be waiting for me to laugh, so I took it as some sort of metaphor, and just nodded. "*Mm-hmm.*"

"But I don't think he's from some other planet. It's like, in space there's this big consciousness, and it sent him here to, you know, 'test mankind' or something. Kinda like the inspection robots that always show up in Hoshi Shinichi's short stories? But he's not a machine or anything. It's just that his body isn't something that exists on Earth. It can, like, turn into anything. So, when he landed on earth, he disguised himself as human and tried to examine the world, but there were a few mistakes, and he didn't quite manage to pull off being human quite right."

"............"

"He's evolved a little too much. He's got more power within him than any human will ever have in a thousand years—no, in ten thousand years! Apparently, space is just so big that they couldn't match him up with Earth time just right, so his true nature came out ahead of time, and the government or some kind of big corporation got a hold of him. But the idiots thought that he was just some mutant, and they did all sorts of experiments on him and cloned him. But, unlike him, that cloned copy turned into a brutal man-eater."

I no longer had the foggiest idea what she was talking about. I elected to keep quiet until I could pick up the thread again.

"He wanted to communicate all this, but he couldn't. He was programmed in such a way that he couldn't talk to humans directly. It was so that he wouldn't reveal his true identity to anyone. Which was fine. I mean, after all, he was sent here to test humans and see if they would be nice to him. He wasn't here to negotiate or make speeches or anything. He was just here to observe, so they named him Echoes, since all he can do is reflect back the words that people speak to him."

"............"

"But the man-eater killed everyone in the research facility and escaped. Now, it's off hiding inside of human society somewhere. But Echoes came after it, and he...and he met me."

"What's he gonna do if he catches it?"

"Fight it, I guess. If he doesn't, it'll just take over the world or something."

"But he's an alien. Why does he care what happens here?"

"Yeah, you've got a point, but...basically, he's just nice."

"That's it?"

"Isn't it enough? Isn't niceness the best motivation that someone can have?" she asked, looking at me kinda solemn. She then let out a sigh. "Half of this is just me reading between the lines.

I think he's got some sort of other complicated reason, too. You know, something about maintaining the balance of the planet. But if that was all...its kinda sad, don't you think?" she whispered pretty downcast. She looked on the verge of tears, which made me uncomfortable.

I felt the kind of tightness in my chest that I thought that I'd left behind in Junior High.

I cleared my throat to hide this feeling, and said deliberately rough, "So, how the hell did this Echoes guy even explain all of this to you? I thought he couldn't talk?" It was a stupid nitpick.

So she said, "*Ah ha ha*! You're too smart! I can't fool you," and cackled.

"That's all?" I asked. The story was a bit too detailed to be dismissed like this.

"Yep, I was just kidding. Just a stupid little fairy tale!" Kamikishiro said with an impish grin stealing over the corners of her mouth.

We sat in silence for a while.

She was the first to break it. "But if Echoes wins, he'll probably go back to his home in the stars."

"Sounds romantic to me. Kinda like the tanabata festival."

"I wonder what he'll tell them about us humans. I don't suppose there's much chance of him saying, 'Don't worry, they're a good species,' is there?"

"Where is he now?"

"Hiding at the school. Don't tell anyone."

I laughed. "Don't worry, I won't."

Stupid promise.

Because of that promise, I got myself suspended and had to lower my ambitions for college. But since I turned all my friends into enemies and spent the rest of school isolated, I had nothing to do but study, and eventually, I used my grades to make up for the poor conduct report.

"The stars are so far away," Kamikishiro said, gazing up at the night sky.

"They're farther away than our lives," I said. I'm not sure what her story really meant, but she'd managed to get the answer that she'd wanted out of me, as I told her, "But if you open your heart to Echoes, then I'm sure he'll learn to like humanity."

"You think so?"

"I want to think so. Because the story you told me leaves us no salvation."

"Yeah. I hope you're right," she said, turning towards me and smiling.

But at the time, I didn't want her to smile. I wanted her to get angry with me for saying something so stupid. I tried to think of something even stupider to say, but instead we headed back home. I walked off down the road to the station, and she went back towards the school, saying that she'd take the bus.

That was the last time I ever saw her.

She didn't come to school the next day. Or the day after that. She never came again.

* * *

Two cups of American coffee appeared in front of Miyashita Touka and me. Miyashita picked up on the waitress' look of keen interest and cooled down a little.

"Sorry, I shouldn't have slapped you. Still..." she said in a hushed tone.

"Don't worry. I know. I'm an idiot."

"I really do think that you need to let her go. She's—what was her name?"

"Kamikishiro Naoko."

"Oh, right. I didn't know her very well, but I think if she really did like you, Akio, that she'd want you to move on now. That's why she didn't say anything when she left. Make sense?"

"That... That'd be nice."

Truth is, I'm pretty sure she never thought twice about me.

Eventually, Miyashita Touka let me go, forcibly exhorting me to cheer up.

We parted at the door to the coffee shop.

"Take care. You know, you really ought to do something about that hero complex of yours. Gonna get you into trouble someday. You've got tests to study for."

"I guess," she said with her head to one side. "But still..."

"Suit yourself," I said, turning to leave. It was then that she called after me.

"—Kimura-kun!"

I looked back and nearly tripped over my own feet.

It was certainly Miyashita Touka standing there, but for some reason, I felt like I was looking at a completely different person—a boy. It was as if she'd transformed or something.

"Wh-what?"

"Kamikishiro Naoko performed her duty admirably. You should perform your own duty, and make her proud. That's the only thing you can do for her," she proclaimed like she was giving some speech on stage.

Then she spun on her heel and was lost in the crowd.

"…………"

I stared after her, watching the throng flow onwards.

* * *

When my bus reached the stop in front of Shinyo Academy, it was already past sunset, and there were no students in sight. Apparently, even the sports teams gave up on practice and called it a day, once it got dark. This must be why none of our teams have ever even so much as qualified for the national tournaments. It hadn't changed a bit since I was last there.

The gates were closed. Outsiders had to identify themselves over an intercom to get in, so I passed right by them.

I entered the school through a gap between the fences that Kamikishiro had shown me.

The darkened school grounds were silent like an abandoned building. The towering school building looked kinda like a giant, looming tombstone.

Until about a year before, I had actually come here every day. But now, I was a stranger.

There's not much good I have to say about my years in high school, but I felt a pain in my chest when I thought about how little connection I had now to my past. I remember Kamikishiro, and the abuse that I took after the incident like it was yesterday, but the rest of it was all far too long ago.

"…………"

Why had I come here? If I was looking for the source of the letter, this place wasn't going to be of any use.

But this high school was the only remaining connection that I had with Kamikishiro. Someone else had moved into her apartment. There were no traces of her left.

There was nowhere else for me to go.

She just wasn't here.

Yeah. Somewhere inside, I had wondered if Kamikishiro herself had sent the letter.

But that was probably wrong. Even here in school, she wasn't around. The letter was nothing but a prank.

Everything was over. It was all in the past.

"………"

I looked up at the sky. It was cloudy, and I couldn't see the stars. And yet, I felt like I could see them like I had when I used to lay with her on the river bank.

She had told me all of her secrets, metaphorically. Told *me*; not Tanaka Shiro, not anyone else. And I never understood what she meant by it.

Wasn't that enough? That's all the reason I needed to love her for the rest of my life. No matter how much I might fall in love with some other girl, she will always live inside of me in the way that she was then—impossible to understand, and more than a little crazy.

"Life is brief, young maiden, fall in love."

I whispered a snatch of the gondola song that she always used to sing while I wandered around the school.

I found myself in front of the gym. Suddenly, I wanted to see the storage room where the interloper had hidden himself. Their exact relationship remained a mystery, but it was the last known trace of her.

I grabbed a flashlight from the emergency supplies, and shone it around the gym. I had forgotten half of the features of the place. Guess I really had wanted to wipe all recall of high school from my mind.

I found some kind of door or cover or something down by the floor, near the main entrance. Figured that must be it. So I hunkered down and opened it.

It was just an empty space. Iron pillars, concrete floor, bare ceiling. The foundations of the gym, I guess. Designed to absorb the impact of an earthquake.

I'd been there three years and never known it was there.

(Guess this isn't it...)

I turned to leave.

But something moved near my foot.

There was a dry rustle.

"*Mm...?*"

I shone the light at my feet.

There was something black and dried. I thought it was a glove at first, maybe forgotten by a workman, but it was too thin for that.

It wasn't meant to be put on over a hand. It *was* a hand.

"........."

I stared at it in shock for a moment...then screamed.

It was a mummified human hand.

(W-w-w-what the hell is this?!)

My knees gave out and I fell on my ass.

When Kamikishiro had vanished, she hadn't been the only one. A number of other students had vanished both before and after her.

I'd never connected them before...but I could think of no other reason why a hand would be lying on the floor of the school.

Maybe it was because I'd kicked it or maybe it was the exposure to the outside air—but whichever the case, the hand crumbled away to dust before my very eyes. And within seconds, there was nothing left of it at all.

(What does it mean? What the hell happened here two years ago?)

But there was nothing to give me those answers. There was nothing for me to do but sit there in the dark, shuddering in fear...

Boogiepop
and others

Chapter Five
Heartbreaker

Niitoki Kei
second year, class F

1.

"Kei, there's a first year boy asking for you," my classmate Mishima said.

I looked up from my book and asked, "Who?"

"Dunno. But he's cute. *Tch*, the discipline committee president, eating all the young boys..." she cackled.

I gave her a pained smile, stood up, and went into the hall.

When he saw me, he bowed his head politely. "Niitoki-senpai? I'm Tanaka Shiro, 1-D."

"Tanaka-kun? You wanted to see me?"

"You were on the gate this morning, weren't you?"

One of the duties of the discipline committee members, which we all took turns doing, was to stand at the gate and monitor the students coming in and out.

"Yeah. What about it?"

"Did you see 3-F's Kamikishiro-san arrive?"

"Naoko-san? I know her, but no, she didn't come today. But she's nearly always late..."

"She's not in class either," he said gravely.

"Really? Must be skipping."

"No," he said, quite sure of himself. "Recently, she had some sort of reason why she had to come to school every day."

(Is this kid in love with her…?)

Seemed like it. Maybe he was gonna ask her out today.

"Hunh. I don't know. If she's not here, ask her tomorrow."

"That might be too late!" he exclaimed anxiously. "You really don't know anything?!"

"You call her house?"

"There's never anyone there."

"*Eh*?"

"Her parents are in the middle of an ugly divorce. Her mother's gone to her parents' house, and her father never comes home."

"Really?"

"Everyone in the apartment building's talking about it. Everybody I asked told me all about it."

"*Hunh…*" I said.

Suddenly, a voice cut in from the side. "You should ask Kirima Nagi."

Both of us swung around in surprise. My kouhai on the discipline committee, Saotome-kun, was standing there.

"Masami? What do you…?" Tanaka-kun said, wide eyed. Later, I found out these two were in the same class.

"I was just passing by; happened to overhear. Thought you might like to know."

"Know what?"

"I don't know any details, but Kamikishiro Naoko-senpai and Kirima Nagi have been friends since Junior High. She's just off of suspension, so she might know something about Kamikishiro-senpai."

I blinked. It was the first I'd heard of Naoko-san being friends with the legendary Kirima Nagi from the class next door. And here I thought I knew about most people in the school.

"How do you know that?" I asked Saotome.

"Oh, I asked Kirima Nagi out once. Picked up a few things back then."

"You asked her out?!"

It took guts to even talk to the Fire Witch. I'll give him that.

"She said no," he admitted.

"What class is this Kirima person in?" Tanaka-kun asked forcibly. Somehow, he'd never heard of her.

"Second year, class D. Right next door."

"Okay!"

"W-whoa, hold on there! No telling what'll happen if you just burst in on her!" I said as if she were some sort of lion. But it was true. She'd punched out one boy's front teeth before.

I couldn't let them go alone, so I followed them to class D. I asked a girl I knew near the door. "Ah, Suema-san. Is Kirima-san here? I've got a first year boy who wants to talk to her..."

"She's not here today."

"Really? She came in the gate." I knew my words to be true. I was on the gate. I'd seen her arrive.

"So, she is here? I haven't seen her come to class, though," Suema-san said, shrugging.

We looked at each other.

"What… what's going on?" Saotome-kun asked.

"Sounds like she *is* involved," Tanaka-kun said in a shrill voice.

"*Hmmm…*" I was seriously worried myself now. Naoko-san and Kirima Nagi… What were they up to?

As we stood there in front of the door, someone asked, "Could I get in here?" We turned around to find Yurihara Minako, the best student in the school, standing right before us.

"Oh, sorry," Saotome-kun said, moving aside.

She nodded, and strode regally into the room like some sort of queen.

The bell rang, so we all split up and headed back to our respective rooms.

* * *

"Naoko's vanished. I can't find her anywhere," Kirima Nagi said in a place steeped in shadows.

The man with her said nothing. His expression never wavered. Nagi grew irritated at his lack of reaction, and shook her head violently.

"I called her cell, but she didn't answer. You don't know anything?" she pressed on.

The man was unable to talk, so he simply shook his head slowly.

"She may have gotten caught in *its* net. That thing Naoko said was your sibling."

"…………" The man did not respond.

Kirima Nagi scowled at him. Finally, she spat, "We should never have listened to you. We should have just called the cops, or the Self-Defense Force. If the world knew about *it*, it would've just washed its hands of the whole business and vanished to some place where we couldn't follow. But if Naoko's dead, then we're already too late..."

She buried her hands in her face, her nail digging into her cheeks and forehead.

"............"

The man didn't move.

"Say something! You talked to Naoko, didn't you?! Try and let me know what you're thinking!" Kirima Nagi shouted, grabbing his collar. It was a Brooks Brothers cotton shirt that Kamikishiro Naoko had bought for him.

"............" Even when she shook him roughly, he did nothing but stare back at her in silence.

"God damn it! I *will* find you, Manticore!" she howled, uncharacteristically angry. "And you're gonna help, Echoes!"

He nodded. But, yes, there was something remote about that motion.

As if he were monitoring Nagi's reactions.

* * *

It bugged the hell out of me, so I took gate duty again that day after school. In the morning, we had to check the cards as they went through, but on the way home, the job was simply boring.

"You are nosy," laughed the first year kid who should have been on duty. He gave up his place happily.

Nosy?

I guess I was.

There's a part of me that can't stand to see something unclear, something uncertain. That part of me wants to fix those things. Once when I was at a friend's house, they left me alone in their room with a half-done jigsaw puzzle, and when they came back, I had already finished it. They'd been pretty angry.

The reason that I was on the unpopular discipline committee—and the president of it, no less—was simply because of this "clarity impulse" of mine.

"Anyone? Who wants to do it?" they'd all ask, but nobody ever raised their hand. They just sat there in silence. And before I knew it, my hand was up.

It's like a disease, I know.

With Naoko-san missing, if I hadn't been asked, I'd never have gotten involved, but now that I had been, I wouldn't be able to sleep until I'd cleared things up.

My friends tell me, "You're like a big sister. There's just something reliable about you," which I took as a compliment (though, they may have been making fun of me.) But the truth is, it's just my neurosis.

(Talking to the Fire Witch is scary, but if I don't, I can't settle down!)

But even when most of the students had gone home, and the sky was starting to darken, Kirima Nagi had yet to appear.

It was well past the time when the gate guard was free to go home, and I was starting to wonder what else I could do, when Tanaka-kun and Saotome-kun came up.

"Ah, senpai! Did Kirima Nagi go home?" Saotome-kun asked.

"No, not yet."

"Oh," said Tanaka-kun, hanging his head.

"Why don't we look for her together? I'm sure she's still in the school somewhere," I suggested.

"That's what we were going to do," Tanaka-kun nodded. "We were talking about it in the classroom."

"I'm a little worried about Kirima Nagi," Saotome-kun said. She may have rejected him, but it seemed that he still liked her.

"But where do you think she is?"

"Somewhere where nobody would notice her—on the roof, or maybe under the gym? Oh, or the pool changing rooms..."

Saotome-kun suggested.

"Why would she be in a place like that?" Tanaka-kun said in an irritated voice.

"I don't know. But everyone knows her, so she must be someplace like that, or somebody would've noticed."

"Let's check them out," I said, and we headed back into the eerily quiet school.

* * *

While on our way to the roof, I couldn't help but ask, "Tanaka-kun, were you and Naoko-san...?"

"*Um*," he said, worried.

"Kamikishiro-senpai asked him out," Saotome-kun interjected.

"What?!" I yelped.

"Masami! That was a secret!"

"Don't worry, senpai won't tell."

I was still reeling as they spoke. "You're joking, right?"

"I certainly thought so. I kept asking her if it was a joke, but she kept saying that she was serious."

"*Hunh*..." I stared at his face closely.

"Please don't tell anyone."

"Okay, I won't. But still..."

"It was pretty confusing, but I couldn't think of a reason to say no, so I ended up going out with her."

"But I could swear that Naoko-san had a different boyfriend..."

"Yeah, she does. Second year guy named Kimura Akio. Never really worked up the nerve to ask about that..."

"Kimura? He picked up Naoko-san, too? But it can't be too serious with a guy like that..."

Kimura-kun was from the class next to mine, and he was an infamous playboy. Legend had it that he'd made a pass at every second year girl in the entire school. He'd even flirted with me—the discipline committee president!

"Maybe, maybe not. Either way, I was never able to figure out what she really wanted."

"Do you like Naoko-san?"

"D-do I?"

"Be clear," my fixation popped right up and out of my mouth.

"If we're going to the roof, the fire escape round back is better," Saotome-kun said, glancing around us.

"Why?"

"The door's locked, isn't it?"

"Oh, right."

As we went round the back, we saw somebody coming down the fire escape.

"*Ah*...!"

We chased after them, but they were gone before we could get there. But they were tall, and probably male, so we didn't chase them any further. Whoever it was had headed towards the gates and was probably going home.

"If he was up there, than Kirima Nagi probably isn't."

"Yeah. Let's check the gym."

We went to the storage rooms under the gym.

They were locked. But luckily for us, I was on gate duty, so I had a master key that would open any door in school.

"*Unh*..." Saotome-kun pushed the heavy door open, and went inside.

"It was closed—I doubt she's in here," I said, peeking in. It was dark, so we turned on the lights. There was just one small fluorescent light, though, and it didn't penetrate past the piles of mats, springboards, and other gym equipment.

"But she might be hiding somewhere," Tanaka-kun said, moving to follow Saotome-kun inside.

But Saotome-kun came walking back towards us, waving his hands.

"Nobody here. And definitely no signs of anyone having been here."

* * *

"—Nothing here," said Saotome Masami. Behind him were the blanket and heater that Echoes had used, and several scattered food wrappers. They were hidden in shadow, and from where they stood at the entrance, Tanaka Shiro and Niitoki Kei weren't able to see them.

"Any cigarette butts?" Kei asked.

Masami made a show of looking behind him, then shook his head.

At his feet was a little bell that Kamikishiro had kept on her school bag.

"Let's try somewhere else."

"Right. Saotome-kun, come on out of there. I'll lock up."

"Mm," Masami said, leaving the evidence where it was, turning out the lights as he left.

"Where should we look next?" Kei asked, locking the door and turning towards the two boys.

"It just occurred to me, but maybe we should use the PA system to summon Kirima Nagi," Masami suggested.

He had confirmed the presence of Echoes, and he knew that Echoes was presumably moving with Kirima Nagi. It was time to move the plan forward to stage two.

* * *

"The PA system?" I said, blinking at Saotome-kun.

"Yeah. That key can get us in the broadcast room, right?"

"Well, yes, it can—but won't we get in trouble?"

"Probably," Saotome-kun admitted. "But there's no other students around, and the only teacher here is the one on night watch. I'd be more surprised if anyone cares enough to yell at us."

"Mmm, well...it *would* be faster. Okay. I'll handle the teacher."

"Thank you for this," Tanaka-kun said apologetically.

"Not like I'm doing it for you," I said. "I'm worried about Naoko-san, too." Why was I being so snotty? I was irritating myself. I was only doing this because I couldn't settle down without making things clear. Only my words were impressive.

But I *was* worried about Naoko.

If Kirima Nagi had gotten her mixed up in something, and if it had gone bad, I had to try and stop it... I'm sounding very much like the ardent discipline committee president, aren't I? I never meant to turn into something like that.

"C-come on," I said, agitated, and set off, the two boys following me.

Unfortunately, being at the head of the party didn't do anything for my image. It made me look even more stuck up. Dang.

2.

"WILL KIRIMA NAGI-SAN, second year, class D, please report to the broadcast office? If you're still in the building, we would like to talk to you regarding Kamikishiro Naoko-san. Repeat, will Kirima Nagi-san, second year, class D ..."

Tanaka Shiro's voice echoed through the darkened school.

Of course, it reached the ears of Nakayama Haruo, the one teacher still in the school on night watch duty.

But all he said was, "*Umph...*" He then slumped onto the table, knocking over his instant ramen, and started snoring.

He was the guardian of the master key that the discipline committee member had, and he was supposed to take it from them and record this in the log, but he was conked out before he could perform his duty.

"*Uhn...nah...*"

But this was not because of any laziness on his part.

His hands dangled towards the floor, much too limply for normal sleep. His face was pressed against the desk, his neck bent as far as it would go, and he was virtually guaranteed a stiff neck in the morning.

"*Uhmph...unh, nahhhhhr...*"

His snores were not considered attractive at the best of times, but now they sounded like a stray dog starving to death.

He was not asleep; he had clearly been knocked unconscious.

Nor was he alone in the room.

There was a girl standing next to him.

"………"

She glared up at the speakers as the voice flowed out of them.

There was a sweet, strange smell in the room. The smell had been enough to knock Nakayama Haruo out, but the beautiful girl with long, black hair did not even raise an eyebrow.

Of course not. She was the source of the smell.

Less than ten seconds after the PA announcement began, she was out the door of the night watch room and heading up the stairs.

For many years afterwards, Nakayama Haruo was to suffer a mysterious phenomenon similar to LSD flashbacks (though he was quite certain that he had never tried any drugs) in which his daily routine was abruptly disrupted by illusions similar to intense migraines.

Certainly, this mysterious "disease" was a curse, but he had no idea how insanely lucky he really was.

The only reason he had survived was by the whim of a killer, the fleeting thought that perhaps she had killed too many people already.

* * *

"——?!" Kirima Nagi heard the announcement as well, and looked up.

She was busy prying open the lockers of every student in the school and searching the contents. Naturally, she was looking for traces of the Manticore. Echoes stood beside her, disguised in a school uniform.

"How do they know I'm still at the school? And what's this about Naoko?"

"Broadcast office..." Echoes plucked the words out of the broadcast, and spoke them.

"Can you sense something, Echoes?!" Kirima Nagi asked. Kamikishiro Naoko had explained to her that he could sense the presence of his clone, the Manticore.

"............" Echoes put his finger on his forehead and tried to sense it, but shook his head, apparently drawing a blank.

"But an obvious summons like that...why the hell would it need to hide?" Nagi said angrily.

Echoes simply shook his head. He knew only that the Manticore had learned far more about human society than he had managed. This was a trap.

"............"

He put his hand on Nagi's shoulder, and pushed her backwards. Signaling her not to follow.

"Why not? It's a trap?" Nagi said. She knew it, too.

Echoes nodded.

"That's why we have to go," Nagi said quietly. "We don't play into this trap and it'll change its face and make a run for it. It'll leave the school. We'll never catch it then."

"............"

Echoes watched the fearless girl carefully. In his heart, he whispered.

(Which is it...?)

But the girl who could hear that voice was no more.

Nagi pulled a pair of leather gloves out of her skirt, put them on, and took a stun gun off of the belt that she wore around her waist. The belt and gloves failed to match her uniform at all.

She squeezed the grip once, testing it.

With a crackle, a two million volt firework flew through the air.

* * *

"She's not coming," Tanaka-kun whispered. It had been at least five minutes since our broadcast.

"The teacher isn't here either. What's going on?" I asked. I was pretty sure Nakayama-sensei was on duty tonight. He was a little neurotic, but he definitely was not the type to let small things go, and an unscheduled broadcast was sure to set him off. Was he asleep?

"............" Saotome-kun stood deep in thought, frowning.

"What now?" Tanaka-kun asked, turning to look at us, unable to wait.

"One more time," Saotome-kun whispered.

"There's no way she didn't hear that. Maybe she *has* gone home." I spread my hands.

"Yeah," grunted Tanaka-kun.

Saotome-kun said again, more forcefully, "Come on, let's do it again!"

But when he reached for the switch, all the lights in the room suddenly went out.

"—*Wah*?!"

There were no windows in the broadcast office. It was pitch black.

"A b-blackout?" I said, recovering slightly.

"Damn, the breakers!" snapped Saotome-kun angrily. I wasn't sure what he meant for a second, but of course, if the circuit breakers went, so would the lights. Made perfect sense. He was clearly a fast thinker.

But why would the breakers trip? Unless it was done deliberately, they only tripped when someone was using too much electricity...

Fumbling around in the darkness, I managed to get the door open at last, and moonlight streamed in through the windows in the hall.

There was a black shadow standing right in front of me.

I didn't even have time to look. The shadow pushed something towards me, and a shockwave hit my body.

"*Hhh*..."

A sound somewhere between a breath and a scream came out of my mouth, and I crumpled to the floor. I couldn't move.

"President?" Saotome-kun cried from behind me. It sounded so far away. The shadow slipped swiftly past me, and launched itself at Saotome-kun.

The impact of him hitting the ground carried through the floorboards to me.

"Wh-who are you?" Tanaka-kun shrieked.

That was the last thing I heard. My consciousness slipped farther and farther away.

* * *

When I opened my eyes, I found myself tied up and lying on my side on a heavily waxed floor.

It was dark around me. But moonlight came in from somewhere, so it was brighter than the main building had been. Wherever we were was pretty open.

There was only one room in the school this large, with big windows along one side and wooden floors. It was the lecture hall.

(—*Wha-what the...*?)

I tried to sit up.

But my body was heavy, leaden. It was clear that I still hadn't fully recovered from the impact.

Saotome-kun and Tanaka-kun were lying next to me. I prodded their backs with my knees.

"Hey!"

"*Unh*," groaned Saotome-kun, stirring, and opening his eyes. "This..." he started to say, but quickly snapped his mouth shut.

"*Mm*? What?" I asked, looking around. I found what had surprised him. Two figures stood in the direction that he was looking.

"Everyone awake?" said one of them. It was Kirima Nagi.

The other one appeared to be a male student. He was wearing a uniform, but I didn't recognize him.

"What did you do with Kamikishiro-san?" Tanaka-kun asked. It looked like he'd woken up first.

"You're Tanaka Shiro, then? Naoko told me about you," Nagi sighed.

"Kirima-san, what...?" Saotome-kun asked.

Nagi glared at him coldly. "I told you not to get involved, Saotome-kun."

"But what's going on?"

"You don't need to know."

"How can you say that?!" I shouted.

Nagi glared at me, surprised. "Committee President, I know why these two are here, but how did you get mixed up in this?"

"I know Naoko-san, too!"

"But don't you think you're trying a little too hard? Caused me no end of confusion."

"I'm the one who's confused!" I shouted, completely forgetting that I was talking to a violence-prone problem child. "Tell me what you think you're doing, right this instant!"

She ignored me, and looked at the boy next to her.

"It's none of them—right, Echoes?"

What did she mean? The boy she'd called Echoes nodded. What a strange nickname.

"None...of them..."

"You'd know, right? Even if it were lying low?"

"Kn-know..."

"None of them have been 'altered.' I see."

Watching the two of them nod at each other pissed me off. "Stop whispering cryptically at each other! And you! You aren't even a student here! I've never seen you before in my life!"

I'm not bragging, but if you're on gate duty often enough, you do end up knowing everyone at school.

Nagi looked at me. "I apologize. We no longer suspect you. Time for you to go on home."

This was much too selfish. "When hell freezes over!" I snapped. Somehow, I managed to get to my feet, despite the ropes binding me. I doubt I could do that twice. It's a stunt you can only pull off when you're too angry to notice.

"*Mm*?" Nagi frowned.

"I told you to explain yourself! How am I supposed to just forget a thing like this?"

"Well, well, well. I guess we see how you became committee president," Nagi said, glaring at me. She looked like a yakuza. "But you need to keep quiet about this."

"Why should I?" I glared back at her.

"For your own good," she said coldly.

"*Raaarh*!" I snarled, contorting my body in anger. Since my hands and feet were tied, this made me lose my balance, and I fell over again.

(Oops...!)

I was just about to fall flat on my face when I felt someone catch me.

It was the boy who'd been standing next to Nagi, "Echoes."

I looked up at him. He nodded, and undid my bonds.

From this close, he had a rather gentle face.

"Th-thanks..." I said, rubbing the rope burns.

He proceeded to undo Tanaka-kun and Saotome-kun as well. We were tied pretty tightly, but he pulled the ropes off like he was playing cat's cradle. He looked frail, but he must have been pretty strong.

For some reason, he reminded me of Christopher Lambert's Tarzan. His hair wasn't as long, but he gave off a similar air. Kind of unworldly.

"Kirima-san, who is this guy?" Saotome-kun asked. Feeling a little jealous, I guess.

"*Mm... uh...* Well...my boyfriend," Nagi replied, clearly lying.

"You can't fool me that easily. What are you doing here? Where's Naoko-san?" I glared at Nagi again.

"R-right! What did you do to Kamikishiro-san?!" Tanaka-kun yelled, turning on Nagi the moment he was free.

"I'm worried about Naoko myself," Nagi said painfully, not meeting his gaze. She clearly knew something.

"Tell us. We can help."

"No, you can't," Nagi snapped.

"Why not?!"

"This is not a normal situation. Unless you're screwed up like me, you can't possibly tackle it."

She didn't hesitate at all to call herself screwed up.

I shrank back a little at the strength of her words.

Saotome-kun spoke up, "Normal still not good enough, *hunh*?" It was clear that he was quite bitter about something.

He smiled a little. I looked at his face, and for some reason, felt the hairs on my neck stand up.

It was just an ordinary, affable smile, but there was something unnaturally relaxed about it, like when you're playing a video game for the thousandth time, and a pattern you're particularly good at shows up. His smile was calm and ruthless.

"*Mm...*" Nagi frowned. She must have said the same thing when she rejected him.

"Is Kamikishiro-san okay?!" Tanaka-kun insisted.

Nagi said bluntly, bitterly, "Shiro-kun, right? You should forget about her."

"What do you mean?!"

"............"

Nagi said nothing else.

3.

NAGI AND THIS ECHOES GUY led us out of the lecture hall.

"Go straight home," Nagi insisted.

"I have to give the key back," I said sullenly. I wasn't finished sulking about not getting an explanation. "Maybe I'll report you."

"Whatever," Nagi said airily.

"What's wrong with you?" I retorted. "What makes you think you have to be personally responsible for everything? Can't you just let things be?!"

"Now, now, Committee President," Saotome-kun said, patting me on the shoulders.

"But—!" I insisted.

But Saotome-kun was completely calm, the exact opposite of my state of mind. He spoke to me like he was soothing a fretful baby. "There's nothing you can do. Kirima-san has things she needs to do." It was like he knew what those things were.

"............"

He was definitely too relaxed.

When I held my tongue, he turned back towards Nagi.

At his steady gaze, Nagi awkwardly looked away.

He spoke to her anyway. "Kirima-san. I do understand." He took a mechanical pencil out of his pocket, and spun it around his fingers, very casually.

"We can never be satisfied with 'normal.'"

"......?" Nagi stared at Saotome-kun, baffled. "What?"

"Looking back, I'm glad you rejected me. If I had been with you, then I would've been her *enemy* when I met her." He sighed, almost happily.

Nagi frowned. "When you met *who*? What are you talking about?" She seemed confused. It looked like something about his turn of phrase had bothered her.

A little smile crept up the edges of Saotome-kun's lips. "In other words, I can't help but put you on the side of 'normal,' now." His shoulders slumped.

Then he moved like lightning.

Before I even realized that he'd turned around, his arm was

reaching out towards Echoes, who stood behind him.

The mechanical pencil was in his hand. His aim was true. The tip of it stabbed deep into Echoes' throat.

"——?!"

Echoes staggered backwards. In an instant, Saotome Masami had buried the pencil all the way inside Echoes' throat. Then he turned his attention back towards Nagi.

"Now, you are our enemy."

A shadow fell towards us from above.

We all looked up, and saw a person dropping down from the school roof.

Someone I knew.

Yurihara Minako.

She was looking right at Echoes.

Falling on him—no, *attacking* him.

"——!"

Blood gushing from his throat, Yurihara Minako cut him open from his shoulder to his waist...with her mere fingers—her nails were hideously long.

She'd fallen more than ten meters, but bounded upwards again like a grasshopper.

There was no *way* she was human.

"*Ah*..." I could do nothing but stand there with my mouth hanging open.

"M-Manticore!" Nagi shrieked, following the leaping monster that looked like Yurihara Minako with her eyes.

That cost her her life.

Saotome Masami was standing right in front of her.

She looked down just in time to see his hand slash downwards.

The knife in his hand flashed.

"——!" Nagi's voice never made it to words. It was a tiny little survival knife, the size of his palm, like a toy, but the blade was sharp, and it sliced her throat open.

"I just changed teams—from the killed, to the *killers*."

I doubt anyone but Saotome Masami himself could understand the meaning behind his words.

Kirima Nagi spun around, blood spraying from her throat. She fell over.

"——!"

His throat pierced, his torso cut in two, Echoes was still watching Nagi. He clearly wasn't human either.

He dodged Yurihara Minako as she attacked again, and dashed to Nagi's side.

Ignoring Saotome Masami, who backed away, Echoes scooped up Nagi's convulsing body, and leapt away. He cleared the roof of the school in a single jump, vanishing into the night sky.

He ran away...?

"Chase him! This is your chance!" Saotome Masami shouted, and Yurihara Minako reversed her course, leaping back the way she had come.

I was dumbfounded.

Beside me, Tanaka-kun wailed, then ran away screaming.

Saotome Masami swung towards me.

I was frozen stiff, and I couldn't move a muscle.

"*Heh heh heh*," he laughed. His smile was exactly the same as it had been a moment before, back when he was on our side.

But this boy had just killed another human being...

My knees rattled. I was shaking with fear.

"To be honest, the plan was for Kirima Nagi to kill me here, but oh well. This way was pretty fun too," he said, grinning. Like everything was normal.

"I could get addicted to doing things myself," he commented, walking towards me, moonlight glittering off the knife in his hand.

* * *

As Echoes fled upwards to the roof, he realized that there was little power left in his body.

The pencil from a moment before—instead of lead, it had been filled with a fatal poison created by the Manticore. He was infected.

"......!"

He quickly pulled the pencil out of his throat. But it was too late.

His feet and hands felt numb. Injuries that his massive regenerative powers should have healed instantly showed no signs of improving.

But what had happened?

That boy was the Manticore's ally?

He hadn't been brainwashed. Echoes was sure of that. But why would a normal human be working with a monster?

Echoes glanced down at Nagi.

She was no longer breathing. Her pupils were dilated, nothing reflected in her eyes. Her lips were half open, a stream of blood flowing out of them. She wasn't moving.

This girl had protected everyone from the shadows, in secret, and it had killed her.

"…………"

Echoes stared down at her ashen face.

(Which is it…?)

He wondered inside. But only Kamikishiro Naoko could answer, and sadly, she was gone.

Yurihara Minako hit the roof behind him, giving chase.

Echoes gathered Nagi up again, and leapt off of the roof.

"You can't get away from me!" The Manticore yelled, following him.

She was smiling. Saotome Masami's plan was going perfectly.

Echoes was running, but he was too badly wounded. He could not hope to hide.

She was an imperfect copy, and would never have been his equal in a fair fight, but now the tables were turned.

When she next caught sight of Echoes, he was abandoning Kirima Nagi's body in the bushes of the school's garden. Clearly, he was trying to lighten the load, but it was too late.

Grinning from ear to ear, the Manticore flung herself at the slow-moving Echoes.

Her kick sent Echoes flying.

* * *

There was a low thud from the school garden.

I snapped out of it.

Saotome Masami was right in front of me, waving a knife.

I narrowly dodged it by rolling on the ground.

I got my feet up from under me and tried to run, but my right foot slipped, and I fell again.

I looked down.

My hands were resting in a pool of Kirima Nagi's blood.

"*Aaaaahhhh*!" and at last, I was able to scream.

Saotome Masami came after me.

I tried to spin around. My fingers touched something.

It gleamed. It was the stun gun that Kirima Nagi had dropped.

"......!"

I snatched up the weapon.

"*Grr...*" Saotome Masami scowled.

"St-stay back!" I pointed the weapon in his direction, and squeezed the switch-like thing on the side.

With a crackle, fireworks spat off of the tip, but they were only a few centimeters long. It was but a tiny little light, and it didn't look at all threatening.

"*Hmph,*" Saotome Masami smiled, coldly. "What are you going to do to me with *that*? That kind of weapon can't kill anyone."

"Wh-what *are* you people? That—Yurihara Minako *thing*... What is it?!"

"She is Yurihara Minako, but she is not Yurihara Minako. The original is dead. She is the Manticore."

"Manticore...?" I could swear I'd heard that name somewhere. In a computer game or something. I'm sure it meant...

...Man-eater.

Oh. God. That meant... That meant Naoko-san was...

Saotome Masami saw my expression, and guessed what I was thinking. He grinned. "*Exactly. She's already been digested.*"

He said it so normally. Without a shred of guilt.

"A-and all the other people who vanished?"

"Mostly. Well, there may be a few girls who just ran away on their own."

"And Kirima Nagi was looking for you..."

That's why she captured us. But she thought we had nothing to do with it, so she released us, without realizing that one of her enemies was hiding among us...

"You used us as cover, didn't you?"

"You had your uses. She was a fool. She allied herself with Echoes, but it never occurred to her that his enemy might have allies as well."

His complete composure put a match to the flames of anger inside me. They soon banished my fear.

"So you lied when you said you loved her?"

"No, that was the truth. *But I no longer need her*. Still, I wasn't going to let the Manticore have her; no, I wanted to kill her with my own hands. Do you know how good that feels?"

"How the hell would I know *that*?"

I thrust my weapon towards him. He dodged easily.

"Beautiful, President. I love your eyes. I love strong-willed, powerful eyes."

Grrr. "You little..." I swung my weapon wildly, not getting anywhere near him.

Then something passed over my head.

It was "Echoes." He slammed into the ground. He'd been thrown there.

He was torn to pieces.

While I was distracted, Saotome Masami kicked my hand.

"*Ah*?!" I yelped, but the stun gun was already flung out of my reach.

From behind me, Yurihara Minako yelled, "Enough, Saotome-kun! I'll finish things."

"Okay," Saotome Masami replied, picking up the stun gun and stepping away. I ran over to Echoes.

He was a wreck. His right arm was half torn off his shoulder, and there were holes all over his body. He was covered in blood.

"E-Echoes?" I said, pulling him upright.

He opened his eyes feebly.

A pained moan escaped his purple lips.

"President, it's no use asking him to save you. He's almost dead," Yurihara Minako—the Manticore—said, laughing.

"That wasn't so hard. You might even have been able to win without any tricks," Saotome Masami said, evidently enjoying himself.

"I never thought he would be this weak," the Manticore replied, amused. "I'm sure he used to be stronger."

I glared at her.

"You aren't human! You're both devils!"

* * *

As he lay dying, Echoes heard the girl holding him shout, "You aren't human!"

Not human. She meant they weren't fit to be called human.

He still didn't understand.

Which were humans?

Humans had captured him for being different, and forcefully and quite mercilessly studied his body. Humans had made the Manticore. But the people who had saved him, the cloaked boy in the black hat, Kamikishiro Naoko, and Kirima Nagi, were all human too.

Which was it?

Which was the truth?

"*Ha ha ha*! You are stupid, aren't you?!" The Manticore laughed, mocking the girl. "I never was human! And Saotome-kun is *nothing* like you foolish humans. Devils? Fine with me! I think I like being called a devil!"

"You will be destroyed!" The girl shouted back, not at all cowed. "I will die here, and so will this man, but there will be other people who will stand in your way! No matter where you hide, there will be people who can't ignore the distortions in the world that you're trying to create! And you will be found again, just like Kirima Nagi found you!" Big tears were running down her cheeks.

She was sad.

Because she was about to die?

Then why was she holding him so tightly?

It was as if she was protecting him from the Manticore.

Like Kamikishiro Naoko had, when she found him wounded in town.

(Humans...)

He had no more time.

He had to make a choice.

* * *

"Like Kirima Nagi?" the Manticore chuckled. "I think I'll be *her* next."

"......?" I didn't know what she meant. I had to ask. "What do you mean?"

"Just that I'll change from Yurihara Minako into Kirima Nagi."

At first, I couldn't comprehend this. My mind went blank. Then I was horrified. "W-what?!"

"She's an ideal specimen. She's crazy, so nobody will say anything if I behave a little oddly; she's rich, and has a vast information network set up. It's perfect. There will be a commotion when Yurihara Minako vanishes, which I would prefer to avoid, but the benefits far outweigh *that*."

"......!" I shuddered, turning to look at Saotome Masami. He had said that he *no longer needed her.* Because *he had a new girlfriend now.*

Saotome Masami stared back at me, expressionless.

I had no words.

"As for *you*, Niitoki Kei," the Manticore continued. "The world will never know you've died. We will alter you, and make a slave of you. You'll be moving around, but you will have no heart. Even if you meet a boy you like, you will feel nothing."

I was horrified again.

I could see it.

The Manticore disguised as Nagi, and me standing beside her as her slave... I could see myself on gate duty, Nagi beside me, whilepointed her to her next meal... Even if the boy I had once loved and his pretty girlfriend came, I would think nothing, simply greet them mechanically...

And that's not all. The Manticore's terrifying words gave me a glimpse of a higher purpose.

She and Saotome Masami weren't killing for their own self-preservation. This was just one part of their plan to take control of the world from us humans.

But if they graduated, and went out of school, what would happen to the world?

She came closer to me.

"......!"

I hugged Echoes' body tightly.

Then...

Echoes slowly raised his wounded arm.

It was shaking. His fist wasn't clenched or open, his fingers just hung there limply.

He pointed his hand at the Manticore.

"What? What's that mean? You still think you can do something to stop me?" The Manticore smirked.

"............" But Echoes wasn't looking at her.

He was looking at the stars in the sky behind her.

And he suddenly spoke, using actual words, not to anybody, but to the *sky* above.

"*My body into information, transmit to source!*"

And the air around me filled with white light.

4.

THAT EVENING, a strange electrical disturbance was recorded in the area. Satellite broadcast monitors all went white, computer hard drives were cleared of all data, and a multitude of other similar unnatural phenomenon were encountered. The television stations and newspaper offices were deluged with questions and complaints. There were several investigations launched, with no real satisfactory results. But a number of witnesses said, "About that time, I could swear I saw the sky glow. It was just for a second, but it was like a bright light launched from the ground into the sky." But these reports were never connected to anything, and were eventually buried and forgotten.

* * *

...I know what I saw.

Echoes changed into light, and that light swallowed the Manticore.

And a second before it did, Saotome Masami leapt in front of the Manticore, shielding her with his body—

I don't know what he was thinking, why he was on the side of the Manticore, and frankly, I don't want to know.

But there was one thing that I did have to admit—he might have killed a number of people for the Manticore, but that casual disregard for life sure included his own.

Saotome Masami was swept up in the torrent of light, his body blown away, not a trace of it left.

He was disintegrated...no, he was erased.

But moments before Echoes had self-destructed, the Manticore had been flung aside by her companion and out of the beam's path.

"......!"

Even as I was flung aside by the shockwave, I desperately struggled to grasp the situation.

But no, I didn't understand *anything*.

From my point of view, there was absolutely no way for me to grasp the first thing about what had just happened.

What the hell was Echoes? How could something that looked like a human turn into light and explode?! And what "information" was he "transmitting"? To who? I simply had no way of knowing.

(What's happening—?!)

I hit the ground and rolled, screaming with frustration inside.

When I finally managed to stop myself, there was no light left around me.

Grunting in pain, I sat up, looked in front of me, and gasped.

She was standing there alone.

Half of her body was burned black, and smoke was rising off of it. The uniform she'd been wearing had been blown away, and beneath the moonlight, every inch of her slim, limber body was exposed.

"............"

She was gazing blankly at the sky.

She didn't seem to be looking at anything.

"............"

Her lips trembled. Like they were scrambling to form words that never emerged.

"*Ah...ahh...*"

There was no expression on her face. It had been replaced by emptiness.

The face of someone that had lost something that they valued more than their own life.

As if half of her body had been torn away.

As if her capacity for joy had been pulled up by the roots.

She looked as if she could no longer perceive any meaning, like there was nothing left for her.

"*Aaaaaarrrrrgggghhhhhhhhh*!!"

Somewhere, her endless scream turned into a howl.

It was the sound of her heart breaking.

The scream seemed to shake the moon.

"…………"

I sat and watched, nailed to the spot.

But then I realized that was the last thing I should be doing.

(G-got to run…!)

As I tried to get to my feet, the gravel scrunched beneath me.

Like a mechanical response, the Manticore's battered face swung towards me.

Our eyes met.

A shiver ran down my spine.

Even by the light of the moon, I could tell her eyes were blood red. The whites were completely soaked in crimson hostility.

"You die…!" she howled. "I'll kill every last one of you!!"

As if her voice had been a trigger, I shot to my feet, and ran for it.

Naturally, she came after me.

I was running, but from the sound of it, she was walking, dragging one leg.

But the sound was getting closer.

(*Waaaah*!)

At the time, I was convinced that fear had finally driven me round the bend.

I was hearing things.

I could hear a melody coming through the bushes in front of me—an impossible, unnatural melody.

Someone was whistling.

Whistling a tune that should never be whistled, Wagner's "Die Meistersinger von Nurnberg."

Unnatural or not, at that moment I had no other straws to grasp at.

I ran for my life towards the sound.

When I was almost there, my leg slipped.

"*Aah*—!" I screamed, pitching forward, falling flat on my face. I smacked my forehead on the ground, and everything went black for a moment.

The whistling stopped.

I could hear the sound of the Manticore's footsteps, several times louder than it had been a moment before.

"——!"

I spun around, and the Manticore's hand was already reaching towards me.

This is it. I'm going to die...!

But just as that thought crossed my mind...

Fwsh!

It was the sound of something cutting through the air.

And then...the Manticore's hand flew off, with a grotesque slicing sound...

It had been severed from her body and was now spinning through the air!

(Wha...?)

I saw something flash.

Like string.

It twisted like it was alive, and wrapped around the Manticore's neck.

It tightened.

"——?!"

The Manticore's expression changed. She snatched at her throat with both hands. But she only had one, and the fingers of it tried to get a grip on the string wrapped around her throat.

It wasn't a string. It was a horrifically thin metal wire.

Ah, I thought. I had my answer. The reason I had suddenly tripped and fallen was because this wire had been strung across my path.

One end of the wire appeared to be tied around a tree.

The other end led into the shadow of the school building. When I looked in that direction, I felt my brains pour out of my ears.

"It can't be—?!" I shouted.

There was a figure there, leaning backwards, pulling on the wire with black gloves. It wore a cape and a black hat shaped like a pipe. It was the very creature that all the girls in my class had been gossiping about.

"...The wrist was charred enough for me to cut through, but the neck seems to be stronger," it said.

The androgynous voice, neither male nor female, was exactly as the rumors said.

But the face...was...

"M-M-Miyashita-san?!"

Yes, it was clearly that of my classmate, Miyashita Touka.

"Currently, I am Boogiepop," she...no, he said clearly, in a boy's voice.

"Gh...?!" gurgled the Manticore, eyes widening in surprise.

She was no more able to take this in than I was.

The wire was sunk deep into the skin of her throat. She was struggling to loosen it with her fingers, but it was cutting the fingers instead, and they were bleeding.

"*Ghh...ghhhh...!*"

"You call yourself the Manticore?" Boogiepop said quietly. "You are much stronger than a human, but I can make free use of the strength that humans unconsciously keep in reserve to avoid exceeding the limits of their flesh. *Since I am only borrowing this body.*"

Then he suddenly shouted, "Now, Shiro-kun! Shoot it!"

I had no time to ponder what he meant. No sooner had the words left his mouth than an arrow pierced the Manticore's chest.

I knew that arrow.

It was a duralumin arrow, that kind that the archery team used.

I spun around, and behind me was Tanaka-kun, who had not run away after all, but was holding a sturdy glass fiber bow, aimed at me—no, at the Manticore.

Her head was trapped. She couldn't dodge.

"Aigh..."

I wonder what the Manticore thought at that moment, when she knew that she had lost.

She didn't look at the arrow in her chest, or at Boogiepop, or at the archer.

I saw an expression steal over that empty face. To me, it looked like...relief.

"Shoot her head!" Boogiepop said, showing no mercy.

He killed her when she was at her most beautiful, before she had a chance to grow ugly; killed her without pain…just as the stories said.

Tanaka-kun let go.

The arrow was flung off the bowstring, and hit Yurihara Minako's face dead center, smashing her head.

For an instant, what looked like cracks ran all down her body, and then she crumbled, changing into a purple smoke.

The smoke drifted in all directions, carried away on the wind.

A little of it drifted past my nose. It smelt of horribly thick, fresh blood.

* * *

"…………"

I couldn't stand up.

Tanaka-kun came running over.

"A-are you okay?"

"*Um*… Y-yeah…" I shook my head, trying to recover some clarity.

But Miyashita-san walked in front of me again in that Boogiepop costume, and my thoughts scattered again.

"Wh-what is that?!" I asked Tanaka-kun, clinging to him like a toddler.

He shook his head. "I don't know. He stopped me on my way back from practice, offered to help—you know him?"

"I…kind of know…*of* him…"

Boogiepop undid the wire from around the tree, and headed to the bushes where Kirima Nagi lay.

"The Manticore said Echoes was surprisingly weak. I wonder why..." he muttered. He (or was it a she after all?) kicked Kirima Nagi.

Nagi had been killed, her throat sliced open...but her body shook, and she sat up.

She'd come back to life.

"He gave you part of his life. You've escaped death again."

Tanaka-kun and I could do nothing but gape.

Nagi moaned and clutched her forehead. She'd lost a lot of blood, and must have been anemic.

"Hello, Fire Witch," Boogiepop said.

"You again," Nagi replied, not at all surprised. She sighed. "If you were out, why didn't you come sooner?"

"Your actions finally allowed me to uncover the nature of the danger."

"I gotta be me all the damn time, but you only bother coming out when the shit hits the fan. You selfish bastard."

"Don't say that," he replied. It sounded like they'd known each other for years.

"Is... Is it over?"

"Yes. Thanks to Echoes' sacrifice and the committee president's courage."

"I see..." Nagi tried to stand, but wavered and fell over again.

Boogiepop made no effort to help her, instead coming back in our direction.

"I leave her in your hands. I'll take care of the clean up," he told us.

"............" We made no response.

Boogiepop picked up the Manticore's hand from the ground. He looked up at me, and made a strange expression, narrowing one eye, like he was smiling, but not quite. It was like he was playing dumb.

"Niitoki Kei—you certainly do have a strong will. It's because of people like you that the world manages to remain a halfway decent place. In the world's stead, I thank you."

It was like a speech from a play. I had no idea what it meant.

Leaving me standing there stunned, he fled like the wind, turning the corner behind the gym and vanishing from sight.

And that was how it ended.

5

"BUT HOW DID BOOGIEPOP become a rumor? He's supposed to be a mysterious figure, his identity a secret. Who started all the legends about him?" I asked Kirima Nagi the next day after class.

"Probably Miyashita Touka herself," Nagi answered. We were alone in the room. Everyone else had already left.

"*Eh*? What do you mean?"

"Miyashita Touka is unaware that she has an alter-ego known as

Boogiepop inside of her. But she knows it unconsciously. You know, like how you talk about yourself, but say it's a friend of yours? Same principle, she just told other people about her other self."

"That's it?"

"You should probably ask Suema about it. Well, not specifically, but she can explain it way better than I can."

"*Hmm*... I still don't really get it."

"I don't know much about that bastard myself," she sighed. "Did everyone make a fuss when Yurihara Minako didn't show?"

"The teacher asked if any of us knew anything, but nobody answered. It's too soon for anyone to realize she's actually missing, so not much is going on yet. But for a straight A student like her, skipping's enough to get the gossip going."

"*Hunh*..."

I'd called Yurihara-san's house the day before, but the answering machine lead me to believe that both her parents were off on business trips. Nobody knew she hadn't come home. It looked as though the Manticore had deliberately chosen to make her move while they were out of town.

But all hell would break loose in a day or two. Yurihara Minako would cause a lot more problems for the school than any of the other girls had.

Saotome Masami would be buried under her shadow. His parents probably already knew he hadn't come home, but he was a boy, so they were unlikely to worry all that much if he was out all night.

"When was the real Yurihara... When was she replaced?"

"Not sure. But a pretty long time ago. She'd always been missing. It was just that up until now, we simply hadn't noticed she was gone."

"I guess that's true..."

We both hung our heads.

It was a strange feeling.

We couldn't tell anyone the truth. If we did, it would just make things worse for all of us. And even then, if word about Echoes got out to the institution that made the Manticore, it would just be asking for trouble.

"So, all it ultimately amounts to is nothing?"

"It's better that way."

"Yeah..."

We stood up.

Most of the other students had gone home, and the sports teams and clubs were all in full session. There was nobody roaming the halls or stopped at the shoe lockers.

We headed for the gates, and the girl on gate duty was very happy to see me.

"Ah! President! Thank god you're here! Could you take over for me for a minute? I really gotta pee!"

I smiled and nodded, and she bolted off into the school.

"Everyone likes you," Nagi grinned.

"Or likes using me," I grimaced. I remembered all the times that Kamikishiro Naoko had talked me into fudging the numbers to make her on time. Which is how we got to be friends in the first place.

"Naoko-san is really…?" I said softly, suddenly horribly sad.

"Yeah…I think so," Nagi whispered sorrowfully.

When Tanaka-kun had left us the day before, he'd said, "I don't know how to say this, but I feel like I should thank you all for Kamikishiro-san. Thank you."

He was almost crying.

"Tanaka-kun, what did you really think of Naoko-san?" I'd asked.

He looked at me sadly. "Truthfully, if we had found her, I would've told her that I wanted to break up. But now…I'm not so sure."

"*Hmmm…*" was all I said.

I couldn't figure out what I should say to her other lover, Kimura Akio. We would probably never speak to each other. If someday someone were to tell him, that would be—

But we all had to return to our daily routine, just exactly as things had been before.

"Naoko said something strange once," Nagi said, looking up at the sky.

"She said Echoes was an angel. That the lord of the heavens had ordered him to investigate, and make the final decision on whether mankind should be allowed to live, or if it should be destroyed. He came here to find out if humans were a benevolent existence, or a malevolent one. If we were the latter, he would end our history."

I was taken aback. "An angel?"

"I mean, I'm pretty sure she was reading a lot into this. She had a tendency to blow everything out of proportion. My guess is Echoes and Manticore were both failed experiments in biotechnology. But if she was right..."

"......"

"We're still here. Looks like we're off the hook this time," she smiled sadly.

She had to say that. She couldn't let her friend's death be in vain.

But I couldn't smile.

Nagi hadn't seen the end of Echoes.

But I had. Clearly.

That light had made it as if Saotome Masami had never existed in the first place. It had turned the nearly immortal Manticore into a burnt crisp.

That was no biotechnological experiment.

It had beamed itself into space, but if something like that were fired at the earth over and over again...

"Then the one who really saved the world..."

"Wasn't me, wasn't Boogiepop...ultimately, it was that lonely little love-struck girl who was nice to Echoes. And we can't even thank her for it now," Nagi sounded almost irritated.

"............"

I had no answer for her. I just stared silently at the sky.

It seemed so far away.

* * *

As Nagi and I stood there staring absently into the clear blue sky, a boy and a girl came walking together towards us. When I saw them, I couldn't stop myself from exclaiming, "*Ah*!"

One of them was Miyashita Touka. The other one was a third year student with a promising career in design that I had fallen for and had my heart broken by, Takeda Keiji-senpai.

He looked a little nervous when he saw me, so I spoke to him first, to show him that he needn't worry about it. "Oh, senpai," I said as cheerfully as I could manage.

"Hey," he said vaguely.

Suddenly, Nagi was standing in front of Miyashita-san. "*Hmm*. So you're Miyashita Touka," she said. It seemed that this was her first time meeting this side of her.

"Y-yes..." Miyashita-san said, nodding, in a cute little voice as far removed from Boogiepop's boyish tones as possible.

"I'm Kirima. Nice to meet you," Nagi said, and held out her hand.

To an outsider, it must have looked like the school delinquent was out to get her.

"Hey!" Takeda-senpai said, stepping up to protect her.

But Miyashita-san shook her head. "You, too," she said, shaking Nagi's hand. Perhaps she understood this unconsciously as well.

"See ya," Nagi said, giving her a wry grin.

The two of them went through the gates, and I let out a big sigh, and stared up at the sky again.

I wasn't able to look Miyashita-san in the eye. I tried to smile at her, but I just couldn't.

There are too many things that just weren't clear.

It should be simple to smile at someone, but sometimes it's a terribly difficult and painful thing to do.

"It's so hard to smile..."

"*Hm*? What do you mean?"

I shook my head. "Never mind. It was nothing."

Nagi looked at me dubiously, but eventually, she looked back up at the sky, and began to whistle.

It was a song I knew. I sang along, softly.

Life is brief, young maiden, fall in love;
before the crimson bloom fades from your lips,
before the tides of passion cool within your hips,
for those of you who know no tomorrow.

The autumn sky was so bright that it made my eyes water.

It'll be winter soon, I thought.

BOOGIEPOP AND OTHERS closed.

Afterword

THE SCHOOL IN BOOGIEPOP

THESE DAYS, I rarely have them, but back in my early twenties, I often had dreams about high school. Dreams in which I was going to high school, not dreams about having gone. I'm talking about in the present tense, as a twenty something adult, putting on a uniform (the old kind with the clasp) and going to school. In the dreams, I knew clearly that I had graduated several years before, but I was pretending not to know and going anyway. Since it was a dream, this pretense was enough to fool my classmates. Not one of them ever noticed that I had no business being at school. Neither did the teachers. I sat in the corner of my class, in the dreams, thinking about how much I really shouldn't be there.

The school in the dreams was not the Kanagawa Prefectural Noba High School that I had actually gone to. Rather, it was a school I had never seen. (For starters, Noba uniforms didn't have a clasp; they were blazers.) Nevertheless, I knew all kinds of things about that school. To make a long story short, the setting for *Boogiepop and Others*, Shinyo Academy, is that school from my dreams, the only part of this novel that is fantasy. The rest is something different.

I think I failed miserably at being a teenage boy. I never once thought I was young, or had a future. (I often do now.) I never actively participated in class or anything else. I just sat there, wondering what I was doing there, and after I graduated, I wondered why I had spent so much time thinking about those sorts of things. I don't particularly understand myself.

So, even now, I don't really get the idea of going to school. I was twenty-eight when I wrote this novel, and over ten years have passed since I graduated. Even if I try to find the answer, I no longer have a school to go to, so the whole thing is permanently out of reach. It's all too late now. It's one of many, but this "what did I do in school?" question is a pretty big trauma for me. It's like my first love that I never asked out. *Augh*! I was a dirty little angst-ridden idiot without a single thought for love. I imagine the reason behind the dreams is my conviction that I would be much better at being a high school student now.

Ultimately, school is a place where you have to be with others. That's all. It ends without you ever really understanding much about each other, but even so, you bump into a lot of people and a lot of thoughts, and you still come back for more. Sadly, schools are not exactly set up to preserve that diversity. (Right, my readers in school?) I can't help but think that's a crying shame, but the entire world seems to work that way, and school isn't that unique of a place in the world. That's why, in my dreams, I'm always thinking, "God, I really hated that guy, but now I wish I'd known him a little better." And I do all this while sitting there in the corner of the room.

(This is less of an afterword than a confession, isn't it?)
(Ah, whatever.)

BGM "HEARTBREAKER" (LIVE VER.)
by GRAND FUNK RAILROAD.

Boogiepop
returns
VS Imaginator Part 1
上遠野浩平
ouhei Kadono

"Is there anything you'd
like me to do? Go ahead,
ask me anything."
– Taniguchi Masaki

"I have no right to dislike anything."
– Orihata Aya

"If you aren't useful to me…
I'll dispose of you whenever I wish."
– Spooky E
"Why am I crying?"
– Anou Shinjirou

"There's nothing in this world that is ever truly decided."
– Minahoshi Suiko

Boogiepop returns

VS Imaginator Part 1

SIGNS

Boogiepop returns

VS Imaginator Part 1

written by
Kouhei Kadono

illustrated by
Kouji Ogata

english translation by
Andrew Cunningham

Possibility, or what we refer to as Imagination, is 99% imitation. The real deal is only 1%. The problem is, this 1% is simultaneously referred to as Evil.

—**Kirima Seiichi (*VS Imaginator*)**

Prelude

ON A VERY COLD AND SNOWY DAY in early March, a girl climbed to the top of our prefectural high school, Shinyo Academy, and proceeded to throw herself off the roof of the building. Her name was Minahoshi Suiko. She was only seventeen.

"Mariko-san, what do *you* like most?" she'd asked me abruptly one day, back when she was still alive.

Without putting much thought into it, I gave her the name of a pop star that everyone was listening to.

"Hmm... Really?"

"Yeah. He's kinda cool," I said offhandedly.

Suiko-san took a deep breath, faced the setting sun, and began to whistle.

Our school is up in the mountains, and it's a place where most students end up taking the bus to get to or from. On that particular day, Suiko-san and I had decided to walk home together, and we had the streets all to ourselves.

The tune she whistled turned out to be the pop star's most popular song. Suiko-san was clearly an exceptional whistler. She made the melody sound quite beautiful, to the point that it sounded much, much better than the actual song itself. When she finished, I couldn't help but applaud.

"That was amazing! Suiko, you're *really* good!"

"Not really. If you liked it, it's simply because you already had a predisposition to liking it in the first place."

She was the type of person who said dramatic things like that, and they came to her quite naturally.

"You must have practiced, though. Do you play an instrument?"

"No, just by ear."

"Then you must have perfect pitch or something. That's so awesome! What do you usually listen to?"

"Stuff nobody's ever heard of."

"Like what?"

"Mm, for example," she said and took another breath, beginning a different piece.

This time, it was more humming than whistling, as if she were a magical instrument that could reproduce any melody in existence.

"......!" I was so stunned just listening to her that I forgot to breathe.

There was simply no comparison to the first song. There was a resonance in my chest, a vibration in my heart that somehow made me feel very sad, all of a sudden. It was a strange melody—both rhythmic and powerful.

When she finished, I couldn't applaud. I was too choked up, with tears welling up in my eyes.

"...What's wrong? Didn't you like it?"

"No...no! It was...it was...uh, I feel sort of embarrassed now. It's like my song was just an imitation of real music..."

"I thought you liked that song?"

"N-no, I think I couldn't have, really. When I heard your song just now, it felt like...this is the first time that I've ever really known that I liked a piece of music. And it didn't have anything to do with what's popular or trendy!" I exclaimed, getting worked up.

"That's nice," Suiko-san said, smiling. She was as beautiful, if not more so, than the song itself. She stood there, backlit by the red light of the evening sky. It was like I was seeing the silhouette of a goddess.

"What song was that?" I asked.

She giggled. "You won't laugh?"

"Why would I?"

"The name of the piece is *Salome*. It's from a ballet."

"What's odd about that?"

"The composer is Ifukube Akira."

"Who?"

"He's most famous for writing the soundtracks to monster movies," Suiko-san said, putting her hand to her mouth, shoulders trembling as she laughed.

This gesture was so feminine that it made my heart beat faster, and I thought, *I could never laugh that naturally*. Truly, there was nobody else I knew who could laugh so beautifully or as unreservedly as her.

But now she was no longer with us.

I couldn't understand it. Why would a girl like her ever want to kill herself?

They said she hadn't even left a note. We don't know if she

had some secret pain that drove her to it, or if she did it just to prove some kind of point.

But I want to know. I had to know.

I can't honestly say that the two of us were all that close. But on those rare occasions when we were alone together, she would always talk openly to me. That was about it, though.

Still, she was without a doubt the most real person I'd ever met, up to that point. I can't think of any other way of describing it. Everyone else was just imitating someone else, trying desperately to pretend that it was their true nature. They were all frauds.

So I thought that there must be some meaning behind her suicide.

That's why I'm going to follow her.

Is that imitation, too? Probably.

What's sad is that I don't even know if I really loved her. And that's the irony; my life is going to end without me really understanding much of anything.

* * *

Komiya Mariko stood on the roof of the school, composing her suicide note in her head, but decided to not write it down.

The sky was dark.

The sun had set a long time ago, and the last traces of light were quickly fading away.

"Suiko-san..."

She looked over the edge of the roof.

Below her, she could still see the white line where Minahoshi Suiko's body had landed. The world around her was almost completely dark, but that line alone seemed to glow, floating upwards.

She swallowed.

Something that Minahoshi Suiko had said to her once popped into her head.

"Mariko-san, there's nothing in this world that is ever truly decided. Birds sometimes fall out of the sky, and sometimes it snows in April. Everything is uncertain, nothing is 'unnatural.'"

I wonder what that meant?

Perhaps I'll understand if I just climb over this fence...!

The white line moved, beckoning to her. It was an illusion, but it seemed too natural to call it that. It made perfect sense to Mariko.

There seemed to be no other logical choice for her doing anything else in life except jumping. The impulse rose up inside her. Her body shook, but not with fear—no, it was excitement.

"Suiko-san...!"

Komiya Mariko grabbed hold of the fence, preparing to climb.

But a voice came from behind her.

"—You wish to follow Minahoshi Suiko? You can't do it that way. It's impossible."

The voice was very strange, like that of a boy or a girl—yet at the same time, neither.

"——?!" Mariko turned around in surprise.

He sat on the other side of the roof, half hidden in darkness. A pipe-shaped black hat half hid his eyes, and he was wrapped in a black cape with a number of rivets attached to it. He wore black lipstick, contrasting with the white of his face.

"If you jump now, you will not end up where she has gone," he said quietly.

"Y-you're...?" Mariko said. She was clearly shaken, but not because she didn't know him. No, she knew all about him. All the girls in school were talking about him.

But for him to be *real*...?

"It seems you know me. That makes things easier." His left eye narrowed, and the right side of his mouth curled up in a strange, asymmetrical expression.

"Wh-what do you mean? Why can't I go to her?"

"Simple. You are about to end your life of your own free will. But Minahoshi Suiko did not. If there is such a thing as heaven, you will surely end up in a different place than her." It would be accurate to describe his voice as chilly.

"She did not end her life of her 'own free will?' What does that mean?" Mariko felt as if the ground beneath her feet were crumbling.

"You know my name, don't you? Then you know what I do." He was half shrouded in darkness. It looked as if he were dissolving into thin air.

"Th-then...you?"

"Yes. I am a shinigami. Minahoshi Suiko did not kill herself. I...killed her."

"Wh-why?!"

"Because she was an enemy of the world."

"......!"

"So now what? Do you still wish to die? Unfortunately, I'm

afraid I have no intention of killing you. You are not even worth that much."

"B-but... But..." Mariko stuttered, confused. She wasn't sure of anything now.

The enemy of the world? Suiko-san? How? What did that mean?

"Alternatively, I could put it this way. Minahoshi Suiko has not yet reached the next world. Unlike me, she was not 'divided'—though she was equally 'automatic.' As for where she is now...I really couldn't tell you."

Mariko couldn't understand anything the cloaked figure was saying.

She hadn't reached the next world?

Reflexively, Mariko looked at the ground below on the other side of the fence. There no longer enough light to make out the white line.

It was crazy. Mariko had seen her—seen what *used* to be her, as the authorities carried her body away under a bloodstained white shroud.

"What does it mean, Boogie—?!" Mariko cried out, turning around—but the cloaked figure was gone.

She looked around, but came up with nothing. The darkness was too complete. It was impossible to tell where the mysterious figure in black had gone.

Or perhaps he had never physically been there at all.

"............"

At last, fear welled up in Mariko's heart.

She glanced at the ground below.

But the fence that had seemed so easy to scale a moment ago now seemed as if it were a hundred meters tall.

"Aah..."

It's impossible.

You will not end up where she has gone.

Minahoshi Suiko has not yet reached the next world.

Her legs shook.

"Aaaaah...!"

And Mariko crumbled, falling to the floor. Tear after tear rolled down her face. She couldn't stop them from coming. They were the first tears she'd shed since Minahoshi Suiko had died.

She had been convinced it was better to die than to cry, but now she couldn't hold the tears back.

"I'm sorry. I'm sorry... I'm sorry, I'm sorry, I'm sorry..." she whispered in a slow rhythm, as she rocked herself back and forth. But her tiny voice was faint and was swept away by the wind, to be lost in the night.

* * *

"............"

The cloaked figure in the black hat watched her from below. Beneath his feet a white line in the shape of a person could be seen. He went down on his knee and ran his hand over it.

"She's certainly not *here* anymore..." he murmured, and stood up. "Are you going to try again? *Imaginator*?"

His black cape flapped furiously in the night wind.

I

If you wish to be good, then do not have dealings with the future. In most cases, that only leads to distortion.

—Kirima Seiichi (*VS Imaginator*)

I.

"SOMETIMES I wake up in the middle of the night," she said. Her name was Nakadai Sawako, and her cheekbones stood out ever so slightly. Her face was very pale, though, and to Asukai Jin, she looked like a withered bouquet inside an oversized jacket.

"Hmm," he said.

"I know it's cliché," she went on, "but I feel like something's sitting on my chest, looking at me. But when I open my eyes..."

"There's nothing there?"

"Yes. I mean, I know it's a dream, but...I have it over and over again. So..."

Sawako's shoulders trembled. In her hair, there were still lingering traces of a two-month-old perm, but she wasn't one to take care of herself, and she had obviously paid little attention to it since getting it. And understandably so: there were only four more months left until her entrance exam. Like so many girls, she would make an appointment to have her hair straightened just before the big day and then strive to take good care of it in order to make a good impression at the interview—but at that moment, she simply didn't have the time to care.

"This...'shadow'..." Asukai said, interrupting her. "Has it said anything to you?"

She looked up at him, surprised. "Yes! Yes, it has. How did you know?"

Ignoring her question, he asked another, "What did it say? Do you remember?"

"N-no, I..."

"You can't remember at all?"

"Right," she nodded.

Not only was the cram school designed to squeeze a large number of people into a very small space to begin with, but the guidance office was hidden in a corner of the building. It was about the size of a prison's solitary confinement cell—and the two of them were all alone in the tiny room.

There was only one window—a long, thin, vertical slit in the wall, through which a single ray of light penetrated. The light was red. It was already evening.

"Hmm..." Asukai said again, shutting his mouth and looking down at the girl's chest.

...She has no roots, he thought. *Very few leaves...only the buds are large, and they're almost breaking the stem...*

Sawako grew uncomfortable in the silence and began locking her fingers together around her knees.

"Um, Asukai-sensei...?"

"............"

He didn't respond.

He had a pointed chin and a thin face with a serene beauty

to it. He was not much older than Sawako, just past twenty. He was a student at a public university, but he taught art part time at this cram school—and he had taken over the highly unpopular position of guidance counselor.

"..............."

She looked up at him timidly. At some point, he'd taken his eyes off her and was staring out the window.

"I-I'm sorry, this all must sound crazy..." Sawako whispered, unable to stand it any longer.

Quietly, Asukai said, "As a teacher, I know I'm not supposed to say this. But maybe you should try to take exams a little less seriously."

"What do you mean?"

"Getting into the best university isn't going to relieve you of your worries—or guarantee your future," he continued, almost like he was reading some inspirational pamphlet. "I know a lot of people who slaved away, got into college, and then had no idea what to do once they were there. All they'd ever done was study, and they didn't know how to just let go and enjoy themselves. So they'd go off to try and pass the civil servants exam or something. They were just pointlessly limiting their options for a...I dunno, a decent future. They meet the person they were supposed to fall in love with, but they don't recognize how valuable they are and before they realize it, they wind up missing out on the most important things in life.

"They're college students, but they can't shake the exam student mentality. And very few people can pass on their first try.

Most people fail. They become ronin. They fritter away their precious youth and end up, frankly, really screwed up because of it."

She just sat there listening, wide-eyed.

"You see?" Asukai asked, turning towards her.

"Um, not..."

"You *already* know this, don't you? But you're doing your very best *not to think about it*. But doing your best and avoiding the truth—they're two different things. We can't tell you not to overdo it, though. The only way to actually pass these tests *is* to overdo it. But it's important not to overburden you with excessive—and frankly, unrealistic—expectations. I know you've heard this all before, but getting into college is not your whole life. That dream about the shadow is a sign that you're unconsciously resisting the notion of getting into college. I just think you need to relax a bit."

"O-okay," she nodded obediently. "But... But still..."

"Yeah. That's why you need to work at it. It isn't a bad thing to want to go to college. It's not like it's an impossible dream, either. But it just isn't healthy to get obsessed with it, you know? At this rate, you're just going to get overwhelmed by the pressure and be in no condition to actually sit there and take the test."

"I... I think I understand," Sawako said meekly.

...The bud relaxed a little, Asukai thought. *If she could just sprout a few more leaves... Not that it would take care of all of her problems, but it would be a start.*

He was looking at her chest again.

He could see something there.

Nobody else could see it, including the girl herself.

After that, they spoke in more concrete terms about how they should go about handling her problem subjects.

"Thank you very much!" she said as she stood up twenty minutes later.

"Your effort is genuine. All you have to do is just stay calm, and keep moving forward."

"Okay. And thanks, Sensei," she said. "I feel much better now. Say, did you ever have some sort of training? Like as a therapist or counselor?"

"Not really."

"Maybe you should consider a new career. You're really smart—and good looking, too." Asukai gave her an awkward smile, and she slapped her hand over her mouth. "Ah! Sorry! I didn't mean to be rude...!"

"I'll think about," he chuckled. "They do say you can't make a living painting."

As she was about to leave, Sawako suddenly turned back, remembering something. "Oh, right! Sensei, have you heard the phrase 'Sometimes it snows in April'?"

"Wh-what?" Asukai said, shocked.

"That's the only thing I remember from my dream. Oh, but it's probably not important. Good-bye!" she said brightly as she exited, her gloomy exterior having finally been shed.

"Sometimes...it snows in April?"

For some reason, those words made something stir inside Asukai.

* * *

When Asukai Jin thought about his strange ability to see the flaws in people's hearts, he always remembered Saint-Exupéry's *The Little Prince*. He had read it when he was three or four years old, but he remembered one line from it that went something like, "The reason this child was beautiful was because he had a rose within his heart."

He felt as if that image had been carved into his psyche and left a lasting impression on him.

His eyes could see a single plant growing from every person's chest. The variety of plant in his vision varied, and they came in all sorts of shapes and sizes, but the problem was not the variety of plant, but the very fact that in every vision, there was some part missing.

Perhaps there was no flower. Or no leaves. No stem. Or, like this girl, no roots. He had never once seen a person that carried a complete plant within their chest.

There was always a flaw.

So, his "advice" was simply to say whatever was needed to compensate for that flaw. If there were no roots, all he had to do was tell them to have more confidence. Everyone would be satisfied by that, and recover their good cheer.

His job at the cram school finished, he walked back to his apartment along a bustling shopping street. He couldn't help but notice the flaws on everyone's chests.

It annoyed him, occasionally.

Human effort was entirely devoted to making up for this flaw. He knew this. But he also knew that what they lacked was never in them to begin with, and that it was something that could never be obtained.

He had looked at his own chest before, but he could find nothing there. Presumably, he was lacking something also, and it was that missing item that was making him so unhappy. Unfortunately, there was no way for him to replace it, either.

"...So that's why *I* said..."

"...What the...?"

"...Ha ha ha! That's so *dumb*..."

Drunks, young people, old people, males, females—they all passed him by. None of them ever thought that they were missing flowers or roots.

(They're happier *not* knowing...)

Since he was very young, he had always felt isolated.

Perhaps he always would.

"—Oh, look! Snow!"

"Wow! It's so *pretty*!"

Everyone around him was cheering at the sky, so Asukai felt obligated to look up, as well.

Something white was falling out of the night sky.

(I do like snow...)

Snow turned everything white. It was one of his favorite things. Perhaps because flowers never bloomed beneath it. He could go about his business without thinking about anything else...or so he felt.

But when he looked happily up at the sky, his expression suddenly froze.

There was a girl standing in the fifth story window of a nearby building.

Her feet were on the window ledge, her body all the way outside, getting ready to jump.

As he stared up at her, their eyes met.

She smiled slightly with her eyes. Then...

"No...!" Asukai tried to shout, but she flung her body outward into the open air.

Reflexively, Asukai ran towards her.

But his feet went out from under him, and he fell awkwardly.

He hurriedly scrambled back to his feet, but as he looked up again, he saw something impossible.

"*Heh heh heh.*"

The girl was floating in mid-air, laughing.

But there was something unique about her smile. Her mouth was closed in a straight line, and her eyes alone smiled, sweet and enchanting.

She was frozen in mid-air, about to fall, but not moving at all.

"Hunh...?" he wondered aloud.

"Hey, wake up! You're in the way," snarled a group of drunks, brushing past him.

"D-do you see that?" Asukai asked, pointing at the girl.

None of them paid much attention. "What are you talking about?"

"You've had too much to drink!"

They were looking where he was pointing, but none of them could see her.

(Wh-what on earth…?)

He stood up, looking up at her, stunned.

Now that he looked carefully, he could tell that she was actually falling, just very, very slowly. Her tangled hair was moving, swaying.

"Heh heh heh."

Those laughing eyes drank in the light like holes in the sky.

"It isn't much fun to see things nobody else can, is it, Asukai-sensei?" he heard her whisper in his ear.

"How…?"

"I know exactly how you feel. I used to be the same."

Asukai stumbled over, until he was directly below the falling girl.

"Th-then you…"

"Just like your extra sensory perception, I can see people's deaths."

Her expression never changed—that tightly closed mouth never moved. It was as if time around her moved at a snail's pace.

"Deaths?"

"To be more accurate, I can see the energy field generated by all living things just before they burn themselves out." She laughed again. "I represent a possibility in which people are able to manipulate death. My purpose is to recreate the world in that fashion, which makes me an enemy of the current world. Even in spring, I bring cold. I make it snow in April."

"Er…"

"Will you help me with my work, Asukai-sensei?"

"What...? What are you talking about? Who are you?!" he shouted.

The people around him looked at him suspiciously. To them, he was shouting at empty space. They must have thought him plastered beyond his limit or tripped out on drugs.

In the air above him, the girl replied, "My enemies call me the *Imaginator*."

And she vanished.

"W-wait!" he cried, reaching out towards her, but his fingers only brushed empty air.

"............"

He was amazed, but then his shoulders slumped in disappointment. He thought to himself that he had finally gone completely insane. Seeing things, it was obvious— then he glanced at his feet and almost shouted.

The falling snow was piled up all around, except at his feet, where a small patch of pavement had been left exposed.

It was like a shadow puppet in the shape of a girl falling from the sky.

* * *

When Asukai got back to his apartment, a girl poked her head out of the window of the room next door as if she'd been waiting for him.

"—There you are! Welcome back!" she said brightly. She was

Kinukawa Kotoe, the apartment owner's daughter and also his cousin. Kotoe had talked her parents into letting her use one of the empty rooms as a study. Her own house was about a minute's walk away.

"Wh-what is it?" he said blankly, still a little out of it.

"Jin-niisan, did you eat yet? I just made some stew; thought you might like some."

"Um, yeah...thanks."

"Cool! I'll bring it over in a minute!" She ducked back into the room.

Kotoe was always like this. Asukai's father had died two years before, and he was renting a room in his uncle's apartment building. But that was the extent of their involvement. Asukai had a scholarship covering his university's tuition, but his art supplies, living expenses, and rent all had to be covered by the money he made from his meager cram school salary. About the only liberty he had taken was to rent the room without a guarantor, but Kotoe had taken it upon herself to look after him.

Seeing Kotoe up and in her usual cheerful mood actually helped Asukai calm his nerves a little.

(Whether that was an illusion or not, it's not like I've never seen anything that outright bizarre before...)

If he kept his cool, he could deal with this, just like he always had.

He entered his apartment, splashed his face a few times with water from his bathroom sink, and turned to find Kotoe coming in with a big pot in her hands.

"Okay! Today's dinner is *especially* good—if I do say so myself!"

She set the table briskly, as if this were her own room, and placed a steaming hot bowl in front of a slightly embarrassed Asukai.

"It does look good. Thanks."

"Jin-niisan, you look kinda tired. Everything okay?"

"Yeah…it's just a busy time of year. My students are all feeling it, and I catch it from them."

"That sucks."

"It's not like you won't be going through the same thing next year yourself."

Kotoe was a second year student at a local prefectural school called Shinyo Academy.

"Yeah, well…I dunno if I'm goin' to college…"

She glanced up at him.

"Or maybe…I just could go to your cram school and you could teach me…"

"When did you decide to go to art school? I teach art history and design, you know."

"But you also do counseling, right? I could use some of that…"

"We can do that here anytime for free. No reason to sign up where I work."

"Really?" Kotoe beamed.

"But the kids I counsel are all very serious people. Not so sure about you…" he teased, winking.

"That's so mean! Like you think I'm some sort of *airhead*!" she said, puffing out her cheeks and pouting. But she couldn't keep it up, and soon they were both laughing.

Kotoe let out a little sigh. "I guess I do come across like that..."

"And thank god you do. You're better off *not* needing my help," Asukai said sincerely, lowering his spoon.

"Mm?"

"I think people need to work their way through their own problems. And with the tests...I'm a cram school teacher, so there's a lot I can't say. I can't tell them they don't need to go to college...even if they really shouldn't be trying..."

He glanced over at Kotoe's chest.

She had no "flower."

What she did have was a bountiful amount of leaves, which were the domain of kindness and warmth, and her stem and roots were equally secure. But there was no flower to be found.

Kotoe was a good girl. She wasn't bad looking. Her parents owned several apartment buildings and were obviously rich. There was no reason at all for her to be unhappy.

But deep in her heart, she wondered, *Why have I never come across anything definitively radiant?* Sometimes she would see a really ordinary, average person who was completely passionate about some insignificant thing. This would devastate her—she would be terribly jealous of them.

But there was nothing she could do about it.

She lacked that passion, and she would never have it.

"Jin-niisan, you just need to chill," Kotoe said, trying to use her usual hip slang to cheer him up. She could never guess what he was looking at, not even in her wildest dreams. "You spend way too much time stressing over other people. You've gotta at *least* try to make things a little easier on yourself, you know." She nodded, oddly forceful.

"Th-thanks. But now I don't know which of us is getting counseled," Asukai grinned.

"Nothing is futile! There is always a path—even if it's towards something that doesn't exist yet," she proclaimed.

"Um...yeah, I guess." Asukai nodded, but with no conviction. "I wish I could think that..."

"But that path may be a trifle...cruel... It might even go against all that this world deems just." Her voice was so certain; it seemed almost scornful.

"...Huh?" Asukai looked up. That didn't sound like something Kotoe would say.

He froze.

The vision at her chest had vanished.

It had been there just a moment before, but now he could see nothing.

And her expression—her mouth was closed in a straight line, her eyes alone sparkling, laughing—

"Wh-who are you?!" Asukai cried out, leaping to his feet.

"Relax. I am only borrowing her body...*temporarily*," the girl with Kotoe's face whispered.

"Wh-what?!"

"This girl's psyche *is not capable of becoming my vessel*," she said quietly. "I must leave her in a moment."

"You weren't a delusion...you were a ghost?"

"No...not a ghost," she said, standing to face him. "To be completely accurate, I am a 'hypothetical possibility given substance.' But for your feeble mind, consider me 'a glimpse of the future.'"

She reached towards Asukai's forehead. She stroked it gently with both hands.

"Asukai-sensei, don't you feel it's time you...*did* something?"

"About what?"

"The flaws found in human hearts."

Her soft, gentle fingertips massaged Asukai's face, firmly.

He moaned. The sensation was sweet and hard to resist.

"What do you think your flaw is, Asukai-sensei?"

".........?!"

"You lack a 'calling.'" Her voice was peaceful, yet firm.

"...Eh?"

"Let me show you a little glimpse of the future."

She pulled his face towards hers, arched her back, and placed her thin lips upon his.

Instantly, *something* opened in Asukai's head.

A torrent of images cascaded past him.

"Ah...aaauuughhhhhh!" he screamed, forcing her away.

She never flinched, simply staggered once and then stared back at him again.

"Hahh...hahh..." Asukai gasped for breath. "Wh-what was that...that spectacle?"

"Your 'calling,' Asukai-sensei."

"L-Like hell! I would never do something like *that*!"

"The choice is yours. But you *are* capable of it. Nothing will change the truth of that. The reason for your birth is *there*...and only there."

"Shut up! What...what are you, some sort of demon?! I...I..." he wheezed, unable to find the words.

"Am I tempting you? No. That's not my intent. It's up to you to decide." Her eyes alone laughed. "But, Asukai-sensei, remember this. Birds do fall from the sky, and sometimes it does snow in April."

"Get away!"

Asukai flung the contents of his stew bowl at her.

She made no effort to dodge, but simply stood there and took it.

A moment later there was a scream. "Ow! Wh-what the heck?!"

Asukai gasped.

Kotoe was back.

"A-are you..."

"Why...why am I...? Gross!!!" Kotoe said, confused; she no idea what was going on. Her memories didn't match up.

Asukai wiped her face off with a towel, trying to keep his body from shaking.

(...What did she call herself? The Imaginator...?)

* * *

He might well be going crazy, but that was no reason to skip work. Asukai was at the cram school again, speaking with yet another student.

"I can't do this anymore. It's not for me. Like, in the middle of the night, I can be taking notes…and my hands just start shaking," the girl said, nodding to herself, over and over.

There was no stem in the girl's "vision." She had roots, but they connected directly into the leaves and base of the flower.

"You need a change," Asukai answered, though he knew it was useless. This girl was afraid that nothing in her being would ever be secure. No matter how often she tried something new, her anxiety would always be there. Whether she passed the exam or not, nothing would change.

"What should I do?"

"Take a break, do whatever you like. Or change the way you study. You've got a good memory, don't you?"

People without stems were good at stuffing things in. But they were unable to turn that knowledge and experience into anything, to nurture it or let it grow. They could put in as much as they liked, but it would just pile up, never changing, never rotting.

"I suppose so…"

"Then spend one week concentrating on solving equations. Halve the number of things to memorize."

"Ah…b-but…" She hesitated. Yet with a clear goal placed in front of her, her eyes shone. Her type had no conscious goals of their own, so they tended to relax if you gave them one. "Will that work?"

"I'm sure you can do it. Your percentile's been going up," Asukai replied. He wanted to add, *That won't save you, though,* but he let the words die in his throat. It was futile.

"Okay! I'll try it. Sensei, thank you so much!"

"You're the one who has to do the work."

"No, it's because you really know how to help people. Everyone says so! Seems such a shame to waste that kind of talent on a cram school."

"Hey, now."

"Asukai-sensei, I think you were meant to do something much more important. Yeah, you probably were."

"Hmm... Who knows?"

You are capable of it. Nothing will change the truth of that.

"I just can't get into it," the boy said, sullenly.

"Hmm... Your first results were pretty good, but they haven't improved at all," Asukai said, looking up from the boy's file and checking the vision at his chest.

No leaves.

This type took no pleasure in life. Since his flower and stem were doing pretty well, he was fully capable of better things, but everything he tried dried up around him.

"I know I gotta do better..."

"Studying bores you, right?" Asukai said bluntly and to the point.

The boy nodded, wryly. "Basically."

"You know why?" Asukai's tone changed, becoming sort of chummy.

"Nope."

"'Cause it's boring. What other reason is there?" he grinned. This was all part of the performance.

"Well, shit, if you put it that way..." the boy said, grinning back. Anyone else would lose their motivation if their teacher talked to them like this, but with this type there was no risk of that.

"Look, I know it's tedious as hell. And you're expected to do whatever us teachers tell you to do...so how's that ever gonna be fun? All we're doing is just following some stupid rulebook anyway."

"Ha ha ha!"

"When you get down to it, passing tests is a matter of understanding the system. You know why I can work part time here, right? It's not like I've got a teaching license or anything."

"Well...you got experience, right?"

"Yep. Few years ago, just like you, I was trying to pass these exams. I kept hitting all these brick walls and I was just banging my head trying to figure out an easy way to pass. Now, I make a living passing on all those little tricks I figured out."

"Ah ha! I get ya."

"See? Studying has some use after all."

"Not just for getting into college, you mean?"

"Exactly. These days, getting into a good college doesn't even mean that much. You only go because you *have* to go. Still, that's no reason to kill yourself studying. But if you look at it as training... Look, I don't know what it is you want to be—but whatever it is, you're gonna have to develop a few tricks—a few *techniques*. Think of all this as, like, a simulation. No, think of them like a game. There aren't that many other times in your life where society itself and all of the people around you will just up and support you, but this is one of those times. It gives you the freedom to experiment."

Personally, Asukai just thought he was talking crap, but the boy sitting across from him was visibly happier.

"Never thought of it that way..."

"Yeah, just think of the test itself as just another chance to gather data and experiment."

"Right..."

"But in that sense, you've got a little catching up to do. On these results, you'll end up in a second rate school. That'd suck, right? Waste of a good opportunity."

This was a little logical slight of hand, but the boy never noticed.

People with no leaves feel like they aren't connected to the world around them. No matter what they do, they can never feel peace of mind when they are around other people. To compensate, they pretty much lose themselves in methodology. They know all sorts of approaches to things and all sorts of tricks, but all they're doing is trying to make up for an inability to communicate with others.

Being nice to them, praising them...it's all useless. Staying firmly on a practical ground worked best.

But the end result of all of their tricks only served to drive them even further into isolation. Since nobody else needed these tricks, they couldn't understand how much work went into them.

Those of the same type were especially cruel—if they happened to be using different methodologies.

None of them would ever find an "ally."

"Okay, I'll try it out." Drawn along by Asukai's friendly manner, the boy was now completely comfortable.

"You've still got plenty of time," Asukai nodded. He didn't dare add, *But all your efforts and memories will never be appreciated by anyone else*. That revelation would only be utterly futile.

"But, Sensei..." the boy said. "What are you planning on doing when you get out of college?"

"Dunno. Probably try and make a living painting."

"Seems like a waste, man. You ought to start your own business, do something big. Seriously." His eyes were serious, no sense of the mocking that this type so often engaged in.

"Maybe."

You lack a "calling."

"I keep having this dream over and over."

"What kind?"

"Um, well. Sensei...have you ever heard the phrase 'Sometimes it snows in April'?"

"Uh...n-no, can't say that I have. Wh-why?"

"In the dream, someone—I don't know who—keeps saying that to me. When I hear those words, I just don't care about anything anymore. This stupid test, this ugly world—they just don't matter to me. Not anymore."

"............"

"But whoever it is, they are a little too nice...and that's sort of scary. When I wake up, it feels like someone just threw a bucket of cold water in my face. *Brrr...*"

"............"

"And after I have that dream, I can't do anything. I had one the day before the last practice test, and I couldn't figure out a single problem."

"............"

"Sensei...is there something *wrong* with me?"

"............"

"Sensei? Uh, Asukai-sensei?"

"—Ah! Oh, uh, hmm?"

"Something wrong?"

"Oh, no. It's nothing."

* * *

When the last student left, Asukai tried several times to sketch *that face*.

Unfortunately, he couldn't draw it well enough, and he crumpled up all of his attempted pages and flung them into the corner of the counseling office, missing the wastebasket.

Afterwards, he knelt down to collect them all and wondered to himself, *What the hell am I doing...?*

He sighed, balled up the failed sketches as tightly as he could, and buried them deep within the office wastebasket.

* * *

Several days passed like this, repeating the same answers over and over for an endless progression of identical worries, occasionally encountering the phrase *Sometimes it snows in April* among them.

Then one day, as he walked along the streets after work, he heard a groan from a back alley.

"Unh...unh...s-somebody..." he heard, faintly.

"...?" He turned off the main road, heading towards the voice.

"Please...somebody..." It sounded like a girl's voice and in great pain, barely gasping out the words.

"Is somebody there?" Asukai called out. There was no answer.

He moved deeper into the alley, and found a girl slumped against the cul-de-sac.

"Unhhhhhhhhh," she groaned.

"What's the matter?" Asukai asked as he went over to her and placed his hand upon her back.

Instantly, his hand was flung off.

The girl sprang up like a jack-in-the-box, launching herself towards him, and slamming his back against the wall. "Don't move," she snarled, with sudden menace. There was a carving knife in her hand.

"You're..." Asukai looked at her face. She was very, very thin—like a skeleton. It was painful to look at her. Her hair was a brittle and matted mess, not at all that of a young girl.

"Heh...heh...that was stupid of you, Asukai-sensei. Even this country's pretty dangerous these days. I knew a sap like you would fall for it!" she sneered, breathing raggedly.

"You were after me...? Imazaki Shizuko, isn't it? You were in my spring course, weren't you?"

She had come to him for counseling once.

"Heh...heh... I'm surprised you remembered." She was gasping for breath. Her eyes were red, bloodshot. It was clear she was on something, presumably some sort of chemical. "But it ain't gonna get you off. Give me all the money you got."

"To buy drugs...? What happened to you? You were such a good student..."

"My dad got arrested for tax evasion or something! Made everything so futile! But what do *you* care?! Just hand it over!!!" The girl screamed, hysterical.

"........." Asukai looked at the tip of the knife. It was shaking. Her grip on it was so tight she couldn't keep it pointed at him. It would be easy to dodge it.

But he suddenly felt a turmoil of emotion welling up inside him.

Everything seemed so ridiculous—directionless anger abruptly gushed forth from deep within his heart.

"No," he said, crisply, before he even realized it.

"What?" The girl said, looking even fiercer.

"Go ahead and kill me," Asukai spat.

"I'm serious!"

"So am I!" he roared. "You think you can escape by taking

drugs? That doesn't do any good! No matter how high you get, there's no saving us!"

"Sh-shut up! You're just scared!" The girl moved the knife closer, touching Asukai's throat.

"Try it!" he yelled, and she put her anger into it, pushing forward.

The knife slipped past, his skin sliced open, and blood came out. She had missed his jugular by a hair's breadth, and he had narrowly escaped death, but Asukai was unaware of this.

The girl toppled over. She didn't have the strength left to keep her footing.

A number of little packets spilled out of her pocket onto the ground—little packets of drugs.

"——!" Asukai frowned down at them. This was hardly for her personal use. With this quantity, there was no reason for her to be trying to mug people. Which meant...

"...Exactly. These are for other people," the girl said, rising slowly to her feet—no, this was no longer the same girl.

Her eyes were laughing, but she had no expression.

"Y-you again." Asukai glared at the thing inhabiting the girl, ignoring the blood dripping from his neck.

"Just to be clear, I took over only a few seconds ago. Most of your encounter was of her own free will," she said coldly. "*If* you can call that free will. It's not like she wanted to do it. She's a girl. If she needed money, there are faster and safer ways for her to get it. But once her body's been torn to pieces like this, those options vanish."

"Shut up!" Despite the fact that the girl had tried to stab him, hearing her insulted made him furious.

"Do you know what these drugs are for, Asukai-sensei?"

The thing inhabiting the girl's body pointed at the ground.

"She was selling them?"

"Exactly. The dosage is too weak for her now—it's beginner's strength. If she wanted more drugs for herself, she had to sell these to other people. That's what they told her. But she couldn't bring herself to do that."

She pointed towards her chest.

"Such a *sad* story. Didn't want to make any more people like her, but what else could she do? So she asked you, the only person she could ever remember being nice to her."

"........."

"But either way, Asukai-sensei, this girl was finished."

"What do you mean?"

"The drugs have destroyed her body. She won't last out the month. She's going to die. Futile, pitiful, miserable, and sad," she sneered.

"........."

"But you might be able to do something," she said, picking up the knife, and stabbing it deep into her own neck.

"——!"

For a second, the girl's blood sprayed out, filling the air; and then she fell over.

"Aiiieeeee!" There was a scream.

At the end of the alley, a woman walking by had seen this. She quickly ran away.

Asukai rushed over to the girl.

She was gasping. Her face was back to normal. *She* was gone.

"Shit...!" Asukai pushed his handkerchief against the girl's wound, but half her blood had already emptied out of her in a massive geyser.

Eyes hollow, the girl whispered, "......It.........t..."

Asukai leaned close, putting his ear to her lips.

"...mn it, damn it, damn it," she swore. Cursing everything in the world. "Damn it, damn it, damn it, damn it, damn it, damn it, da—!"

Asukai stared down at the girl. She had no choice but to stay angry until the very end.

He grit his teeth, and put his hand on her chest.

It was so much easier than he'd thought.

* * *

"Let me get this straight... Moments after she assaulted you, she suddenly stabbed herself in the throat? That's your story?" The detective asked. He was speaking to the key witness, who had stayed by the side of the body until the patrol cars arrived.

"Yes," Asukai said instantly. There was a bandage around his neck, applied by the doctor at the police hospital.

"You say you knew this girl?"

"Yes. Her name is Imazaki Shizuko. She's about eighteen. I don't know her address, but it's probably still in the files at the cram school. I taught her last spring." He answered smoothly, without faltering. No emotion.

"Did she have something against you? Any idea what?"

"Maybe. She came to me for counseling, but I guess I didn't help her much."

"Well, from what we've been able to ascertain, her family situation was at the root of it," the detective admitted. He'd decided Asukai's calm responses proved his innocence. "She had reason enough to kill herself."

"Suicide?"

"Yeah. She wouldn't have lasted much longer, anyway. The drugs had wrecked her system. The way she died was comparatively pain-free. Overdosing's a nasty way to go. Truth is...we'd had our eyes on her for dealing for a while now. I can tell you that she wasn't much good at it. Heart wasn't in it."

"You knew about her?"

"She was low level for another pusher that we're after, but the big man still hasn't shown his face."

You knew, but didn't save her?! Asukai's poker face hid this thought perfectly.

"You'll be free to go soon. We've got a witness, so we know you didn't kill her. Soon as we wrap things up here, you can leave."

"Thank you," Asukai bowed his head.

The investigation was over soon enough, and he signed and stamped his statement as directed. Asukai rose to leave.

"Oh, Asukai-san... This is just my own personal question, but..." the detective started.

"What?"

"While she was dying, did you say something to her?"

"What do you mean?"

"I don't mean anything. Just that girl, dying that way...her face was awfully peaceful. Like the thorns in her heart had all been plucked away. If something you said put her mind at ease, then you must be one hell of a teacher." The aging detective nodded keenly.

"Sorry, I... I didn't say anything," Asukai replied quietly, and left the room.

* * *

Soon, Asukai found himself walking through the evening streets again.

For every alley he found, he stopped, and peered down it looking for some sort of sign. His eyes never missed a thing, like the eyes of a hawk searching for its next target.

Then he heard a sound, like something falling over. Like the girl's moans, the sound was so faint nobody else around even noticed.

"————"

But he turned instantly, and went down the alley towards the sound's origin.

He found some people there. Seven in all—six boys and a girl.

Something was clearly going on—the girl's clothes were torn, her naked and vulnerable upper body exposed. Five of the boys stood around her, reaching towards her. One stood to the side, dazed, blood running from his mouth.

"Well, *this* is easy to figure out!" Asukai's voice boomed.

All the boys spun towards him.

"—! Wh-who are you?!"

"Just to make sure, I'd better ask. You there," Asukai pointed to the odd boy out, the one who'd clearly been beaten. "Do you want to save this girl?"

The confidence in Asukai's voice brought the boy out of his daze. He quickly nodded, "Y-yes."

"Then take her and run!" Asukai said, walking straight through the boys, taking the girl's arm, and pulling her out.

"Hey!" The boys said, lurching towards Asukai.

"Hmph," he snorted, and *did something* to one of them, too fast for anyone to see.

The boy fell over backwards.

"——?!"

The others shrank backwards, surprised. Asukai pushed the unresisting girl towards the bleeding boy. "Go! Get out of here!!"

"Th-thank you," the boy mumbled, scrambling away. He grabbed the girl's hand,and ran.

"Wait!" the others shouted, but when they tried to follow, they found Asukai between them.

"You wait," he said, a fearless smile on his face.

"Oh, yeah?!" they shouted, pulling knives from their pockets.

Asukai didn't bat an eyelash at the blades. "I've got no grudge against you," he said. "But I need a few more samples."

* * *

One minute later—

Everyone else was sprawled on the ground. Only one of the boy thugs was still standing.

Strangely enough, all of their injuries were caused by each other's knives.

"Ah...ahhhh..." the last boy moaned, his teeth chattering together. Asukai came over to him, waving his right hand over his chest.

"Wh-wh-wh-what did you do to them?" the boy asked.

"You wouldn't understand. But I haven't hurt them. I've given them happiness."

His words, his calm, scared the boy more than anything else in his short life.

"Wh-what the hell are you?"

"Mm? Let's see... What was that name?" Asukai looked behind him.

The girl hanging in the sky above him replied, "Imaginator!"

"Right...*that*," Asukai grinned...and his right hand snapped out towards the boy.

There was a muffled scream.

Boogiepop returns
VS Imaginator Part 1

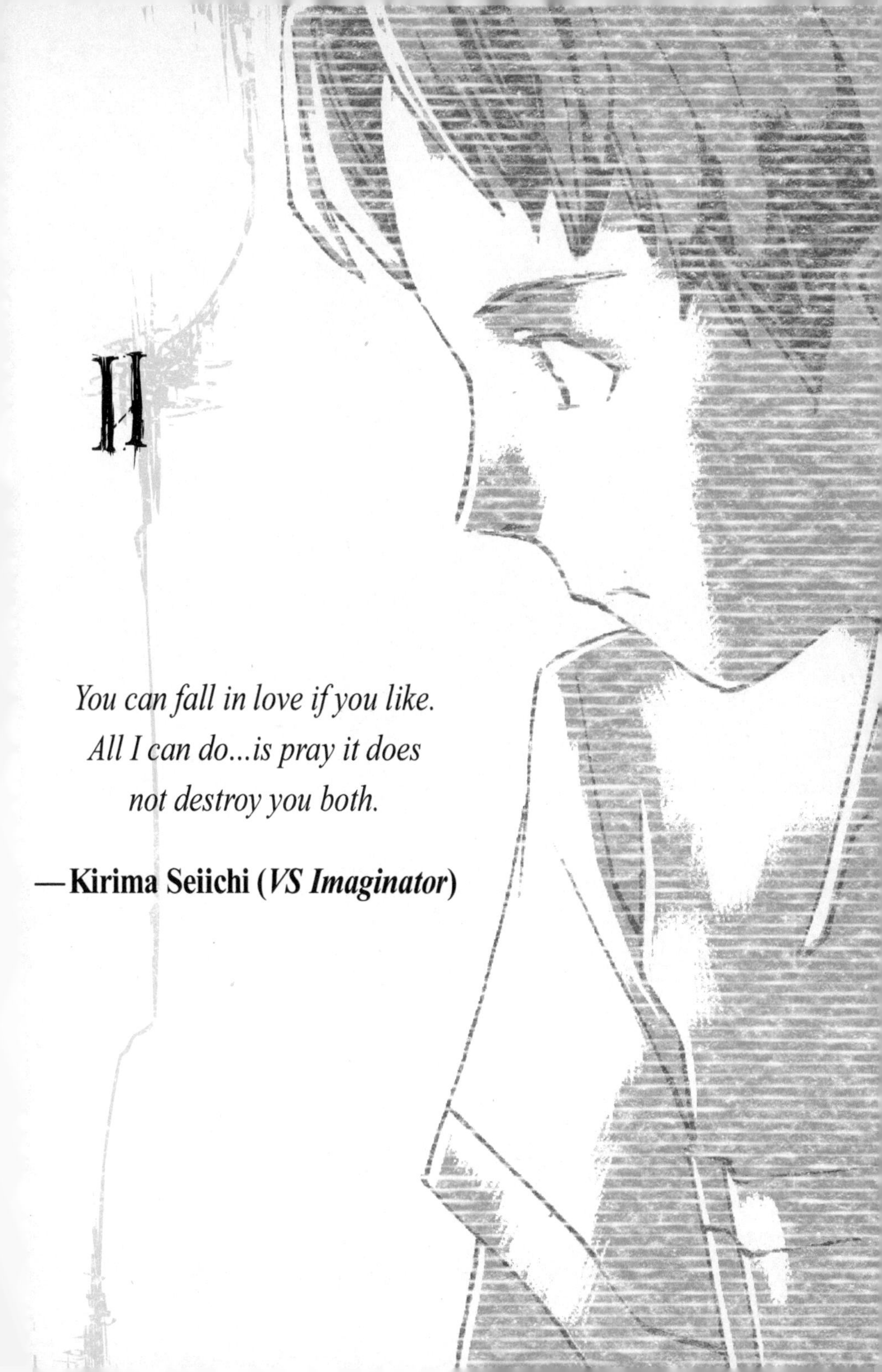

II

You can fall in love if you like.
All I can do...is pray it does
not destroy you both.

—Kirima Seiichi (*VS Imaginator*)

II.

HER NAME was Orihata Aya.

She had big striking eyes, with large pupils—though, they almost never looked at you directly. Very beautiful, but an incredibly reckless personality, and she always spoke in a very terse fashion. She was the same age as me, which is, well, fifteen, but there was a sort of sobriety about her that even most adults never manage to develop.

"Masaki, why are you interested in me?"

"Um, I just thought we could...I dunno, be friends, you know?"

"You want me?"

"Hunh?!"

"Do you want to have sex with me?"

"Hey, Orihata—!"

"We can if you want to."

"............"

Yeah, many of our conversations were a lot like this.

She seemed like she didn't even have friends at her school, and until she met me, I had my own doubts whether she'd ever had a normal conversation before.

Oh, right... My name's Taniguchi Masaki, and as you can probably guess, Orihata and I...we're complete opposites. It's funny, though; Orihata and I met in the most messed up kind of way.

At the time, I had just returned to Japan to get ready for high school after having lived abroad with my parents for a while, which was in this place called Phnom Penh. I was not really all that comfortable with my surroundings yet, and I'd heard horror stories from my parents about how other Japanese students had this tendency to keep their distance from returnees.

Luckily, I also have a sister—who isn't actually related to me—who's spent her entire life in Japan. She said, "Sadly, that's true. They're all pathetic losers, afraid of anyone who does something different or thinks about crap in a different way. You'd better be ready."

So I was prepared for it and just kept quiet.

Even when I didn't feel like it, I always tried to help people, and I was careful to always maintain an easy-going attitude. And somehow, I ended up getting really popular with all of the girls in class. If they had something they didn't understand, or something in the study guide that didn't make sense, they'd always come to me for help instead of the teacher.

"Oh, Masaki's so smart! Must be all that studying abroad."

I hadn't really studied abroad in the traditional sense of the term, but for some reason, the idea stuck.

Honestly, I was a bit out of my league. I couldn't push the girls away, but the guys in my class—in my entire school—all started to look at me funny.

By this point, high school entrance exams were right on top of us, so I wasn't exactly bullied by anyone (not much, anyway), but when I left school grounds, things would get a little...argumentative. In school, lowerclassmen would never bug an upperclassman, but once school was over, that line just vanished. I got glares from all directions.

It wouldn't have been so bad if I didn't always have a group of girls crowding around me. But all they ever did was just squeal and treat me like their own little toy—never like a true friend. I was pretty fed up with it by then, but I stuck with it anyway.

Then one day, I slipped up. Guess I must've been tired or something.

I had to swing by the station, so I cut through a back alley, and found myself surrounded by five guys.

"So, Mr. Study Abroad. You've been doing pretty well for yourself, *haven't* ya?"

"Getting a little bit too much attention, see?"

You'd think these guys would be dressed all trashy, but they weren't. No, they were all wearing pretty expensive jackets and didn't look like delinquents at all. So I hadn't realized what they were up to until it was too late and I was already surrounded. And by then, they already had switchblades open.

I wasn't sure how old they were, but they had to have been younger than me. One of the kids' voices had barely even cracked. Still, that didn't make the others any less menacing.

"Right," I said. "I'll be more cautious."

I'd blown it. I'd been so careful not to let myself get into a situation like this that I had walked right smack dab into one... and now they had me.

"You'll be careful? How are you gonna do *that*?"

"I'll try not to get as much attention?"

They all cackled.

Then suddenly, one shouted, "Don't you fuck with us!" And a hard punch connected with my cheek.

I saw his fist coming for me easily enough, but I let him hit me. I swung my body back a little and softened the blow.

The punch had connected enough to cut the inside of my cheek. There was blood in my mouth...but my teeth were fine. He hadn't hit any key points, so I wasn't even shaken.

This guy was nothing much. In Phnom Penh, I'd been studying a sort of undisciplined form of karate—kind of a child's self defense class, if you will—for a pretty long time. I'd learned to size up my opponents just by looking at them. Their shoulders alone were a good indicator of just how much damage a person could really do.

The most effective technique in this self-defense class was to yell for help as loud as you can. I considered this, briefly. If these were professional kidnappers, it might work—but this was Japan, and I felt that with opponents as inexperienced as these guys it would just provoke them. Plus, people tend to ignore cries for help, anyway. The only real way to get anyone's attention is to just lie and scream, *Fire!*

What *really* had me worried was that these guys probably went to the same school as me. If I kicked their asses, they'd just come back in larger numbers, and then the trouble would never let up.

And just as I was trying to figure out if hitting them four or five times would settle things or not, someone spoke up.

"Hey," they said.

She was talking to all of us at once. Both the attackers and little ol' me—the victim.

"That looks boring."

Surprised, we turned and found a girl just standing there.

The first thing I noticed was her unruly hair, which seemed to have been just left there at a sort of arbitrary length. It seemed to flow out of her.

We were in a dirty back alley that stank of piss and ditch water. The sky was dark and cloudy, and I was hunched down like a sad frightened rabbit.

No matter how you looked at it, my first meeting with Orihata Aya was...anything but perfect.

* * *

"............"

I gaped at her for what seemed like an eternity.

The girl with her arbitrary hair never even glanced at me. She just walked briskly towards us.

"Wh-who are you? Study Abroad's girlfriend?" one snarled.

She didn't even blink. "What is your purpose? What failing of his caused this behavior?" Her voice was flat, devoid of emotion.

"Hunh? You don't know this guy?"

"What do you think you're doing here?" asked another classmate.

"I asked for a reason," she insisted.

"Hey, this guy thinks he's Don Juan. Looking like this, tricking girls into falling for him."

Obviously lies, but I fought back the anger.

"Hunh..." she said, and at last looked at me.

For some reason, I found myself glaring back at her.

She frowned. She looked at me like I puzzled her.

I thought she was pitying me, which made me angrier. I could tell my expression was growing harsher as I fought against my feelings.

She frowned harder, put her head to one side, then sort of drooped before looking back at the group around me.

"So, he stole your girlfriends, then? The cause of your anger is sexual frustration?"

She didn't even bat an eye at what she was saying.

It was so out there that we all just sort of stared.

"Uh...what? What did she say?"

"I'm asking if this attack is a way of forgetting that your sexual partners all hate you."

Her tone was so level, it couldn't be taken as deliberate provocation. She was just throwing the words out there.

They stood silently for a moment, but then their faces turned red, their fists shook. They were getting angry.

"You...*bitch*!" They all went for her, reaching out to grab her.

And she did something none of us could have predicted.

She grabbed her own shirt, and tore it off, exposing her bare chest to the chilly night air. Her body was pale and beautiful, as if it was drinking in all the light that shone around it.

"If you have frustrated desires, I can fulfill them," she said, still completely calm. The thing is, there was much more expression on her face just moments before when she had looked at me. At this moment, it was like she was wearing a mask.

"Uuuum..."

"H-hey..."

The boys froze in mid-lunge, bug-eyed.

"Whoa, *wait* a minute—!" I said, flustered. I didn't know what the hell was going on, but I was not about to stand by and let them do as they pleased with her.

But at that moment, a loud voice came from the far end of the alley.

"Well, *this* is easy to figure out!"

We spun around, and there was a young man in white clothes standing there.

He strode towards us confidently.

"—! Wh-who are you?!"

"Just to make sure, I'd better ask. You there," he pointed at me. "Do you want to save this girl?"

I quickly nodded, "Y-yes."

"Then take her and run!" he snapped, strode right over to her, and took the bare-chested girl by the arm.

"Hey!" one of the boys said, and moved towards him—but

with blinding speed, he reached out toward the boy's chest...and that alone sent him flying.

Even I couldn't see what the man had done. This guy was something else.

While I was still stunned, he shoved the girl towards me.

"Go! Get out of here!!"

I managed to say, "Th-thank you," as I took the girl's arm and ran. She followed, unresisting.

When we were almost on the main street, I quickly shrugged off my jacket and covered her body with it.

"Are you okay?" I asked.

She seemed a little out of it. She stared back at me, and asked, "Why?"

"Eh?"

"Didn't you hate me?" She looked puzzled again.

I didn't get it, but I couldn't leave that man to handle those boys all by himself, so I put her on a bench in front of the station, which seemed safe enough, told her to wait for me, and hurried back.

But halfway there a hand grabbed me from behind.

I turned around, and it was the young man.

"Hey," he said, smiling. There was not a scratch on him. No dirt...not even so much as a wrinkle on his crisp white suit. Who *was* this guy?!

"Are...you okay?!"

"Yeah, it's all taken care of. I doubt they'll bother you again," he said airily.

I gaped at him. I'd been gone less than two or three minutes. And there'd been five of them.

"Um, y-you..."

"I think you ought to worry more about her than me. How's she doing?"

"Um, I don't..."

"Better hurry back. The girl's much less secure than she looks. Her roots and stem have merged, and you can't tell them apart. Plus, she's got very few leaves and just a hardened bud in place of a flower."

He'd lost me completely. All I could manage was a dumbfounded, "What?"

"It's not important. If she says horrible things to you, I wouldn't pay too much attention. That's the trick for getting along with her. Bye." Leaving this further cryptic comment behind him, the man in white turned and walked away.

"............"

I stood there stunned for a moment, but soon collected myself, and hurried back to the girl.

She was sitting in exactly the same position as I'd left her, with both hands on the front of the jacket, holding it closed.

"—Um, are you feeling better?" I asked rather stupidly, unable to think of anything else.

"............" She didn't answer.

I didn't know what to do, but now that I thought about it, she had effectively rescued me, so I said, "Uh, th-thanks. For, uh... for back there."

"Why?" she asked, looking up at me. She looked puzzled again.

Man, I couldn't get this conversation rolling at all.

"Well, you saved me, didn't you?" I said, smiling hopefully.

Her eyes widened, then for some reason she looked down, and mumbled, "...I thought you hated me."

"Hunh?" I gaped back at her. "Why? Why would I hate you?"

"I can't be hated by anyone. Not by any normal humans," she said, oddly intense. Her eyes were serious.

"...I don't hate you."

"But you glared at me..." she said, very sadly.

"I did? Oh...but that wasn't about you. I just was angry with myself, so...I... I mean..." I stumbled, trying to clear things up.

Still looking at the ground, she whispered, "I'm sorry."

"Why are you apologizing? It's all my fault! *I* was worried that you hated *me*!"

She looked up. "—Why?"

"I mean, that was pretty pathetic back there, right? That's why I was angry at myself. Nothing to do with you. I was so angry because I was sure you hated me." The more I babbled, the more pathetic I came across.

She quietly watched me flail about, but said nothing.

"And then because I couldn't make up my mind, you..." I trailed off, shoulders slumping. "But it's over now. I'll pay for your clothes. Um..."

I reached for my wallet, and remembered that the reason I'd been heading for the station in the first place was that I had no money and needed to swing by an ATM.

"Ugh, crap...the ATM's already closed...!"

"Don't worry about money. I have some," she answered as she stood up.

"But I can't just do nothing..."

"Really. If you could lend me this jacket...I'll give it back."

"Oh, no—take it! But that doesn't really pay you back at all... could you at least give me your address? Or phone number? I'll call you later and I'll pay you for the clothes then..."

"........." She stared at me levelly. I was taller than her, so she had to look up at me slightly. It could be taken as a glare.

"Ah, no, I don't mean it like that. Uh...if you'd prefer to call me...yeah, we should do it that way."

"Orihata."

"Mm?"

"My name. Orihata Aya. You are...?"

"Oh, uh, I'm Taniguchi Masaki."

"Masaki...that's a nice name," I said, and at last she smiled. A very small smile, the corners of her mouth turning up ever so slightly—but there was enough power in it to grab me by the heart.

Was this what they called love at first sight?

* * *

"I... I got tickets to a movie that's supposed to be really good. You... You wanna come?" I asked, finally working up the nerve to ask out Orihata. It was over the phone, but you have to go with what you have.

"Are you sure? With me?" The voice on the other end of the line said, faintly.

Hiding my tension, I replied cheerily, "I still haven't thanked you for last time. If you've got other plans, I… I understand, but…"

"…Thank you. Okay."

"You'll… You'll come?! Awesome!!!"

"But Masaki, I'm really…"

"Mm? What?"

"No…never mind." And she fell silent.

Further details were basically all decided by me, and she simply agreed to everything I suggested. I couldn't think of any clever way to say good-bye and ended the call by hanging up awkwardly.

I heard someone giggle behind me. At some point, my sister had come downstairs. My parents were still living abroad, so the two of us were alone in the house.

"And here I thought you were a playboy. Awfully stressed for a simple *date*, aren't we?"

"It's not nice to eavesdrop."

"I couldn't *not* hear you. Your voice was so loud, I heard it upstairs. I thought something had happened."

Considering that she spent basically all her time poking at computers in her room, she was awfully nosy at times like this.

"None of your business, Nagi! Leave me alone."

"Okay, okay. I'm not *that* bored," she said, playing dumb.

* * *

On the day of our date, we got to the movie theater and realized we had underestimated the situation a bit. There was a huge crowd with the line snaking all around the theater and back out onto the street.

"The end of the line starts here," shouted a theater employee at the end of the line. "Please be advised that there is a four-hour wait!"

"Oh, wow... What should we do?" I clutched my head. I'd blown our first date. "Should we try some other day?" I asked.

Orihata looked puzzled. "Why?" she asked.

"We'll have to wait a really long time. It'll blow our whole day."

"You don't want to wait?"

"Well...doesn't it make you tired?"

"Then I'll wait in line. You go play somewhere," she said calmly, and took her place at the end of the line.

I was a mess. "What?! I can't do that! I should be the one who waits!"

"I don't mind. I'm used to doing nothing."

"No, I mean... This is supposed to be me...thanking *you*." Even as I spoke, several people got in line behind her.

"Right!" I made up my mind. I turned and ran back towards the station.

The road was filled with people. I looked around me as I ran.

"Oh, Study Abroad. What are *you* doing here?" someone asked. I spun around. It was one of the guys from my class, Anou.

"Ah, um, you know."

"Yeah, I do. You're making some chick wait for you, huh?"

The boys in my school didn't like me in the first place, but this Anou guy was one of the most aggressive. Usually, I could handle him okay, but I had no time for it today.

"Sorry, in kind of a hurry," I said, brushing him off, and dove into a fast food joint. I bought an assortment of food and drinks, and hurried back.

"Excuse me! Excuse me! Coming through..." I wormed my way through the line, earning the hatred of every single person I passed, and finally caught up with Orihata. "Sorry to keep you waiting, heh heh..."

"I thought you weren't coming back."

"We need an endurance strategy for this. Thought we ought to at least have lunch." I showed her the bag.

"But you didn't like waiting."

"Not really. But if..." *But if I'm with you, I've got no time to be bored*, I started to say, but got embarrassed, and fell silent.

"What?" Orihata asked, head to one side.

"...So, uh, what'll you have?" I said. "I brought a bunch so you could choose...what do you like?"

"Anything."

"You like everything?"

"I have no right to dislike anything."

There she went again with the cryptic stuff. I couldn't get her to explain this. It was like her heart was locked down somewhere, and I couldn't get in.

So I grabbed a double cheeseburger at random and handed it to her and began scarfing down a hot dog myself.

She began nibbling at the burger, neither reluctantly nor happily. I felt like I was feeding a rabbit, which made me uncomfortable.

I finished my hot dog in three bites, and had nothing left to do. My eyes wandered upwards towards the sky.

Suddenly, Orihata looked at my face, and exclaimed, "Ah!" Before I even had time to wonder why, she reached up, her face came close to mine, and she licked the ketchup off the side of my mouth...with her tongue!

I was stunned. She looked like nothing at all had happened.

"Now you're clean," she said. She wasn't at all embarrassed, and she wasn't joking around, either. It was as if she had decided her tongue would be the most effective tool, since her hands were busy holding the burger. Her job complete, she turned her attention back to eating again.

Meanwhile, I had turned bright, bright red.

I'm not sure how many hours we waited, but at some point we finally managed to make it into the theater. Before I knew it, the movie was over. I couldn't tell you a single thing that happened—I spent the entire time in a complete daze.

When I snapped out of it, we were outside, and it was already night.

All it took was Orihata telling me, "Bye," outside the theater to bring my attention crashing back to reality.

"Eh? Going home already?" I'm sure I sounded a little whiney.

Orihata looked a little surprised. "But...we already saw the movie."

"Yeah, but...we could go to a cafe or something," I said, wistfully.

"Really?"

"Of course! It'll be on me!"

"Not the money... You don't think I'm boring?"

"No, not at all!" I said, flustered. I thought she must be angry with me, since I'd been so out of it.

But Orihata looked relieved, and said, "Good. I was worried. I thought you hated me."

I never in a million years thought she would say that, so I panicked a little. We somehow made it into a nearby cafe, *Tristan*, ordered some coffee, and at last, I settled down. This was the chance I needed to sort everything out, so I tried talking with her.

"Orihata, you don't think...*I'm* boring?" Oh god, that was terrible. Still, I couldn't not ask that.

But Orihata didn't answer. Instead, she suddenly took my hand. Her gentle touch wrapped around my wrist.

I was taken aback, but I couldn't snatch my hand away, so I just sort of jumped in my seat dramatically.

"Masaki...your skin is warm," she said with a peaceful expression on her face, like an old lady who had just sipped some really good tea.

She was a mystery. I understood nothing about her.

* * *

And that's basically how Orihata and I started going out,

although it was a strange sort of relationship, and I'm not really sure you could call it dating.

First of all, her house...

No matter when I called, she always answered instantly—right in the middle of the first ring. I had barely finished dialing, and the call was connected, and BAM! There she was, saying, "Orihata," with absolutely no emotion at all.

"Um, it's Taniguchi..." No matter how many times I called, I always started out tongue-tied.

"What?" she always said, curtly.

"Um, well, I thought this Saturday..."

Our relationship was awfully like this phone call. I got all excited and chased after her, but she was completely neutral.

But even though the high school entrance exams were right in front of me, I spent all of my free time with her. In my case, I had already been successfully admitted to a private high school a year before—but on the condition that I graduate from a Japanese junior high, which was why I'd moved back here—so I had nothing to worry about. Still, I was a little worried about her. I asked once, but she just shrugged.

"You haven't decided?" It was already mid-January.

"I'll be taking a test, but I don't know which school yet," she said, as if she was talking about someone else.

"Are your parents strict?"

"I don't have any."

"Hunh? What?"

"Parents."

"But that..." Apparently she had no parents, and lived alone. In high school, sure, I could see that—but in junior high? "No relatives at all?"

"............" No answer.

"Sorry, I... I shouldn't have asked," I said apologetically.

She turned towards me suddenly. "Sorry, Masaki," she said, rather urgently.

"About what?" I asked, surprised.

She looked at the ground. "I'm sorry. I can't tell you," she murmured.

I couldn't ask further. It hurt me to see her sad. Whenever she did, I would get really cheery and try to slide past it. "Gosh, the sky is really beautiful today, huh?!" I might say, in a stupidly loud voice.

She almost never smiled, but when we separated, she always asked if we could meet again, so I guess she didn't hate me. At least, that's what I kept telling myself.

Eventually, I don't know how, she decided to go to high school at Shinyo Academy.

"Oh! Congratulations!" I said happily, when she told me on the phone that she had passed the test.

"I'm glad you're happy, Masaki," she replied. She almost never sounded like she was having fun, but that day...she did.

"We should do something to celebrate. What do you think? Meet in a few at the usual place?"

"Yes, okay."

Happily, I rushed out to the park where we always met. I had no idea what was waiting for me.

* * *

"Yes, okay. Mmhmm...mmhmm...bye."

Orihata Aya hung up her cell phone after her conversation with Taniguchi Masaki.

It had been the first time she had ever called him. Until now, she had always waited for him to call, but Masaki had been worried about what high school she was going to, so she thought she should let him know.

He had been happy. That made Aya happy. He was unaware that "higher education" was merely a camouflage for her "mission." She was not happy about it. She did not feel anything about it. But if something she did made Masaki happy, then Aya was happy too.

She moved quickly towards her closet.

Since she met Masaki, her wardrobe had increased dramatically. If she wore something nice, Masaki would tell her it was cute, so Aya began paying attention to her clothes.

There was nothing else in her room. With the exception of the furniture provided by the building's landlord, there were no other furnishings. No TV, no table, not even a bed. There was but a single sleeping bag lying on the floor.

She changed, and went out, allowing the muscles in her cheeks to relax slightly.

People hardly ever came to the park where they always met. It was a large green belt surrounded by three highways, which made it a little scary for parents to take their children out to play. Unfortunately, it was also a tad too out in the open for young people, so it was like an empty air pocket smack dab in the center of the city.

Aya sat down on a bench.

Waiting for Masaki as the rays of the afternoon sun came through the trees above her, Aya entertained the brief fantasy that she was a normal, happy girl.

She didn't know exactly what Masaki thought of her. But when she thought of the secrets she was keeping from him...she knew that, no matter what he wanted from her, he would still be important to her.

If he knew the truth, would he still be her friend? This was her greatest fear.

With her head down, Aya waited for Masaki, not moving.

She was always worried that he wouldn't come. But she couldn't possibly arrive after him. It would be awful if he hated her because of that. So she always came an hour before they were supposed to meet. But today's meeting had come up quite sudden, so she only had to wait another ten minutes or so.

As Aya glanced at her watch, a shadow stood before her.

She thought it was Masaki, and looked up, blushing slightly.

Her expression froze.

"———!"

It wasn't him. It was a very fat man, with graying hair and a broad grin. Big, round, glittering eyes.

"What are you doing, 'Camille'?" the man said to Aya, in a high, reedy voice. The black leather jacket he wore was open at the front, but looked ready to burst apart at the seams at any moment.

It shone with a tasteless gleam. There was a belt round his waist with a number of pockets hanging from it, each of which had a cell phone in it.

"Nothing of any purpose," Aya replied, dutifully answering to the name 'Camille,' eyes down towards the ground.

"Meeting a boy?" The fat man sneered. "Remember who you are." His eyes didn't budge as he laughed, but stayed perfectly round.

His fat lay entirely on his head and belly, which were perfectly round, but his arms and legs were thin and long like poles. He looked very unhealthy. He had almost no neck and strongly defined features and swollen cheeks, like he'd placed pads on the sides of his face.

At that moment, a gust of wind swept by, lifting his long, greying hair. His right ear was missing. There was only a jagged wound, like it had been torn off.

The man straightened his hair, hiding the injury.

"........." Aya's head was still down.

"Look up," the man said, and she obeyed, moving jerkily.

He glared down at her frostily. "Have you done him?"

"...No, not yet."

"What are you waiting for? Let him have you. You're in no position to make a big deal out of something like that."

"Yes..."

"Well, not like *that mission* has to be in any hurry...but the other one does. Have you found any clues?"

"No, I—" Aya started to say, but was abruptly cut off as the man punched her in the face.

Aya fell off the bench, and sprawled on the pavement. Her lip was split and bleeding.

"…………"

But her expression registered neither pain nor anger.

"You just don't get it, Camille, *do* you? What are you? *Mm?* You don't perform your duty. You're nothing but a defective product."

He waddled over to her slowly and kicked her in the side. He kicked her again and again, and each time her body shook.

"…………"

Even so, her expression never changed.

"You see? I'm not letting you stay alive out of pity. If you aren't useful to the Towa Organization…if you aren't useful to me…I'll dispose of you whenever I wish. We've got a lot more where you came from!"

He grabbed Aya's collar, and yanked her upwards, putting his face right in hers.

"Now you listen to me. He's in this area." His voice went low and quiet, like a knife twisting in her gut. "I don't know why, but all the young girls in this area know about him. It's idle gossip, but they know of him. There must be something. Finding out what that is…is your job. Not walking around and just wasting time with a guy you're not even having sex with. Got me?"

"I understand, Spooky E." Aya answered quietly, emotionless.

And then, someone called out, "Hey! What are you doing?!"

Spooky E twisted his head towards the voice. It was Taniguchi Masaki.

"Let go of her!" he screamed, running towards them.

"......! N-no!" Aya cried, terrified.

"Mm?" Spooky E frowned at her emotion, but quickly grinned, and dropped her. "You must be lover boy."

He turned towards Masaki, on his guard.

"What did you do to her?!" Masaki yelled, furious, and uncharacteristically came right at Spooky E, swinging his fist.

"No, Masaki! Run away!" Aya screamed, desperate.

"Hunh..." Spooky E made a light step sideways, dodging the blow.

Spooky E tried to punch Masaki in the back, but Masaki had read the movement and was able to twist his body enough to dodge the blow and recover his distance.

"......!" Spooky E looked alarmed.

Masaki got his balance back, and hit a stance.

But he was far more tense than the fat man.

(...this guy's pulling back...but I still barely dodged him.)

He should never have been able to move like that at his weight. However...

Masaki's instincts told him to ignore common sense. This was clearly no ordinary opponent.

"...Mmph..." Cold sweat ran down his brow.

Spooky E spoke to the fallen Aya. "Is this guy some sort of stupid martial artist? Or is he an MPLS? Is he an enemy of the Towa Organization?!"

"——!" Aya's face turned white. "Nothing like that! Masaki's a normal human!" she almost shrieked, like Masaki's life depended on her answer.

"Ah, so he's just some average Joe that thought he'd learn a little kung fu."

"......?" Masaki glanced at Aya. These two *knew* each other?

Aya avoided his eyes.

Spooky E took advantage of this drop in his guard and lunged at him.

Too fast for the eye to follow, he closed the gap between them.

"Wah!" Instincts screamed danger as Masaki made no attempt to guard. He simply fled the attack.

He rolled on the ground.

But this took him farther away from Aya.

"———! Oh no!" He wasn't thinking clearly.

He tried to get near her quickly, but Spooky E was right there in his way.

"You can't leave her and run away alone, eh? What a hero."

"............"

"If you were an MPLS, I might have to be careful...but an ordinary human? Let me show you why they call me...Spooky Electric." He opened his fists.

On his palms, his blood vessels stood out unnaturally. Blue and red lines ran all across them.

Masaki thought he could hear a crackle coming from them...

"O-Orihata! Run!" he yelled, sensing danger.

But Aya just slumped, making no attempt to stand.

"Shit...!" Masaki rushed forward, desperately.

Grinning, Spooky E waited for him.

Inside, Masaki thought, *To hell with it*, and, grinding his teeth, he aimed a kick right at Spooky E's unguarded crotch.

His karate master had told him, *If you really need to, don't hesitate.*

Masaki's toes struck directly at every man's weakest point.

But...the sensation his foot met with was all wrong.

"—Hunh?!" He looked up at his enemy's face.

The grin was still there, the same as ever.

"Too *baaaad*," Spooky E said, and with a quick little jitterbug of a step, he put his palms on Masaki's head, one on each side.

Everything went black before Masaki's eyes, and he passed out.

* * *

My head throbbed.

I could hear voices, but they seemed so far away...

"Please, let him be. We haven't yet. There's still a chance..."

"He got to you pretty good, huh? But if that boy knew what you've been up to, he won't think the same..."

"I know...but please...spare him."

"Huh? You aren't even human. What are you thinking?"

"Please..."

"Okay, then. I'll let him live...on that one condition."

"Thank you."

"But don't forget, Camille. Your primary mission is to find *him*. Find that——"

That was all I heard. After that, I knew nothing more.

* * *

And when I woke up, it felt very warm all around me.

"Uh......?" I opened my eyes, stretching. Orihata's face was right above me.

"You woke up," she said, gently.

Surprised, I sat up, looking around. We were in the park where I had apparently fallen asleep on a bench.

On her lap no less.

"Wh-what? Why am I sleeping here?"

I shook my head, but the last thing I could remember was getting a phone call from Orihata and suggesting we celebrate her getting accepted into high school. I couldn't remember what I'd done after that. I couldn't even remember arriving at the park.

"I think you got sunstroke. When I got here, you were already asleep," Orihata said calmly.

"Really? I was sleeping?"

"It surprised me. I thought you were dead..."

"Wow... I'm s-sorry. But sunstroke?" It was sunny enough, but it was barely spring. Much too early to get sunstroke, right?

"Sorry, this is all my fault..." she said.

"N-no it isn't! I'm the one who passed out!" I said hurriedly. It seemed like I was always showing her these awkward undignified moments. "S-so we were going to celebrate, right? Is there anything you'd like me to do? Go ahead, ask me anything," I said, cheerfully, grinning, trying desperately to cover.

She looked suddenly very sad.

She stood up from the bench, turning her back on me.

There was a long silence.

"............"

Her figure seemed to absorb the rays of the setting sun, like she was melting into the backlight.

She looked very fragile, almost like a ghost.

After a minute of silence, I gingerly asked, "Wh-what's wrong?"

"Masaki...you're really strong, aren't you?" she whispered, not turning around.

"Um?"

"When we first met...if I hadn't saved you, you'd have been able to get out of that on your own, right?"

Suddenly, I found myself in a very awkward position. "Uh, w-well, that's not..."

"Masaki, can I ask you a favor?" Her voice came over her shoulders.

"Yes. Anything!"

"Masaki, you're friends with the girls in this area, right?"

"Uh, yeah...I-I guess."

"I wonder if you've heard anything from them...rumors of a mysterious shinigami."

"Rumors?"

"Nobody knows where he appears, but all the girls know his name." She turned around. The backlight hid her face, and I couldn't make out her expression. "They all know about Boogiepop."

Boogiepop returns

VS Imaginator Part 1

III

Do not doubt your work.
No matter how pointless or unrewarding it may appear to be, anything is better than knowing for certain that is actually is.

—Kirima Seiichi (*VS Imaginator*)

"UM, SO IF X is an imaginary number, then the range of y is...a complete mystery. Suemaaaa! Help meeee...!"

One day late in March, my friend Miyashita Touka and I were hunched over our study guides in a quiet corner of the freshly emptied cram school. There was nobody else around.

This year's students had mostly taken their tests and stopped coming, and next year's crowd wouldn't start attending seriously until next week. It was like a little breathing room between tests.

"We've only been studying twenty minutes. It's too soon to give up."

"Yeah...but I have. My head's already spinning from all those numbers. If I see another equation, I'm gonna hurl!"

"Not like you're a drunk or anything..." I giggled. Touka was at best artless and at worst...a little on the rude side—but still, I thought she was refreshing. At least she always admitted when she didn't understand something.

"Come on, help me here, Kazuko-chaaaan! How does this thing work?" With a labored expression, she glared fiercely at the study guide, poking at it with the tip of her pencil.

This year, we would finally be seniors. While we'd effectively been so since January, once April came around, we would officially make the switch from being laid-back high school students to stressed-out exam students.

I met Touka back during the winter course at this cram school, and that was where I learned that we went to the same high school. Previous to that point, we had somehow managed to completely avoid running into each other—and even now, we pretty much only saw each other at cram school.

Still, we hit it off really well. I'm a little warped because of some stuff in my past, but she came over to me despite all that.

"Well, this one..." I leaned over and started explaining the problem to her.

"Uh huh. Uh huh." Touka sat up, and leaned her entire upper body onto the table. From the side, we must've looked like we were about to arm wrestle. The very thought amused me.

"Got that?"

"Umm... Well...kind of."

"Then explain it back to me."

"Eh heh. That... That might be pushing things," Touka replied, looking extremely embarrassed.

"Tut tut. You've got to understand this properly," I said.

Touka giggled. "I'm sorry. It's like I'm turning you into my own private tutor. And you're not even getting paid. Still, if I didn't make smart friends, I'd be totally screwed..."

"You aren't gonna sweet talk your way out of this."

"Ah, you noticed."

"Yep. So, how do we use that equation to solve this problem?"

"Um... Pass!"

"You can't do that! We're not playing shogi here..."

Studying for exams was never easy, but at moments like this, it could be a lot of fun.

While Touka was grappling with the problem, I glanced away, turning my gaze to a painting that was hung on the wall.

It was a strange picture of a large number of people holding hands, sprawled on the ground of a wasteland. The style was pretty rough, with a lot of pencil traces left in it. To me, it felt awfully dated for such a hip cram school.

It was an abstract oil painting. The title was "Snow Falling in April." The painter was Asukai Jin, who was one of the teachers that worked here. This painting had won some kind of an award and was probably just hanging on the wall to make the school look more important than it was.

Because of certain events in my past, I got pretty interested in criminal psychology and the unconscious psyche. This fascination has led me to read all I could find on those subjects, so it was out of habit that I started analyzing the painting in-depth.

(Hmm... The sky is cloudy...it lacks width. Must be a very closed off painting. But there's something cheerful about it. Or maybe just shallow. The wasteland clearly represents a feeling of emptiness, so why is it I get a hint of deep conviction behind it?)

And with all those people, why weren't any of them looking at each other?

"It's a weird painting," Touka said, following my gaze.

"Yeah…something about it I just don't *like*," I said in a snobbish *Oh, I hate this painting* sort of way. It might be a good painting, but I just couldn't bring myself to like it.

"Not your type, Suema?"

"No, I think…the guy that painted this hates people like me."

Or maybe…yeah, he was the same as me. It was a natural aversion.

"That's beyond me," Touka laughed.

"Too strange?"

"Nah, it's cool. Go with your gut."

In the past, more than a few people have told me that I was strange. But Touka always accepted what I said without question. You wouldn't believe how happy that always made me feel.

"I bet he likes you, though," I said.

"Is that a confession?" she joked, and we cackled.

A voice came from behind us, "Um, are you Suema Kazuko-san? From Shinyo Academy…?"

We turned, and there was a girl who looked about our age.

"Yes, and…you are?"

"I'm Kinukawa Kotoe. I… I go to Shinyo Academy, as well. I wanted to talk to you about something, Suema-san…" She opened and closed her hands. Clearly this was really important to her.

"What about?"

"Well…you know a lot, don't you? About, you know… And Kinoshita-san said you…"

"Kinoshita? You mean Kyoko?"

Kinoshita Kyoko was a former classmate of mine.

"Yes! She said Suema could keep a secret, and was very nice, and was very smart... So she said you could help me out!" Kotoe said earnestly, waving her hands around like she was worried this wasn't enough.

"Um, well..." I hadn't done that much for Kyoko, really. Just listened to her problems and told her what I thought. The person who had helped her out when she was really in trouble was another girl.

"Please, Suema-san. Help Jin-niisan!"

"H-help who? Touka, do you have... Touka?" I turned around to find Touka completely gone.

Somehow, she'd gotten up without my ever noticing, and was standing right next to this Kotoe girl.

"Sit down, Kinukawa-san," she said, and handed her a cup of coffee from the vending machine.

When the heck had she bought that?

"Th-thanks..." Kotoe bobbed her head, and took a sip of coffee from the paper cup.

"Feel better now?" Touka asked, sounding oddly masculine.

"Y-yes, thanks." Kotoe bobbed her head again.

"You need her help?" She pointed at me with her chin.

"Y-yes. And I am sorry, but, um..."

"I understand. I'm in the way. I'll leave you two alone."

"W-wait! Touka...!"

"Kinukawa-san needs your help. You should at least listen to her." She sounded like she was on stage. Touka gave me a strange, asymmetrical expression, somewhere between innocent and mocking. I got the strangest feeling that I wasn't looking at Touka—heck, that who I was looking at wasn't even a girl. It was very unsettling. "Adios," she said, and was gone.

"............"

I stared after her like I'd seen a fox.

Kotoe pressed forward, "So..."

"Mm? Oh, right... Okay. If you're friends with Kyoko, then, sure, I'll hear you out," I sighed.

* * *

"—Asukai Jin?" I said, eyes wide. This was the first name out of Kotoe's mouth. "The painting guy?"

"Yeah. He teaches here. You know him?"

"Just the name. They say he's a pretty good counselor."

I'd heard the rumors. You went to him for guidance counseling, he'd give you very specific advice. Neither Touka nor I had ever met with the guy. A fine arts course teacher didn't really have much contact with those of us in the national science course.

"I've...heard that too. I don't really know much."

"And you are his...niece? Or cousin?" I wasn't sure which. The gist of her introduction had escaped me.

"Our parents didn't really...get along. So Jin-niisan and I haven't been friendly for all that long, but...the first time we ever really spoke to each other was at his father's funeral. But I knew pretty much instantly that he was this really amazing guy."

"Huh..." Her story just wasn't coming together. I had to try to make sense of it somehow. "So, why does he need help?"

"Suema-san, you know a lot, right? If somebody...changes... then, I dunno...it's, like, you know, that sort of thing."

"That sort of thing?" I asked, perplexed. I found myself looking at the painting again.

There were a number of goats among the crowd. They were munching on the rose bushes that grew out of the wasteland. Black goats.

From what I know, roses are sturdy enough, and they could pretty much bloom anywhere—though, the quality of the flowers would probably suffer. So, seeing thorny rose bushes wasn't all that surprising. But the black goats...those were usually an allegory for the devil.

They were eating the roses—flowers, leaves, thorns and all.

The picture itself didn't give off all that unpleasant of a feeling... it was pastoral and peaceful. But something about it bugged me...

"Has he suddenly become stand-offish?" I asked.

"Not that...it's like he doesn't worry anymore."

"He used to?"

"Yeah, all the time," she said forcefully. "Maybe I shouldn't be telling you this but...his father, which was like his only family... He died in kind of a strange way..."

"How?"

"Well..."

"If you don't want to talk about it, that's fine. Lately, I've been trying to avoid those kinds of stories, anyway," I said, honestly.

Kotoe looked relieved. "I knew I could count on you. You seem so with it."

"Never mind that. Why do you think he's stopped worrying?" I never did like getting compliments. Especially about this type of subject. It felt like those times when somebody would tell you how cute you used to be when you were a child. It's irritating because these people are all so lost in the past.

"Mm..." Kotoe told me that Asukai Jin had been staying out all night recently. It seemed like she was monitoring his behavior pretty closely.

"And when he does come home in the morning, he just claims to have spent the night at a friend's house?" I said. "No other details at all? I mean, uh, couldn't that just be what young guys do?"

"It doesn't seem like he's got a girlfriend! When he comes home, there's always...stains on his clothes. Dark red stains. They might be..."

I gulped a little at this one. "You mean, blood?"

"But he's never injured! And his clothes never look torn, so..."

"He goes out every night and comes back covered in other people's blood? That sounds like, I dunno... Like a vampire or something." I shivered.

"But if I talk to the police, Jin-niisan might get arrested, and my father's always looking for an excuse to just kick him out. Please, Suema-san, I... I don't know what to do anymore!" Kotoe buried her face in her hands.

This was starting to sound a little dangerous.

I got this feeling sometimes—like a pounding in my chest,

like an itch racing all over my body—and I had to remind myself, *Come on, Kazuko! You're an exam student! You don't have time to go poking your head where it doesn't belong!*

But...one time, I'd almost been killed by something I'd never seen, and I didn't find out about it until it was all over. And because of that experience, I have this weird compulsion of mine.

A compulsion to face off against darkness.

Before I could stop myself, I said, "Um, Kinukawa-san, why don't you just leave everything up to me, okay?"

* * *

And so I found myself alone just outside the cram school's guidance counseling office, which was essentially Asukai Jin's personal domain. I'd sent Kotoe home minutes before. I knew that if she'd tagged along, she'd just have gotten in the way.

There was not a soul left in the building at this time of day.

I tried the door and it opened. It wasn't locked or anything.

(Pretty careless...or is there simply nothing in here worth stealing?)

I went in. I'd been a student here for three months, but this was my first time ever setting foot inside this office. It was tiny and dark.

It's like one of those police interrogation rooms from TV, I thought.

There was a desk next to the teacher's chair, and a computer on top of that. I almost turned it on, but thought better of it. It was probably password protected, anyway.

(There must be something...a clue as to why he's changed...)

I poked around his desk. But there was nothing there but cram school pamphlets and various papers with notes scrawled on them about students' scores for different schools—nothing to do with Asukai Jin himself.

"Hmm..."

Had I underestimated the situation? Was this too simple a way of gathering information?

"Agh...!" I said, flopping down in his chair. I slouched down a bit, but my skirt started rising up, forcing me to twist my body a bit...

And then I saw it.

There was something white under the desk, crammed all the way towards the back. Like a scrap of paper crumpled into a ball.

"Mm?"

It caught my interest, so I dove down to fish it out.

I flattened it out. It was a page of sketchbook paper with a drawing of a girl penciled on it. The artist's initial guidelines could still be seen below the face. Clearly a failed sketch.

"............?"

There was something creepy about it.

I felt like I'd seen it before.

Like I *knew* this girl.

(Who is she?)

As I sat there thinking, I heard footsteps from the hall.

(Uh-oh...!)

I panicked. There were no other rooms in this hallway, and

the only reason anyone would come down here was to come directly to this very counseling office.

(What should I do? Um...um...)

In hindsight, I should have just left the room casually. After all, the door wasn't locked, and I was a student here, so it wouldn't have been at all strange if I had just simply come by for some counseling. I could always say I'd come in for a session, but nobody was there.

But since I was feeling a little guilty, I just stayed and hid under the desk. It was a fairly large desk—it filled about a sixth of the room—with enough room for a large computer and plenty of desk space left for paperwork.

I hunched down in the shadow of the drawer, and breathed as quietly as I could. I was completely hidden.

The footsteps stopped in front of the door, and several people came in.

"—But Asukai-sensei, we really are friends. We don't hate each other at all, right, Yuriko?"

"Y-yeah..."

Sounded like two girls and a man. The man must be Asukai Jin.

"Mm, maybe a bad choice of words. See, almost all humans hate each other. I just meant that you were no exception. I'm not making it out like you two are a special case or anything."

Asukai Jin's voice was very calm, a clear, beautiful tenor.

"But, that's so..."

"........."

One of the girls was pretty outgoing, while the other one mostly did whatever she was told, it seemed.

"Shall we get started…? What is it?"

"Um…er, are we really going to…?" The stronger girl asked, sounding a little nervous.

"Everyone else is. I'm not forcing anybody, if you don't want to join them."

"No, we'll do it!" The follower said.

"Yu-Yuriko?"

"Let's do it, Misaki. I don't want to be just an exam student anymore…!"

"Yuriko…"

"What do you think?" Asukai asked. "This is your choice to make. I can't make it for you."

"Tell me exactly what to do. That way I can…"

(What the hell are they talking about?)

Completely forgetting that I was supposed to be hiding, I started to get annoyed by the incomprehensible conversation.

Asukai continued, detached. "I can't. The Imaginator doesn't force anyone. It's a simple choice. You can influence events, or you can be swept along by them."

Imaginator?

A word I knew suddenly popped out, surprising me. That name was from the work of a writer I had been a big fan of. I wasn't sure if it had the same meaning here or not, though.

Forgetting the danger, I poked my face out a little, peering up into the room through the gap between the chair and the drawer.

The girl called Misaki was biting her fingernails.

"Asukai-sensei, can you do me alone?" Yuriko asked. The two girls had similar hair styles and faces.

"Hmm?" Asukai Jin's face was hidden from my vantage point. All I could make out were his white clothes.

He was moving slowly towards me. I stiffened, but he didn't pull the chair out. Instead, he sat down on top of the desk.

Inches from my face, he started swinging his long, slim legs. I'd never seen a man's legs this close up before. I could feel my cheeks burning, for no reason.

"Then you'd need a different partner, someone other than Kitahara-kun."

"I'll find one!"

"Wait, Yuriko!" Misaki yelped. I couldn't figure out why she was so upset.

What were they up to? What were they talking about doing?

"Like I have a choice! You don't want to?!"

"But I..."

"Get out!"

"Eh?"

"You have no right to be in the same room as Asukai-sensei!" Yuriko yelled harshly. It was no surprise he had said that they hated each other.

"N-no! That's just...okay, I'll do it! Please Sensei, I'll do it!" she said, turning her gaze above me, presumably looking Asukai Jin in the eye.

"All right. I respect your decision." Asukai Jin stood up.

Suddenly, he reached out his hands to the girl's chests, and started undoing the buttons, stripping their shirts right off.

(What?! Whaaaat?!!)

I panicked. I'd been worried it was something like this, but for it to be this sexual...

But the bare-chested girls turned not towards Asukai Jin, but towards each other.

They closed the gap between them, and placed their hands on each other's shoulders.

"Stop there...now, don't move," Asukai directed, just as their breasts were about to touch.

He turned his back towards me, and reached out towards their breasts.

Their transformation was dramatic.

Simultaneously, the girls flung their heads back, mouths gaping wide like some sort of animal, the air quivering at their soundless howls. The hands resting on each other's shoulders clenched up tightly, nails digging into the skin, drawing blood.

I swear this was not the kind of transformation that pain or pleasure can cause. It was like they had temporarily ceased to be human, like—like something was being torn away from them.

Asukai Jin quietly stood before them, calmly doing something I couldn't see.

Every time his shoulders shifted, the girls shook, bodies convulsing.

Like he was tinkering with them. But near as I could tell, he never touched their bodies directly. What on Earth was he *doing*?

"————!!!"

The girls gave one last great spasm, and Asukai Jin moved away.

Worn out, the girls leaned against each other. They were covered in sweat.

They were panting...but their faces looked human again, reason restored.

The girls looked at each other...and giggled.

Their expressions were so terrifying that I felt like something had its hand around my heart.

They looked *exactly* the same.

The features of their faces had not changed. In fact, their expressions were so identical that the resemblance between them that I had noticed before had grown far *less* pronounced.

But that expression—the emotion the muscles in their faces were shifting in reaction to—I couldn't help but feel like it was identical.

"How does it feel to be true friends?" Asukai Jin asked.

"Nice..."

"Completely wonderful."

Smiling, the girls stood up, and began dressing each other.

"That's good," Asukai Jin replied, and I swear I heard a flicker of a smile in his voice.

"Asukai-sensei, we're no longer afraid of anything."

"We feel like we could change the world for you right now."

They came over to him.

They took his hands, and kissed the back of Asukai Jin's hands like a pair of princesses swearing their allegiance to some heroic knight of legend.

I was shivering violently. It took all my self-restraint just to keep my teeth from chattering. I couldn't move for a full three minutes after they left the room.

(Wh-what was that? What just happened here...?)

Stiffly, I crawled out from under the desk and spread out the drawing once again as my hands trembled.

I remembered her now. The girl in the sketch had gone to my high school.

Her name was Minahoshi Suiko.

But she had killed herself. She was long gone.

The sketch was clearly Asukai Jin's, though... So how in the world was he connected to her suicide?

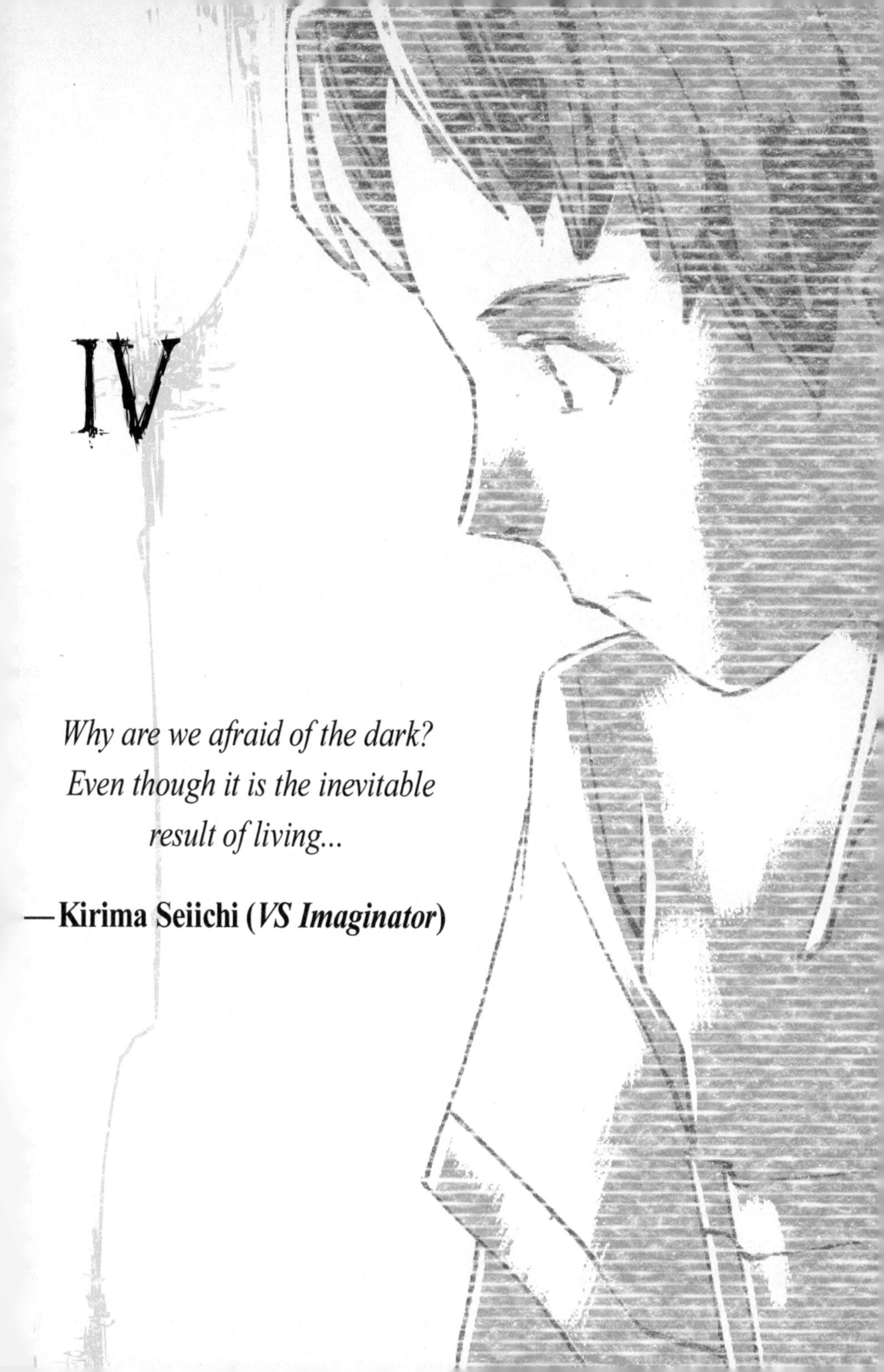

IV

Why are we afraid of the dark?
Even though it is the inevitable
result of living...

—Kirima Seiichi (*VS Imaginator*)

IV.

It's often said that every town has two faces, one for day and one for night. That's true enough, I suppose, but realistically, the difference is not so distinct, not so clear. Sadly, there is really no easily understood line drawn between the territory of safe, happy daylight and the sinister domain of the night.

For example, right now there's a girl sitting on a bench in front of a train station, sunlight gleaming brightly all around her. She's wearing traditional casual fashion, and anyone who looked at her would think she was a very ordinary, middle class girl.

She appears to be waiting for somebody. She's got a town events guide rolled up in her hand, and she keeps tapping the ground with the toe of her shoe.

But if you watch the girl long enough, you'll begin to see a pattern hidden in the tapping. There's a rhythm to it, the same spacing between the taps, repeating.

Wait a little longer, and at last a boy comes over to her. He looks ordinary as well, clothes and hairstyle pretty bourgeois, like he gets a decent allowance.

"Yo! Waiting for someone?"

Not the most natural pick up line ever, but not likely to attract much attention if overheard.

"Yeah, at one o'clock," the girl nods. Mind you, the time is well past three.

"Okay, this way," the boy says, jerking his chin for her to follow.

This particular location has a police box in it, and there's never been a fight here. It's just that kind of place.

Whether she'd been waiting for him, or waiting for someone else, they leave the square together and head into town.

They look like any other young couple. They don't stand out at all. Why, they are the most ordinary pairing in the world.

They wander towards a deserted area of town, a zone slated for redevelopment.

The old buildings haven't been knocked down yet, and they're surrounded by dingy office spaces and crumbling stores that have long since shed any sign of what they used to sell.

The whole lot is surrounded by ropes with "no trespassing" signs hung on them. Yet the young couple pays them no attention and ducks right under.

They turn down a narrow space between two buildings, where several men are waiting for them.

"There you are."

"Only one today?"

These "men" all appeared to be less than twenty years old.

The boy quickly goes over to them, and they all look the girl over for a moment.

She stands and takes it. "........."

"So, how much do you want, girl?" the oldest looking of the men asks. He wears a leather jacket and flashes her a sleazy grin.

"Everything," the girl answers back, emotionless.

"Huh?"

"*I'd like you to give me everything you have*," the girl says without a trace of hesitation.

The men look a little put out. "Girl, do you even know what you're doing? You know who we are?" the guy in the leather jacket says fiercely.

"I do. You're flunkies for a drug dealer. You sell drugs to whoever gives the signal." Her face is completely calm, no eagerness, nothing unnatural.

"Flunkies?! What we got here's gonna go for a few million. You got that kinda cash?"

"No," the girl says flatly.

This outlandish declaration leaves the men gaping. "What?! What'd she say?!"

"I have no money. But like I said, I'll be taking all your drugs now." You could even call her voice chilly.

The flabbergasted men's shoulders gradually start to shake. Obviously, from anger.

"You asked for it!"

"Little bitch!"

The men launch themselves at her.

She turns and runs.

"Wait right there!"

"Don't even think about getting away!"

"I don't need to," the girl says, and turns the corner.

The first man after her rounds the corner, and the moment he does, he goes flying over backwards.

"———!"

The men's eyes bug out of their heads.

A figure stands before them in a very strange outfit.

He's dressed in a long, black cape and wears a black hat shaped like a pipe atop his head. His face is covered in make up, white face contrasting with black lipstick. It's a hideously embarrassing outfit, completely stupid.

"Um, don't do anything idiot. You cannot defeat me," the cloaked figure stammers. It's clear why the first man went flying—this cloaked figure packs one hell of a punch.

"What the hell are you?!" The men gape. Understandably.

"I'm calling myself Boogiepop...apparently," the weirdo says, with a strange lack of confidence.

"Huh?"

"You some kinda cosplayer or somethin'?"

"Of course you've never heard of me," the weirdo mutters to himself. "Only the girls know."

"What?"

"Oh, never mind."

The girl comes up behind the weirdo. And like she's reading a script, she exclaims, "Boogiepop! These people are bad! Get them!!"

"Right, I've had just about enough of..." The men move to attack. Several of them are clearly experienced fighters. They know what they're doing.

...So I couldn't hold back.

* * *

As soon as all the men had been thoroughly beaten, the cloaked figure went through their pockets, and removed a large number of little plastic bags filled with drugs.

Stuffing these into the pack on his side, the weirdo darted away.

His breathing was ragged, less from exhaustion than panic and at last, he took shelter under a rarely used pedestrian overpass.

The girl was waiting for him there—Orihata Aya.

"Thank you, Masaki," Orihata said, smiling.

The cloaked weirdo took off his black hat.

That weirdo was me—Taniguchi Masaki.

"Ugh! This outfit is freakin' hot!" I griped. "You have no idea how hard it is to fight dressed in this thing!"

"But according to the rumors, this is the outfit he wears," Orihata said, moving around behind me and untying the cloak.

"Girls' rumors! I bet they never put any thought behind them at all. *Grr.*"

"Towel," she said, handing it over. I scrubbed my face with it, and the make up came off soon enough. I felt much better already.

Obviously, I had been following them since Orihata left the station.

As soon as she entered the redevelopment zone, I quickly hid in the shadows and changed...even went to the trouble of putting black lipstick on to seal the effect.

What was I doing, you say?

Well...I was playing super-hero.

I was punishing all the evildoers in town. But please, don't ask me why. It was all Orihata's idea.

She took the pouch off my hip, scooped the drugs out of it, tore open each of the bags, and poured the contents out in the nearest ditch. The brown water dissolved the white powder relatively quickly, and there was no sign of it a minute later.

Millions of yen, they said, I thought, absently. Not that I thought it was a waste, or that I wanted that money. It was just that for most people, I could see how that amount of cash could easily become a motive for doing something illegal.

"You're a hero, Masaki," Orihata announced.

"I... I guess."

"Thanks to you, about a hundred people have been saved from drug addiction. That's a *good* thing." She sounded like she was still reading off some invisible cue cards plastered nearby. And the tone of her voice made it hard to tell if she was being serious or still playing along.

I just didn't get it. She had known all the signs and code words for that transaction earlier—but how the heck would a girl like her know that kind of crap? I asked, of course, but all she said was, "Almost everyone knows."

"Oh? Your hand..." Orihata's gaze stopped on my left hand. I had grazed it, and there was a little fresh blood on the surface.

"Just a scratch."

"I'm sorry. It's all my fault," she said, taking my hand gently, and tending to the wound with a first aid kit she'd brought with her.

Her hand was so soft, and her face was close enough that I could feel the warmth of her breath.

Beneath the deserted walkway, it was just me and a girl standing close together, bound by a shared secret. The sad thing is, I'd never even held her hand.

And before I knew it, I was a hero.

What am I *doing*...?

* * *

"—They all know Boogiepop," she said. It was the first time she had ever used that name. "Do you?"

"Never heard of it. Uh, what is it?"

"They say he's a shinigami. Or a killer."

"A...?" I gaped at her.

She just continued on. "It's just an urban legend, some sort of monstrous character, but they say this boy kills people when they are at their most beautiful, before they have a chance to grow old and ugly. That sort of thing."

"Weird." It certainly sounded like the sort of thing that would show up in girls' horror stories. I bet *he* was supposed to be pretty, too. "So what?"

"Masaki...will you *become* him?"

"Uh, ex-excuse me?"

"I know you can do it. You're so strong. You might be a little tall, but not by too much."

"W-wait a sec! This is a killer, right?" My mind reeled. I couldn't follow the first thing she said.

"No, the killer thing is nothing more than reputation. In fact, he seems to *save* people more often than kill them."

She was talking like this guy actually existed.

"Y-you want me to s-save people? From what?"

"Anything."

"Anything?"

"Anything we can."

"............"

"You're strong, Masaki. You can become Boogiepop." She stared at me intently.

Overwhelmed, I fell silent.

Her gaze suddenly shifted away. "I'm sorry. I know I have no right to ask something like this of you..."

She hung her head. Her shoulders shook.

Deflated like that, she looked so small. I felt like my chest was being torn apart.

"So if I...become this Boogie-whatsit, will that...make you happy?" I asked, unable to bear the silence.

She looked up. "Will you?"

"Sure, I'll do it. I don't know what it is I'm doing, but I'll do what I can."

"Really...?"

"Yeah," I replied, too embarrassed to add, *If it makes you happy*.

"I'm sorry, Masaki," she said and buried her face in her hands. "I really am. This is too much to ask..."

"I said it was okay. We're friends, aren't we?"

"I'm so sorry..."

She always seemed so sad. She apologized so often that I felt I had to do something. Still, I couldn't shake the feeling that I'd taken a step into some strange new dimension.

* * *

At that time, I was unfortunately still unaware that Boogiepop wore such an embarrassing outfit.

Orihata bought a huge swath of black cloth, almost like a theater curtain, at a do-it-yourself fabric shop, and fashioned a cloak and hat out of it. I was appalled when she showed it to me. It was hideous.

"You want me to walk outside...in *this*?"

"You will change before you 'appear.' Until then, it can remain hidden...in a sports bag or something."

She produced a big Nike bag from out of seemingly nowhere.

"W-wait, I... I really have to put this stuff on?"

This was like what a street performer would wear from some long forgotten decade.

Despite my concerns, Orihata simply said, "That's how it goes."

I took the cloak, the decorations clattering, thinking again that this was a step I shouldn't be taking.

It was well made. She'd sewn it carefully, and the fabric was doubled over. It was really thick. You would never think for a minute that it was handmade, which made it all the more serious—and all the more embarrassing, to boot.

"But what if someone I know sees me?" I asked, still underestimating my predicament.

Orihata answered that one easily. "Don't worry. You'll be wearing make-up. No one will ever recognize you."

* * *

This all brings us back to the here and now, with Boogiepop roaming the streets.

The first thing we tried was to have Orihata walk down backroads at night and try to attract would-be molesters, which I would then proceed to beat the ever-loving crap out of. As heroic as it sounds, I felt like I was working some sort of con. Still, if someone tried to attack Orihata, I wasn't about to just stand there and let them have their way with her.

"I thought you could do it. You're really strong," she said.

I am a guy, after all, so I can't say that hearing that didn't make me happy.

So, we kept it up, like today.

Until I started doing this, I really had now idea how dangerous this town really is. Don't believe what people tell you. Japan isn't nearly as safe a place as the government and media leads you to believe. The proof was in how easy it was for Orihata—our "bait"—to lure in prey.

If you must know, my karate master had been forced to leave

Japan after an epic bout of violence, but a man with as powerful a sense of justice as he had could hardly have lived in Japan without getting mixed up in stuff. I was no different than my master at this very moment. Which is why if he only knew his student was following in his footsteps...he'd be furious!

As for why, exactly, Orihata wanted me to do this—that was something that I couldn't for the life of me figure out. The most worrisome thing of all was the more that I did it, the more I found myself enjoying this little "game." And not just because I was with Orihata...

"School's going to start up again pretty soon. What then?" I asked, as I stood there in a back alley, letting her apply my Boogiepop make-up.

"............" She didn't answer. After covering my face with skin cream, she began patting white foundation all over it.

"Be honest—how long can we really keep this up?"

"............" She said nothing, calmly applying my eyeliner.

Her face was inches from mine. Her lips were slightly puckered, as if she were about to kiss me.

"What do you say?"

"............"

Boogiepop's face was apparently very, very pale. Below the eyes there were black lines, or blueish shadows. Then on top of that, he wore a hat that covers his eyes, making him look inhuman—like a ghost. If I met him on some darkened street at night, I'd probably wet myself.

"Well?" I kept asking.

She looked away, and then I heard her say, "Masaki..."

"Yes?"

"Is there anything you want me to do?"

"That came out of the blue..."

"I'll do anything. Ask me anything at all. Anything you want to do, Masaki...we'll do it." She never looked at me, but the words burst out of her.

I was stunned.

"I know it won't be enough. But if there's anything I can do... I'll do it...anything and everything you desire, Masaki. I'll do everything you want from me..."

I'd never seen her so desperate.

Her profile trembled. She seemed so wretched. I felt a pain in my chest, like it was on fire. I felt a surge of misdirected emotions.

"In that case, I'll play Boogiepop as best as I can," I said, shoulders slumping.

Her head snapped up, and she stared at me. It was her usual response, "Why?"

"Well...to tell you the truth, it's getting kinda fun." It wasn't a lie. I'd only recently come to that very revelation myself.

"Masaki..." Her hands reached towards me...then stopped, flailed around in the air a bit, and dropped limply to her sides. "You're an idiot, Masaki," she whispered.

"I know," I grimaced.

Call it irresponsible, but whatever happens, happens.

* * *

That day, they caught nothing. Aya went to dangerous spot after dangerous spot, but nobody came after her.

"I'm a little relieved," Masaki said. "If you got attacked every time, that'd be pretty crazy. Not to mention *scary*." He took off his outfit and handed it to Aya, like always. It was her job to look after the outfit. She would patch up any rips or tears, but today there weren't any.

"Masaki, how do you..." Aya started to ask, standing on the darkened night street.

But Masaki was busy wiping the make-up off his face and didn't hear her.

"Uh, what'd you say?" he asked, rubbing cleansing cream over his skin.

"Nothing," Aya said, letting the question remain unspoken. She had almost asked, *How do you feel about me?* But no matter what the answer might've been, Aya could do nothing about it... because she was lying to him.

"I'll take you home, then."

"No need."

"Don't be silly. After all the times you've been attacked, I'm not letting you go anywhere without me," Masaki smiled. They had this exchange every time.

They went to the bus terminal near the station, got on a late night bus, and headed towards her apartment.

They said nothing as they rode.

Aya couldn't figure out what to talk about and Masaki felt no need to talk. Aya glanced over at him from time to time, and every time his eyes were always there looking at her with a smile on his face. It was as if just being with her was fun enough.

Whenever Aya saw that carefree grin, her chest hurt.

She didn't know what to do.

"I'm sorry..." she whispered, inaudible above the noise of the bus.

He leaned in, "What?"

"Nothing," she said, shaking her head.

At length, the bus reached their stop.

They got off, and Masaki walked her all the way to the elevator door.

But that was all. He followed her no further.

"Night."

"Good night." Aya could think of nothing else to say.

With the Nike bag with the Boogiepop outfit inside slung over her shoulder, the elevator doors closed, and headed upwards.

She bit her lip.

Something moved inside her jacket. Her phone was ringing.

She jumped, and answered, "Orihata."

"Camille?" That voice was always hostile.

"Y-yes."

"You still haven't caught him?"

"At...at this point, there has been no contact," Aya's voice trembled slightly.

"Hmph. I thought a fake was too cheap a gambit for him... We need to put a bullet in this plan."

"Which means...?" Aya felt her backbone turn to ice.

The malevolent voice continued, "We've got a different use for Taniguchi Masaki. Time for you to cut him loose."

"......!"

"Soon enough, we'll need to sterilize the area. I'll have further instructions for you. Until then, keep things going." He hung up.

".........!" Aya stood frozen in horror.

The elevator stopped, and the doors opened, but her legs were shaking so much that she was frozen in place. Seconds later, the doors closed again in front of her.

Boogiepop returns

VS Imaginator Part 1

V

It is easy to become carefree.
All you have to do is lose your soul.

—Kirima Seiichi (*VS Imaginator*)

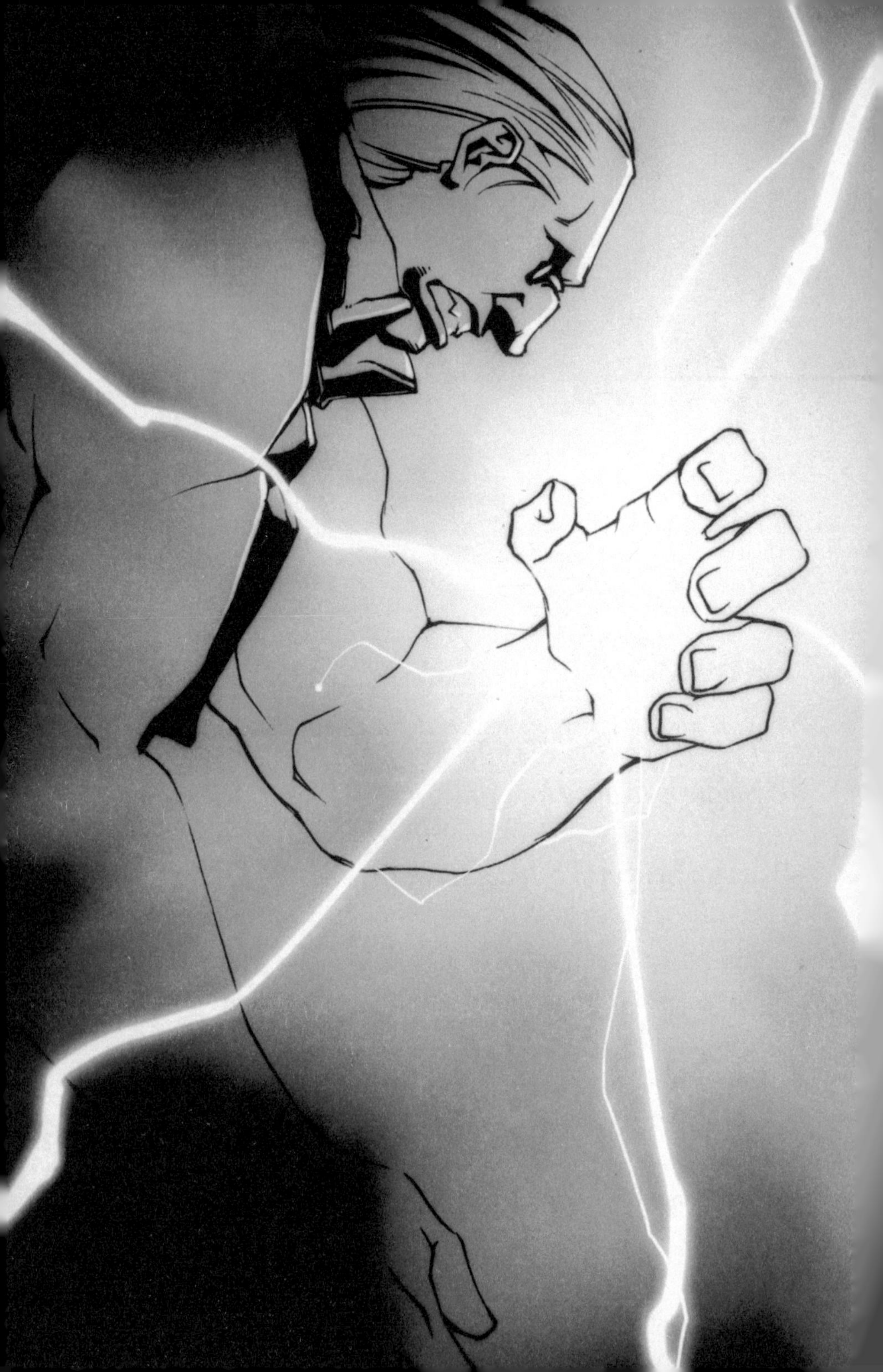

V.

WHEN HE FIRST SET EYES on the individual who had just transferred into his third year junior high class, Anou Shinjirou felt like someone had grabbed him by the heart. It was love at first sight.

"My name's Taniguchi Masaki. It's nice to meet you all," the new boy said, and gave a gentle smile. Shinjirou thought he was going to fall into those eyes. He could barely breathe; his throat was dry.

But a moment later, all the girls in class shrieked, and he was jolted back to reality.

(What am I *thinking*...?)

Until that moment, Shinjirou had believed himself to be just a normal ordinary boy. No sirree, nothing particularly unusual about him—which is why he didn't understand the feelings being born inside him at that very moment.

"He's not so great..." the guy behind him muttered, watching Taniguchi Masaki grin weakly back at the lovesick, squealing girls.

Shinjirou quickly exclaimed, "Y-yeah, I hate him already." The moment the words left his mouth, he was certain they were true. He hated the guy. That was all.

And yet every time he looked at Masaki, his chest began to pound. What could that mean?

Taniguchi Masaki was still bowing, saying "Hello," and giving everyone a vague, embarrassed smile. Shinjirou didn't think it suited his handsome features at all, but all the girls just kept yelling stuff like "Oh, wow!," and "He's so cute!"

He couldn't stop himself from feeling immensely irritated. The very sight of Masaki giving his feeble little friendly smile was unbearably unpleasant for him.

Shinjirou shouted inside himself, *Stop doing that! Stop smiling!! It's not right!!!* An incomprehensible urge to strangle Masaki fluttered deep in his heart.

* * *

Taniguchi Masaki was soon idolized by almost all the girls in the school.

For starters, the boy should have been going to a much better school than this one. On top of that, everyone was right in the middle of exams, so the girls bombarded Masaki all at once with pleas to check their homework. He hardly ever refused, and as a result, he was almost always surrounded by throngs of ladies whenever he was at school.

(Shit...)

Shinjirou spied the action all from the desolate safety of his far corner seat. It was clear that every glare he gave in Masaki's direction was always filled with icy anger and resentment.

If only he could talk to Masaki like that...he found himself thinking.

"Doesn't he just piss you off?" the guy next to him would ask.

"Mm?" he started, turning towards his classmate.

The guy nodded, "I know how you feel, man. Guy pisses me off to no end."

"Y-yeah..." Shinjirou had, somehow, become the boy in school who hated Masaki the most. Despite never having actually fought with him, he'd somehow earned that reputation.

And thus, all the girls hated him.

"What the hell is Anou's problem?"

"Oh, he's just *jealous*."

"Never heard of anything so *pathetic*."

Their whispers were easily overheard and only served to direct his anger even more.

Even Masaki thought Shinjirou hated him. That blow was the one that hurt Shinjirou the most.

But he still didn't understand his own feelings.

He couldn't work out why Taniguchi Masaki preyed on his mind like this. The conscious knowledge that they were the same gender prevented him from grasping the true nature of his all too obvious emotions. His previous lack of interest in other men besides Masaki was another big reason for his sudden confusion.

His environment didn't give him the latitude to work things out. Even if he had understood the true nature of his feelings, there was nowhere and no one he could ever go to where those feelings would be accepted.

If his classmates found out, he would be shunned. They already didn't like him much, and if they knew...he would be considered less than human.

If his parents found out, they'd disown him or worse...haul him off to a psychiatric ward.

Shinjirou's mind was a thunderstorm of confusion and doubt. Fear of the unknown meant he couldn't act on his feelings. As a result, he made no real attempt to ever sort things out.

But despite his ignorance, the feelings kept surging up inside him, unconsciously causing him pain.

He wanted to talk to Masaki. He wanted to be near him. He didn't know why, but he knew he had no choice.

(Aahhhhhhh...!!!)

Miserable, he began yelling at people for absolutely no reason, he disobeyed his teachers at every turn, and he got into full-blown fist fights over the most trivial things.

Then one day, the pressure got too much for him, and he managed to convince all of his club's kouhai into mounting an assault on Masaki. They all had a grudge against "Study Abroad"—Taniguchi Masaki—to begin with, so they didn't need much persuading.

"Heh heh—let's do it."

"That asshole's been on my shit list for a while."

"We'll show him how far his pretty face can take him."

"Good," Shinjirou grinned—but in fact, he was planning to burst onto the scene and rescue Masaki.

He wanted to make friends with him. If this gave him a chance to do that, then he didn't care what crap he had to take from his kouhai afterwards—his emotions left him no choice.

This "strategy" went into motion a few days later after school.

They followed Masaki on his usual trip home, and when Masaki ducked into his usual back alley shortcut to the train station, Shinjirou signaled to his five kouhai—"Go for it."

The five boys quickly snuck into the deserted alley. By the time Masaki realized he was being followed, it was too late...he was already surrounded.

"So, Mr. Study Abroad. You've been doing pretty well for yourself, haven't ya?" It was obvious they were trying to sound tough.

But things didn't progress as Shinjirou had originally hoped. He had been so sure that Masaki would be scared out of his wits that he never considered the possibility that maybe, just maybe, Masaki would instead take the scenario in stride and be totally calm and collected. "Right...I'll be more careful," Masaki replied, just standing there and accepting their aggression.

They threatened him, they pushed him, but no matter what they said...his response was completely serene.

(——?)

Watching this from the sidelines, Shinjirou started to fret. Ladies' men weren't supposed to act like this.

Eventually one of his kouhai lost his temper and let loose, punching Masaki in the cheek.

(Ah—!)

Shinjirou almost shrieked. He had never planned to let it go that far. He quickly stepped forward, intending to intervene...

But something happened.

A girl appeared, entering the alley from the side opposite to where Shinjirou was hiding.

"What is your purpose?" she said, her voice empty, dispassionate. "What failing of his caused this behavior?" She spoke like a windup doll.

(Wh-who the hell is *she*?)

Shinjirou gaped at her, completely blowing the timing of his entrance.

"Hey, this guy thinks he's Don Juan," his kouhai snarled, switchblade in hand. "Looking like this, tricking girls into falling for him."

"So, he stole your girlfriends, then? The cause of your anger is sexual frustration?" What in the world was this girl's problem?!

"Uh…what? What did she say?"

"I'm asking if this attack is a way of forgetting that your sexual partners all hate you."

"You…*bitch!*"

The situation was rapidly spiraling in a sinister direction. Shinjirou didn't know what to do, and he couldn't force himself out of hiding.

As if things weren't confusing enough already, the girl suddenly tore her own shirt off and stood there bare-chested.

"If you have frustrated desires, I can fulfill them," she said in the most deadpan voice. This girl was out of freaking control.

"Uuuum…"

"H-hey…"

"Whoa! *Wait* a minute," Masaki yelped, flustered. He had

been totally unfazed when he himself was in danger, but once the girl got mixed up in it, his attitude changed.

Watching this, Shinjirou thought, *Oh, crap!*

He knew he'd made a terrible mistake.

Quickly, he took a step forward, but even as he did, someone even stranger appeared on the scene.

"Well, *this* is easy to figure out!"

A young man in white clothes, positively exuding confidence, strode directly into the alley.

"—! Wh-who are you?!"

"Just to make sure, I'd better ask. You there." He pointed at Masaki. "Do you want to save this girl?"

Masaki nodded, "Y-yes."

"Then take her and run!"

With lightning speed, the man pulled the girl out of the ring of kouhai and shoved her towards Masaki.

Taking the man at his word, Masaki took the girl's arm, and fled the scene.

(Wahhh?!)

Shinjirou was horrified. They were running straight towards him.

But they were going too fast and ran right past him without ever noticing that he was there.

(Wh-what's going on?)

He was a little relieved, but now more confused than ever. Things were playing out in a way that bore no resemblance to his original plans, and he could no longer follow anything.

He looked back at the man in white, and somehow, all his *kouhai* had already been defeated, and were lying in a bloody heap on the ground.

"Eeek!" Shinjirou let out a little shriek, and the man turned towards him.

"Can't say I think much of your methods," the man said, like he had been well aware that Shinjirou had been hiding there all along.

The man smiled. It was a villainous, heartless smile.

"Aaaaugh!" Shinjirou ran for it.

He ran as hard as he could, not stopping until he reached the square by the side of the station.

Feeling safe, he relaxed...and realized that Masaki and the girl were sitting together on a bench on the other side of the square.

"Ah...!" he wailed.

He had been right.

It was obvious that they were drawn to each other—especially Masaki, whose heart had been stolen by the girl. It was written all over his face. He'd never looked like that at school, all red faced and smiling.

"............!"

In that very moment, Shinjirou felt all of the energy drain out of his body.

* * *

A few days afterwards, Masaki went on a date with the girl.

Shinjirou watched from the shadows, having followed after Masaki every day since the incident.

(Augh...)

He ground his teeth as he watched the couple head for the movie theater. Masaki appeared to be quite surprised by how crowded the theater was.

They talked for a moment, apparently arguing.

(Oooh...)

Shinjirou waited hopefully. The girl joined the line on her own, leaving Masaki just standing there.

After a moment, Masaki turned and walked towards the main road.

Pleased by this turn of events, Shinjirou quickly followed after him.

Masaki looked all around as he walked, as if searching for some place in particular. With his heart pounding, Shinjirou took this opportunity to walk over to Masaki and speak to him. "Oh, Study Abroad. What are *you* doing here?" His tone was rather aggressive, out of habit.

"Ah, um, you know," Masaki replied, scrunching up his face unhappily.

Shrinking back from this reception, Shinjirou said, "Yeah, I do. You're making some chick wait for you, huh?"

But Masaki just answered, "Sorry, in kind of a hurry," and rushed off.

"Ah...!" Shinjirou wondered where he was going, but Masaki just ducked into a fast food place, and after a few minutes, popped out with a large paper bag and some drinks, and headed back to where the girl was waiting in line.

They began happily munching away on their burgers.

"............"

As Shinjirou watched vacantly, the girl suddenly kissed Masaki. To be strictly accurate, it wasn't technically a kiss—she had actually licked off a blob of ketchup from Masaki's cheek with her tongue—but to Shinjirou, this sudden display was far more erotic than any old kiss.

"............"

Shinjirou's face turned white as a sheet. He was trembling.

Unable to take any more, he turned and fled.

* * *

"Ah, that'd be Orihata. She's in our school, yeah."

Shinjirou had called everyone he knew, trying to find out the girl's name. And now he had it. He had the hateful name of his archenemy's girlfriend—Orihata Aya. The very name only drew more questions. "What's she like?!" he urged.

On the other end of the line, a friend of his from elementary school hesitated, "Um... Well..." Then he sniggered, meaningfully. "You did her, then?"

"Huh? No, nothing like that..."

"Better be careful, man. Everyone knows about Orihata. Hee hee hee."

"What do you mean?"

"She looks all good girl, right? Like some choir chick? But she's a *total* slut."

The rude word caught Shinjirou totally off guard. "Wh-what?"

"I know dozens of guys who say they've done her. Hee hee."

"Really?"

"She'll do anyone that asks. Go for it, man. Say her name and she'll follow you anywhere. Course, you gotta watch out that you don't catch somethin' from her... Hee hee hee hee."

"————" Shinjirou couldn't answer.

Did Masaki know about this?

Ever since meeting her, Masaki had appeared more alive, even from a distance—like his life had taken on new meaning. It seemed like he was really in love with her, and that made his every waking moment enjoyable.

Additionally, his previously reluctant reception to the girls who flocked around him shifted, and he spoke to them warmly. Living proof of the old counselor's maxim that the better your life is going, the nicer you are to other people. This made him even more popular than ever, but Shinjirou was way past being jealous of that.

Masaki was in the midst of the kind of love that comes along only once a lifetime...and the girl probably didn't deserve any of it. Surely lurking in his future was a horrendous heartbreak. But what could Shinjirou do?

(—Just leave them be? Yeah, a guy like that deserves to be put through the wringer by some lying, evil bitch!)

Yes, sometimes he thought like that. But at other times, he

thought he might be able to take advantage of the situation and somehow get closer to Masaki.

(Auuuugh...)

The test was right on top of them, but Shinjirou never thought of anything but Masaki and Aya, and as a result, his scores plummeted.

He abandoned his studies to do nothing but obsessively follow Masaki—and, of course, Orihata Aya, who was almost always with him. Gradually, he started keeping an even closer eye on Orihata Aya than he did Masaki. He would lie to his parents and tell them he was going to cram school, but in reality, he would venture out and stand outside Orihata's apartment building, beneath the wintry night sky, feeling the north wind slice his body to ribbons.

"Aaugh..."

He had no conscious recognition of how creepy his behavior was. No, he was merely following Orihata Aya because he was desperate to know the truth—why did Masaki like her? But the meaningless irritation pouring out of him prevented him from understanding.

"I'm gonna figure out who she is..." he muttered to himself in the darkness. The lights in Orihata Aya's room were off.

From Shinjirou's stalker-ish observations, he gathered that Orihata Aya must live alone. He'd never seen any sign of other family members in the apartment, and the lights inside were never left on—whether Orihata Aya was there or not. After a date with Taniguchi Masaki, the lights would go on for about ten minutes, presumably while she was in the shower, but they'd be turned off right afterwards.

Does anyone go to sleep that fast?

At first, his perverted mind thought that she might be doing something naughty, and this fantasy excited him initially—and the knotty mess of that feeling made Shinjirou hate himself even more. But as his observations continued, he realized that this occurrence happened each and every time she came home, like clockwork, and he began to doubt that possibility. No one masturbated like that, not even Shinjirou.

The most troubling thing about these observations was realizing how dull Orihata Aya's life really was. She never watched TV or anything. She just sat there in total darkness. Did this girl even have a private life?

On days when she didn't meet Masaki, she would come directly home from school, go out to buy a bento at the convenience store for her dinner. The lights would go off shortly after she returned home with it. Most of the time, the bento was a plain nori bento—nothing to spice up her meals at all.

It was like this girl did nothing. She just went through the normal motions of life, but never actually *lived* it.

(Why would anyone go for an expressionless mannequin of a girl like her...?)

One thing Shinjirou realized quite quickly from his observations was that his friend was a liar. There were no signs of the mythical parade of men his friend had so playfully spoken of. No, there was only Masaki. There were no indications at all of her ever going off with other men, and this left him with absolutely no evidence at all to confront Masaki with.

(Shit...)

Teeth chattering in the cold, Shinjirou carried on stalking her. Had anyone seen him, they would certainly have called the police.

* * *

Then one night...

Shinjirou was staring up at Orihata Aya's room when the door slid open. The lights inside remained off.

It was really cold, so it couldn't possibly be an attempt to air the place out.

He held his breath, watching, and Orihata Aya came out on the veranda alone...in her underwear.

Her hair was a mess. She looked like she'd just woken up. Didn't she have anything else she could sleep in besides her underwear?

"............"

Silently, the girl put her hands on the railing, and stood there, not moving. She was immobile, stiff, staring down from her veranda.

(.........?)

Shinjirou looked up at her through the binoculars he had with him, and shivered.

Orihata Aya's trademark mask-like face was gone. She was biting her lower lip so hard that it had turned blue, and she was shaking like a leaf. He could tell from the uncanny light shining in her wide-open eyes that it was not because of the cold.

Something was tormenting her...but what?

She looked as though she was about to jump.

(H-hey—)

Shinjirou gulped, but kept watching.

Her lips parted, and she whispered something. The same words, over and over and over.

She kept on whispering and whispering until eventually Shinjirou couldn't stand it any longer. He had to get in closer.

Shinjirou quietly scampered towards the building's outer wall, and it was there, carried on the chilly wind, that her "spell" reached Shinjirou's ears.

It went as follows:

"I have no right to fall in love. I have no right to fall in love. I have no right to fall in love. I have no right to fall in love. I have no right to fall in love. I have no right to fall in love. I have no right to fall in love. I have no right to fall in love. I have no right to fall in love. I have no right to fall in love. I have no right to fall in love. I have no right to fall in love. I have no right to fall in love. I have no right to fall in love. I have no right to fall in love. I have no right to fall in love. I have no right to fall in love. I have no right to fall in love. I have no right to fall in love..."

On and on and on it went, like she was spitting out blood.

Shinjirou was bewildered.

(Wh-what the hell...is she *saying*?)

He couldn't comprehend it...but deep inside his body something made him shiver, and it wasn't the cold. Something in him had responded to her single-minded intensity. Something perhaps very similar to what Taniguchi Masaki had felt about her.

But it was beyond Shinjirou's capability to understand it.

"So you're the one who's been following Camille around? You got a crush on her or something?" A voice snarled from behind him.

"——?!" He spun around in shock, but he wasn't quick enough. The hideously fat man behind him—Spooky E—reached out with both his hands and grabbed ahold of the young stalker.

Electricity raced through Shinjirou's body, and he passed out instantly, crumpling to the ground.

"Huh..." Spooky E sneered, picking Shinjirou up in one hand like a shopping bag. He carried him around to the building's garbage dump.

Above them, oblivious to their presence, Orihata Aya struggled desperately to crush her feelings for Taniguchi Masaki, shivering in her underwear, whispering over and over, "...I have no right to fall in love..."

* * *

Spooky E stood in the darkness, hands either side of the unconscious Anou Shinjirou's head. His fingers slowly, slowly moved across the boy's scalp.

With each movement, bits of Shinjirou's body would twitch. Once, the ring finger on his left hand curled; another time, his right eyelid opened, then shut.

"O...o...aahhh..." His mouth opened, meaningless sounds spilling out. "O...o...rihata...Orihata...Orihata Aya..."

When the words acquired meaning, Spooky E grinned. He had reached the part of Shinjirou's brain that knew about her.

Spooky E briefly removed his hands, stuck his fingers in his mouth, and licked them all over. Once they were covered in saliva, he placed them back on Shinjirou's head.

Spooky E's hands generated a very low power electromagnetic wave. He could use this to shock the cells in someone's brain, and manipulate their memories and their very psyche. His power was called "Spooky Electric." It was this that his code name was derived. He was a synthetic human. By licking his fingers, he was able to increase the conductivity of the very electromagnetic wave he was generating.

"Okay, Anou Shinjirou. You will no longer pay the slightest attention to that girl or anything to do with her," Spooky E said. He had discovered the boy's name from the student ID card in his pocket.

"I will not."

"From now on, you will have no personal desires," Spooky E whispered, massaging the boy's frontal lobes.

"I will not."

"From now on, you work for the Towa Organization as one of our living terminals."

"I am a terminal."

"The sex drive that troubles you no longer exists," Spooky E's fingers slid between Shinjirou's forehead and his eyes, hunting for the hypothalamus and the limbic system.

"No sex drive."

"You are no longer lonely."

"Not lonely."

"You don't want a lover...you don't want friends."

"I don't."

These quiet statements and responses continued for another thirty minutes.

Eventually, Spooky E whispered in Shinjirou's ear, "You will enter Shinyo Academy and await instructions."

"I will."

"Programming complete. Reset all systems, reactivate in ten minutes."

"Complete."

And with that, Shinjirou's body toppled over, immobile.

* * *

"I'm home."

Hearing the voice from the doorway, Anou Kumiko jumped up from the sofa. She had dozed off.

It was the unexpected voice of her son, Shinjirou. She hurriedly looked at the clock, but soon realized that he was home more than an hour earlier than when cram school should have let out. She had not overslept.

"What's wrong, Shin-chan?" she asked. "Did something happen at cram school?"

Her son looked much more relaxed than usual. The closer the

test got, the more stressed out he'd become, but that seemed to have vanished.

"No," he said. "I quit."

Kumiko freaked. "EH?! Wh-what's *that* supposed to mean?"

"My scores have been taking a nose dive. I realized I was going to the wrong school," he answered readily.

"B-but...all on your own? And wasn't it your idea to go in the *first* place?"

"I switched to a different school. The one by the station." He mentioned the name of a big school that handled college entrance exam students as well.

Kumiko was taken aback, but when she heard that he'd already done all the paperwork and paid for the course fees, she frowned. "With what money?"

"I had some savings."

"How much?"

"Two hundred thousand yen."

She was staggered. She had known he had that kind of money saved up from New Year's presents and the like—but for him to use that money on studying was unthinkable.

"I want to get into a prefectural school, at least," he continued, composedly.

"Sh-Shin-chan..." Kumiko couldn't decide if she should be happy at her son's newfound maturity or to continue freaking out over his rash decisions.

"But first, what's for dinner? I didn't get anything on the way home..."

He ate twice as much as usual.

"Um, Shin-chan?" Kumiko asked, hesitantly.

He looked up from his third bowl of rice. "What?"

"Which school are you thinking about?"

"Shinyo Academy. I should be able to make that level...if I start now."

"You... You really want to?"

"It's worth a shot. I've been dragging my feet way too long, though..." He shook his head.

Kumiko wasn't sure why, but she couldn't stop worrying.

When he finished dinner, he went straight to his room and started studying.

Kumiko snuck a peek, and found him actually at his desk, without the headphones he always had on, plugging away at his study guides and notes.

"............"

She held her breath, unable to tear herself away from the crack in the door. Yet her son never moved, continuing to study away in exactly the same position for hours like he had become some kind of machine.

Eventually her husband came home, and Kumiko hurriedly told him what was happening.

"Mm? Sounds great. Finally found some motivation."

"But there's something strange about him. Like... Oh, I can't put it into words..." She must have looked very high strung at that moment.

Her husband frowned in irritation. "Come off it. You're his

mother. He's the one taking the test. You put too much pressure on him and he won't be able to concentrate," he snapped.

"Yes, I know, but..."

"Sounds like you've got a case of exam nerves. Just take a deep breath and relax, dear."

"Okay..." Kumiko nodded in agreement. It *was* true that she wanted him to study more, and she couldn't deny that the current developments were a bit of a relief. And really, it wasn't *that* strange...

And with that, the intuitive doubt that had arisen inside her was washed away in a flood of sensible analysis.

* * *

General opinion of Anou Shinjirou abruptly improved. Everyone noticed that he had become more serious. This more motivated turn not only impressed the teachers, but also softened the views of his classmates. Most of all, everyone kept expressing surprise at his sudden lack of interest in Taniguchi Masaki.

"Well, I thought about it, and realized I was just jealous. And you know, that's really not cool..." Shinjirou said, and since Masaki's number one enemy had changed his mind, the other guys began to think differently as well, and soon none of them were openly bad mouthing Taniguchi Masaki.

The first group to come around to Shinjirou were the very girls who had treated him like an insect before. "Huh... Anou-kun's not a bad guy after all..."

"All that conflict between him and Masaki-kun was just some stupid rivalry," they said, spinning things positively all on their own.

Taniguchi Masaki himself was probably the only person who didn't pick up on the sea of change. His head was full of Orihata Aya, and he had no time for anything else.

Anou Shinjirou himself cared little for the reaction it provoked. He was simply plugging away at his studies, gradually getting closer to the benchmark for the high school he was aiming for.

"Well, Anou, you're doing very well. You should have no problem at all getting into Shinyo Academy," his teacher said, during one of their counseling sessions.

"But I can't slack off now," Shinjirou replied calmly.

"Hey, that's my line! Ha ha ha! But true, very true. Keep up the good work."

"Yes."

"You're living proof that all you have to do is put your mind to it. Don't think about anything else; just concentrate and you'll get there."

"I think so, too," Shinjirou nodded quietly.

But his teacher frowned at him. "Hey...is something wrong?"

"What?"

"You're crying."

"Huh?" Shinjirou put his hand to his eyes. His cheeks were wet. "I am? But why?" he murmured.

"You getting enough sleep? I mean, I'm glad you're working so hard, but maybe you ought to try and take things a little easier now."

"..........."

But Shinjirou had no answer. He just sat there, tears rolling down his cheeks, staring into space, unable to understand why he was crying.

* * *

"Dear Anou Shinjirou-kun,

I'm sorry to send you a letter like this so suddenly. I know this is a busy time for everyone, and no one has time to spare, but I have something I need to say to you.

I think I'm in love with you.

Is that strange? I don't even know my own feelings. I know I softened the sentiment with a dumb phrase like, 'I think,' but that's the truth of it.

Until just a while ago, I was like everyone else, and totally misunderstood you. You just seemed to always be angry about something, so it was hard to ever get near you. But..."

"........."

This letter was resting in his shoe locker when he left school. When he opened the letter, a whiff of perfume emerged. The paper was soaked in it. He started reading the letter with no reaction at all, and soon he realized it was a love letter.

"But recently, I started watching you, and I realized that you were only angry because no one understood the

true nature of your feelings.

Am I right? I'm sure I am. I understand...because I feel the same way.

I know I might be making this all up, but I feel like you're the only one who can understand my feelings. I hate to trouble you, but will you meet me? Just this once?

Please give me a chance..."

The letter continued, giving a date, time and place to meet... but no name.

"........." Shinjirou remained expressionless, just standing there holding the letter. He didn't know what to do, so he remained motionless.

Eventually, he moved stiffly over to a nearby phone booth.

Automatically, he dialed the number implanted in his brain.

The call was answered the moment it connected.

"State your name," the high-pitched voice on the other end of the line said.

"D1229085. Urgent communication for Spooky E," Shinjirou said, in a flat, mechanical tone.

"What, something happened?"

"Emergence of Emotional Circuit Response Case F. Disturbance level A."

The man on the other end of the line clicked his tongue in irritation. "Report details."

Shinjirou did so mechanically.

When he finished, the voice said, "Hmm. So this girl was drawn to a loner like you? Go for it, take her invitation. I'll permit it."

"Understood. Permission received."

"Where did she want to meet?"

Shinjirou told him, and Spooky E made a pleased chuckle. "Rather a lonely place for a romantic tryst, mm? Bet you anything that girl wants you to do her. Hee hee hee hee."

"…………"

"Okay, that place might do just fine, but if it looks like there are other people around, try and lure her out to some place deserted. I'll 'condition' her."

"………"

"Do you understand?"

"I understand."

"Okay. When you hang up the phone, you will return to normal mode in twelve seconds. You will forget about the letter until it is time for the meeting."

"I understand. I will hang up."

He hung up, put the letter in his bag, stood for a few seconds absently, and when he hit the twelve second mark, he snapped out of it and left the school, heading for his cram school, same as he always did.

He sat through classes like always, and during the short lull between classes, he found a spot on a bench in the rest area and ate a hamburger.

Around him were several kids his age and a group of high schoolers studying for college.

Right next to Shinjirou, one such girl said, "Oh god, what *is* this? Help me, Suemaaa!"

"Touka! At this stage of the game, you *have* to know *this*!"

"I know, but..."

The two girls were studying together. Their uniforms were obviously from Shinyo Academy, which is where he was planning to go to high school, but he paid them no attention.

"........." While he ate, he flipped through his vocabulary book.

But his hand stopped for a moment.

His gaze was drawn to a painting hung on the wall opposite him.

It was a painting of a great crowd of people sitting in a wasteland, holding hands. There were several black goats around them, eating the rose bushes that grew in the wilderness.

"..........." He couldn't take his eyes off it.

Eventually the bell rang, and everyone got up and went back to their classrooms, but Shinjirou just sat there, motionless. Left alone, as if frozen to his seat.

"..........."

Ever since Spooky E had "conditioned" him, Shinjirou had stopped thinking on his own. He simply followed the implanted instructions and the expectations of those around him, dutifully.

So why was he just standing there, looking at the painting, like he had been nailed to the floor?

"..........." He stared up at the painting.

From behind him, a voice said, "What you are experiencing is what we call 'emotion.'"

Shinjirou turned around. Behind him stood a young man in white clothes.

"Uh..." He could swear he'd seen the guy somewhere before, but he couldn't remember where. Yet he *had* seen him. Where was it...?

The man seemed to think they hadn't spoken before. At the previous meeting, the man had been unable to see Shinjirou, so he didn't recognize him. Neither one of them knew that they were crossing paths for the second time.

"Your heart was moved by something in that painting. But you've had no such experience in your life before, so you had no sample data inside to tell you how to react," the man in white said quietly, walking towards Shinjirou.

"............" Shinjirou said nothing. He was unable to express any reaction to this man, as well.

"You're Anou Shinjirou, right? From the public school last minute preparation course?" The man in white sat down next to Shinjirou.

"Yes, I am."

"My name is Asukai Jin. I'm in charge of the national art school preparation course here. I've had my eye on you, Anou-kun." He smiled gently.

"Why?" Shinjirou asked.

The man raised one eyebrow, as if joking. "You probably don't know."

"Know what?"

"That you have absolutely no hope," he said, calmly, but with a trace of sadness.

"What does that mean...?" Shinjirou asked.

But the man didn't answer. He stood up, slowly turned his back, and whispered, "The man who played with your heart worked for the Towa Organization, correct?"

This word was implanted deep inside Shinjirou. The moment he heard it, his body moved automatically.

His lungs screamed at the sudden motion, but he ignored them, flinging his body towards the man.

Even though his back was turned, the man stepped lightly to one side, easily dodging Shinjirou's lunge.

Shinjirou's body was carried onwards, flying into the tables and chairs opposite.

There was a huge crashing sound.

Bleeding from several places, Shinjirou sprang to his feet again. There was no trace of emotion on his face.

His head turned, looking for the man.

The man did not run, but instead, he stood his ground.

"Hmph..." A cruel smile appeared on his lips.

Shinjirou—or rather the body being controlled by implanted instructions— launched himself towards the man again.

This time, Shinjirouf grabbed him. He pushed him over, and tried to put one arm around his neck to strangle him.

But before he could, the man's hand reached out to Shinjirou's chest.

"————!"

A moment later, Shinjirou's body suddenly bent over of its own accord, and flung itself backwards.

There was another tremendous crash.

"Pathetic..." the man said, unmoved. He stood up, and brushed the dust off his clothes.

He came over to where Shinjirou lay unable to move, and got down on his knees. He peered into the boy's face.

"What was that sound?"

"Asukai-san, what happened?"

Several other faculty members had come running.

"He fell over. Looks like anemia of the brain..." Asukai replied, helping Anou Shinjirou up, and over to a comfortable sofa, where he laid him down flat.

"Is he okay? Should I call an ambulance?"

"Better ask the manager. If he lies down for a minute...he should be okay, I think..." Asukai answered, well aware that an ambulance pulling up to the cram school was hardly a desirable event.

"W-wait right there, I'll go ask," and the other teachers ran off.

Once again the lobby fell silent, if only for a short while.

"........." Asukai Jin slowly rubbed Anou Shinjirou's chest. "I've no idea of the true nature of your suffering, Anou-kun. But I promise you, your wordless pain will be buried when the snow falls in April...when the whiteness falls on *all* of mankind," he whispered kindly, yet firmly.

Behind him, floating in the air, a vision of a girl wavered.

* * *

When Shinjirou awoke, he was lying on a sofa at his cram

school. His mother was sitting next to him, peering at his face with a worried expression. Apparently, someone had called her.

"Shin-chan, how do you feel?"

"...Umm... Wh-where...?"

"Cram school. You... You passed out," his mother said.

He looked around him. Everything felt strange, like his eyes wouldn't quite focus.

"Cram school..." he got to his feet unsteadily. He stood there, looking puzzled.

"Should we go see a doctor?" his mother asked.

He didn't appear to be seriously injured, though, so they simply headed straight home. They went for a check up the next day, but the doctors found nothing amiss. Just to be safe, they gave him a mild tranquilizer and then sent him home. The diagnosis was simply stress. He had been studying far too much.

"Thank goodness."

"Yeah..."

"The test is pretty close, but you don't need to work too hard. The teachers all agree... You'll do fine."

"Yeah..."

* * *

When they got home, Shinjirou did as the doctors had suggested and went to bed.

He awoke soon after, and stood up. He reached for his bag, untouched since he'd come home the day before, and emptied it out onto his bed. He planned to reorganize the contents by priority.

Text books, study guides, notes...and a letter he didn't remember getting.

"..........."

As tempting as the letter was, he did not open it. He simply stood there, holding it in his fingers, looking off into nothing.

* * *

Two tall office buildings and a department store that housed a number of specialty shops had been piled on top of each other into one giant complex known as the Twin City. It was one of the many areas planned for during the redevelopment of the station area and the only one yet completed.

On a daily basis, tens of thousands of people came here. Customers for the department store, businessmen with deals to be done—they all flooded in and out of the building in a constant stream.

But once a month, on the third Wednesday, the department store would close for the day, and the place would be completely and utterly deserted...just a vast, empty space. The business hotel's rent was far too expensive, and it had hardly any tenants.

The roof of the department store was open to the eighth and ninth floors of the tenant buildings. This "connection space" was also deserted that day. The department store was closed, but the elevators in the office buildings were operating, so the roof was still accessible. The game centers and yakisoba shops that catered to the passing businessmen were all closed, and nothing visited but the wind.

Nonetheless, this monthly void in the middle of the city was where the girl in the letter had promised to meet Anou Shinjirou.

At four in the afternoon, the sun was already setting, painting the world red.

The elevator, which any other day stopped at nearly every floor, took him directly to his destination.

"............"

There was a gust of wind as Shinjirou came onto the roof. It was always windy this high up, but today exceptionally so. One of the screens that used to break the wind had come loose and was flapping noisily, but there was nobody there to fix it.

"Um... Hello?" Shinjirou looked around, searching for signs of life. There was nobody there, no signs of anyone having *been* there.

The meeting spot was in the center of the rooftop, near some round, squarish, enigmatic sort of abstract sculptures. Shinjirou headed towards them.

Long shadows spread out like stripes across the floor. A girl was seated alone on one of the sculptures.

"You... You wrote the letter...?"

"........." The girl nodded, silently. She wore a thick navy blue coat and a thick wool hat. Her hair was bound in two braids, and she wore glasses.

He'd never seen her before.

"Um... So, what did that letter mean?" Shinjirou asked.

"..........." She didn't answer. She just stared at the ground.

Shinjirou made no attempt to approach, stopping a good distance from her.

"I thought someone was making fun of me at first, but you're actually here..."

"..............."

"But when did you put the letter in my bag? I don't remember leaving it lying around..."

"—What?" The girl's face snapped up. For a moment, the setting sun glinted off her glasses. "What did you just say?" Her voice sounded more like a boy's.

"Huh?"

"You found the letter in your bag? *That's why you came here?*"

"What about it?" Shinjirou stared at her blankly.

She suddenly yelled, "*Look out*!" and dove towards Shinjirou, knocking him aside.

"Waah—?!"

A moment later, something black and round cut through the air where Shinjirou had been standing.

The impact of its landing shook the roof, and then it stood up—Spooky E.

The monstrous man had planned to crush Shinjirou on his dive. But he had failed.

"——?!"

Spooky E swung his fist towards the girl who had spotted his attack.

But his punch met only fabric—the girl had tossed her coat, and was no longer there.

Instead, her hat and glasses spun in the air, falling to the floor of the roof.

Something like a thick black rope landed on top of them—the braids that had emerged from under her hat. They were fake.

"What—?!" Spooky E yelled, stomping on the glasses and fake braids, glaring around him.

There was no sign of the girl—if she even *was* a girl.

"............" Shinjirou stayed on the ground, making no sound.

Spooky E turned towards him. "How the hell did you escape from my control?"

"Er..."

"You said you found the letter in your bag...but I made you forget that letter. So how did you find it again?! You should've only come here because I *ordered* you to!"

"Wh-what?" Shinjirou had no idea what the man was shouting about. He'd never seen him before in his life.

Spooky E reached his hand towards Shinjirou. Something flashed in the air between them.

"———!"

Spooky E yanked his hand back quickly. But it was too late; there was already a long, thin cut on his arm, deep enough to draw blood.

A microfilament wire.

It had moved at a frightening speed, slicing open Spooky E's arm the same way a copy paper can sometimes slice your fingers. Worst of all, it had prevented him from getting close to Anou Shinjirou.

From somewhere around them came a whistle. Shinjirou had no taste for classical music, so he didn't know the tune, but it was "Die Meistersinger von Nurnberg."

"You're not nearly as tough as the Manticore," a voice said. Just like the girl, it was an androgynous voice, impossible to tell if it was male or female.

"Wh-what are you?" Spooky E spun around and found a black shadow standing on one of the sculptures, cloak flapping in the wind.

Its left hand was on its head, holding its pipe-shaped hat as if it had just put it on.

"You should know who I am by now. After all, you are one of the Towa Organization's synthetic humans." The cloaked figure brushed its fingers across its lips, leaving them covered in black lipstick. It was as if this figure was performing some sort of magic trick.

The figure let out a strange, asymmetrical expression.

"Y-you're Boogie...!" Spooky E started to scream, then suddenly flinched, leaping backwards. "Unnh!"

Something glinted in the air, following him.

A piece of paper blowing in the wind was neatly sliced in two.

Frantically, Spooky E rolled away, then forced himself upright, pulling a small gun from his pocket and firing at the cloaked figure.

The figure leapt away a moment before the gun was aimed. There was a crunch, and bits of the statue shattered as the bullet ricocheted off of it.

The cloaked figure slid nimbly from shadow to shadow, between the statues.

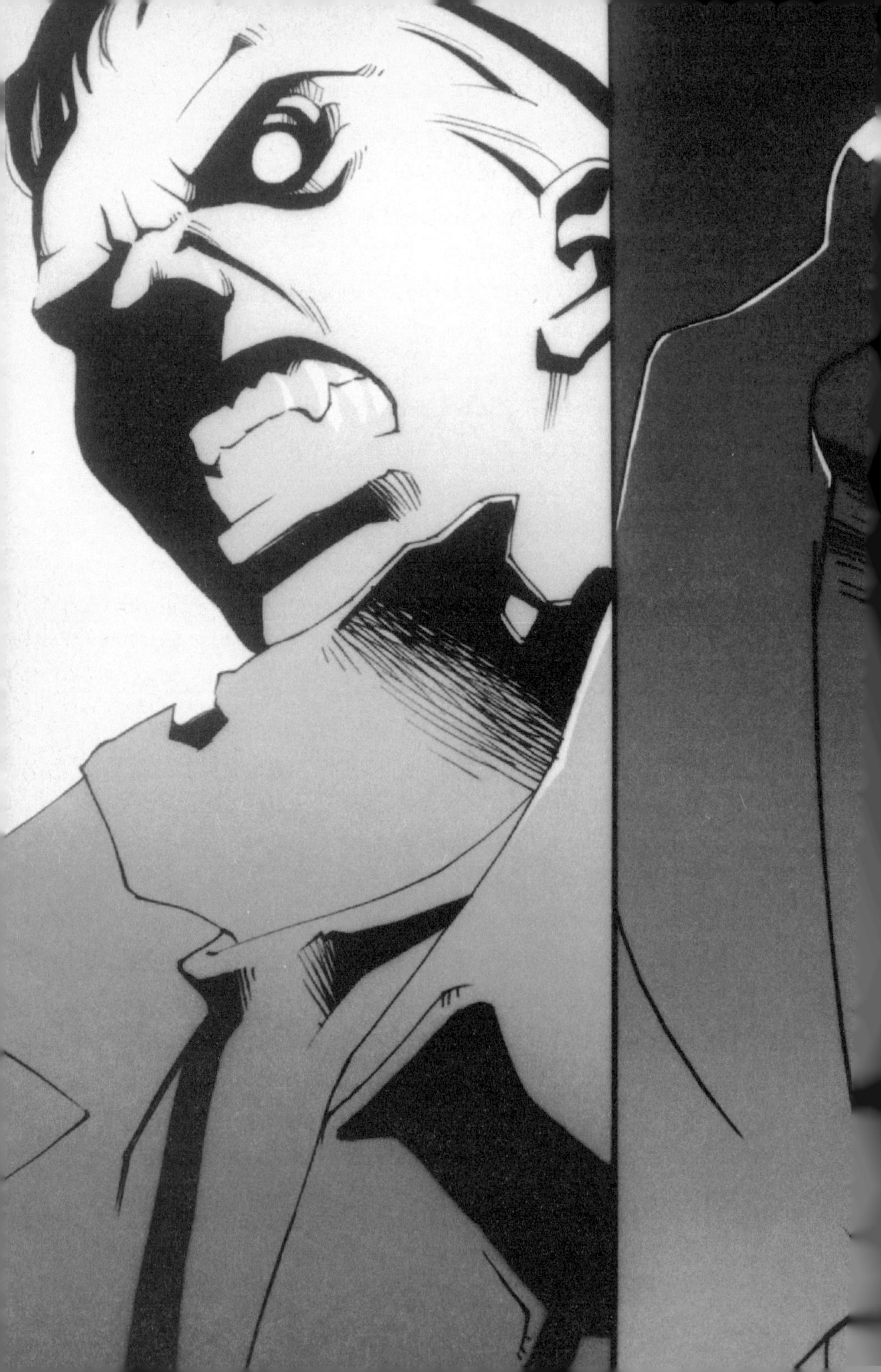

"Shit shit shit!" Spooky E yelled, firing into the darkness. There was a silencer on the end of the gun, and it made only a vacant, hollow whistle as it fired.

"My primary objective is the Imaginator's reemergence. I should not be bothering with the likes of you," that creepy voice echoed from somewhere.

"But with one of your victims right in front of me, I can hardly ignore matters. I do apologize for the second class treatment, but I'm going to have to destroy you."

"Grrrrrr!" Spooky E ground his teeth.

There was a click as the hammer struck an empty chamber. He tried to reload, but a wire came undulating through the air, wound around the gun, and pulled it from his hand.

"——!"

"Are you ready?" the voice whispered, seemingly right in his ear.

"S-screw this!" Spooky E turned his back and ran headlong in the opposite direction from where the cloaked figure had last been, in a mad attempt to flee the roof.

In front of him, Anou Shinjirou was still sprawled out on the ground.

Shinjirou lifted his head and yelped, "Uh oh...!" Just the sight of Spooky E running back towards him was enough for him to pull himself together. He scrambled to his feet, tried to run—

But something grabbed his ankle from behind.

"Augghh!"

"You can't get away from me, boy!" Spooky E yanked Shinjirou towards him, but there was the shrill sound of something slicing through the air...

Spooky E ducked his head, a moment too late.

There was an unpleasant squishing sound.

Spooky E's right ear was torn clean off his head, spinning through the air.

"Naaaaaarrgghhh——!!!"

But Spooky E did not waver. He spun Shinjirou's body, and flung him right towards the flapping windbreaker, where a gaping hole opened onto the fifty meter drop.

"Waaaugggh?!" Shinjirou screamed.

As he flew, he thought over and over, *This is a dream! This is a dream!*

He refused to believe his life would end like this.

A newspaper headline fluttered across his mind's eye.

Junior High Student Buckles Under Exam Pressure, Commits Suicide.

Everyone would be talking about him, saying stuff like, "He was always worried," and, "He couldn't handle the stress."

And they'd all be wrong.

The idea that he died from getting mixed up in a fight between two mysterious inhuman creatures was just beyond imagining. None of them would ever guess.

He would die alone...misunderstood.

(N-no! I don't want *that*!)

From the bottom of his heart, he knew.

He had still not done anything of any real worth.

He screamed something, but he couldn't catch the meaning of his own words. He might have begged for help, but what could he say that would help him? His scream did not even reach his own ears—

* * *

Suddenly, he felt his arm twist violently backwards, his body forcefully thrust in a very different direction. Like a bungee cord reaching its length, he was shot back up into the air and yanked onto the roof.

He landed awkwardly on his back and let out a howl of pain.

Still beside himself with panic, he stared up at the black figure perched on the edge of the roof. Had it saved him? Or just deflected the enemy's attack?

"............"

The setting sun behind it kept him from seeing its expression. A strong gust of wind blew its cloak around, but failed to move the figure itself.

Glumly, it whispered, "He got away..."

Shinjirou looked around, but the hideously fat man who had raved incomprehensible things at him was nowhere to be seen.

"Oh well... At least he won't go near you again. He knows if he does, there's surely a risk of crossing paths with me again."

The cloaked figure came towards him. It was shorter than he'd thought at first.

But now that he thought about it, the girl who had been waiting for him was actually this guy in disguise, so of *course* he was tiny.

Then the letter had all just been a ruse to draw out the mysterious blubberball?

"........." He stared vacantly up at the cloaked figure.

Halfway to him, the cloaked figure bent over and picked something up off of the ground. It was the blubberball's ear, freshly severed. The cloaked figure tossed it lightly into the air, like he'd picked up a ten-yen coin.

"How did you get out from under his control? *That's* what interests me the most. Although, if I ask, I doubt you'll know. They'd hardly leave such an obvious clue."

Shinjirou was unable to grasp any meaning from those words.

The cloaked figure stopped just in front of him, reached into its cloak, and pulled out not an ear, but a letter.

"This is the real letter. You should have it. The meeting is not for today, but for the day after tomorrow. Make sure to be there," the figure instructed as it handed over the letter to Shinjirou. "I apologize for infringing on your privacy, but will you forgive me? I had no choice."

He took the letter absently, and opened it. It was in the same handwriting, and had the same words. Only the date was different.

"What does this mean?" he asked, looking up.

But the cloaked figure was gone.

There was nothing left but the wind.

* * *

Two weeks later, Anou Shinjirou passed the entrance exam for Shinyo Academy.

Boogiepop returns

VS Imaginator Part 1

VI

Not all confusion will ever be cleared up.
Sometimes it will solidify, still confused,
and attempt to judge the world.
Like a curse, affecting the world with no
rhyme or reason…

—Kirima Seiichi (*VS Imaginator*)

VI.

"PLEASE, SUEMA-SAN. Save Jin-niisan..."

I couldn't get Kinukawa Kotoe's earnest appeal out of my head. And Asukai Jin's strange behavior at the cram school...that drawing of the girl who killed herself...

I couldn't forget. Even if it wasn't someone like me—a recovering abnormal psychological behavior addict—I don't think anyone else would be able to distance themselves from the matter that easily.

Early in the morning the day after Kinukawa Kotoe had made her request, I went to the place where Minahoshi Suiko had killed herself. It was spring vacation, so I thought the place would be empty, but there was quite a crowd around the gates.

"What's going on?" I wondered.

My friend Miyashita Touka had come with me. "New students getting fitted for uniforms, and handing out the ID cards—you know, orientation crap," she said.

"Oh, yeah." Come to think of it, two years before we had done the exact same thing. I had completely forgotten.

They all looked like they were having fun. That wouldn't last long. Soon they would be back to the stress of exams, or job hunting, like we were.

"Not the mood for checking out a suicide, is it?" Touka said. "What do you think, Suema? You can go home if you like. I gotta swing by the library."

The reason she'd come with me was something about a book she'd forgotten to return. Wanted to get it back early before we had to head to cram school.

"Nah, I'll come with you."

"Okay then. Ah..." Touka made a face as we reached the gates. "That girl's here. Dang it!"

"Mm? Who?" This was unusual. Touka was not the kind of girl who disliked people easily or avoided them.

"Discipline committee president," she muttered, glumly.

I was even more surprised. "Really? Niitoki-san? But she's so nice!"

"Nah, it's all me. This and that." She put her palms together. "Sorry, gotta go!" she yelled, turning her back and darting off.

"B-but...?!" I stammered, abandoned.

Oh well, I thought, as I turned back towards the school.

The new first year students were all happily gathered around the gates which, as anyone who's ever visited our school would know, are set up with gate checks like those found at a train station. You have to actually run your ID card through it just to get in. It's completely useless! And here all the new kids were just *oohing* and *aahing* over it! If you looked really closely though, you could see only about half of them were actually excited about it—the rest seemed pretty darn alarmed.

"Excuse me, coming through," I said, pushing my way towards the gates.

"Morning, Suema-san," said the apparently problematic discipline committee president, Niitoki Kei. We've known each other since we were first year students.

"Morning. You get roped into this just because you're president?" I asked.

She laughed. "I'm not president anymore. But even so..."

"Ah, right, your term's over. It just seemed like something you'd do..."

"What's *that* supposed to mean?"

"I mean, you know, the big sister thing."

"Pot calling the kettle, Doctor."

We looked at each other and laughed.

"So what brings you here, Suema-san?"

I couldn't answer. It wasn't something to tell just anyone about. "Um... Just, you know, *stuff*."

"That Miyashita-san with you?" she said, suddenly.

I was taken aback. "Uh... Um, well..."

"She doesn't want to talk to me, huh?"

"Yeah... What's going on there? You two don't seem like you'd rub each other the wrong way..."

"Nah, that's not it. Just, uh... This and that," Kei said, meaningfully and a little forlornly.

"Is this about a boy?" I asked, on a hunch.

Kei's eyes nearly popped out of her head. She gave a nervous giggle. "...You're scary sometimes, you know that? Like you can read my mind."

"Oh... I didn't mean to..." I scrambled for the right thing to say.

But it seemed like she hadn't taken it that badly."Bingo," she said lightly. "Her boyfriend turned me down. No room for doubt—just clear and direct."

"Oh, the designer guy?"

I'd met him. He was... Well, not a *bad* guy—but that was about the extent of my impression. I think there's something about your friends' boyfriends that makes them hard to get to know.

"Right, that one," Kei said, somehow refreshed.

She was free now, I realized. She'd let him go. I was impressed. I doubt I would manage my heartbreak so neatly. I bet I'd be dragged around by it for ages, but here Kei had already put it behind her.

"If only Touka could be so relaxed about it," I muttered.

Kei laughed. "If only that were all of it. If only that were all."

"Eh? There's more?"

"I know who that girl *really* is," she said, naughtily.

"Uh... Wha—?" I asked, but the buzzer on the gate went off.

"Sorry," Kei said, and turned towards the noise.

There was a boy standing in front of the gate, looking blank. He had forgotten to run his card through.

"What's wrong?" Kei asked him.

"Ah... Nothing," he said, like his eyes weren't focusing.

The other kids were starting to cluster around.

"You all go on ahead, find your classrooms," Kei said, loudly. Her manner brooked no questions, and everyone did exactly as they were told. She had more authority than most of the teachers.

Kei pulled the boy over to the side. One girl followed him. "What's wrong, Anou-kun?" she asked, worriedly, putting her hand on his shoulder. They wore the same uniform. Looked like they were a couple moving up from the same junior high.

I don't know why, but I thought to myself how nice it must be to be a carefree youth. I was a little jealous.

"N-no...just, um..." Anou-kun stuttered, apparently shaking his head.

"........."

I knew it was nosy, but I couldn't stop watching them.

"...I just thought, why am I *here*?" Anou-kun said, like nothing made sense to him.

"What do you mean?" Kei asked, puzzled.

"I just... I feel like I lost something really, really important to come here. I don't know what..." Anou-kun muttered.

"Are you okay?"

"Anou-kun had a rough time last year," his girlfriend said.

But he just carried on, like he hadn't even heard her. "I can't figure out what it is. I haven't lost anything. I know that. I know that, but... I don't know what it was, but it was really important. The first time I'd found it..." It was like he was delirious.

Then tears started pouring down his cheeks.

I was surprised, and so were Kei and Anou-kun's girlfriend.

"Wh-what? What's wrong?"

"Anou-kun?"

"Huh?" He looked up, apparently surprised by his own tears.

He rubbed his cheeks, amazed. "Why am I crying?" he asked, bemused.

I moved away. I just couldn't watch anymore without feeling guilty.

* * *

I went around the back of the school. It was quiet. There was no one else around.

Just to be on the safe side, I looked around, making sure that I couldn't be seen.

"Okay..."

I clambered up and over the railings of the locked fire escape behind the school. This was the only route left to the roof these days. The door to the roof from the inside set of stairs was locked, and you couldn't get outside. It was locked because Minahoshi Suiko had jumped off the roof, killing herself.

The fire escape made a racket as I climbed, surprising me, so I put my feet down as softly as possible.

It was windy on the roof. Keeping my hair out of my eyes, I headed towards the spot where Minahoshi Suiko had jumped.

I knew I would gain nothing by coming up here. I wasn't Sherlock Holmes. *I can't claim that a simple visit to the scene will tell me everything, my dear Watson.*

But I hoped I would at least catch a feeling.

To be honest, despite all the books I'd read on abnormal psychology, I didn't know *squat* about suicides.

Of course, I had read interviews with the survivors of botched suicide attempts, but that was ultimately just the words of people who *didn't* die. More than half of those people made no further attempt at suicide, and just went on with their lives.

But those who actually succeeded must be dramatically different. For example, I had read an essay by a writer who had been involved in a number of attempted suicides before finally managing to die. He wrote, "I myself do not particularly want to die, but I am pulled along by my obsession with the woman." Then when he did manage to die, it was in a botched display of attempted suicide that had apparently succeeded.

But the real deal, the ones that *intentionally* die...even if they leave a note, it feels to me like they die without ever really communicating the true reason.

But what about Minahoshi Suiko?

Was she for real? Or was it a failure? Or had everyone misunderstood her, and it was only an accident? Or even worse, was it actually...

I shivered as I walked slowly forward. Then...as I reached the spot, I nearly shrieked. "————?!"

There was a girl standing there, hands on the railings, with a face so desperate she looked like she was about to jump right then and there.

* * *

Orihata Aya never asked Spooky E why she suddenly had to go to Shinyo Academy.

Even if she had, she could hardly have disobeyed, and as far as tests went, she had enough academic ability implanted in her to pass any test put in front of her, so that was no problem.

"…………"

She had come for the new students' orientation, but there was still some time left before it started, so she had gone up to the roof. She wanted to see the sky. Why the gate was barred, she didn't know, but she simply climbed right on over it.

Since she had met Taniguchi Masaki, she had begun to like looking up at the sky. When they were walking together, he would often say, "Gosh, the sky sure is beautiful." And sure enough, she had begun to think it was.

"……………"

When she looked at the sky, she felt like her body was melting, like things would be easier.

She sometimes almost believed Masaki might forgive her…

"…………"

But that was impossible.

She was unforgivable.

When she thought of all the danger she had put him in, how she had deceived him, how she had kept him from the truth… Even if he killed her, she could hardly complain.

And somewhere deep inside, Aya *wanted* Masaki to kill her.

She thought, *If that happened, what a weight off my shoulders that would be.*

Before she knew it, she was gripping the railing around the roof tightly, shaking like a leaf.

"Uh... Um," a voice stuttered from behind her.

She turned around, and a girl from this high school—her senpai—was coming hesitantly towards her.

Aya remembered her face. She had seen her before. Not directly, but in a file. Her name was Suema Kazuko.

"Yes?" Aya asked.

"No, um... I know I might have read things wrong and this may just sound stupid, but..." Suema Kazuko ventured. "But, um, if you're thinking about jumping, then, uh, please don't. Someone already jumped from there. And... And that's not good..."

"........." Aya's eyes widened.

"I... I know there's no guarantee that things will get better if you live, so it's too simple to say so. But, I mean, if you die, then the things you hate, and all those things you can't tolerate...they won't go away. So, uh, my point is..."

While Suema was rambling, she closed the gap between them, and suddenly grabbed ahold of Aya's arm.

Aya looked at that powerful grip and then at the other girl's face.

"Dying is useless. That's all I can say," Suema said forcefully, staring directly into Aya's eyes. She showed no signs of letting go.

"..........." Aya had no idea of how to clear up the misunderstanding.

Was it really a misunderstanding?

Had she, deep down, really wanted to jump?

She wasn't sure.

But either way, Suema Kazuko probably wouldn't let go. She was sure of that.

"Useless...?" Aya said, quietly.

"Yep. Perhaps you think your life doesn't have any meaning, but dying has even less."

"............"

Was that true? If she died here, then at least Masaki would be protected, indirectly.

Aya hung her head.

"I want to die," she said, letting herself say it.

Suema frowned. "Really?"

Aya nodded weakly.

"I see. But you can't now—because I found you."

Suema pulled on her arm, dragging Aya to the center of the roof. She forced her to sit down.

"I'm sorry, Suema-san," Aya whispered.

Mm? Suema looked at her, startled. "You know me?"

Oops, Aya thought, but her conditioned reflexes took over, and she said smoothly, "Yes, I know someone who goes here. They told me about you. You are Suema Kazuko-senpai, right?"

"Who...? What did you hear? Oh, nah—never mind. I can guess," Kazuko said ruefully, a little exasperated.

"I'm sorry."

In fact, her photograph had been in the follow-up subject data file. She had nearly lost her life in an incident six years before, but Suema herself had been unaware of that, so she was not even on the Towa Organization's checklist.

"No need to apologize," Suema gave her a gentle smile.

Aya was silent for a moment, then asked, "Um, Suema-senpai, can I ask you something?"

"What's that?"

"What do you think about Boogiepop?"

"Er..." Suema looked confused. "What do I think? Don't take this the wrong way, but that kind of rumor's a little..."

"You don't believe it?"

"Mmm... Yeah, basically. But more than *that*, I just don't know anything about it."

"Really? But all of the girls..."

"Yep, all of them. Except me," Suema sighed. "They all think I'm morbid... Like, I know everything there is to know about murder. So nobody ever thinks to tell me about stuff like 'Boogiepop'..."

"Oh..."

"But you know, like, that sort of killer, or shinigami or whatever... It's so *blah*. Typical adolescent imagery. Everyone's anxious about something, so part of them feels like it would be just great if everything around them were destroyed. Like they want to be killed."

"........." Aya stiffened.

"And grown-ups are all irresponsibly saying crap like, 'This period of anxiety is only a phase. Things will get better soon.' Ha! Like that helps. Things just aren't that easy, right?" Suema's shoulders slumped. "That's where he comes in."

"Huh...?"

"Boogiepop. *That's why he exists.* To protect an unstable heart and... And keep it like that. That's all he is, I think. Course, you're probably happier believing in him," Suema added with a shrug, as if joking.

This unexpected answer confused Aya. "Protect?"

"Even though he's a shinigami? But that kind of thing's the product of romanticism, bred without much knowledge of actual assassins. Anyone who's actually killed someone would never put on some goofy ass costume. I mean, *seriously*!"

"............" Aya lowered her gaze. Whatever Boogiepop was, she didn't think he would protect her. "Senpai, can I talk to you?" Her mouth moved before she thought. She had never before tried to talk to someone of her own accord like this.

"Sure," Suema nodded, so readily that Aya's little mouth opened.

"A boy...likes me," she said. "I think."

"Mm."

"But I... I'm no good. I can't do something...like that."

"Mm."

"I'm no good for him... But I don't know what to do."

"Mm."

"I'd do anything for him... But there's just nothing I can do. And instead, I'm just causing all sorts of problems for him. What can I do...?" As she talked, she found herself shaking again. Her hands clutched her own shoulders, but that couldn't stop her trembling.

"Mm," Suema nodded.

"I can't be hated by anybody. That's the way I am, but if this goes on, he's going to hate me..."

"Mm."

"But the only thing justifying my existence is that nobody hates me. But there's nothing I can do...nothing left for me to do. I'd be better off if I wasn't alive..."

"Impossible," Suema spoke at last. "It's impossible to live without someone hating you," she declared.

"Eh...?" Aya looked up.

Suema stared at her, peering into her eyes. Not accusingly, though. No, it was like the gaze of a mother looking at a sleeping child. Yet Orihata Aya had never been looked at that way before, so she was quite flustered.

"Being alive means you have to come into contact with other people. No matter how hard you try, you will end up hurting some of those people. There's nothing we can do about it. That's just life," Suema explained calmly. Her direct—yet gentle and soft—gaze made Aya feel like she was naked.

"B-but..."

"I'd bet good money that you've already made yourself several enemies. And not just any enemies. I'm talking people who hate you so much that they want to kill you," Suema said, the softness of her tone contrasting with the harshness of her words.

"..........." Aya was floored. She could form no answer. Her mouth opened, but barely formed words. "Wh-what...do you...?"

"That's the way things are," Suema said, answering without

really answering. Yet it sounded awfully convincing. She continued, "The very idea of living without being hated is detestable. You may not mean it that way, but trying to not be hated is like violating another's right to hate you. See what I mean? *You're* the one hurting *them*," she said, heatedly.

"..............." Aya simply stared back at her. Suema's gaze never wavered.

"Not to change the subject or anything, but have you ever heard of a writer named Kirima Seiichi?" Suema asked.

"Huh?" Aya snapped out of it.

Suema nodded, "Well, he's a novelist—though, uh, I still haven't gotten to actually reading any of his fiction stuff. Anyway, in one of his psychology books, he wrote: 'There certainly is *something* out there. Something that makes people believe that they have to know their place in life. This knowledge gets in between people, and rocks the very foundations of this world.'" Suema spouted this quote off smoothly from memory. She thought it was perfectly normal, but her ability to produce things like this at the drop of a hat was one reason other people were so creeped out by her. She was pretty oblivious to that fact, though.

Going on, she said, "'...If there is anything that gives value to human life, it is the struggle with that "something." In the battle with the Imaginator that does your thinking for you, *VS Imaginator* is the starting line upon which all humans must stand.' Which is pretty hard to grasp, I know. But the point is, humans are all bound by the chains of common sense far more than we realize—and this is what makes us suffer."

"Chains...?"

"Right. If we're bound by something, we've got to cut ourselves loose; that's what he's going on about." Suema spoke of this writer like most people do when using a friend as an example.

"............"

"I'm sure you have something you have to do, something that you can't live without doing. I'm not gonna ask you what that is, but that boy who likes you...he doesn't want you to be tying yourself into knots like this. That much I'm *sure* of."

"Yes." Aya nodded, hooked on Suema's words.

Suema grinned. "This is gonna sound pretty pompous, but I really think you're missing the concept of that 'struggle.' And you really need to get that."

"Yes..." Aya said. But how could she get it? Despite her uncertainty, she grit her teeth—Aya knew this girl was right.

"You can die after you fight," Suema said. "For now, let's get down from here. You're a new student, right?"

"Yes, I am..."

"Oh, no! The orientations have already started! We'd better hurry!"

* * *

I grabbed her hand and led her down from the roof.

When we reached the ground, she turned to me and bowed.

"Thank you. I don't know if I can do anything, but I'm going to try," she said.

I was a little flustered. I'm not really the best person to be dispensing life counseling. I'm more of the type to receive it. Yet it seemed like something I said must've sunken in.

"Yeah... Sorry for rambling on like that," I said, honestly.

She shook her head. "No...um, senpai...?"

"Yes?"

"If the one I have to fight is Boogiepop, then should I still fight?" she asked, deadly serious.

Naturally, I replied, "Absolutely." I knew nothing about her, but I was making sweeping declarations.

"Thank you," she said again, and turned and ran.

Suddenly I realized something, and called after her, "What's your name?"

"Orihata Aya," she said, stopping, and bowing once more.

"Good luck, Orihata-san," I waved.

And for some reason, I had the strangest feeling that I would meet her again. I don't know how I knew this, but the sharp pain in my chest said I would.

Boogiepop Returns - "SIGNS" closed.

To be continued in Boogiepop VS Imaginator

Afterword

THAT THING WITH THE POP AND THE BOOGIE

THERE'S SOMETHING CALLED pop culture. It's made up of novels, and manga, and movies, and games, and music—and just about anything else, really. Art? Nah, that's a little, you know, too artsy. Frankly, pop culture is a bit better at rocking people emotionally than the better part of the so-called fine arts. The sole standard of judgment in pop culture is the ludicrously simple concept of "what sells wins," which is nice and honest. Sells is sort of an "*eh*" term to me, so instead let's say that it finds an audience. It's a very pop culture thing to establish yourself by finding an audience. Which is true, and I tell people this, but I bet they'd say *everything* works that way. In our world, however, there *are* things that are just really damn good—no matter *what* other people say. And that sort of thing is not called pop culture. No, that's known as a lost masterpiece, or a legendary performance, or by all sorts of other names. It's not that these things aren't great—they just aren't pop.

I'm saying this in full knowledge that it might be misunderstood, but most pop culture is kind of half-assed. "The real thing is stuff, so fake stuff is better." Is that logical? People fully capable of making something real are deliberately pulling back and putting out something fake. What does this tell us? Thinking about that scares me, so I'm not going to, but this very half-assed approach is also sort of "blowing away the petrified past and opening a path to the future." (Nobody's got any idea what I'm talking about, right?) (Okay.)

The best thing about pop culture is how hard it is for it to achieve any kind of legitimacy. It's not that it never earns it, but it *is* pretty rare for it to do so. Something that was king of the hill a moment before is cast onto the compost heap a second later, while something that was long ago pronounced dated is resurrected and declared, "Innovative!" people wondering "Why did those idiots forget about this?" That's what pop is. It's pretty crazy, but within that whirlpool you do get a sense of a certain kind of necessity. Something appears, becomes huge, and then explodes, and is gone completely. Like a bubble...with a pop. Hmm, a fitting name. There's no cheap trick to get something established. A novel might win some big award, but that doesn't have the least bit of effect on sales.

To be perfectly honest, my own tastes have always been a bit disconnected from my generation. I'm the least pop person ever. I'm running around listening to stuff from twenty years ago, thirty years ago, screaming, "Awesome!" and reading books from fifty years ago. shouting, "Coool!" Yes, that kind of guy. These things aren't connecting to the pop of today at all; the only one getting excited is me. I'm a little worried about that. As someone who's trying somehow to make a living as a novelist, naturally I'm worried, and I'm trying to make myself more pop, but it just isn't working. As I can imagine you can tell from the general tone of this essay, I admire pop and have a sort of complex about it, really. But since my personality's gone and twisted itself, everything I make people say is something along the lines of "Well... it's unique," or "Is this supposed to be funny?" Which is usually followed up with "Well, *we* can't publish it..." And they're still saying it, even now.

Still, I've got to aim for pop. This is the theme of my life, so it can't be helped. If everything I make ends up being more boogie, it's not my fault... That's what I'd like to say that, except it is my fault, really. But I'm going for it, anyway. Even if it's a kind of boogie pop, then someday, I still might make the real thing.

(This guy just writes whatever crap he wants to...)
(Whatever.)

BGM "CHILDREN of the SUN" by MAYTE

Boogiepop
returns
VS Imaginator Part 2
上遠野浩平
ouhei Kadono

"I need you to be a sacrifice."
– Asukai Jin

"It is my function
to remake the world."
– Imaginator

"You don't need a reason
to do the right thing."
– Kinukawa Kotoe
"I'm not big on giving out
my name as much as he is."
– Kirima Nagi

"Is that a confession?"
– Miyashita Touka
"I have to save her…"
– Suema Kazuko

Boogiepop returns
VS Imaginator Part 2
PARADE

Boogiepop returns
VS Imaginator Part 2

written by
Kouhei Kadono

illustrated by
Kouji Ogata

english translation by
Andrew Cunningham

A new possibility…
occasionally consumes all things like itself…
before self-destructing.

—Kirima Seiichi (*VS Imaginator*)

Prelude

One year earlier...

JUST BEFORE DAWN, the coldest wind of the day swept across the world.

A girl was standing at the edge of the silent school roof.

"............"

The wind whipped her long hair about roughly, as if trying to tear it out.

Unaffected, she stared back at the shadowy figure that stood with her on the roof.

"It's a shame, really," she said, a thoroughly groundless and unsettling smile on her face. She wasn't smiling because she was happy, or was amused, or even because she was *actually* much too sad—there was no reason for it. She just smiled, but with her eyes alone—her mouth remained locked in a straight line.

"Ultimately, you are also unable to free yourself from the 'here' and 'now.' Such a shame."

"............" The other figure remained silent. It resembled a pipe more than a human with the shadow of the school building enveloping it, leaving it only partially visible.

"But no matter how long you wait, nothing will ever begin. Eventually, you will float mournfully away, just as your name suggests—vanish with a little *pop*."

She put her hand to her mouth. Her shoulders shook slightly.

She was laughing.

The gesture was incredibly natural. How was it possible for anyone to laugh so unaffectedly? It was quite a mystery.

If her feet shifted a mere ten centimeters, they would find themselves heading swiftly towards a sharp impact with the ground below. But this precarious position had no influence on her laughter.

"………"

The shadow beside her didn't move. It showed no signs of emotion. It was as if it didn't even know what laughter was.

"Don't you agree, Boogiepop?"

Addressed by name, the shadow stepped forward. "Say what you will," it said. "Either way, you are finished here. There is nothing else for you." The shadow's voice was somewhere neutrally between that of both male and female genders.

"Hmmm… Finished? Really?" The girl failed to flinch before the advancing shadow. She stood her ground. "I think I've barely begun. I don't even have a name yet…"

A cloud lit ever so slightly by the rays of the rising sun passed by in the darkened sky above. The wind was extremely strong.

"Then I shall name you now. Existences like yours were dubbed 'Imaginator' by the father of the Fire Witch."

The shadow continued towards the girl, feet never pausing.

The girl was unmoved. She nodded quietly, and said mockingly, "I read that book, too. But it's an awfully prosaic name, isn't it? It lacks romance. How unlike you."

The wind was now pulling her long black hair at an almost perfect right angle to her head, as if pouring ink into the river of air around them.

"Romance...? I know of no such thing. Only *normal* humans do," the shadow said, producing an arm from beneath the cloak that covered its body. There was a knife in its hand.

Faced with the blade's sinister gleam, the girl's lips at last curved upwards, into a look of pure confidence.

"'Love is like snow that falls in April. Unexpected, yet not unforeseen...out of season, it chills you to the core.' Who was it that said *that*?"

"......!" The shadow stopped in its tracks.

The girl had taken a step backwards, there was nothing behind her and nothing below her.

"The end of the beginning is also the beginning of the end, Boogiepop," she said. "You stopped me here—but that is just the beginning of the next ending."

With a broad smile on its face, the girl's body plunged from the roof, toward the garden below.

There was an ugly, unpleasant sound. The sound of something splattering.

"............"

The shadow stood where it was. It did not rush to the edge and look down. It did not need to.

A vision of the girl floated in thin air in front of the shadow.

"I have plenty of time before I actually hit the ground. Will you be able to find me before I do?"

The vision smiled—once again, only with its eyes.

Then it gradually faded away, melting into the air.

"............"

Left behind, the shadow stood, knife in hand.

The wind stopped.

The sudden silence gave the impression that all movement had left the world.

On the ground below, a body lay, broken open like a flower in bloom. The stain it left behind would take a great deal of time to remove.

But that was all a year ago...

I

Nightmares begin before you are aware of them. They are extremely difficult to predict or prevent.

—Kirima Seiichi (*VS Imaginator*)

I.

THE MOUNTAIN WAS NOT FAR from the city center. It had been carefully leveled off, with staircases built up the slopes. But despite the size of it, there was nobody there. The earth was exposed, with nothing growing or living on it besides a few tufts of brown grass barely managing to get through the winter alive. In a few more weeks, weeds would spring up everywhere, and the ground would look even less pleasant, but for the moment, it was simply desolate. Piles of steel and other building supplies lay abandoned, never to be used, near half-constructed towers left to forlornly rust away.

Five years before, there had been plans to turn this mountain into an amusement park; the groundwork had been completed three years previous. But after problems with the developers, the bank had repossessed the land. They had tried to put the land up for auction, but had been unsuccessful. Unable to find any buyers, the lot ended up abandoned, the amusement park construction frozen, waiting absently in the faint hope of things getting worked out.

The land was surrounded by a tall fence that cast long shadows in the sunset, like stripes across the ground.

A large, round patch of darkness fell across those stripes. Leaping down inside the fence came the silhouette of an almost spherical human. As he vaulted the two and a half meter tall fence, his graying hair flew upwards, displaying the torn up flesh where his right ear had once been.

It was Spooky E. An overloaded convenience store bag hung from his left hand. He cliczed his tongue, and fussily straightened his hair, scratching at his wound through the knotted tangles. Blood welled up, getting into his hair, but Spooky E paid it no mind and kept on scratching, putting his nails into it. It had been almost a month since his ear had been sliced off, but his incessant scratching had prevented the wound from healing. As a synthetic human, Spooky E's healing abilities were far greater than those of an average human, but he scratched it so persistently his abilities were unable to compensate.

As his fingers carved away, he walked further into the unfinished amusement park. He reached a strangely-shaped tower, like a spiral reaching towards the sky. Its entrance was blocked—not just bolted shut, but also wrapped in chains.

"..........." Spooky E never even glanced at it. He took a short step backwards, crouched down, and took a flying leap—just as he had with the fence—all the way up to the third floor and through the empty window frame.

The floor inside was covered in dust. Garbage carried by the wind was strung here and there. Kicking the mess out of his way, Spooky E stumped across the floor towards the inner staircase. The elevator was an empty shaft—though, even if it had been finished, there was no power with which to operate it.

He climbed to the top floor, which was the only one that had had glass placed into its window frames—as if the construction crew had been working from the top down.

"................."

At last, Spooky E stopped picking at his wounded ear and sat down in the middle of the empty floor, taking onigiri and a pair of sandwiches from the bag. It was his lunch, and he was starving.

As if a thought had just struck him, he took one of the cell phones that hung at his waist and dialed at an unsettling speed—all ten digits in less than a second.

The phone barely had time to ring before a girl answered. "This is Kasugai."

"Command 700259," Spooky E said, cramming an entire ham sandwich into his mouth.

"Understood," the girl said, her voice suddenly mechanical. "Command accepted. Preparation complete. Awaiting details."

"Go to the city library and get the key hidden between the Hungarian dictionary and the Hungarian phrase book."

"Understood."

"The key is for a coin locker at the station. Take the medicine inside and pour it into the drinks at the fast food restaurant you work at. One tab for every three liters."

"Understood."

"That's all. Command 700259, transmission complete."

"Understood. Transmission complete. Proceeding to action."

Spooky E hung up.

He put the phone back on his belt, took off another one, and dialed a new number.

"Who is it?" snapped an angry-sounding boy.

"Command 5400129," Spooky E muttered.

"Understood," the boy said instantly, his voice turning mechanical just as the girl's had.

"How many members are currently on your team?"

"Seven."

"Not enough. Make it twelve. This week."

"Understood. How?"

"I don't *care*. Threaten them, force them—just get them in your group."

"Understood."

"When you have twelve, take to the streets and cause a disturbance between Sixth and Eighth Street. Report who fights back."

"Understood."

In this instance, "disturbance" meant extortion and theft.

As he was speaking, a different phone on Spooky E's waist began vibrating.

Unhurriedly, Spooky E continued his conversation with the boy. Finally, he concluded with, "That's all. Command 5400129, transmission complete."

"Understood."

Only then did he answer the incoming call. "What?!"

"FS450036 Periodic Report." The voice sounded like an adult woman in her late twenties. Once again, it lacked expression and was totally mechanical.

"Any problems?"

"70% of the spiked cream has been sold. 70% of all customers have come back to the shop, but there have been no noticeable changes."

"Send the details like always. Begin stage two on the spiked customers, regardless of results."

"Understood."

Spooky E continued thusly, munching on convenience store junk food in the forgotten, deserted location while giving instructions to the "Terminals" he had brainwashed and hidden throughout the city. He made a seemingly endless series of calls and received an equally endless number. How many people had he brainwashed? An unimaginable number, apparently. He was like a scalper with tickets for all the hottest gigs.

His contacts were divided into roughly two camps: those who gave people drugs and those who observed the results.

But there were also a few unrelated calls:

"They say he comes out near the expressway overpass."

"Someone saw him running along the river."

"Rumor has it a shadow like him was seen on the Twin City roof."

Such calls always made Spooky E sullen—especially the third one, during which he shouted, "I know!" into the phone.

"Shit!" he roared, once the flood of calls subsided. "God *damn* that Boogiepop!"

He ground his teeth so hard that blood spurted out of his ear stub. He thrust his hand into the plastic bag, but it was empty, simply making a dismal rustle.

"Son of a bitch!"

He tore the bag to pieces.

Flinging the garbage aside, he stomped up to the tower roof, footsteps echoing.

(Unforgivable! I'm gonna tear him apart with my bare hands!!)

On the roof, a strong wind was blowing, just like it had when he had faced his "enemy."

(He mentioned the Manticore, that fugitive Tarkus was after. But it sounds like he already finished it off… I'm not telling Axis about him, though! He's *my* prey! Nobody else's!)

He glared at the seven cylinders that stood on the roof.

They didn't really stand out much among the other building supplies left abandoned there. Even if someone were to notice them, they would never have guessed they had been placed there much later. But inside each of them was a disinfectant strong enough to bring "death" to every living thing in the surrounding area.

(If it comes to it, I'll use these on him if I have to.)

Blood spurted out of his ear stump again. He stopped it with his hands and whispered, "But… but that other name he said… 'Imaginator.' What the hell is *that*?"

Spooky E stood glumly for a moment, then his expression suddenly sharpened and he glared down at the park below the building.

"Mm…?"

Someone was standing at the locked gate at the park's entrance.

It was a woman—no, a girl. And it looked as though she was dressed in her uniform, on her way home from high school.

She did something at the gate and—surprisingly—the lock opened. She had a key.

"Well, now…" Spooky E grinned and watched the girl enter the park.

"Ow! Damn, cut myself!" Kinukawa Kotoe sucked the tip of her finger, scratched by one of the barbs on the fence surrounding the abandoned amusement park. The taste of blood filled her mouth. "What am I *doing*?"

She reached into her school bag and took out one of the band-aids she always had with her, decorated with cartoon rabbits, and wrapped it around her wound.

She felt very childish. Like she was three years old again.

Nobody knew she had a key to the half-finished Paisley Park construction site. One of the countless companies with a claim on the ground belonged to her father and when he had brought the master key home, Kotoe snuck out of the house with it and made a copy.

Ever since, it had become her secret hideout when she was feeling depressed.

The buildings in the park had been abandoned just after construction began, so they looked more like abstract sculptures than anything else, and the curved walking paths were all bare, waiting patiently for beautiful tiles to be laid upon them. But as Kotoe felt as if she was about to cry a river as she walked by and looked at the buildings.

It was a very lonely place, and while she might have been a cheerful girl at home and at school, something about the desolate, deserted park tugged at her heartstrings. She had never told anyone about it, but...part of her was convinced that she belonged in a place like this. It was like there was something fundamental missing inside of her—a draft blowing through the cracks in her heart.

This place, where they had tried to build a spectacular amusement park, was now a forgotten, pathetic little dream—the kind of dream everyone has when they are young, but never achieves, only to become abandoned with time. Kotoe felt like she had never had that sort of dream at all.

Of course, this seventeen-year-old girl was not consciously aware of this. But she indistinctly felt it, and this sadness remained inside of her, refusing to melt away.

She walked on through the ruins, painted by the light of the setting sun.

As she did, she thought about the only thing she *ever* thought about these days—her cousin, Asukai Jin.

(Jin-niisan...)

She first met Asukai Jin when she was five years old, and she remembered it clearly, even now.

Jin's father had come to borrow money from his younger

brother—Kotoe's father—and Jin had come along with him. He must still have been in elementary school.

She had only seen him from a distance.

Kotoe's father had taken his wife's name, Kinukawa, and behaved like the rightful heir, much more so than Kotoe's docile mother. He had thundered, "Stop begging," to his brother.

But Jin's father had persisted until Jin had said, quietly, "Uncle Kouji's right, Father. Nobody would lend money to someone who just wants it and has no plan for how they're going to use it."

When that clean boy soprano cut through the tension in the drawing room (decorated perfectly to her father's tastes), Kotoe had the strangest feeling that this boy would take her away from everything—away from this life where she lacked nothing but could scarcely breathe.

Much to her father's surprise, his brother agreed with his son Jin. He abandoned his attempts to beg for money based solely upon familial blood ties and instead began to explain the details of his business plan.

Kotoe didn't really understand the conversation from that point on, but ultimately, Kotoe's father did end up lending his brother some money. What Kotoe remembered especially was how Jin's farewell showed far better manners than his father's.

He seemed so noble.

He was her first love.

She had looked forward to seeing him again, but it turned out that the start-up business that Jin's father had founded with the borrowed money had gone bust. They didn't return to Kotoe's house for a very long time. Occasionally, her father would refer to his brother as "that good-for-nothing," which always made Kotoe extremely sad.

Four years passed before Kotoe met Jin again.

Father and son called at the Kinukawa home once more. The father was extremely well-dressed, and—surprisingly—he returned the money that he had borrowed. Plus interest.

Kotoe's father muttered, "Normally, you would also have to pay damages..." but was clearly happy to have the money back.

"But how did you get it?" he asked, but Jin's father just grinned.

His son sat next to him, in the uniform from his junior high school. He didn't appear bored by the grown ups' conversation, but he also did not appear to be excessively interested either. He blended in so easily. Kotoe, who was watching from the shadows, was mystified by this.

"Say, Kouji, would you like a painting?" Jin's father asked.

"Painting?"

"First rate artists only. I'm in that line of work now."

"*You* sell paintings? You got a D in art! How do you know you aren't selling fakes?"

"I leave all that up to him," Jin's father said, pointing at his son. "He's a genius. He's won all sorts of awards for his paintings."

"Really? But even so..."

"His eye is amazing. We buy stuff up at paltry sums, and a year later that artist explodes and we sell it for ten times the price," he said proudly.

Even when praised, the boy stayed quiet.

"Oh? So someday you might become a great artist like Picasso, Jin?" Kotoe's father asked, addressing his nephew for the first time.

"That's my dream, sir," the boy replied, without a trace of arrogance. His manner proved that he was the most together person in the room, Kotoe thought.

He knew what everyone in the room was thinking, and acted accordingly. He was perfectly at ease, yet never gave off even a hint of being such.

The evening developed into a drinking party, and Jin and his father spent the night at Kotoe's house. Kotoe wanted desperately to talk with Jin, but he never left his father's side, meaning she had no chance to do so.

Only once, when Jin went to the kitchen to get a glass of water for his father's stomach pills, was she able to say, "Um..." There she was, standing in front of him, the moment she'd been longing for.

"Oh, sorry. Can I get some water?" he asked politely.

"C-certainly!" Kotoe replied.

Her mother said, "What a good boy," and handed him a cup of water.

He bowed his head, and left.

Kotoe wanted to call after him, but she couldn't think of anything to say, and so she could only watch him leave. But that evening, when Kotoe woke in the middle of the night and came down to the kitchen for a drink, she found Jin standing alone in the garden, looking up at the night sky.

It was winter outside, and all he had on were the pajamas they'd found for him, so it must have been terribly cold out.

He looked so sad. She'd never seen him look anything but calm, so Kotoe was a little shocked.

She wanted to know what he was thinking about, but she thought it must be something difficult that she wouldn't be able to understand. This meant she didn't know what to do. So she stood there for a while, and eventually he turned and spotted her.

"Ah...!" she exclaimed, and he bowed his head, and came over to the outside of the house.

Kotoe hurriedly unlocked the window. "Wh-what are you doing?" she asked. When she opened her mouth, a white cloud came out.

"Sorry, didn't mean to surprise you," he said. "I was just wondering if it would snow."

"Snow?"

"Yeah. It looked like it might, but..."

"You like snow?"

"Yeah. Childish of me, huh?" He grinned.

"Aren't you cold?" she asked and instantly regretted it. What a stupid question.

But he didn't seem to notice. "Sure, it's cold. I was just about to come inside," he said softly, bobbed his head, and walked away.

Kotoe watched him go once more.

At the time, they were just relatives. They had no other connection. So once again, quite some time passed without the two of them seeing each other.

(But...)

Kotoe stopped in front of the most eye-catching remnant,

a spiral tower that was to have been named "The Ladder." Like Asukai Jin had done as a boy, she looked up at the sky.

But of course, it was not snowing—it was April, after all.

(But...Jin-niisan's father, so awful...)

His cause of death was still unclear.

He had been walking along the street and then suddenly vomited up blood and fell over. It was all so sudden that the police suspected he'd been poisoned.

But there were no traces of anything like that. Witnesses had said that just before his death, he'd eaten lunch at a perfectly ordinary family restaurant. Nobody who worked at the restaurant had any connections to him. It clearly hadn't been poison.

Even so, the whole ordeal had left Asukai Jin orphaned.

"We should help him," Kotoe said.

Her mother asked, "Why don't we adopt him?"

But since her father had married into the family, he felt it would never do for him to take in his brother's child. Besides, Asukai Jin himself refused to entertain such notions, telling them not to worry.

His father's business was handed off to others, and most of the inheritance went to various debts and obligations, but Jin quickly secured a full scholarship to an art school, and a job as a cram school teacher took care of his living expenses. Very efficient.

Kotoe was somewhat relieved. If they had adopted him, then she would have become his sister. It was a dream, sure—yet as long as they were cousins, the possibility remained.

But no matter how quickly Asukai Jin had taken charge of his situation, that sad boy who stared up at the night sky remained. Kotoe could still see it in him.

He had some sort of burden. He'd carried it for a very long time.

(And yet...)

Recently, Jin had been acting strangely—wandering around all night long, coming back with what looked like bloodstains on his clothes...and even worse, he was oddly cheerful. Of course, he had always been affable, easy to get along with, and well liked, and none of that hadn't changed. But still...

The only person who had listened to her problems was a girl from her school named Suema Kazuko. They weren't close enough to be called friends, but she had listened carefully and told her, "Why don't you leave things up to me?"

She had telephoned later and added, "I'll clear things up, but until then, you'd better stay away from him." Which meant Kotoe hadn't seen Jin for a while.

Suema Kazuko seemed reliable, and she would probably be able to figure things out far better than Kotoe herself could ever manage. But she still missed him.

"Jin-niisan..." she whispered, looking up at the red sky.

"Is that your man's name?" a voice asked from behind her.

Surprised, she tried to turn around, but the electric monster's hands had already latched onto each side of her head.

There was a crackle, and then she could feel her brain's functions rudely interrupted.

"............?!"

Kinukawa Kotoe was unconscious.

"Her name's Kinukawa Kotoe, and she's seventeen, eh?" Spooky E had gone through the pockets of his newly acquired prey, and found her Shinyo Academy student ID.

"So *that's* how she had a master key," the monster whispered, glancing over towards a sign at the side of the park. The name "Kinukawa Enterprises" was printed on it.

"Damn, she's loaded..."

Had she been awake, she would have shuddered at the sight of the sinister smile that split Spooky E's face from ear to ear. His big round eyes stayed wide open, making it even more horrible.

"That means she's got cash. Perfect. I can use her to find this 'Imaginator.'"

The monster licked his fingers, and thrust his saliva-drenched hands into Kotoe's beautifully treated hair.

The next thing she knew, Kinukawa Kotoe was walking along the street at night. She was herself again.

"..............."

However, she failed to wonder what she had been doing all this time. She was neither surprised nor confused.

"..............."

The street was filled with clusters of people, freed from the stress of the day: older men, faces already flushed with booze, young lovers chattering happily in cafes...

She ignored this peaceful world, headed straight for an ATM, and began withdrawing money. It was early in the month, so there was no one else in line.

The machine had a limit of 300,000 yen per transaction; she withdrew this in full ten times. Three million yen in all. Without so much as flinching, she put the bills into her school bag and headed directly to a nearby dance club.

Once before, a friend had taken her there. Kotoe herself had been unable to get swept up in the crowd's enthusiasm for the indie band's passionate, but unskilled performance, and she had never gone back. But now, without the slightest trace of hesitation, she headed straight down the stairs to the dimly lit basement entrance. She paid the five thousand yen cover charge (which came with a free drink) and went in. Her ears were instantly filled with a horrific noise. Kotoe never glanced at the band wailing away on stage, or the audience, bobbing their heads and waving their arms around. No, she headed straight for the drink counter.

"'Sup?" asked the spiky-haired, punk-styled guy behind the counter, listlessly. He put a paper cup in front of Kotoe.

Ignoring the drink entirely, Kotoe said, "I have a question."

"Mm?"

"You ever heard of the Imaginator?"

The punk's expression changed the moment the word left her mouth. "Wh-what...?"

"You have?" she said.

"No, never!"

"Liar," Kotoe declared.

The punk flinched. He leaned over and whispered in her ear,

"I don't know where the hell you heard that anme, but you really shouldn't say it out loud. It might—"

Before he could finish, a man sitting in the corner interrupted, saying, "What? The Imaginator?" He was a two-meter tall skinhead. "Where'd you hear that name, high school girl? You know where that asshole is?"

The man advanced on her, the thick soles of his boots so loud they were easily heard above the racket on stage.

"That asshole? This Imaginator is an individual?" Kotoe said. Clearly, the man had failed to frighten her in slightest.

"*I'm* the one asking questions!" he yelled, grabbing the collar of her uniform and lifting her into the air. "Don't piss me off! Everyone in my band's screwed up now, all thanks to that Imaginator freak! What the hell did he do to them?!" The veins stood out on his bare scalp.

Swinging around at the end of his arm, Kotoe shook with the waves of his anger. But all she did was simply ask, quietly, "So, the Imaginator does something to people and moves them over to its side? Is it through religion or something?"

The skinhead frowned at her, puzzled.

"How exactly were they changed?" she continued.

"Girl, who *are* you?" he asked, putting her down.

He'd been sure she was just some cocky kid, but there was something far stranger about her behavior.

Kotoe gave an enigmatic smile. "Just in case things aren't perfectly clear, I'm not asking for any favors." She pulled a wad of cash out of her bag. 100,000 yen. "I'm *buying* information."

The skinhead's eyes bugged out of his head. "Who *are* you?" he said again.

"No friend of the Imaginator," she purred.

"...I've never seen the Imaginator directly. But I know a guy who saw something goin' down on some back road."

They had shifted location to the empty locker room, where the skinhead had started talking.

"Something?"

"His words. He wasn't really sure what. But there were several of them, and the Imaginator sent them all flyin'. Yeah, that's what he said—not punched, not kicked, not even beat—he just sent them flyin'!

"The guys who got beat weren't pussies or anythin'. This isn't just some tough guy winning a street fight. This is bigger than that. After the dudes went flying, they all stood up and started pinning down their buddies that were still standing. Their own buddies! This Imaginator turned them against each other!

"So no matter how badly you get messed up, you can never lay a finger on the Imaginator. Everyone that's crossed paths with that creep ends up slammed into the pavement, pukin' blood. I seriously don't know what he is. Must be some kinda monster. Like Dracula, or somethin'."

"What happened to the people he beat up? Have you talked to them?"

"They... they were... I mean..."

"Your friends were different?"

"I saw Tsuyoshi only once after. He was walking through town alone. We never really got along that well, but since everyone else had up and vanished on me, I called out to him. He turned around, looked happy to see me."

"How is that strange?"

"He's the type that always snarls, 'Shut the hell up' when you speak to him. Least if he's alone. He's usually always with some chick. But that time he was grinning, like someone had...stripped all his thorns off. Creepy calm."

"Where had he been?"

"He said he hadn't been anywhere in particular. Insisted it was just a coincidence we hadn't bumped into each other until then. At the time, I still hadn't heard about the Imaginator, so I didn't know Tsuyoshi'd gone up against him. I only heard about that later. So at the time, I was just confused. But I haven't seen him since. He won't answer his damn phone."

"You been to their houses?"

"Nope. No idea where he lives. Never asked."

"Is that what bands are like these days?"

"Hey, I thought it was a little sad, too," the skinhead protested weakly. "But everyone else seemed cool with it, so I guess I just went with the flow, you know? Anyway, everything else aside, it seemed like he was basically a nice guy deep down."

Kotoe sniggered, "So? This Imaginator... This guy heard him give his name?"

"Yeah..."

"What did he sound like?"

"Prim and stuck up, apparently. Said, 'If you must, you may call me the Imaginator'—whatever the hell *that* means."

"He didn't see him?"

"Nah, he was hiding. Oh, that reminds me..."

"What?"

"White. He said he saw a figure in white."

For reasons she didn't understand, Kotoe was badly shaken by this. "WHAT?!"

The skinhead was surprised by her sudden, strong reaction.

"Wh-what? You know someone that wears white?"

"........." Kotoe had been programmed to suppress all unnecessary memories, so she was utterly unable to determine the cause for her surprise. She had a vague feeling that she knew a man who always dressed in white, but she couldn't remember who.

The faint roar of the musicians and the audience, like the sound of a swarm of insects, swirled around her, hurting her ears.

"N-no..." Kotoe said, shaking her head as if trying to clear out the confusion. "Never mind."

"So who are you?" the skinhead asked. "Why are you after the Imaginator?"

"Don't you want revenge?" Kotoe suddenly asked, out of left field.

"For those guys?" The skinhead looked dubious.

"You'd rather leave them to their fate?" she said. "Fine by me..."

"Not that!" he yelled, turning red. He leapt to his feet, kicking over the folding chair he'd been sitting on.

"Then do as I say," Kotoe smirked, looking up at him.

She opened her bag, and took out the rest of the money. She dumped it on top of the table.

The skinhead gaped.

"Use this to gather all the people you can. We're going to hunt the Imaginator down."

"That's… that's a lot of money," the skinhead gulped.

"Not to me," Kotoe said, unperturbed.

"What if I take the money and run?" he asked. Like good guys always do.

"No skin off of my teeth," Kotoe said, cool as cucumber. "I'll just know you're a *coward*."

"…………!"

"But if you're going to swindle me, you should wait a little longer. There's more where that came from," Kotoe said, broadening her grin. No matter how big her smile became, her eyes never narrowed.

Just like Spooky E.

Boogiepop returns

VS Imaginator Part 2

II

Rather than ask yourself
if you are correct,
It is far more realistic to think
about how you are mistaken.
Most humans have not been
designed to be right very often.

—Kirima Seiichi (*VS Imaginator*)

II.

MY NAME IS Taniguchi Masaki. I became a high school student this past April, and about a month ago, I began imitating—okay, maybe just cosplaying as—the legendary Boogiepop.

It was the first time I'd ever fallen in love with a girl, so I got carried away and did whatever Orihata Aya told me—even if that meant dressing all in black like some sort of shinigami and walking around acting like a superhero. What's crazy is that I still have no idea why she wanted me to do all this.

But every time she called me, I'd come running. I made fun of myself awhile for it, but just being with Orihata was the best time I'd ever had.

Then, early one Sunday, as I was tying the laces on my sneakers and getting ready to leave, my sister popped up behind me.

"Hey, Masaki..."

"What, Nagi?" I said, not turning around.

"You've been out of the house a lot lately."

"Have I?"

"And back late, too. What's going on?"

My sister always sounds a little harsh, but she's fundamentally a nice person.

"*You're* out all night too, Oneechan," I said, smiling.

But this time she wasn't letting me get out of it that easily. "Same thing, every time?"

"Same what?"

"You don't look like you're off to meet a girl. Your clothes aren't nice enough. You used to dress better."

"………"

I was wearing a pretty shabby T-shirt, a pair of 3,000 yen jeans, and a cheap windbreaker. I'd be disguised as Boogiepop anyway, so I hadn't put a lot of thought into it.

"Where are you going?" she asked, leaning forward and peering into my eyes.

Less peering than glaring.

"N-nowhere special," I said, feeling a bead of sweat roll down my neck. This was not how my sister usually acted. She was a lot more intense today.

Nagi grabbed my hand. It was so sudden that it startled me.

"Wh-what?" I stuttered.

"Nice calluses," she said, stroking the back of my hand. "You practicing karate?"

"Um, y-yeah. A little. I'd been slacking off for a while, so…" I stammered to a stop.

"You're pretty strong," she said, like she was accusing me of something.

"Oh, not really…"

"Sakakibara-sensei warned you about the danger of being strong, yeah? Get cocky, and you'll get creamed."

Sakakibara-sensei was my karate shishou, and an old friend of Nagi's deceased father.

"Yeah, I remember. He said that so many times I still hear it in my sleep."

"But do you really understand it?" She moved her face right up against mine. My sister's a beautiful girl, and we aren't actually related, so when those red lips came towards me... But the atmosphere around us was about as unerotic as you could get. The air was chilly, and it left me shivering.

"Y-yeah," I gulped, nodding. I felt like a frog transfixed in a snake's glare.

"Then...okay." At last, she let me go.

I fumbled as I tied my laces and staggered out the door.

On my back, where she'd touched me, there was a wet patch of sweat, like I'd been standing next to a fire.

(They say girls are scary, but Nagi-neesan's freaking terrifying!)

I shivered again, lowered my head, and plunged into the chilly April wind.

When I entered the cafe where Orihata and I were supposed to meet, I saw something unexpected.

Like always, Orihata had arrived first; she was sitting there, waiting for me. No matter how fast I tried to get there, she was always there first. That wasn't the unexpected part, though.

No, today, there was someone else sitting next to her. Not

across from her, mind you. No, the other side of the counter was empty. This person was next to her, and it was another girl.

"Oh, is that your boyfriend? Ha ha! Right, he *is* handsome," the new girl said, looking at me, then grinning at Orihata. I disliked her instantly.

"Masaki, this..." Orihata stammered. She couldn't figure out what to tell me.

"Friend of yours?" I asked her, carefully avoiding eye contact with the other girl.

"From school... My senpai."

"Kinukawa Kotoe," she said, standing up and holding out her hand. "Nice to meet you, Taniguchi Masaki-kun."

"Yeah," I said, reluctantly shaking her hand.

She giggled. "Boy, you sure don't hesitate to take a girl's hand, do you? Must be experienced. Will make things easier for Orihata-san someday, huh?" She said lewdly. It wasn't like she was making fun of me—it was more like she was trying to provoke me.

"Who are you?"

"Orihata-san's friend. Just like you."

"...?"

She released my hand and slapped me on the shoulder. "Right, Boogiepop-san?"

I looked at Orihata. She gave me a tiny nod. "Kinukawa-san knows everything."

"Orihata-san told me all about it," "Kinukawa-san" said brightly. "I knew I had to help."

This wasn't exactly working for me. "What do you want?"

"You don't need a reason to do the right thing," she said reasonably, but the phrase, in this case, was just screwy.

"........." I silently picked up the check. "Uh, Orihata, come with me for a minute."

"Oh, I don't mean to get in your way," Kinukawa laughed.

Sullenly, I said, "I'll pay for this, so take your time."

Then I took Orihata's hand and pulled her out of the seat.

We left the shop, and Kinukawa waved at us through the window. I walked quickly away and hid beneath the bridge.

"Um, Masaki..." Orihata tried to say.

I interrupted her. "What did she do to you?"

"Nothing..."

"Who the hell does she think she is? Did she threaten you?"

"Nothing like that, really," Orihata said, looking distressed.

I backed down. "Then what? She doesn't look like a friend at all."

"........."

"If you're in some sort of trouble, I could..." I began, hands clenching into fists.

"No!" Orihata cried, turning pale, and grabbing my hand.

I took a deep breath. My sister's voice floated through my head, "Get cocky, and you'll get creamed."

"O-okay, then... Sorry. But at least tell me why that girl knows about Boogiepop," I asked, staring at her.

She avoided my gaze, staring at the ground. She looked like she was searching for a lie, which pissed me off.

"...She saw the clothes," Aya managed, obviously lying.

"Where? At school?" Masaki asked. The edge in his tone made it clear he didn't believe her.

"In my apartment. She's my landlord's daughter."

This was true, but she couldn't tell him that her personality had been changed by Spooky E.

"What?" Masaki asked, surprised. This rang a bell. He growled, "There *was* a sign saying Kinukawa Enterprises..." He had been to Aya's apartment building several times, and seen the sign next to the door. "So what does she want?"

"Well..."

The truth was this:

Yesterday, she had received orders from Spooky E, saying that a girl named Kinukawa Kotoe would be coming over and that Aya should do whatever she said. Kotoe had shown up at Aya's apartment shortly after.

The moment she laid eyes on her, Aya knew Spooky E had spent quite a lot of time working on her. Her expression was exactly like Spooky E's, but she was less his arms and legs and more like an independently functioning copy.

"It's a good thing you live in Kinukawa Kotoe's territory," what should have been Kotoe herself said, laughing. "We're gonna use this as a base while we hunt down the Imaginator."

"The Imaginator...?"

"You don't need to know. But there will be a few men coming by, so let them in, and do whatever they ask you to."

Aya stiffened at this. She was sure "whatever" covered a lot more than cooking.

"B-but then Masaki will..."

"Like I said, you're almost finished with that boy. Time to cut him loose. Or are you still going on about how you don't want him to hate you?"

"Th-the Towa Organization t-told me not to be h-hated by anyone, so..."

"The Towa Organization? You still think you're working for them?"

Kotoe shoved Aya hard. She fell over backwards.

Kotoe then kicked her in the cheek. Aya couldn't dodge at all, and the blow cut the inside of her mouth, spilling blood out from between her lips. Kotoe continued to hurt Aya, and Aya never resisted.

Had Kotoe had any free will left, she would have undoubtedly shrieked, "Stop!" in Aya's place. But no one there was capable of halting the violence.

"The Towa Organization forgot about you years ago! You are nothing but a tool for me—for Spooky E, to use how *I* see fit!"

"Yes..."

"And where the hell do you get off, getting all picky about men *now*?! Can you even count how many men you've taken since you left the institution?"

"No..."

"All on the pretext of some experiment to see if normal and synthetic humans could crossbreed—but you never managed to get knocked up, did you? Which means you're just a useless whore!"

"Yes..."

"All the successes I've had and I get no luck at all! Why should a failure like you get to have all the fun? You piece of shit! You little bitch!"

Rage that had nothing to do with Kotoe's body, but everything to do with the knowledge and personality overwriting hers, came pouring out.

But all the expressionless Aya did was answer mechanically, "Yes..."

The beating continued a little while longer, but at last Kotoe grew out of breath, and she stopped.

"Hmph! Get up and make me some food. Kinukawa Kotoe's body has moved too much and is demanding nutrition."

"Yes..."

Swaying, Aya got to her feet.

She took her own convenience store bento and put it in the almost unused built-in microwave. Standing there, waiting for it to warm up, Aya's eyes were vacant. But her lips were faintly trembling. Not from fear, but rather because she was whispering something under her breath. She spoke quietly that no one else could hear, so quietly the sound did not even reach her own ears, repeating over and over:

"I must save Masaki, I must save Masaki, I must save Masaki, I must save Masaki, I must save Masaki, I must save Masaki, I must save Masaki, I must save Masaki, I must save Masaki,

I must save Masaki, I must save Masaki..."

...And then this morning, Spooky E had ordered Aya to bang Taniguchi Masaki. It was her last chance to test if crossbreeding with him was even possible. The cruelest joke he could make, though, was to send his copy, Kinukawa Kotoe, along to watch. It was like pouring salt directly into her wounds.

But she couldn't tell Masaki any of this.

"I..."

"You can't tell me?" Masaki said, sadly.

"It... it's all my fault," she managed.

"Okay," Masaki nodded, like he had made up his mind about something.

Aya hoped that this had made Masaki hate her. After all, Spooky E had said her orders (to not be hated and to not make trouble) were no longer active. There was no one to criticize her for being hated. If hating her saved him, then she wanted him to hate her.

Her own feelings were another problem.

"In that case, we should stop playing Boogiepop," Masaki said, curtly.

"Yes," Aya said, still staring at the ground. This was for the best, she thought.

But his next words shocked her...

"So, I'll take that," he said, and took the Nike bag out of Aya's hands.

"Hunh?" Aya's eyes widened. The Boogiepop costume and makeup were in the bag.

"I'm going to keep doing this without you," Masaki said.

Ultimately, I was just angry.

Kinukawa's attitude had pissed me off, and I was annoyed that Orihata couldn't tell me about it. But more than anything, I was furious with myself for happily dressing up as Boogiepop without once trying to figure out why Orihata wanted me to do so.

"M-Masaki?" Orihata asked, surprised. "What do you mean?"

"Like I said...I'm going on alone. I don't need your help anymore," I snapped.

I had assumed I was playing Boogiepop because Orihata wanted me to.

But judging from that Kinukawa woman's attitude, Orihata had not been doing that of her own free will.

I'd been useless. By trying to make her happy, I'd simply driven her into a corner.

"But why?! You don't have to do anything anymore, Masaki!!"

"No, *you* don't!" I shouted, angry. "Why didn't you ever tell me you really didn't want me to be Boogiepop? If you'd just *said* something, you never would've had to have been bait!"

"I..." Orihata stammered.

"I didn't *want* to put you in danger like that! But I thought it was what you wanted, so...!" I trailed off, losing track of what I wanted to say.

Both of us stood there in the darkness, glaring at each other stupidly, shaking.

Finally, "Why... why are you... I just..." Orihata whispered, sounding exhausted.

For no real reason, this made me angry again.

"Goodbye!" I roared, turning my back on her, and walking away. I couldn't bear to be in that conversation another second.

All she'd done was use me—and for something she hadn't even wanted. That's how I understood the situation. So what did that make me?

All I'd done was to think cheerily that being with her was all I needed.

"Shit, shit, shit, shit, shit!"

I swung the bag filled with Boogiepop stuff around me as I ran, tears streaming down my cheeks. I was incredibly ashamed. Dressing up as Boogiepop was far less embarrassing than this.

In my mind, I screamed, *I'll be a superhero as long as I damn well feel like it!*

"Masaki!" Aya shrieked, and tried to chase after him.

But someone grabbed her shoulder roughly from behind.

"Wait, Camille," he said. It was Spooky E. He had been secretly watching the entire time.

"L-Let go of me!" She tried to fling him off. But Spooky E was inhumanly strong, and Aya's body might as well have been in a vise for all the freedom of movement he'd left her.

"Change of orders. Forget about him," Spooky E sneered.

"Eh?"

"Looks like he's going to keep doing Boogiepop on his own. Saves us the bother."

"What do you mean?"

"Sooner or later, they're gonna find Boogiepop's corpse lying in an alley somewhere. Then everyone'll know the truth behind the legends. It was just some heartbroken idiot!" Spooky E guffawed.

Aya's face turned white. "W-was...?!"

Was *that* what "cut him loose" meant? Kill Masaki as the "real" one publicly, and make the real one "fake"? Was that Spooky E's plan? If that drew the real Boogiepop out of hiding, then great—and if not, well, at least Spooky E would have cheered himself up.

He was planning to kill Masaki!

"Y-you can't!" Aya cried, grabbing Spooky E. The shoulder he was holding felt like it was going to pop. A second later, electricity ran from Spooky E's hands, coursing through Aya's body. It rattled her bones, her spinal cord, her brain. Every one of her nerves shook, and her skin quivered.

"Aaaauuuugh!" Her head flung back, the walls of her nostrils tore open, and blood shot out.

(M-Masaki...!)

Even now, her immobile body was struggling to escape Spooky E's shocking grasp.

Electricity raced through her again.

"———!" She fell unconscious.

"Bwa ha ha ha ha ha ha ha ha ha ha ha ha ha ha ha ha ha!" Spooky E's laughter echoed on and on through the deserted space below the bridge.

But what was Boogiepop?

"Hah...hah...hah..." I ran till I was gasping for breath, then collapsed on the sidewalk, and started thinking.

Orihata had no family, apparently. But there had to be some sort of reason why she could live in such a nice apartment building.

And if that reason had some connection to the crazy legends of a black cloaked shinigami boy...

(...Then what?)

How the hell did that have anything to do with that ludicrous outfit?

Certainly not money. She'd thrown away drugs worth millions without so much as a second thought. If it was that type of syndicate, they'd hardly do something so wasteful. But her actions themselves did seem productive as far as cleaning up the city.

You're a hero, Masaki. Aya had said to me once, and those words suddenly echoed through my head again.

(Damn it!)

Tears welled up once more. She'd been acting, but I couldn't stop the burning feeling in my chest. But this was no time for crying.

I had to calm down, and decide what to do.

I looked around myself, and made sure no one else was there, then sat cross-legged on the pavement. I closed my eyes, and began meditating.

My shishou once said, *When you are in trouble, at least maintain the appearance of control. Pretend to be calm. This may actually trick you into cooling down.*

For a karate instructor, he never once said anything about spirit or mental focus. He'd get angry every time he saw me frowning. All in all, I must say, it was a rather strange way of learning.

Imagine a staff in your heart. Decide your direction by letting it topple over. The less logic you force into your imagination, the better the results.

But the staff in my heart just spun round and round, and never once started to fall.

At times like this, the way you are tackling the problem is mistaken. You are trying to decide something that cannot be decided. The first thing you need to do is look for that which you can.

...I was starting to feel like shishou was whispering in my ear.

(*Okaaay...*)

Did I hate Orihata?

...No, I didn't.

Did I dislike being Boogiepop?

...Not true either.

Was I trying to poke my nose in something way over my head?

...Yeah, probably.

Was this because I wanted to be Boogiepop, so I could beat up people?

...No, not really. Not that at all.

Then what?

...I don't know. But I can't just do nothing. I think I have to do something.

What was it I had to be careful of?

...Don't get carried away. Shishou always said that. And...

"—Nagi-neesan," I said aloud and opened my eyes. "Right. I can't go home, then." I couldn't get her mixed up in this. That had been bugging me.

(She'll be pissed...)

I stood up, dusted myself off, and managed a feeble grin.

Here I was, just starting high school, and already I was gonna be skipping.

If I'd known I was gonna end up like this, I wouldn't have been so careful in junior high...

"Ha ha! I sure was an *idiot*!"

Hoisting the Boogiepop bag over my back, I headed off down the street.

Boogiepop returns

VS Imaginator Part 2

III

When humans think something
is absolutely correct,
In most cases, that truth is
already in the past.

—Kirima Seiichi (*VS Imaginator*)

"WHAT IS IT, SUEMA?"

We were waiting in line at the bus stop in front of our school when I suddenly stepped out of line, much to the surprise of my friend Miyashita Touka, who was standing behind me.

I didn't answer. I just kept walking forward, abandoning my place in line.

"Wait, Kazuko!" Touka yelled, grabbing my sleeve.

"Just remembered something, Touka. I'm skipping cram school today," I said, not even turning around to look.

"Hunh? Why?"

"Just let me borrow your notes later, okay?!" I said breathlessly and quickly ran away.

If I didn't hurry, I'd lose sight of her— one of the girls I'd seen with Asukai Jin. I knew it was her the moment I'd spotted her walking down the hill that our school's built on.

Her name, I'm sure, was "Kitahara Misaki." She went to our school?

No, I'm sure the last time I saw her, she was wearing a different uniform. Which means...

(She's in disguise? Sneaking in?)

Why on earth would she do something like that?

Plus, to get into our school, she would need a card. If she had managed to get one, then this was going to be be pretty hardcore.

"Misaki" was moving down the hill at a good clip. I managed to keep her in sight, but at this speed, I stuck out like a sore thumb. Not only that, but I was wearing leather shoes, while she had on sneakers. I was obviously less natural than her.

After a few minutes of this, Misaki turned off the road into a park. It was a collecting ground for water in the event of a flood, and there was nowhere to hide. It was right below the school, in full view of the staff room—so students hardly ever went near the place.

(Uh-oh.)

There was nothing I *could* do but keep on walking. A short distance away, however, I bent over, doing a bad impression of someone whose shoelaces have come undone.

I glanced sideways into the park. Misaki was there, talking on her cell phone.

"...No, she's not here. She's been absent for the last few days..."

A gust of wind carried her words to my ears, but quickly dissipated a moment later, leaving me unable to hear anything.

("She"...?)

She was looking for someone?

A second later, Misaki ended the call.

She headed towards me, so I hurriedly stood up and began walking before she caught up with me.

I gave up walking quickly. After just a few minutes, Misaki had caught up and passed me. Clearly, I couldn't chase her any further than this. She'd seen me.

I was sure she was headed for the cram school and Asukai Jin.

I just went back to school.

Touka was still standing there at the bus stop.

"Um?" I said, eyes widening. Yeah—the bus had already left, and Touka hadn't gotten on.

"Thought you'd be back, Suema," she said, grinning.

"Why?"

"'Cause you forgot your bag. You didn't notice?" she said in astonishment. I gaped. Now that she mentioned it, my hands *were* kind of empty.

"Ah...!" How stupid of me. I was so preoccupied with chasing after Misaki that I hadn't even remembered that my bag was lying on the ground.

"Here you go," Touka said, handing it over. My face was bright red.

"Th-thanks. Sorry. So, uh, you waited for me?"

"Yep. I thought you'd be back," Touka nodded.

She's such a nice girl, I thought. So I said it aloud, "You're really nice, you know that?"

Touka snorted, "What?"

"No, really."

"Oh, please," she said and tackled me playfully. As her fist bounced off my head, I frowned.

Touka's bag caught my eye.

It wasn't the school bag that she normally carried, but rather a huge Spalding sports bag.

I wondered what was in it, but...

"So, what now? Still skipping cram school?" she asked.

"Eh? Uh... Ahhhh...nah—let's go."

To be honest, I wanted to see if Asukai Jin was there or not.

Touka and I lined up at the bus stop, which was empty, since a bus had only just been by.

I changed my grip on the bag Touka had been holding for me.

(But I don't remember putting it down...)

True, it hadn't been in my hands. When I started off after Misaki, Touka had grabbed my sleeve, and I hadn't had it then...

(Hunh...)

There was a hole in my memory. I felt like someone had picked my pocket.

"So why'd you run off like that?" Touka asked. "You looked pretty serious..."

"Eh?" I pulled out of my thoughts and turned to look at her.

She was grinning. It was one of those blameless sort of smiles.

"Um, I thought I saw someone I knew from junior high...but I was wrong," I lied.

"Really?"

"Y-yes! Some boy I knew."

"Your first *love*...?"

"Uh, maybe."

"Oooh? I demand details," she insisted, grinning.

"Maybe sometime later. Not right now."

I couldn't let Touka get mixed up with Asukai Jin and the unfathomable strangeness clustering around him. She was a good friend. I couldn't put her in harm's way.

"Oh, all right," Touka nodded, resigned.

Then she gave me a hard-to-describe, asymmetrical expression.

"If you're up against something you can't handle, you should consult your friends. That's what they're here for," she said, as if performing a speech on stage.

I felt like someone had wrapped their fist around my heart. It was like my nuclear core had been pierced.

"I-It's nothing like that!" I protested hastily.

"Sure," she said, shoulders slumping, and then her face went back to normal.

"............"

I found it rather hard to calm down. For some reason, I thought Touka had wanted to warn me about something. I had no real reason to think that, but I just couldn't shake that impression.

We got on the bus, got off at the station, and just before we entered the school, I said, "Uh, there's a study guide I need to get. I'll catch up with you, okay?"

"Want me to come?"

"Nah, you go on in."

"I'll save a seat for you."

"Thanks!"

We split up. I waited for about thirty seconds after Touka went inside, then I snuck into the building after her.

I avoided the elevators and went up the stairs instead.

Asukai Jin was not in the guidance office.

(His day off?)

I tried to remember if Asukai Jin had been off this day last week, but I couldn't be sure.

"Hmmm..." I hesitated for a moment, but then went back down the stairs and used the pay phone in the lobby to dial the phone number to Kinukawa Kotoe's house.

I didn't really want to cause any more worry for a single-minded girl like Kotoe, but she lived next door to him, so she ought to know if Asukai Jin was there or not.

It rang several times, but at last someone answered. "Kinukawa residence."

Sounded like an older woman, probably her mom.

"Um, my name's Suema... Is Kotoe-san there?" I asked. Halfway through the sentence, I heard a gasp on the other end of the line.

"She's not here," she snapped, her tone suddenly becoming very harsh.

I was a little taken aback, but asked, "Do you know where she is?"

"..............." There was no answer.

"Hello?"

"What do you want with her?" she suddenly shrieked.

"Uh..."

"What were you going to do with her? Where are you now?" she screamed.

"Whoa! H-hang on! What are you talking about?" I asked,

flustered. She asked where I was again, so I said, "The cram school by the station."

"The cram school?" she asked, mystified.

"Yes," I said, nodding into the phone.

"You are...Kotoe's... What?"

"Um, we both go to Shinyo Academy. Different classes, but... we're friends. My name's Suema Kazuko."

"You're at the cram school?"

"Y-yes, I'm an exam student."

"Kotoe hasn't been to school. You didn't know?" her mother said, surprising me.

"Eh...?" I said, stunned. "R-really?!"

"Her sensei called... She hasn't been to school in three days!"

"H-has she been home?"

"We had a fight and she ran away," her mother said, sounding like she was about to cry. "She's always been such a good girl. She would never have stayed out all night, or taken money out of the bank without permission..."

"............!" I was floored.

That girl?

The girl who'd cried and begged me to "save Jin-niisan"?

"I-I don't believe it..."

"Do you have any idea where Kotoe might be?"

"H-how long has she been gone?"

"Four days..."

"O-okay! I'll go look for her!"

I hung up, badly shaken.

I forgot to take my telephone card out, and the warning buzzer echoed through the lobby for a few minutes. At last, I realized it was for me and reclaimed it.

(Wh-what's going on...?)

Had Asukai Jin done something to her?

(No... If he wanted to, he would have done something a long time ago. She's been right next to him all this time.)

Been thinking about him for so long...

Staying out all night and withdrawing money?

"..............."

Trying to calm my spinning head, I ground my teeth.

(What now? Obviously, I've got to find Kotoe. If I don't talk to her, I can't begin to figure this out...)

I picked up the receiver again, and called everyone I knew who might know Kotoe, anyone who was in her class this year.

"Eh? Kinukawa? Dunno... She's got a pretty bad rep lately, been throwing around how rich she is and all..."

"That girl asked me if I wanted to go out partying with her. Who is she *kidding*? We have *exams*! She said she'd pick up the tab, though, so I won't say I wasn't tempted! Ha ha ha!!!"

"Sorry, Suema. Should never have introduced her to you. I was a little worried about it, so I asked how things were going, and she just looked at me blankly. Last time, she was almost crying! Something's strange about her. You hear anything?"

"Yeah, I saw her leave school with a bunch of lower classmen. No, all boys. Most of them scary looking, rough types. Why? Dunno—after her money, I guess..."

"Don't even talk to me about *her*. She used to be okay, but now she's just another rich bitch. Oh, get this: I asked her what she was doing for college, and she said, 'Who gives a shit?' Bet you *anything* she has some back road in."

I gave everyone non-committal replies, but inside I was just flabbergasted.

The opinions varied, but the general consensus was the same.

Kinukawa Kotoe had changed—and with unbelievable speed.

Completely confused now, I flopped down on a leather bench in the lobby.

What the hell had happened to her? What was going on?

If what everyone said was true, then she had probably already forgotten that she ever asked me to help, forgotten she was worried about Asukai Jin. She must have. Kyoko said she had, and Kyoko's the one who sent her to me in the first place.

Even speaking generously, I'm not that great of a person. Something I'm passionate about one day, I'll more than likely grow tired of the next. I'm always thirsty for something new.

Maybe Kotoe had just fallen prey to what adults always describe as, "Kids these days."

But...

I knew I could count on you. You seem so with it.

The way her eyes sparkled when she said that... I couldn't believe the girl who said that could be this shallow. This wasn't anything to do with belief—it simply didn't parse. I couldn't even begin to figure it out.

"..........."

I balled up both fists in front of my lips, stared at nothing, and thought as hard as I could.

But my thoughts cut off suddenly.

I had seen someone come in the automatic doors at the building's entrance. Someone wearing white clothes.

Asukai Jin.

"...........!"

Reflexively, I stood up.

Asukai Jin noticed that there was a high school girl—me—glaring at him.

He smiled at me. "Hey. You a student here?"

"..........."

"Something wrong? You look pale," he said, as he started walking towards me.

"Asukai Jin?" I said, before I knew it.

"Yes?"

"I need to talk to you. Do you have time?" Like I was not myself. My voice was so quiet, so calm.

"Oh, sure. Counseling...?"

"No."

I took a step towards him.

"As Kinukawa Kotoe's friend."

One hour earlier—

Asukai Jin was sitting alone in a cafe near his university, drinking coffee and flipping through the pages of a paperback.

The place was pretty crowded. Most of the customers were

groups of two or three, and the place rang with girls' voices raised in laugher or exclamation. Asukai was the only person sitting in a booth alone.

The cell phone in his breast pocket rang.

"Yes?" he said, answering it at once.

"It's Misaki," a girl's voice said.

"How was it?"

"Just like you said—'she' wasn't here."

"Really?"

"Yes. She hasn't been to school for a few days."

"Did she call in sick? Is she at the hospital?"

"I don't know. Nobody seems to know what's happened to her, including her teachers."

"And this is not because she's a new student or hasn't got to know anyone yet?"

"No. Everyone knew her, but she didn't talk about herself much. They described her as mysterious and more than a little remote."

"Hmm..."

"It seems like she didn't have any friends. I asked several people, but none of them could think of any."

"Okay, thank you."

"What should I do next?"

"Can you change on the way? Just throw that uniform away and meet me at the cram school."

"Okay."

Asukai got off the phone and looked up to find the waitress had come to refill his cup.

"Refill?"

"Yes, please."

The waitress bent over to fill his cup and put her lips near his ear. "New orders came."

"……" Asukai Jin nodded faintly.

"A girl will arrive soon in his 'stead.' I'm to do as she says."

"A girl?" Asukai bobbed his head, and took a sip of his coffee.

He knew the waitress well. She'd been a student of his at the cram school the year before. Starting this spring, she'd become a college student, but she had been working at this cafe since she was a ronin.

"There's no medicine in this one, right?" Asukai whispered, smiling.

The waitress grinned back. "You never know. There's always a chance I might slip you something..."

"Scary," he said, ducking slightly. She went away.

He silently drank his coffee for a few minutes, then looked back at the book in his hands.

The book's title was *The Victor's Principle: The Victim's Future*, by Kirima Seiichi. It was a thin book, only about 150 pages.

He flipped through the pages one way, then back the other. He read nothing, but kept opening it to one passage, then closing it again. It read:

"...but all hopes, ultimately, are achieved in the future. Everyone dreams, desires the realization of those dreams, but it is not the dreamer that obtains that realization. It is the following generation. Furthermore, for those that receive the fruits of that success, it is no longer a dream, but established fact. All hopes must therefore become the sacrifice of the victor, but this is how humanity has advanced. Our only road is ahead of us, for people cannot live in the past..."

The grammar was so twisted it was impossible to tell if the writer was resigned or optimistic.

"............"

Without reading it, without even displaying interest in it, Asukai flipped back and forth, aways returning to that passage.

"Sacrifice, hunh?" he muttered at last, so quietly no one could hear him. "That may be the only way..."

His phone rang again.

"Asukai speaking," he answered at once. Nodding to himself, he listened to the other speaker, but suddenly his eyes narrowed. "What?! Really?" His voice was tense. "And? You don't know where 'she' is at all?" He paused, listening, then said, "Okay. No, don't worry about it. I'd get away from there if I were you. She probably won't come back," he said quietly, calmly. But the worry was clear on his face.

At last, he hung up, and for a moment, did not move. The hand holding the book clenched, crushing it.

"Jesus... So that's the 'girl.'"

He stood up.

The waitress from before was at the register and took his check. Asukai whispered in her ear, "When the 'girl' comes in his stead, tell me at once. If you can, take her captive."

"Okay. How?"

"Up to you. But try to do it so you don't leave any evidence."

"Got it."

"Thank you. I'll be at the cram school."

He left the cafe and headed straight for work.

(What now...?)

As he walked, his expression was peaceful. But it was the kind of tense quiet that could snap at any second.

(If I'm going to help her, I'll have to hurry... But...)

From time to time, his teeth ground together.

He reached the school, and entered the building. A girl sitting in the lobby stood up and glared at him.

For some reason, Asukai was badly shaken.

She was clearly an ordinary girl, but he felt like she had some unfathomable power. Like a warrior headed for the battle of her life, sword drawn. She stared right through Asukai.

The girl introduced herself as Suema Kazuko. A friend of Kinukawa Kotoe's.

"...Kinukawa-san has not been herself recently. Have you heard anything?" she asked, the moment they entered the tiny counseling room.

"Yes... I mean, I just found out a few minutes ago."

"What do you think?"

"What... what do you mean?"

"Kinukawa-san is in love with you," Suema announced.

"............"

"Yeah, I know. She's the one who ought to tell you. But I figured you already knew. Right?"

"Yes, vaguely..." he said.

"I've no intention of asking you what you think of her. That's none of my business. But do you think her transformation has anything to do with you?"

"...I don't know."

"Kinukawa-san thinks nothing of you, now?" she asked.

"So it seems," he said.

"I think you know."

"What?"

"The reason," she said.

"Why do you think that?"

"It's written all over your face," she responded.

Asukai froze. Was this girl like him? Could she see *something in people's hearts*?

After a moment, she sighed."But seriously...it's not that simple. I just got the feeling you did."

"I'd honestly like to know the reason," he said. "But..." It was true. Why did she have to be a target? He didn't know. There should have been no chance for *him* to get near her.

(If he was after money, there must have been better candidates.)

"Kinukawa-san was worried about you," Suema said.

Asukai was slightly taken aback. "Worried? Why?"

"I can't tell you. I promised her."

"........."

"But now that I've actually met you, I think I understand how Kinukawa-san feels," Suema said, staring at Asukai. "She has changed, but I suspect you have as well."

"Possibly… I guess I'm not going to be able to return her feelings," Asukai said, looking down.

Suema shook her head. "Not that. I don't think you would have been collected enough to be concerned about her. That's part of the reason why she liked you. She wanted to help you."

"…………"

"You were caught up with your own mess," she said.

"…………"

"She liked it that way," Suema continued. "She knew that's the kind of person you were—until you changed. You found something. That gave you time to poke your head up above surface. And when she realized that…"

Asukai was beginning to shudder. He thought this girl was far more collected than he was.

How much did she know?

Or was she also working for *him*?

"Are you…" he started, but then he saw something.

Suema's hands were locked together on her lap, but her fingers were trembling.

She was afraid, but was forcing herself to be brave.

"What are you doing, Asukai-sensei?" she asked.

"Why do you want to know?" Asukai replied, trying to get in control.

"Because…"

"You said you were friends, but you clearly haven't known her that long. You have nothing in common. In fact, I imagine you would find her rather irritating," he said, recovering his cool. She was just a girl. Not worth being afraid of.

He'd been looking at her for a while, and this girl had no "flower." She was the same type as Kotoe. This type never liked each other.

Suema failed to answer.

Asukai pressed forward. "You're a pretty smart girl. You proud of that?"

"N-no!" I said, feeling like someone had stuck a knife in my chest.

"I can't believe you would have any respect for a girl like Kotoe-chan. Especially after you found out how much she's changed. You just can't figure things out, right?"

"I... I just..."

"You want an answer."

"Th-that's probably part of it, but..." The entire conversation had been me on a roll, and the moment I started to lose my footing, I stumbled. Asukai Jin's eyes looked like they could see right into my soul.

"Oh, I understand," he said. "I'm not criticizing you for it. But I'm more worried about Kotoe-chan than you are. I'm just grateful it was worthy of your attention."

I had no idea how to respond to that."A-Asukai-sensei...?" I said.

"What?"

"Do you really... Are you sure you don't have anything to do with her transformation?" Even as I spoke, I realized this wasn't the question I wanted to ask.

"I feel a little guilty. I'm sure it's my fault somehow," he said, sounding pretty sincere. Like he was really a good guy.

But that's what bugged me.

It was unnatural. And no matter how you looked at it...he was hiding something.

"Then does it have something to do with that painting?" I babbled. Even I wasn't sure what I meant.

"What?" Asukai Jin asked, puzzled. "Which painting?"

"'Snow Falls in April.' That picture is your... How can I put this..." Basically, I just felt like I had to say something. If I stayed silent and let him keep talking, I'd completely lose control of the conversation and not able to argue anything at all. "It's a part of you that Kinukawa-san could never touch. Don't you see?"

"............"

"A-and she felt like there was something about you she couldn't handle."

"............" Asukai was expressionless. He didn't react at all.

What was I trying to say?

Was I being the archetypal excitedly stupid high school girl, who speaks without thinking?

But I felt like I was right. That picture said something about this man...

"That picture," Asukai Jin said.

I snapped out of it. "Wh-what?"

"Do you understand it?" he asked, his voice so quiet and calm—and a little mocking.

But I snapped, "I don't know everything, but that picture... yeah. I do." If he was going to make fun of me, I might as well speak my mind.

"Pray tell," he said. I got the feeling he was pulling a little away, flinching back.

"I hate it," I snarled, going for the big blow in the hopes of knocking him over.

But he just said, "Harsh," in an airy voice.

I was off balance now, but I couldn't pull back. "I'm right, aren't I? Did you actually want to draw a picture like that?"

"I wasn't exactly planning on selling it."

"But you were trying to capture something external. Right?"

"............"

"It's an awfully lonely picture," I said.

"You're the first person who's said that about it."

"But that's what I think. No matter how you look at that picture, there's no trace of the painter's intentions." When did I suddenly become a hypocritical art critic? I was so unconvincing.

"...I see." Asukai Jin nodded anyway.

"What were you thinking when you drew that thing?" I asked, growing uncertain as to why I was sitting here having this conversation.

"Why are we talking about this?" Asukai Jin asked, clearly thinking the same thing.

I managed to find some words and turn them into an answer. "Because we want to help Kinukawa-san. That's why I want to know more about you."

"What is it that makes you work so hard for Kotoe-chan?" Asukai Jin had been staring at me this whole time. Unable to hold his gaze any longer, I broke eye contact.

"That's...the second time you made that implication," I said.

"Mm? What do you mean?"

"That I'm not really that close to her. But if I ever want to be closer to her, then I have to help her now." No sooner had the words left my mouth than I felt a pain in my chest. I had a strong sensation that I was a horribly pathetic life form.

The thought that I needed a reason to simply get closer to another human being just seemed like the saddest thing in the world.

I found myself staring at the floor and shaking.

This had to stop.

I couldn't deal with Asukai Jin. There was no way I could ever understand the secret Kotoe had wanted to know.

Suddenly, Asukai Jin asked, "Do you want to be saved?"

"Hunh—?"

"Do you want to know what I am doing?" He stared directly at me, missing nothing.

I was transfixed. I couldn't move.

"I am trying to change the world," he said, his eyes completely serious.

"…………"

"I am trying to heal the flaws in human hearts. And I'm doing it the only way I know how—by planting the right type of flower in their souls."

"…………"

I remembered something I had thoughtlessly said back when Kotoe was telling me about Asukai Jin. *He goes out every night and comes back covered in other people's blood? That sounds like, I dunno… Like a vampire or something.*

And now, I found myself nailed to the wall, trapped in his gaze and totally immobile.

"It's a problem of balance. I've been searching for that. I've got all kinds of people 'cooperating.' And finally I found it. That balance—a gentle, modest 'seed' that can be planted harmlessly in almost everyone."

"…………"

"It has no shape, and it won't ever help you achieve your desires…but that's what allows it to meet all of the requirements. The perfect 'seed.'"

"…………"

"Fortunately, I had already found that balance. I met a 'girl' who had it. Now all I have to do is find her."

"…………"

"I will take this seed from the 'girl' and propagate it across the world… The 'seed' will lay down roots and before they know it, everyone in the world will be without flaws. To achieve this, I have to sacrifice the girl, but that is a necessary evil."

"…………"

"Your heart is flawed as well," he said to me. "You realize that, don't you?"

"............"

"What if I told you I could fix that...?"

"............"

"What would you say?"

"I... I would..." I could hear my own heart beating furiously. Beating so hard it felt like it was about to leap out of my mouth. "I have already *been* saved by someone else!" I shouted.

Asukai Jin frowned. "Oh? Who?"

"B-Boogiepop!" I said, well aware that I was babbling like a lunatic. The person who had actually saved me had said that name. But did shinigami actually save people?

"Oh, *him* again?" Asukai chuckled. It sounded like he'd heard the rumors.

I could feel my face turning red. "Not like that!"

"He's a superhero, right?"

"H-he's not that simple..." I tried to argue, but in truth I knew nothing about him. "A-and before you make fun of him... I mean, you just said y-you were going to change the world..." As the words left my mouth, I realized something.

(What——?!)

What had he just said?

The true impact of his words sank in.

Asukai Jin stared at me silently.

"............"

I gulped.

He slowly reached his hand out towards my chest.

I felt like I was frozen to my chair—I couldn't get away.

Asukai Jin's fingers began to turn, like he was grasping something I couldn't see.

(Wh-what is he...?!)

What was happening? I stiffened, and Asukai Jin's fingers bunched together like he was holding a pen—then moved, like he was drawing a line in the air.

It was like he was drawing a picture.

My jaw dropped, and he shrugged.

"I'm talking about a picture. I wanted to surprise people with it. The world might be aiming a little high, but every painter has that desire secretly lurking deep within, telling them they're an artist."

"............" I was stunned.

"The girl is just a model. She's nothing more than that to me, personally—but I wonder if Kotoe-chan didn't mistake her for my girlfriend. That might have caused her to act out like she has. So I plan to find Kotoe and talk to her, clear things up."

He smiled softly as he spoke.

"I...see," I said and managed to nod.

I felt like a decisive moment has just passed me by.

"I apologize for being so harsh earlier, but, you see, I was embarrassed. I didn't really doubt your friendship with Kotoe-chan," Asukai Jin said, and bowed his head.

"............" I couldn't answer.

There was nothing left for me to say.

No matter how much I asked, he wasn't going to give me any more than what he had.

There was nothing else for me to do.

"Thank you," I said, weakly rising to my feet.

As I was about to leave, I turned back. "Oh, one more thing... What did you mean by 'sacrifice?'" I asked. "You said, 'I have to sacrifice the girl.' That's not exactly a pleasant image."

"Well, she's a model," he explained. "She has to remain in exactly the same position for eight hours, and I always feel a little guilty asking that of people. But what else can I do?" he said, without hesitation.

I bowed awkwardly, and left the room.

And then I ran.

I'm not sure where to, but I couldn't stand being there a second longer.

(Damn it—!)

I knew something was horribly twisted, but had no idea what it was. This was the second time in my life I had ever bitterly regretted being nothing more than some boring and ordinary girl.

(Damn it! I'm an idiot! Such a shithead! Stupid, stupid, stupid, stupid, stupid stupid...!!!)

I raged internally, cursing myself.

"Why did I let her go...?" Asukai whispered to himself, left alone in the guidance counselor's office.

"There was nothing about that girl to make her special." Asukai looked at the door she'd left through. "So...how did she know?"

It's an awfully lonely picture.

No matter how you look at that picture, there's no trace of the painter's intentions.

"How did she...?" he wondered out loud.

She said she wanted to save Kinukawa Kotoe, and she meant it. She was serious.

That seriousness had left Asukai feeling utterly defeated.

"Yes, Suema Kazuko-san. Exactly as you say," he murmured. His face looked like that of a badly hurt boy's. Like he was about to cry, struggling furiously to stop himself.

At that moment, his phone rang.

His face snapped up, and he answered quickly.

He listened for a moment, then nodded. "Okay."

The person on the other end said something else, and he shook his head. "No, it seems we have to move quickly," he said. "Yeah. At this point, we can't avoid a fight. Yes, I'll take Spooky E out personally."

Boogiepop returns

VS Imaginator Part 2

IV

Once something
has begun to crumble,
There is nothing to be done but
rebuild from square one.

—Kirima Seiichi
(*VS Imaginator*)

IV.

When I could sleep, I would go into a movie theater, and sit on the side in the very front row, where nobody would ever come. The times were always different; sometimes in the morning, sometimes at night. I doubt I ever snored. Nobody ever woke me up.

At night, I would find a 24-hour family restaurant and wait for sunrise. I'd sit there reading manga or something, to keep from being noticed. I was hardly the only one doing this, so I didn't stand out too much.

I wondered if my sister had filed a missing person's report with the police, so I started wearing glasses as a disguise—but I never met anyone who seemed to be looking for me.

And when I wasn't resting...I was Boogiepop.

Kids my age would attack drunken businessmen in groups to steal their money and prove their strength. Suddenly, their attack would be interrupted by a dark, cloaked figure, which would spout haughty bullshit like, "How sad you are," and then beat the crap out of them before fleeing like the wind.

Obviously, I did this because I didn't want the people I saved to get a good look at my face. Half the time, though, I didn't know which side was to blame, but I always took the side of the underdog.

But if the people I saved seemed like they were going to exact revenge, I'd put them down, too. Then I'd blow a whistle, like the kind police use, and vanish before anyone arrived.

As soon as I was safely away, I'd slip into the shadows, whip off my costume, and stuff it into my bag before walking away with as innocent an expression as I could muster, always thinking:

What am I doing?

Man, I'm certainly getting good at running away...

And the like.

I'd given up the makeup. It was dark, and no one would be able to recognize me anyway. Besides...it was always Orihata who was putting on the makeup. Without her here, I could never get it right.

"Ow..."

I glanced at my fist, and found I'd hurt it again.

My movements were becoming wild. My shishou always said there were no moves in karate that would allow you to injure yourself—and that if you did, that was a sign you had not yet trained enough, or you were losing control. Both were true for me now.

I put some cold spray on the bruise and put a pair of gloves over it, the sort of first aid Orihata had once done for me. Damn, I was thinking about her again.

"Argh..."

My opponents were nothing much, so I was just narrowly scraping by. If I actually ran into anyone dangerous, though, I'd be in serious trouble. Most weapons, like knives, I just had to dodge—but if someone had a gun, I'd be a goner.

And then what would happen to me? Would this be what Orihata needed?

Absently munching on spaghetti carbonara (plus salad), pondering things, a thought struck me.

Is this a roundabout way of killing myself...?

I knew I was pretty desperate, but did I really want to die?

"............"

Carbonara sauce is made from soft-boiled eggs and tastes terrible cold, so my mouth never stopped moving the whole time I was thinking. I even asked a waiter for a refill on my coffee.

"............"

I added a lot of cream and sugar, and took a sip.

Even I was amazed at how low my sense of danger was.

I was ultra calm.

I didn't know what the hell I was trying to do and no one was ever going to praise me for it. I was gradually forgetting the correct movements for karate, flailing wildly and becoming a menace to myself.

(Hunh...)

I knew all of this, but I didn't seem to care.

Why not? Was something wrong with me? Well, that much was obvious, but exactly what was wrong?

(Hmmm...)

I thought about Orihata. I felt no anger towards her. I wasn't playing Boogiepop to get attention. I was actually hoping that she'd forgotten all about me.

When I remembered how I'd fawned over her, I was embarrassed. I couldn't forget how pathetic I was with my head in the clouds.

(Okay...)

I think I'm playing Boogiepop to apologize to her. *If what I'm doing is in any way useful to her...* That was the thought that was driving me.

(Man, what self-centered logic.)

I was unable to suppress a self-deprecating giggle.

Here I was, fully aware that the girl I'd been going out with had never really been in love with me at all. Yet, I couldn't stop letting her memory dictate my every move. God, I was a loser.

(So stupid...)

I giggled again, but by this point I was pretending to read a manga anthology so that nobody would look at me suspiciously. Damn, but I was getting too good at this.

The waiter passed by, and I ordered another cup of coffee.

"It's him. No doubt about it," Kinukawa Kotoe said, looking at Taniguchi Masaki, sitting in the window of a family restaurant.

She and six others were standing on the other side of a four-lane road across from the restaurant.

From the side, they looked like they just happened to all be waiting for the light to change so they could cross.

The other six were all thin men. Their ages varied, as did their clothes, from suits to school uniforms, leather jackets and jeans. The only thing linking them together was their singular lack of expression. This was the only thing, yet this distinguishing feature made it plain to see—they were all Spooky E's "terminals."

"Heh..." Kotoe grinned, seeing Masaki's glasses. "What a crappy disguise. Still, he was pretty good at running and hiding. Took some doing to track him down."

"............"

"............"

The men behind her made no response.

The light changed, and a motorcycle pulled to a stop in front of them.

They stepped forward to cross the street, but Kotoe said softly, "No, wait..."

Masaki was about to leave the restaurant. It looked like he was going to prowl a little more tonight.

"He looks serious. Split into three groups and tail him."

They started across the street, passing in front of the stopped motorcycle.

There was nothing strange about the motorcycle at first glance, but on closer inspection, the driver was a little unusual. She wore a leather jumpsuit and safety boots. The kind people wear in a factory to keep their feet intact even if several tons fall on them. There was a military style backpack slung over her shoulders.

Her face was hidden beneath a full face helmet, but she was clearly female.

Kotoe's group reached the other side, and started following after Masaki. He had the Boogiepop disguise in a bag on his shoulder. Two of them took the lead, and the others took side streets, temporarily staying out of sight.

The signal changed.

"—————"

The biker girl made a sudden sharp turn into the other side of the road, and roared off back the way she had come.

(Only two following me...?)

Of course, I had noticed.

The moment I saw that woman—the girl who had been so snide with Orihata, Kinukawa Kotoe—I knew the moment I'd been waiting for had come. Luckily, it looked like they didn't know that I was on to them.

I made a show of heading to a deserted area of town, like I'm sure they hoped I would, and then turned into a shopping area and had some fun going up and down elevators for a while.

It looked like there were several of them trading off, but I wasn't worried. I knew someone was after me the whole time, so I didn't bother trying to distinguish between them.

(Okay. Now what?)

I was having trouble deciding. I did have an idea, but it was a tad...out there.

(Right, then—still not gonna change the fact that I'm pathetic.)

I left the main streets for a stretch of dimly lit back roads.

I knew the area well. It was the type of place I'd often patrol as Boogiepop. And the alley leading down to the station had a special place in my heart. I hadn't been there in almost six months, though...

Yet it still smelled of stagnant water. You could never call it beautiful.

"............"

It made me a little sad.

I was doubtless far too young to reminisce, but if I had no future, then who cared if I acted like an old man? I just went for it.

This was the place where I'd been surrounded by kouhai from my junior high school, where I'd been saved by Orihata Aya—where I first met her...

(Man, she sure bowled me over. I mean, just look at how she...)

I could feel my face turning red at the thought of that memory. I brushed it off with a chuckle to myself.

Footsteps came towards me from behind.

I grinned, and dove into the shadows.

The footsteps sped up. They were on the offensive. They weren't going to just follow me around any longer.

Another set of footsteps came towards me from the opposite direction. They had me surrounded.

"Where is he?"

I could hear voices.

"He's gotta be hiding somewhere!"

"Don't panic. Every way out of here's a dead end. He must be here somewhere!"

I started counting.

(One, two...six in all. Almost the same number I saw from the window.)

All men.

"We split up and search?"

"No. Wait. I have a plan." This was Kinukawa Kotoe's voice. That made seven.

They were all here.

I started to move, slowly and carefully. Her voice grew louder.

"Hey! Taniguchi Masaki-kun! Are you still in love with Orihata Aya?"

I didn't answer.

"Do you know what she really is?" Kinukawa continued. "She never let you screw her, did she? Such a shame. After all the experience she's had with those other guys... You know what they call her behind her back? The public toilet."

She was trying to provoke me. Trying to make me mad.

I didn't answer.

"You've got a pathetic sense of duty to a bitch like that? How can you be fooled by that little goody two-shoes exterior of hers?!"

In the darkness, I grasped the Nike bag, now much lighter.

For a second, I closed my eyes.

In my mind's eye, I pictured her.

You're really strong, aren't you?

Masaki...will you become him?

Orihata was wrong.

I'm strong at all. Truth is, I don't have any idea what's right.

Only way I get by is from paying close attention to the expressions of the people around me.

But I think I can "become" him. When you said that... When I was with you...

It might just have been a delusion. But I didn't care if it was—even without evidence, without proof... *Isn't that what* this *is?*

"That girl's better than anyone at fooling men," Kinukawa said. "I almost feel sorry for how you jumped right into her trap. You're the saddest person in the world—"

As she was talking, there was a sudden noise from behind her.

The men rushed towards it. One of them kicked over a pile of wooden crates, exposing something hidden in the shadows.

The empty Nike bag, lying right where I'd flung it.

"——!"

The men stiffened—their backs to me.

Surprise attacks are over in seconds.

I kicked them in the back, right between the spine and ribs, three of them in less than two seconds.

"GUH!"

All three of them went flying.

The other three turned towards me. As I'd expected, they all had guns.

But I was very close to them. I could attack as fast as they could aim.

I bent down and swung my leg, sweeping the legs out from all three of them.

All three lost their balance and fell over.

I leapt on them, slamming my knee into two of them.

Leaving them crumpled, I slammed my elbow into the third.

When I stood up again, all six of them were unconscious.

"————"

I quickly picked up one of the dropped guns.

Spinning around, I released the safety, and aimed it right at Kinukawa Kotoe. And yes, I'd held a real gun before, back in Phnom Penh, and I was ready to use it.

She froze instantly. "...T-taniguchi Masaki," she stammered. "I think I may have underestimated..."

"I'm not Taniguchi Masaki," I interrupted, quietly.

I wore a black hat and cloak. In this outfit, "I am Boogiepop."

I stepped slowly forward, and placed the barrel of the gun against her chin.

But she wasn't the least bit frightened. She gave me a confident grin. "Okay, point for you. You've earned my respect. If I told Axis about you, they'd probably pick you up, convinced you were the real thing."

I had no idea what she was talking about.

"Tell me what you did to Orihata," I said, trying to suppress my anger, but well aware that I was failing. I was that close to the edge.

"But I just *did*. That was all true. She really has been with any number of men."

"Did you make her do that?!"

"So what if I did? She still didn't tell you; she still betrayed you."

"Augh......" My eyes misted over.

I suddenly understood what she had meant all those times she'd said she was sorry.

But I was a fool. I hadn't noticed. All this time, she'd been asking for help.

"I'll ask you again... *Where is Orihata*?!"

"Wouldn't you like to know?"

"Fuck you!" Ignoring the fact that she was a girl, I smacked her with the butt of the gun.

She spat blood and fell over into the ditch water.

Even then, she smiled.

"Hee hee hee hee... Go ahead, *kill me*. After all, I've had my way with your woman all along!"

"Graah!" I could feel my head ignite.

My hands were shaking so hard I could barely keep the gun pointed at her.

I could pull that trigger at any second.

"I'd planned to leave a corpse for everyone to blame, but I'm just as happy leaving you a murderer—how about it?" she wheedled, venomous.

"Sh-shit...!" Wave after wave of hatred poured out of me. I couldn't stop it.

With a will of its own, my fingers pulled back the hammer.

With a click, it was ready to fire.

"Rrrrrrrrr!" Grinding my teeth, I could hear my blood roaring in my ears.

"...Mm?" Kinukawa Kotoe frowned, puzzled.

Even though I looked ready to shoot her any second, her gaze was directed not at me, but at something behind me.

Alarmed, I spun around.

Too late.

Someone had snuck up behind me. They touched my neck, moving much faster than me. A shock ran through my body.

"GACK—?!"

Suddenly unable to move, I toppled over.

Electricity—a stun gun.

"Idiot," said a voice I'd heard before—a young girl's voice.

But could it really be her...?

I struggled to turn my head, and at last succeeded. It *was* her.

"I thought you were up to something dumb, but Christ... If I let you kill someone, how the hell could I ever face your parents?"

Only one girl talked like a boy and ran around in a leather jumpsuit and safety boots, heedless of how they looked.

"N-Nagi-neesan...?" My sister.

"I *told* you—don't call me 'Neesan,'" she snarled. No one else talked like her. "And why in god's name are you dressed like *that*? I dunno who the hell put you up to it, but you are a grade A dumbass." She spat out her words, tearing Boogiepop's hat and cloak off me while I was still paralyzed.

"Who the hell are you?" Kinukawa Kotoe asked, trying to get to her feet. But Nagi poked her with her stungun, which was the rod kind, much like a police truncheon.

"You aren't going anywhere, Kinukawa Kotoe."

"Whaaat?! You know me?" Kotoe stared, amazed.

My sister snorted. "Thought so. Girl like Kinukawa Kotoe, suddenly acting crazy..."

"What do you mean?!"

"*You* aren't Kinukawa," she said quietly. "You're just borrowing her face, or maybe you brainwashed her. I dunno, but absolutely every student at Shinyo Academy knows who I am."

She looked awfully used to this.

"What are you?" Kotoe asked.

"I'm not big on giving out my name as much as *he* is. And I'm the one asking questions. Who's controlling you?" she asked, pointedly.

I was confused now.

What the...?

Brainwashed?

So it wasn't this woman who'd done something to Orihata?

"............" Kotoe fell silent.

Then her face twisted into a smile again."Oooooh... I get it," she said. "I found you, buried down in Kinukawa Kotoe's memories. You're that 'Fire Witch.' Didn't seem that important at the time—but I guess I blew it, not leaving that in the conscious registers. Never thought the class delinquent would be doing something like this."

This was nothing like the way Kotoe had been talking—she sounded like a middle-aged man with the face of a girl.

"Answer me," my sister said, unmoved. Was she always going around, doing stuff like this?

"My, my. First him, then the Imaginator, now you... Problems everywhere I turn." Whatever was inside her grinned at us. Her eyes stayed perfectly round, which made the smile that much more sinister. "Good thing I took the precaution of sending in two teams."

She snapped her fingers.

"......!"

My sister suddenly flung herself to the side.

And from above, something—no, someone—fell on her, first one and then another.

Punk-styled men were attacking from the air!

(WHAT—?!)

I looked up. From the building beside us, put of the second floor staircase window, came a swarm of punks, skinheads, and yakuza-looking men all leaping down into the alley. Like the first bunch, this motley crew seemed to have nothing to do with each other.

The six men I'd knocked out earlier were just the main course? These others had all been waiting on standby?!

"N-Nagi-neesa—!" I tried to tell her to run, but...

"Hmph!"

Making a noise somewhere between a grunt and a chuckle, she dodged every nail-ridden bat they swung at her. Then she kicked them, zapped them with her stungun, dodged a blow from behind without even looking...

It was all so fast...

She was taking on five or six at a time, never flinching, never hesitating—knocking them down like bowling pins. She was insanely strong.

(Wh-who the hell *is* she?)

By any standard, she was far stronger than me, and it wasn't because she had a weapon. No, she was good without one—but *with* a weapon, it was like it became an extension of her own body, a clear sign of just how good she was.

Now that I thought about it, I remember once asking my shishou what my sister, the daughter of his friend, had been like as a child.

Shishou had laughed, and said only this: "I couldn't keep up with her."

But I'd never thought he meant it *literally*.

"…………"

Both body and mind now stunned and unable to move, Nagi suddenly grabbed me by the front of my shirt and flung me across the alley.

Aaah! I thought, and a second later a skinhead landed where I'd been lying. She'd saved me getting trampled.

Now *that* is true strength.

Bam, bam, all the punks went flying, kicked or zapped.

"……"

I no longer understood anything, but did my best to move, trying to keep out of my sister's way.

Suddenly, a yakuza-looking guy landed right in front of me.

I panicked for a moment, but he was out cold. Wasn't even twitching.

Just as I started to get angry with him for startling me, I noticed the key holder hanging from his alligator belt.

There were a bunch of keys that looked to go to various motorcycles and cars, and so on, but the one my eyes had latched on to, was...

"Th-that's..."

I forced my frozen arm through horrible pain, and grabbed the key.

I'd seen that key before.

I'd seen her holding it, once.

"Oh god..."

It belonged to Orihata. It was her apartment key.

"Shit—! What *is* she?!" Kinukawa Kotoe snarled, watching the terminals get pulverized by one girl. Kotoe picked up the gun Taniguchi Masaki had dropped, and fired it in the girl's direction.

It hit the girl square in the back.

"Unh!" She fell forwards...and turned it into a forwards somersault. She was back on her feet in a second flat.

Bulletproof clothing—!

She spun towards Kotoe, and glared at her.

"Sh-shit!" Kotoe fired the gun a few times. But the enemy was moving too fast, and none of the bullets hit her. Most of them hit her allies, the terminals, who were not bulletproof. They toppled over, spurting blood.

"Stop it!" the girl roared.

(I'm finished...!)

Kotoe fled, abandoning her allies.

"Wait!" the girl called, but *that* wasn't going to happen.

"Keep her here!" Kotoe yelled at the terminals.

They did as they were told, flinging themselves at Taniguchi Masaki's sister, despite their wounds.

"Argh!" she roared, knocking them aside, one after the other.

When the last one went down, she looked around her.

There was no sign of Kotoe.

"Damn," she muttered. Then she noticed her brother was missing too. "That *idiot*!" she said, irritated, but her tone was more worried than annoyed.

"Okay. Guess I'll have to take care of you boys first," she said, looking down at the groaning terminal in front of her.

She poked her stun gun against his head.

"If this is the guy I think it is, this ought to fix things," and a weaker burst of electricity coursed through the terminal's head.

She repeated this with all of them. Even those with gunshot wounds—none of the wounds were fatal, so she let them be.

"Okay..." she said, looking up. She checked to see just how many power lines were running overhead.

Then she picked up the five guns lying on the ground. They all had silencers on them, so she unscrewed them and held the pieces in both hands.

She fired and fired until there were no bullets left, leaving the street echoing with more gunfire than a yakuza flick.

Kinukawa Kotoe heard the noise as well.

"What—?!"

She had already fled onto a different street, but the noise carried like the wind.

Everyone in earshot knew something was up.

(What is that crazy bitch thinking...?)

The people around her were turning their heads, and moving towards the noise. Presumably they had never heard real gunshots before. In this respect, Japan was still a peaceful country. Kotoe, however, had no intention of turning back and making sure of anything. She wanted to get away as quickly as humanly possible.

Kotoe started up the road in a temporary vacuum as everyone around her headed towards the noise, but then her feet suddenly stopped.

A man was standing in front of her.

He was not heading towards the noise, but looking right at her, waiting quietly.

He was wearing white.

"............"

Kotoe could not understand why this had such an impact on her. To be strictly accurate, the surface consciousness Spooky E had imprinted on Kotoe did not understand.

(Who...is this again?)

She was mystified to find herself fretting because he'd seen her.

"............"

The man in white moved slowly towards her.

He looked very sad. Kotoe felt that expression was very familiar.

Like something she had long since left behind...

"Wh... wh-who...are you?!" she shrieked.

Right there in the middle of the street, heedless as to who might see her, she pulled out her gun and pointed it at the man.

"............" The man in white kept walking toward her.

Kotoe took a step backwards, helpless. She couldn't let him get close to her. She couldn't even look at his face.

She had to run away. She turned her back on him and took a step...

And he grabbed her hand.

"—Kotoe-chan," he whispered.

When she heard his voice, Kotoe burst into tears. "L-Let go!" she screamed, but it was a very feeble scream.

The man in white did as she asked.

Kotoe staggered, tripped over her own feet, no longer able to walk.

The man was in front of her again.

"I've known how you felt for a long time," he said, quietly.

Kotoe could not answer. Consciously, she was unable to understand anything he said, but her body had frozen, unable to react.

"Wh-what...?" The word slipped out of her mouth despite her immobility, but he ignored it completely.

"I know that you were, in your own fashion, quite serious about me. But at the same time, *I could see you*. So I knew very well that, even if you loved me, you would never become happy." His voice droned on and on, like some sort of machine.

"Ahhhh..." Kotoe began shaking.

"Your feelings are, sadly, nothing more than childish admiration, Kotoe-chan. You will never be able to truly love anything. That's the way you are. Half of your feelings for me were nothing more than pity. You were only able to convince yourself that this was love because you are still a child."

"Aaaah..."

"And you will always be lonely. You will never understand why you seem to be incapable of being truly passionate about anything...which will be an eternal source of sorrow. That's why I interested you. I appeared to be sad, and you wondered if I was the same as you—but that was a delusion."

"Aaaaaaaahhhh..."

"I never really felt sadness. Only despair. I lacked a future, but had no feelings like yours. Whatever you wanted from me, I could have given you nothing."

"Aaaaaaahhhhh... Aahhh..."

From the moment he started talking, Kotoe had been bawling. Her face was frozen and expressionless, but her tears were pouring down her cheeks.

"There is no world where we can be together," he said and closed his mouth at last.

"Ah... Aaaaah... Aaaaaaaaaaaaaahhh..."

Kotoe shook so hard she almost fell over and had to grab onto the man for support.

"...H... he......help......" her expression shattered, and she struggled to say something through her tears. "...Help... help me... help me, Jin-niisan...... Help me!"

A name she should not have been able to say escaped her lips.

Like a lost child who has at last found its parents, she clung to the man—to her beloved Asukai Jin.

"—If I only could," he said, in the same quiet voice. "I've been hoping I could for a long time now. If only I could help you—but I can't. I still have no idea what to do for you. I know that you should not be with me. Regardless of what you felt that night you spoke to me, when I was waiting for snow alone outside."

Only this last line showed any trace of warmth.

Kotoe was well beyond her stress limits, and was unable to stop her consciousness from fading away. "Jin...nii...sa...n......"

The world in front of her darkened. From the darkness, she heard a voice, unchanged from a moment before, ask, "Where is Spooky E?"

Kotoe might have said something in reply. But she was no longer capable of knowing what.

For a second, she felt as if she were being embraced, but it may just have been her imagination.

"I'm sorry. Goodbye," came a voice from so far away it may well have been in the next world. It was the last time she ever heard it......

When people came back, they found a girl lying in the middle of the road. She was taken away in an ambulance and regained consciousness a few hours later. She attempted to explain herself to the policeman sitting by her side, but he only nodded kindly.

"We've figured out most of it by now."

The gunfire incident concluded in a rather odd manner, since almost everyone involved had received an electric shock, and was unable to remember anything about it. The forensics team believed that one of the bullets had struck a power line, which in turn had sent a current running through the ditch water left standing in the alley. The area was a mess, and they were unable to find any further evidence.

There were a few witnesses, but all of them just said stuff like, "I didn't see anyone else come out of there." So they were forced to conclude that the scuffle had ended in this extremely unusual fashion.

The reason for the scuffle was lost in a sea of confusion, but at least a few of the people lying there were known drug dealers, which made things simple. The punks, skinheads, and indie musicians lying around them remembered being asked by the girl to look for something. The police in turn concluded that she had been the leader, and had been investigating ties to a possible drug syndicate. As further evidence, a strange outfit often described by recently arrested drug dealers was found lying at the scene.

"The only thing left is motive, which we heard as well. Your cousin cooperated with us once before. He was involved in a case where one of your friends died. He told us you were unable to let that situation rest."

"Really?"

"Yep. It was pretty bad. She was so far into withdrawal, the pain led her to stab herself in the throat. I know just how you feel."

"My friend..." she said absently, lying still in her hospital bed.

She was a little out of it.

The police were not surprised. "You've done a few things we could probably charge you for, but really—why? Mitigating circumstances are good enough for me. The people who helped you will get off with a suspended sentence as well, I think. After all, you have managed to completely destroy a drug operation."

"............"

"I'm gonna let you take it easy and start recovering from shock now," the policeman said kindly.

All she could do was thank him, in a voice without emotion.

Boogiepop returns

VS Imaginator Part 2

V

A perfect victory is difficult to obtain,
But it is even more difficult to lose well.

—Kirima Seiichi (*VS Imaginator*)

V.

TRYING NOT TO PUKE from the lingering effects of the stun gun my sister had zapped me with, I boarded a bus and headed straight for Orihata's apartment building.

(Urp...)

The more you try to suppress the urge, the more attention you attract. I barely managed to look normal.

I had lost the Boogiepop outfit Orihata had made me.

That felt strange.

I felt like that had been the link between us, and without it, I couldn't settle down.

But I could no longer rely on it. Either way, Kinukawa Kotoe had been taken into custody, and there was no way for me to ask her where Orihata was.

I got off the bus, and walked the route to Orihata's apartment, which I had followed countless times before (though I always turned back at the entrance).

I was a little worried that someone would stop me, but no one did, and I was soon standing outside the door to her apartment.

I rang the bell, my heart pounding.

There was no answer...

I rang it again.

Still nothing...

I grit my teeth, pulled out the key, and unlocked the door.

Now that I thought about it, Orihata had never once actually come over to my home—and this was my first time ever entering hers. Yeah, all things considered, we had had a rather strange relationship.

"Hello?" I whispered, stepping in.

My feet stopped almost instantly.

"Uh...?!"

The room was empty.

There wasn't a trace of anyone living here.

"W-wait a minute," I said, flustered.

This was absurd. I had dropped her off here almost every day, and the key was the right key, so... Feeling myself beginning to panic, I looked around the apartment again, and found a sleeping bag lying in the corner of the empty living room.

I gulped.

I crept over to it and picked it up by the corner.

I sniffed—I know, kinda creepy—and it smelled like her hair did whenever she leaned in close to powder my face in makeup.

(Orihata—slept here?)

I dropped the sleeping bag and peered around the room.

Her Shinyo Academy uniform was hanging on the wall.

I opened the closet, and found the rest of her clothes. I'd seen everything in there. It was all of the clothes she'd ever worn on our dates.

And that was it...

Nothing casual, nothing for around the house. No sweatshirts, no jerseys, no pajamas. Nothing.

"............"

Hesitantly, I opened what I assumed was her underwear drawer.

Only one type, and they were all lined up. It was as if she'd bought them on sale somewhere.

"............"

I glanced back towards her clothes.

I had seen all of them...but one set was missing.

"Where are the clothes she was wearing the last time I saw her...?" I said, unease gnawing at my gut.

I went into the kitchen. The stove looked barely even used, so I looked in her garbage. It was filled with empty convenience store *bento*. I flipped through each of them.

No recent dates...

The most recent one was the day before I last saw her.

"........." I felt suddenly dizzy and fell over on the floor.

(What does this *mean*—?)

Where was Orihata?

I felt like I was overlooking something important.

But what?

What was I forgetting?

Meanwhile, in an abandoned, half-finished, suburban amusement park near the city, another man was equally confused.

(What's going on?)

Spooky E was furiously dialing one number after another, his always pasty features even paler, trying to contact the "terminals" he'd brainwashed.

But not one of them would respond. Every phone was turned off.

(Shit! How did this happen?)

Blood spurted out of the wounds where his right ear had been. His teeth chattered away.

His hair had gone from simply graying to completely gray.

Fear.

It was the one thing tormenting him now.

If his terminals did not respond, then his power over them had been lifted.

Which (to him) meant he had lost all proof of his existence.

This had happened before—a boy had somehow slipped out from under his control, but he had convinced himself this was an isolated occurrence and merely coincidental.

No, he had *tried* to convince himself.

Without his power, he was in the same position as the object of his abuse and scorn, Orihata Aya—if not worse.

Orihata Aya would be able to carry on somehow, testing to see if cross breeding were possible, but he had no chance of anything like that.

He would be completely useless.

And, probably, disposed of.

(This can't be happening!)

He opened his hands, and let electricity crackle across his palms. He could see the sparks, hear the sound of air burning.

(It's still working—I'm not finished yet! So why——?)

He forced power into his jaw, and managed to stop his teeth from dancing.

Normally, this would be no time to be holed up in an abandoned, half-finished amusement park like this. He should be down in town, trying to work out what was wrong. But...

"D-d-d-damn you..."

He couldn't do that.

He was too scared, too frightened to see things with his own eyes.

"Damn it... Damn it!"

What worried him the most was the lack of response from Kinukawa Kotoe, who he had spent so much time on. Even if the others fizzled out, she had been a virtual copy of himself, so how could she possibly escape his control?

"Impossible! It's completely impossible!"

Blood glurped out of his ear wound again.

He sat trembling in the darkness a while longer, but at last he got control of himself and stood up.

He walked slowly to the top of the tower he was hiding in.

The roof of the half-finished tower was covered in building materials, and he made a b-line for one particularly innocuous-looking pile.

"If it's come to this..."

There were seven canisters, none especially large.

Each one contained enough bioweaponry to wipe out every living person in the area.

Specifically, it was a toxic virus genetically engineered to dissipate and die within three hours of being released into the air—or thirty minutes in daylight.

But during that time, the virus would multiply explosively, infect every living thing it came into contact with, and melt every cell in their body. Eventually, the virus would begin to cannibalize itself, leaving nothing untouched in its wake.

It was described as the ultimate "antibiotic"—one so powerful that it could disinfect life itself.

But Spooky E was hardly concerned about such details. His body already had immunities to the virus—so no matter how much "death" he spread, he would never feel so much as a sniffle.

"I could use this..."

If he killed everyone, he might be able to hide the fact that his ability had failed...!

He reached his hand towards the valve on top of one of the canisters.

"Then...!" There was a gleam in his big eyes.

But his hand suddenly froze, like something was pulling it back.

He raised his head, and stared around him.

"What...?!"

He heard footsteps. Someone was here.

Quite a lot of people were here.

He looked over the edge of the tower at the ground below.

His expression stiffened.

"........."

There was a crowd of people staring up at him.

He recognized at least half of them.

Naturally, they were the people he had brainwashed.

"Wh-what the *hell*?!" he roared.

But none of them made any response. It was as if they hadn't even heard him.

They simply stared calmly up at him, in silence.

"A-answer me! What the hell are—!" he shouted hysterically.

A voice from behind him said, "At last we meet, Spooky Electric-kun."

It was a young man's voice. Spooky E twitched like he'd been jolted with electricity, then spun around.

A man in white clothes—Asukai Jin—was standing at the entrance to the roof.

"Wh-who are you?!" Spooky E screamed.

Asukai Jin did not answer. He stared at the canister behind Spooky E.

"Oh, I see. The 'disinfectant.' You were going to use that? Cut it close then."

"What the hell are you?!" Spooky E shrieked, and at last Asukai met his gaze.

"That's a strange question."

"Wh-what?!"

"I thought you were looking for me. Was I wrong?" Asukai said, shrugging. "If you must say something, it should be, 'I guess the time has come,' or something like that."

"Th-then...y-you are......" Spooky E took a step backwards. He bumped against the canister.

"You know me as 'The Imaginator,'" Asukai said, grinning.

Spooky E gasped. "What...did you do? How—?!"

He knew the man in front of him was his greatest threat.

"I'm just better than you," Asukai said quietly and with utter confidence.

"Guh...!"

"The Towa Organization, was it? Your syndicate—no, system?" Asukai trilled.

"Y-you know...?"

"Not any specifics. Just that this system is...'observing' things. I must say, you've got quite some people working for you."

Spooky E made another choking sound.

"What are you observing? What conditions are you searching for?" Asukai asked, peacefully. "I've thought of many things, but have only been able to come up with one working theory."

Spooky E was shaking like a leaf.

"'Transformation.' What else? Anything that changes? That's what you're watching, correct? You give ordinary, innocent humans drugs and observe their reactions, and then you investigate how much they change...am I right?"

"Unh..."

"From which we can determine that the Towa Organization

operates on a scale much too grand to be referred to as a mere syndicate. Essentially, everything in the 'present'—whether they hate all things new and different, or whether they are trying to bend these new things to their will—has collectively produced what is known as the Towa Organization. Obviously, this means their power is incredibly vast. However..." Asukai shot Spooky E another grin. "In this area, at the moment, there is only you. Correct?"

He smiled with only his eyes, his eyes declaring that Spooky E would not be saved, would not be able to escape.

"Grrraagh...!" Spooky E ground his teeth, blood spraying out of his missing ear again. "Y-you... you know that much...but do you have any idea what that means?"

"Mm?"

"No matter what you do to me, you have no future!" Spooky E bellowed. "You can't survive long with the Towa Organization as your enemy! When you end my life—you end yours!" His shrill voice was almost completely swept away by the high wind blowing across the tower roof.

"............" Asukai Jin just kept on smiling, staring at Spooky E. "My enemy?" He nodded to himself. Then his mouth twisted into a smirk. "My enemy!"

"What's so funny?"

"Speaking of enemies... Do you have any idea?"

"Of what?"

"How many people died because of the 'experiments' you've been conducting? People who coincidentally had an allergic reaction to the drugs you fed them...or who went into shock. Here's a hint, it's no small number."

"So what? They aren't important!"

"True. They aren't," Asukai agreed, calmly. "The percentage of deaths is much lower than traffic accidents, or disease. You could certainly say that anyone that happened to die that way was simply unlucky...nothing more. But every human has someone who depends on them. Don't you understand? They have friends... family."

"...?" Spooky E frowned, unable to figure out what Asukai was driving at.

"He certainly was unlucky. He always did have bad luck," Asukai said, his gaze drifting marginally skywards. "He had no 'roots,' you see. Everything he tried, he did timidly. Yet his 'flower' was gigantic, which meant he'd jump on board any fool's dream, get tricked again, and just wind up in trouble. I had to cover for him so many times." A self-deprecating grin passed across his face. "But that was all in vain. No matter how hard I worked, I could not make up for his utter lack of fortune."

"What do you mean? What are you talking about?"

"I suppose it was he who gave me *The Little Prince*." Asukai sighed and fixed his gaze on Spooky E again. "Enemy? No, this is revenge. This is the irony of fate."

"So tell me what you mean!"

"Just a little history," Asukai said suddenly.

"What...?"

"Have you ever considered who it is who ultimately wins? Is it the strongest? Is it the one who kept everyone under his thumb? What do you think happens to people like that in the end? I'll tell you...*nothing*. When they win, they use too much power, and collapse. Their victory is snatched away from them by someone else. When you face your enemy, you must make a more intelligent choice."

Asukai's smile vanished.

"The second option is to carefully surrender. You have plenty of power, but not enough to take on your opponent, so surrender is the best way to stay alive. But the first option—"

Unsmiling, his gaze was so pointed it seemed to pierce the other man's skin.

"Turn your enemy into your ally. This is the wisest, most effective method."

Spooky E's big eyes opened even wider. "Wh-what...?!"

"You and I are a lot alike. We're almost exactly the same. We have the same kind of power. Our abilities compliment each other."

Asukai spread his hands.

"In other words, as long as I keep doing the same kind of things, then as far as the Towa Organization is concerned, there is no real difference from when you did them."

"............!" Spooky E's expression twisted. "Y-you can't mean...!"

"Yes, I can. I'm going to use you as cover while I take over the Towa Organization. Through you, I shall spread the Imaginator throughout the Towa Organization—at least, that's the plan."

Asukai took a step towards Spooky E.

Spooky E slid sideways past the canister at his back, trying to keep his distance. "B-but that's..."

"Forget can or can't. I have to. If I want to make snow fall in April everywhere in the world, I absolutely need a vast organization backing me."

"S-snow...?"

To any sensible human being, Spooky E was a monstrous being of unfathomable mystery...yet now he faced something far more inscrutable than himself for the first time since he had come into this world.

"Simply put, I plan to standardize humanity's psyche—putting an end to all the sadness, all the disconnections, all the misunderstandings that arise between us."

"Y-you're insane! You've completely lost your mind!"

"So what if I have? If you think yourself sane, then do something about this madman before you start insisting you are," Asukai said, grinning.

"Ah...rraaaaaaaaah!" Spooky E bellowed as leapt at Asukai, electricity sparking from both hands.

Asukai...did not dodge.

Spooky E's electric palms slapped him on the head like a sumo wrestler, knocking him over backwards.

(What—?!)

After all the confident speeches, Spooky E was completely thrown by his enemy's extreme weakness.

But he couldn't hesitate now. He attacked again.

Grabbing Asukai's head between both hands, he sent electricity—

Or at least, he *tried* to, but Asukai suddenly sprang forward, and Spooky E reflexively shrank backwards.

"Unh..." Big drops of battle sweat rolled down his fat cheeks and forehead.

"Pretty intense," Asukai said, shaking his head. Something fell off it.

Something that made Spooky E's eyes bulge out of his head.

A wig, with smoke pouring off of it. The inside was covered in strips of something.

It was a glossless texture that Spooky E knew very well.

"A-anti-magnetic sheets?"

These were stickers designed to shield floppy discs from the magnets in purse latches and the like by halting all electromagnetic waves. Piling these on top of each other had effectively left Asukai's head wrapped into a sort of papier-mâché helmet.

"Exactly! I had surmised that your ability was based on electromagnetic waves, so I came prepared," Asukai taunted. Without the wig, his hair looked exactly the same. He was busy shaking debris out of it, fragments fallen from the anti-magnetic sheets.

"........." Spooky E stared at the wig for a moment, but at last snorted loudly, then broke into a wild guffaw. "Bwa ha ha ha ha ha ha ha ha ha ha ha ha!!!"

"Is it funny?" Asukai asked.

Spooky E went right on laughing. "Ha ha! You were nothing

more than a fraud all along! How can I *not* laugh? You had me running scared!"

"Am I?"

"Without that little trick of yours, you can't block my attack. We may be equally matched in the brainwashing department, but you're not even in the ballpark when it comes to fighting!"

"Ah, you could put it that way. Yes." Asukai hung his head.

"Give it up! You can never..." he started to say, but...

(......?)

Spooky E noticed something odd.

In Asukai Jin's right hand was a single rose. Held delicately in his fingertips.

(Where'd that come from?)

The rose had no roots. But it had not been cut; instead, the stem grew steadily smaller, tapering off to nothing. It was like an artificial flower, but was too realistic, too fresh.

"Other people may not be able to see my 'visions,' but I imagine you can," Asukai said, twirling the rose around in his fingertips. "After all, this...is your 'psyche.'"

"More magic tricks?" Spooky E bellowed, and lunged at Asukai again.

Again, Asukai did not try to dodge. This time there was nothing on his head to protect him.

(Don't need to hold back! Full storm power, fry every cell in his stupid brain!)

Spooky E reached out with both hands.

Asukai stood there, waiting for the blow to fall—

But just before it did, Spooky E's body froze in place.

(Wh-what the—?)

He was right in front of Asukai Jin. His hands were just centimeters away from grabbing onto him...but he couldn't close that gap.

"Gr...rrrrr...?"

Clearly, it wasn't some invisible wall between them. It was more like Spooky E's body had become incredibly, amazingly heavy—too heavy to continue moving.

"M-my body...it... it won't move...!"

"Not your body. *Your mind*," Asukai said quietly, the rose still in his hand.

"Wh-what did you do to me?"

"Right now, no matter what, you will not be able to work up the motivation to attack me. That's all. The only thing stopping you from moving is your own will. Your *own* unconscious will."

"H-how...?!"

"I removed the 'thorns' from your 'flower.' That's all."

"............?!"

"But that seems to have *removed your very capacity for aggression.*"

Asukai spun the rose in his hand again. There were no thorns anywhere on the rose's stem.

"Th-that's impossible..." But even as he spoke, Spooky E toppled feebly over and with a thump, he was sitting on the floor of the roof.

"Unh..." He couldn't even roar.

Now he got it.

He knew why Asukai had used another cheap trick like those anti-magnetic sheets... It was so he couldn't run away.

First, he needed to make him attack, and then stop that attack. But he only needed to stop it once. If he managed to get close enough to Spooky E even for a moment, then he could take his "rose."

"Your power—this thing where you control a person's brain with electric shocks—is incredibly backwards," Asukai said, glaring down at Spooky E. "It lacks the concept of the 'soul.' You pay no attention to the principle force driving human behavior. You just jam a bit of information down on top of their minds, without ever really changing them in any real sense of the word. Compared to the Imaginator, you're just second rate."

"Unh..."

"You never thought to even do what I can—to perceive the flaws in human hearts and discover how to repair them. Your method is like striking water with a hammer. The key point is to change your method depending on who you are working with."

"Uuuuunh..."

"Told you I was better," Asukai said.

"Uuuuuuunh," Spooky E moaned, reeling. It was just as Asukai said; he had no urge to attac, and no strength anywhere in his body.

"Yet...I should admit that I do have to do much the same thing as you do with your lightning. There are just too many humans in this world."

"Wh-what have you done...? What are you going to do now...?" Spooky E managed, listlessly.

"Grafting. You know the word? Where you take two similar plants, touch the parts that bear fruit together, and create an entirely new plant. Same principle. I have been taking groups of two or more and using them to plant a small piece of what each of them lacked. Everyone I've done this for has been very happy, since their hearts are now perfect. And naturally, all of them have become my allies."

Asukai smiled gently.

"I can do the same thing for you. As soon as you find a partner, I can give you the 'roots' you lack. In return, I will take just a little sliver of your 'stem.' Of course, it'll cut down that strong mental power...but you'll hardly even notice. Not with the joy you'll be feeling once your flaw is healed."

"..............." Spooky E looked dazed. "I don't...understand."

"Even you will understand soon."

Spooky E looked up at Asukai, his eyes unfocused. "What I don't understand is how you can be enjoying this. I, at least, was acting on orders from the Towa Organazation—but you..."

Asukai frowned, sharply.

Spooky E ignored him, dropping his gaze again. "Nah... Well, that's really not important... There's only one thing left for me to look forward to."

He held his hands up in front of his face, staring at them.

"What's that?"

"Something I've wanted to do for a long time," he muttered. "But my hatred for *them* was too strong, so I never could. I couldn't do it while they were still living. But now those feelings are gone. Maybe because you took my 'thorns.' So for that, I guess I'm grateful to you..."

"What are you talking about?" Asukai asked, puzzled.

"Let me give you one warning...Imaginator! Boogiepop is after you," he said, and then Spooky E grabbed his own face.

Sparks flew.

"——!"

By the time a flustered Asukai reached his side, Spooky E had already burned out all the cells in his brain with his own electricity. Blood poured out of his eyes and nose. Smoke trailed from the wound on his right ear.

He was dead.

".........Ah," Orihata Aya moaned, opening her eyes. She thought she had heard faint screaming coming from somewhere.

The world around her was still pitch black. There were no windows or lamps in the room she was imprisoned in.

She was sprawled out on the dust-covered floor, her hands and feet handcuffed from behind. Spooky E had put her here.

She could no longer tell how long she had been sleeping. Despair seemed ready to tear her open.

"Mmph," she mumbled, twisting herself upright.

Dust flew, and she coughed.

"I have to... I have to get away..."

It might already be too late. The thought made her teeth chatter violently.

"I have to go... I have to tell him..."

Tormented by anxiety and fear, she moved like an inchworm, looking for the door.

But it wasn't that simple. The door was locked, and there was no other way in or out.

"Augh...!"

She was shivering violently. It was cold, she was exhausted, and she was powerless.

But she kept on moving despite the handcuffs, frantically searching for a way out.

As her body twisted, something fell out of her jacket pocket.

Her cell phone.

Spooky E had forgotten to take it away from her, but regardless of how brightly the low battery light was shining...there was still hope.

(Aaah...!)

Aya quickly planted her face next to the phone. With this, she could tell him...!

She prayed there would be a signal.

(P-please......!)

Using the tip of her tongue—the only part of her she could move—she tried to push the buttons.

Suddenly, there was a click from the door.

Aya's face jerked.

"......!"

It was no good. She had no time. She couldn't hide the phone in time...!

The handle turned, and the door swung open.

Light poured into the dark room.

But the silhouette standing before her was not Spooky E.

"Wh-who are...?" Aya thought she had seen this tall man in white clothes before.

"We've met before," the man said, agreeing.

"You are—!" she remembered.

The man who had saved them the day she first met Masaki.

"Why are you...?" she murmured, then her head jerked up. "P-please! Help me!"

"I'm sorry, but I can't do that," the man said quietly.

"Eh...?"

"I need you to be a sacrifice," he said, sounding very lonely.

"Wh-what do you...mean?"

"I don't have much time...I didn't expect Spooky E to die. Sooner or later, another Towa Organization agent will come here. I need to be ready for them. I have at least brought 'lightning' to this town."

Aya couldn't understand most of what the man said, except for one thing...

(He's dead...?)

She was sure he'd said that.

The man who had bound her like this was dead?

Then that meant... that meant *he* was...

"Um, excuse me...!" Ignoring the man's sinister promise to sacrifice her, Aya tried to ask for the one thing she cared about.

And then the phone in front of her lit up and began to ring.

"......!"

Aya knew instantly.

Only two people ever called her phone number, and one of them was Spooky E.

The man in white reached out, and picked up the phone.

He answered the phone—and just like when headphones are yanked from a stereo, it got really loud, and a boy's frantic voice filled the room.

"Orihata! Orihata, is that you?!"

It was Taniguchi Masaki.

(Ahhhhh……)

Relief stole all the strength in Aya's body.

"………"

Asukai had heard the voice that came gushing out of the phone before.

(That boy…)

He looked back at Orihata Aya.

She looked completely and utterly relieved.

(She had been about to ask me if the boy was safe.)

He nodded. That was more important to the girl than her own safety.

"Hello…? Hello! Orihata?! Say something, please?!"

"…………"

Asukai listened wordlessly, and at last held the phone out… to Aya's ear.

"…?"

She looked surprised. Whoever this man was, he didn't seem

like he planned to forgive her. So why was he giving her the phone?

Asukai gazed down at her coldly. No trace of pity or pride.

"Orihata?! Orihata?!!" the boy's voice continued, nearly shrieking.

Asukai Jin and Orihata Aya looked at each other as the voice between them rang out——

VI

Just as no truth is certain, there is no such thing as a perfect lie.

—Kirima Seiichi (*VS Imaginator*)

VI.

BECAUSE I'M a complete *idiot*, it took me half the day to sort things out.

I just sat in Orihata's empty apartment, flat on my ass, trying to work out what was bugging me.

(What is it? There's gotta be something...)

When I got hungry, I ate some Calorie Mate I had left in my pocket. I pondered as I ate. But as I thought, I guess I must have dozed off. When my eyes snapped open again, several hours had passed.

"Sh-shit...!"

I looked at my watch, panicking. It was broken. I must have smashed it on something during the fight, or maybe the stun gun my sister hit me with took it out. I had only just now noticed.

(When I got to the bus stop, the bus had come right away, so I never even glanced at my watch...)

I looked around the room.

Nope, there were no clocks. No TV or stereo either.

What now? I couldn't just sit here. I had no clues, but just as I stood up to go out and look for her anyway, it finally hit me.

"Oh..."

I was standing in the middle of an empty room.

There was nothing in it.

Nothing at all...

I looked along the walls towards the corners, and that's when I found it.

The phone jack had the lid down. There was nothing hooked up to it.

There was no phone in her apartment...

But I had called her here many, many times. Which means...

"I wasn't actually calling her home phone!"

I'm such an idiot.

I bolted out of the apartment and onto the road, looking around frantically.

Nothing.

"Shit!"

I ran and ran, and at last, five hundred meters down the road, I found a pay phone in front of a convenience store.

I grabbed the receiver like an infant grabbing his mother's knee, jammed my phone card into it, and stabbed the phone number I had seared into my memory.

"Come on, pick up... Pick up...!"

Orihata's phone was a *cell* phone.

She might still have it with her. Wherever she was, I could call her!

It rang and rang and rang.

"Damn it! Pick up...!" I shouted, fretting.

I'm sure it was less than twenty seconds, but it felt more like twenty minutes to me.

At last, there was a click as someone answered.

"Orihata! Orihata, is that you?!" I cried.

There was no response.

"Hello...? Hello!" I could feel my voice rising, getting worked up.

I kept on calling her name.

After what seemed like an eternity of silence, at last I heard a faint voice on the line go, "Ah..." And I knew instantly. It was Orihata's voice. I almost burst into tears. It was her.

"Hello? Orihata, it's me, Taniguchi Masaki!"

"...Yes, I know," she said, sounding very distant.

"Are you safe, Orihata?"

"Y-yes... N-no. Why do you ask?" she said, awkwardly. It sounded like she had nodded, then corrected herself?

"Kinukawa was arrested by the police...did you hear?"

"Really...?"

"What about you? Are you in any danger?"

"Not really."

"Kinukawa-san was brainwashed apparently, so..."

"—Yes. Please, don't blame her..."

"Is someone there with you? Are they...making you do anything?" I didn't know how to ask this.

"............"

"I might be out of line saying this, but I want to help you. I want to save you."

Sort of a corny line, but I genuinely meant it.

"............"

"Orihata, you... I mean, maybe you're just fed up with me by now, but I really don't mind being used. So, just go ahead and use me anytime you want to. I really did like being with you, and that was enough for me... So anything more than that, I... Your..."

As I babbled, I could feel my sentences making less and less sense.

I felt like nothing I said was getting through.

No matter what I said, no matter how much I meant it... it was never enough.

"Masaki..." she said, quietly.

"Y-yes?"

"That's enough. I don't need you anymore," she said, bluntly.

I felt a sharp pain in my chest.

"You should find yourself a better...normal girl. You shouldn't see me anymore."

"N-no, that's not... I don't..."

"No. We're finished."

"Uh, Orihata—"

"You know by now? What I've done?"

"I-I—"

"No matter what they told you, it's all true. It never occurred to you that I was like that, did it?"

"Well—"

"I'm sorry. That's what I am. I don't know what you expected from me, but that's all there is."

"But—"

"I lied to you. I betrayed you. Wake up and look around you, Masaki. You're an idiot!"

"But...I'm in love with you!" I shouted, forgetting everything but that truth.

"...............!"

The voice echoing out of the phone momentarily robbed Aya of words.

The pretense she'd barely managed to maintain was crumbling beneath her. Her face flushed, her throat trembled. She couldn't talk.

Her hands were still handcuffed behind her, and someone else was holding the phone for her. She was speaking into the receiver Asukai Jin was silently holding out for her. Her hands were empty, but covered in sweat. She balled them up, trying to stop them from shaking.

"H-how can you say..." she managed, stifling the quaver in her voice.

She had to.

She couldn't rely on Masaki here.

She couldn't drag him any further into this. She couldn't bear it any longer.

She could never tell him how she felt.

"Where are you, Orihata?"

"N-none of your business!"

She wanted to see him.

One more time, with her own eyes.

But those feelings were her enemy now.

She could only protect Masaki if he hated her. That was the only way.

She remembered what Suema Kazuko had said, on the roof of the school.

It's impossible to live without someone hating you... You're missing the concept of that "struggle." And you really need to get that.

Now was that moment.

She had to fight her enemy, had to struggle with her own emotions.

"F-forget about me—leave me alone...!"

But she couldn't say it forcefully.

"Orihata...!" Masaki's voice didn't falter.

Aya couldn't talk anymore. "G-goodbye..." she managed. Tears made her voice sound funny.

"............"

Asukai Jin watched Aya's suffering with mechanical detachment.

When it became obvious that Aya was not going to speak anymore, he held the phone to his own ear.

"...Is someone else there?" the boy's voice asked, with surprising perception.

Asukai did not reply.

"I know you're listening. I don't know who you are, but you're standing right next to her, aren't you?"

"............"

"I don't give a shit who you are. You do anything to Orihata, and I guarantee you that I'll be your enemy. And I *will* fight you for her!"

"..............." Asukai looked down at Aya.

She had not heard this last speech. Her head was down, her body quivering—she was crying.

He looked at her, but this did not change Asukai's expression.

"Hey! Are you lis—" and Asukai hung up, cutting the boy off.

A second later, he heard the distinctive roar of an airplane passing through the sky over the Paisley Park construction site.

The noise grew in strength, and was soon easily identifiable.

(Did he hear that...? No, it was still too faint. He won't have recognized it...)

The phone rang again, but Asukai shut it off.

He spoke to Aya. "Satisfied?"

"..............."

"You were happy to hear his voice."

She looked up at him and—surprisingly—nodded. "Yes."

She wasn't forcing herself. She honestly meant it.

"Okay. Then your life was not in vain. In that respect, you have the advantage on me," Asukai said, smiling faintly.

"............!"

I looked up.

Nothing. I couldn't see any sign of it.

(No! It's gotta be there! It's gotta be somewhere close!)

With a feeling bordering on faith, I searched the sky. If

anyone had seen me, I must have looked like I was searching for UFOs.

At last I found it.

A black shadow, high up in the air. The sky was gradually darkening, and I could just make out the flashing lights on the tips of the wings.

I took the direction it was flying into consideration...

(It's heading this way, so...it must have been over there... which means...)

The more I thought, the uneasier I grew.

I heard an airplane—I think. I was hardly certain.

But airplanes can be heard over an absurdly large area. Was I going to search it all?

(Like I have any choice...)

The lights of the airplane were getting closer, and now I could pick up the sound.

"——!"

Oh—!

Even when you can see the airplane, you can't necessarily hear it yet. Light travels faster than sound. There's a gap between the moment you see it, and the time the sound actually reaches your ears.

(So that means...it was further away than it was when I found it...)

My imagination sprang into action, making a mental map of the air.

(That means...it came from outside of the city?)

There was nothing but mountains there. Nobody lived out there. It was completely deserted.

(Or wait... I did hear something about an abandoned construction site...)

I felt myself getting excited.

That was it. It had to be!

"That's where she is!"

I started running.

I burst out onto a nearby street, saw that it was deserted, found a motorcycle parked by the side of the road, and crouched down to look at the lock.

The key wasn't in the ignition or anything, but I knew how to get the engine started. You tend to pick up a few tricks when you spend your time living abroad.

Sure, I didn't have a license or anything, but I'd driven one before.

"Sorry. Next time, use a chain!" I muttered to the absent owner, and opened the throttle.

"...I was *so* worried about you. Oh, well. At least you're safe..." Kinukawa Kotoe's mother said, happily arranging flowers in Kotoe's private hospital room.

Kotoe stared absently at the ceiling.

"........."

It was white, but the slanting rays of the sun gave it a reddish color.

She was still under the supervision of the police. Once she

was released, she would have a lot of questions to answer, but her father was in a prominent position in the city, and she was being treated well. It was very easy for people to get permission to visit her like this.

"Is there anything you'd like me to bring you, Kotoe?"

"Mom..."

"Yes?"

"What's going to happen to me?" she whispered.

"Don't worry! You have nothing to worry about. Your father said so! He didn't even need to put any pressure on anyone. The police just took care of everything on their own. There's even talk of them actually giving you some sort of award!"

"........." That wasn't what she'd meant, but Kotoe didn't try to explain herself.

"Oh, that reminds me. About Jin-kun..." her mother suddenly said.

Kotoe turned to look. "Jin-niisan? What about him?"

"It sounds like he's suddenly decided to study abroad!"

"Eh...?"

"He came by this morning. He said they can only take so many people, and that he has to leave immediately. He told me to say, 'Hi' to you. That boy is doing so *well*!"

"He's...gone?"

"Yes...he said someone would be round to pick up his things at the apartment later."

"............"

"You were friends with him, right? You'll miss him?"

"Yeah..." Kotoe nodded, expressionless.

There was a knock at the door.

"Yes?" her mother said, opening it.

There was a policeman in the hall. "Excuse me, but there's someone asking to see her. Is that okay?"

"Someone?"

"Says she's friends with your daughter," the policeman said, turning sideways so they could see the girl standing behind him.

"I'm Suema Kazuko. I spoke with you on the phone, once..."

"Oh, yes, I remember you! I recognize your voice."

"I wanted to speak with Kinukawa-san, if I could..."

"Just a moment." Her mother went back into the room. "Your friend Suema-san is here," she said.

"Suema-san...?"

"If you're too tired, we can ask her to come back."

"Uh, n-no... I want to see her. Please, let her in. And Mom...?"

"Yes?"

"C-could we have some privacy?"

Her mother was slightly surprised, but agreed pleasantly.

Suema Kazuko came in as her mother left, and closed the door.

"How are you feeling?" she said gently, following the standard progression of a sickbed visit.

"Fine."

"That's good," Suema said and smiled.

There didn't seem to be anything lurking behind that smile, so Kotoe relaxed a little.

"S-surprised? Didn't think I'd end up like this...?" she asked, hesitantly.

"Yes, well. I guess it was a bit unexpected," Suema said, very sweetly. "But not as surprising as it was earlier."

"Earlier?"

"When I heard how everyone's opinion of you had changed."

Kotoe looked down. "I can imagine..."

"They *were* pretty harsh."

"Yeah..."

"'Course, soon as your warrior legend spreads, that ought to change pretty quickly. People's reputations can change just like *that.*" Suema was grinning now.

Kotoe felt like something warm was rising out of her chest. She had been right, she thought. This girl would accept anything.

"Thank you. So, uh, did you come to cheer me up?"

"Nope," Suema shook her head. "I needed to ask you something point-blank."

"What?"

"Who or what was controlling you?"

I asked Kotoe, as directly as I could.

I knew it was a leap, but I was sure of myself.

Kotoe's eyes widened.

But I didn't flinch. I'm used to people thinking I'm weird.

I stood there, staring at her silently.

After a long pause of nothingness, she asked, "How did you know?"

This was hard to explain, but I had to say something before she would answer.

"Um, how can I put this... Humans tend to follow certain patterns. I don't mean stuff like, 'that girl's pretty, so she's stuck-up,' or anything like that. No, I mean everyone has a good and a bad side, you know? They're sensitive to some things and totally clueless about others. We all have a certain balance."

I'd found this out when I was almost killed. The person that was going to kill me was just an ordinary guy, with an ordinary job—maybe too ordinary. I'd thought a lot about why he had tried to kill me, but I could only come up with one explanation.

He was too ordinary.

That was it. There was no other reason.

I believe that was his balance.

"So your balance, or whatever you want to call it, didn't match up with the way you changed. If you changed, you would change in a different way. Sure, I might be wrong, but..."

But every time I started talking like this, I would start to wonder if it wasn't me that was the strange one.

Despite what I was saying, I didn't believe for a second that because Kotoe was a nice girl she wouldn't do anything strange.

But if she ever did do something strange, it would have been something else. That's all.

"............"

Kotoe's eyes were still wide open. Guess she hadn't followed my drift. I'm not entirely sure I had myself, so that was probably only natural.

"Putting it a little more bluntly, you're a bit dense and haven't really realized what it means to be pretty and rich, like you are. I'd be surprised if you were actually able take that in quickly."

"...!" Kotoe gasped.

I couldn't blame her; even I thought it was a little harsh.

"Sorry, it's just...that's what I thought," I said, apologetically.

Kotoe hung her head, but said nothing.

I couldn't think of anything else.

After a long pause, Kotoe at last said, "But..."

"Mm?"

"But I... I don't...remember very well."

"Starting when?"

"You called me once, right? I know I was normal then. A little after that... I don't really know what I was doing anymore," she said slowly, but surely.

I was again impressed by her strength.

I'd been so critical of her, and she had just sat there and took it. It's amazing.

"Right after I called?"

"No...awhile later. You told me not to see Jin-niisan, and I remember being shocked by that..."

"S-sorry. That was..."

"No, forget it. I... Right, I went where I always go when I'm depressed, and I remember staring at the sky...wondering silly things like, is it going to snow? That's the last thing I remember. After that, everything's just a strange blur." She looked very sad.

"Where is that?"

"Paisley Park. The amusement park they never finished. There's a tower there, called The Ladder. You know it?"

"Yeah, I do. Your father was part of that?"

"Yes. I had a key... I didn't go there because I'm rich or anything." There was a note of sadness in her voice.

"S-sorry. Please forget I said that."

"No, I don't mean that... I just thought, I'm so stupid. So childish," she said. Her head was down. She was trembling. "I can barely remember... But Jin-niisan said goodbye to me."

"..........."

"We won't meet again. I know that, but...I'm so childish, so stupid—"

Her shoulders quivered with a tiny, shriveled, lonely shiver.

"Kinukawa-san...are you still in love with Asukai Jin?" I asked.

She shook her head. "I don't know. I really don't know...not anymore... But... but..." Her grip tightened on her sheet. Tears began dropping on her fists. "But I want to see him again. I want him to laugh at me and make fun of me with his, 'Kotoe-chan, you're so shallow.' And then, I want to fight about it... I want him to laugh at me for getting angry..."

After that, she couldn't manage any more words.

I went over to her and gave her a hug.

I brushed her hair quietly.

"Don't worry. I'll do something. I promised, didn't I? I'll do something."

I felt like her loneliness was being transmitted directly to me with each tremble.

When I reached the first floor lobby, my friend Miyashita Touka, who'd come with me, came running over.

"So? How was she?"

"Touka... Sorry, but can you go home ahead of me?" I said, so harshly it must have sounded rude.

"Why?" she asked, surprised, peering at my face. I didn't have the freedom to worry about her feelings.

"There's somewhere I have to go," I snapped.

"Wh-where?"

"To look for The Ladder."

I couldn't wait here. I had to go there *now*. I knew that much.

I was furious.

I'd only met the man once, but I could have killed him.

I wanted to tie a rope around Asukai Jin's neck and drag him back down here to apologize to Kinukawa Kotoe...!

"Suema, w-wait—!" Touka's flustered voice called after me as I burst out of the hospital and into the sunset outside.

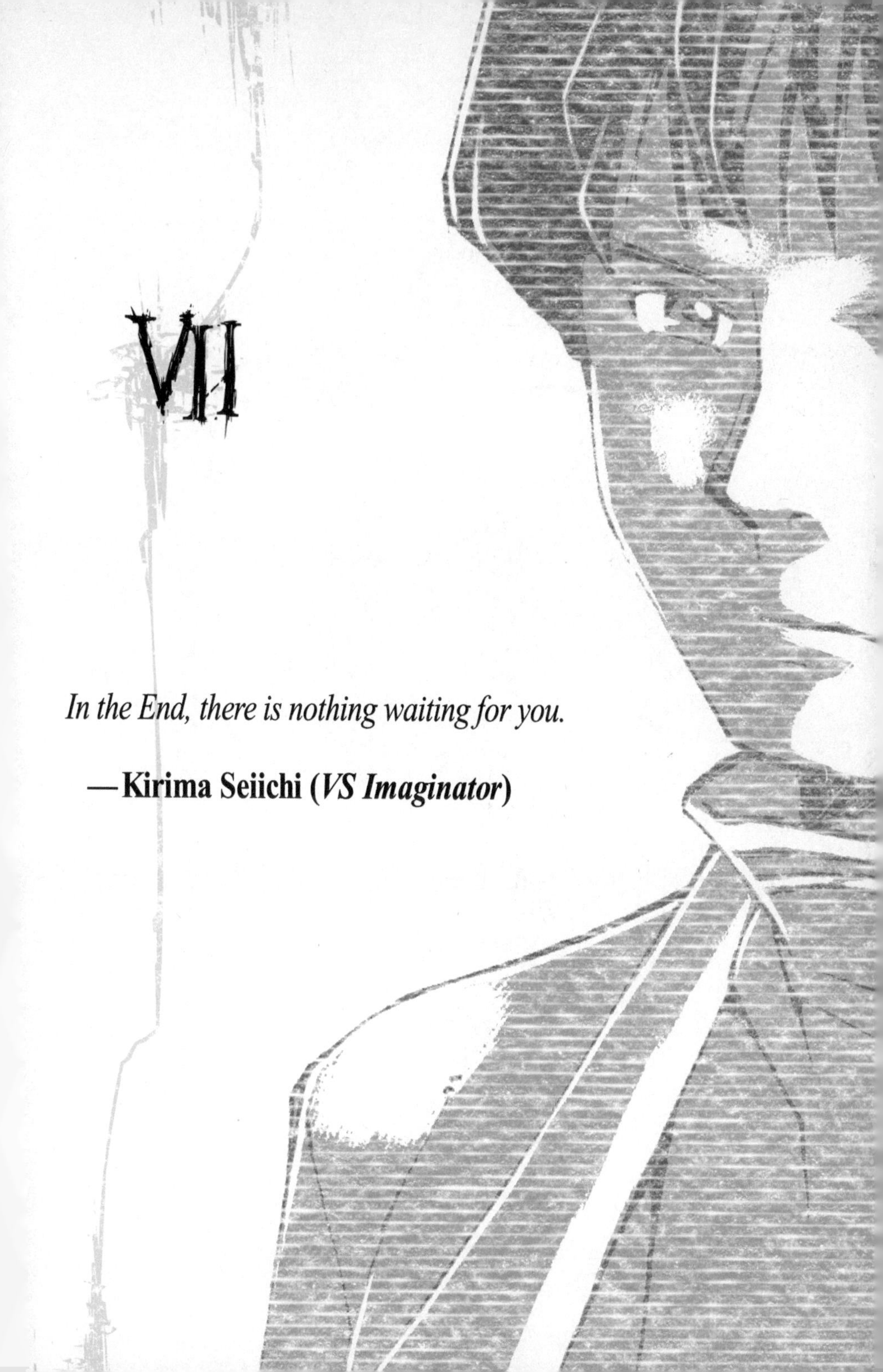

VII

In the End, there is nothing waiting for you.

—Kirima Seiichi (*VS Imaginator*)

VII.

"Just a little longer," the girl standing behind Asukai Jin said.

Her body was transparent, and few people could actually see her. Even Asukai, who had originally been able to see her quite well, could almost never make her out these days.

"Just a little longer."

The girl's feet were floating just above the ground.

No matter where she was, wherever people could stand, her feet would be a few centimeters up in the air.

But she had almost reached touchdown.

"I can almost get through."

No one could hear her voice.

Or perhaps she never intended it to be heard.

"Mm?"

As Asukai Jin took Orihata Aya up the stairs of The Ladder, he thought he could almost hear a voice he had not heard for awhile.

He stopped and turned his head, but there was nothing there.

"………?"

Her hands still handcuffed, Orihata Aya looked up at him, confused. "Are you going to kill me here...?" As always, her manner of speaking was extremely distant.

"N-no...not yet." Asukai shook his head and began pushing her ahead of him again.

He was already beginning to think that the spectral girl had been nothing but an illusion. His own unconscious had produced a delusional "counselor" to help him make full use of his ability.

The moment he had begun moving of his own accord, he had almost entirely ceased to see her.

In retrospect, the key phrase, "Snow Falls in April," was one he'd heard from students before. Some common fragment of the female students' unconsciousness had been giving him remarkably similar dreams, and he had allowed them to influence him.

So he had no one to help him with what he was about to do.

He had to find his own resolve and become the Imaginator. He nodded to himself. He already had.

"Technically, I'm not going to kill you," he said, in a low voice. "I'm just going to tear away your heart. You will no longer be yourself, but rather something not even worth calling human."

"............" This sinister declaration failed to have any effect on Aya's expression. "Human..." she said under her breath.

"Mm?" Asukai didn't hear her. "What did you say?"

"........." She didn't answer.

Asukai grunted in irritation, but didn't ask again.

What Aya had almost said was, *Human? I was never...*

"We have a little more time. It's still early in the evening.

People are out and about. This may cause quite a panic, so we'll wait until most people have settled down—till the middle of the night," Asukai explained. "I should have some time before the Towa Organization notices that Spooky E has failed to report in and sends someone to take care of the other systems they have placed throughout the area."

"........." Aya wondered if she even factored into those plans.

"The seed I'll make from your heart will only be strong enough to influence the people in this town. But that's enough. As long we can tell *them* from whatever the Towa Organization sends. As for the next seed, well, I'm sure a suitable candidate will emerge from the people I've planted yours on."

"How strong...an influence?" Aya asked quietly.

"Not that much. None of them would even notice. Their pain will just abruptly vanish."

"Oh..."

That was fine.

Then Masaki would be able to forget her.

They reached the roof of The Ladder. The place Spooky E had chosen as the perfect spot to disperse his "disinfectant" commanded a panoramic view of the city and of the people's lives within it.

The sky was darkening rapidly. Aya looked up into that sky and thought of how, when that light had completely vanished, she would no longer have a meaningful existence.

Man, it's a beautiful night!

She thought she heard Masaki's voice echoing in her ear. He

had said that shortly after they met, back when they were out walking together.

She smiled faintly at the memory. It was enough.

"………"

Asukai Jin looked down at her wordlessly.

This stability, even when facing her own end, was exactly what he needed.

The phone in his breast pocket rang.

"What?" he answered. Only his followers knew this number.

"Someone's approaching."

"Who?"

"Him again—the boy playing 'Boogiepop.'"

"Okay…" Asukai frowned. *So he did come,* he thought. When he spoke again, however, his voice had not lost its quiet. "Deal with him as planned."

The person replied, "Roger," and hung up.

Aya had not heard their conversation. She had not even appeared interested, as if nothing was worth paying attention to ever again.

If I told her… Asukai thought, staring at her fragile profile. *If I told her, what would she do?*

For a moment, he was tempted to find out. But of course, he said nothing. He just toyed with the notion in the back of his mind.

The motorcycle ran out of gas partway up the mountain.

"Shit—!" I swore, and dumped the bike. I climbed the rest of the way on foot.

There was no green anywhere on the mountain. It had been completely cleared, and parts of it were already paved with asphalt.

A big sign that read, "Paisley Park Construction Site" came into view, and behind it, I could see several towers and other constructions, glowing eerily in the light of the setting sun.

It was surrounded by heavy-duty fences. They looked hard to climb. Too tall, and made of smooth vertical poles leaving no footholds.

"Shit, shit, shit!" I fretted, walking along the fence, looking for a way in.

I had hoped that shaking the fence would dislodge it or knock it over, but it wouldn't budge, even though it must have been there for years.

I lost my temper again. "Damn it!" I yelled, kicking the fence.

And about ten meters away, I heard a creak.

I snapped my head towards the sound, and found a section of the fence slowly opening—an emergency exit of some kind.

(Did the latch break when I kicked it?)

I darted towards it—but heard a faint rustle and skidded to a stop.

What was it?

"............"

I moved forward again, slowly...carefully.

The sound kept going, like whatever it was was increasing.

I gritted my teeth.

The door had been opened deliberately. They were welcoming me in.

Common sense told me to retreat.

But if I had had any of that, I never would have come here in the first place. The fact that someone was waiting for me was, really, proof that I had guessed correctly. Orihata was here.

So I had to go in.

"______"

I felt briefly like I was missing something. Which embarrassed me—because I was missing my outfit. When I was wearing it, it was much easier to take on something unnatural, like I was now. It was easier to concentrate, kind of like I was hypnotizing myself into bravery.

But it was gone now. I had to do this by my own force of will.

"Let's do this," I said softly, and slipped through the fence into Paisley Park.

The half-finished, skeletal buildings cast complicated and sinister patterns across the ground in the near horizontal rays of the setting sun.

Just walking on those patterns made me feel drunk.

I hadn't noticed on the motorcycle—or while I was rushing forward—but the wind had gotten really strong.

"Orihata!" I shouted, but the wind stole my voice, and it went nowhere.

I was gonna have to check every one of these buildings.

I started walking.

Behind me, a footstep crunched the sand that lay piled on the asphalt.

Scrunch, scrunch—more than one. Several.

"............" Ready for anything, I turned around.

And was completely surprised.

"Wh-what?!!" I blurted. The five figures behind me were...

A bear.

A panda.

A penguin.

A cat.

A dinosaur.

All costumes, obviously.

And they were coming towards me.

"Wh-what the hell?!" I shouted, confused. A second later, they lunged at me, so I had to dodge quickly.

"——!" They may have been dressed like a joke, but their movements were completely serious.

Their kicks and punches were extremely accurate.

"Unh...rah!" Moving backwards, I kicked the penguin in the stomach.

But the costume cushioned the blow, absorbing the impact.

But it also twisted my foot...

Uh oh, I thought.

They weren't dressed up like this to mess with me. It was for protection! And just like I'dd with my own outfit, they were also using theirs to remain focused. They had probably found them stored somewhere in the park. After all—the stranger you look, the easier it is to do something crazy.

(So, the people inside these things are...normal?!)

Who was attacking me?

I tripped the bear and tried to run away to give myself time to figure things out. I figured the costumes would be hard to run in.

I figured wrong.

My passage was blocked by a group of clowns.

"G-gimme me a break…!"

I understood the logic behind it, but it was still bad for my heart.

I changed direction and dashed off again.

But again and again, wave after wave, people in bizarre costumes and clothing, with their faces painted purple, or yellow, or some other weird-ass color, just kept coming at me.

"Augh! Get away!"

I scrambled to avoid them.

"Nothing to be afraid of, Boogiepop-kun," one of them—too many to tell which—said.

"Nothing to be afraid of."

"Don't be scared!"

The others joined in, like a relay race, or a game of telephone.

"St-stay away!" I shouted, finding myself surrounded.

"There's no reason to be frightened, Boogiepop-kun—" they said, the same thing, over and over.

"You'll understand soon——"

No matter how many I punched or kicked, they kept on coming. It was as if they'd never heard of using caution.

"St-stop this—!" I shouted, trying to punch a new guy in the face, but he just grinned at me.

"——!"

The face under the makeup was that of a girl's. Young, probably high school.

Thrown completely, I stopped moving.

Seizing the chance, several others piled on me from behind.

"Sh-shit! Let go!!"

I slammed my elbow into them, but they were the guys in costumes, and my blows had no effect.

"Don't be afraid—"

"It'll be over soon—"

Each of my limbs was pinned down by at least three people, and I was completely unable to move.

"D-damn it!"

As I struggled, a male clown brought something towards me.

A needle.

Some sort of drug inside it.

".........!" I gulped.

"Don't worry, Boogiepop-kun. When you wake up, you'll be one of us—" he said and stuck the needle in my arm.

"N-noooo!" I screamed. But the clown's fingers pushed the end of the needle relentlessly, injecting the liquid inside into my veins.

(O-orihata—!)

Filled with rage and despair, the world grew dim before my eyes.

There was a sudden pain in my arm.

I swung my gaze that way and saw that the needle, still stuck in my arm, had been broken in two.

The clown was staring at his empty hands in surprise.

Half the needle was still stuck in me, yes—but the other half was floating in the air above my chest.

"Eh?"

The needle suddenly leapt away, like something was pulling on it.

I looked in that direction—and watched the needle fall to the ground in front of a shadowy figure.

Before I even realized what it was, I thought, *Oh, I get it. He must've yanked the needle out with some sort of microfilament wire, and that's what caused it to break and go flying towards him.*

How was I suddenly able to make such a calm analysis? My only explanation was that my brain was in such a state of panic that it couldn't figure out what else to think about.

Why? Because the shadowy figure—standing there, looking more like a pipe than a person, as if it had risen directly out of the dark ground—was a figure I knew well. All *too* well, in fact, as now I had no earthly idea of what was happening.

Did I know it?

How could I *not*?

After all the time I'd spent—

"Wh-who are you?" the clown screamed.

The figure in the black cloak answered quietly, "You already know who I am."

From the voice, it was impossible to tell if it was a man or a woman.

He reached his hand out from under the cloak. There was

a stopwatch in it. Glancing down at it, the cloaked figure said, "Three, two one," and then waved his hand.

A horrifically loud noise rocked Paisley Park.

It was—

I, Suema Kazuko, was riding up the mountain road in the evening, on the scooter my parents had bought for me.

At first, they had been opposed to me even getting a license, but once I started going to cram school and coming home so late, I was able to easily convince them it was much safer at night if I was driving something. It's at moments like this that you realize just how strangely useful it is to have such a horrible thing happen to you in the past.

Of course, my real goal was to broaden the area I could move in. I wanted to see and know all kinds of things, and this feeling was driving me onwards.

"Um?" I stopped for a moment. There was a motorcycle abandoned by the side of the road.

I put my hand on it—the engine was still warm. It looked like it had just run out of gas and been abandoned. From the way it was lying on its side, it looked like the driver had been in quite a hurry.

"Something's definitely going on," I said, swallowing.

Just as I got back on my scooter to drive on, I heard music from up ahead.

".........?" I listened closely.

I'd heard the tune somewhere before. I don't know a lot about music, but this piece was famous enough that even *I'd* heard it. It had been used in some kind of commercial or something.

"Is it Wagner...?"

"'Die Meistersinger von Numberg'?!" Asukai Jin gaped, the flamboyant music roaring all around him.

It was playing on every speaker they'd installed in the half-finished park.

There should have been no power, but the music thundered on even so.

"What's going on?!" Asukai dialed his phone, trying to figure out what was happening, but nobody answered.

Presumably the electricity had been left connected, the breakers shut off. But someone had clearly flipped them back on again.

There should have been watchmen posted throughout the park. Yet—

"——?"

Orihata Aya blinked her eyes at the bizarrely lively flood of sound.

The composer was known for extremely long, tempestuous music, and one of his loudest, most flamboyant pieces of music seemed to be trying to bring this dying park back to life.

The image in front of me wobbled.

The needle. A quarter of the contents had entered my bloodstream. Presumably, it was an anesthetic.

(Unh......)

The scenery seemed to be swaying.

Events unfolded around me like an illusion.

The clowns rushed at the cloaked figure, who waved a hand—and with that, all the clowns started falling over. And as they fell over, they slid across the ground, moving into one big pile, freezing into place like some sort of dog pile.

Like magic.

The cloaked figure started moving. The guy in the dinosaur costume leapt toward him. The cloaked figure moved his hand again, not even touching the dinosaur, but knocking him over all the same.

There was a trick to it.

He was using thread. An extremely strong, extremely thin wire.

I knew this, but... but he was barely moving, standing bolt upright—yet the way he was grabbing their legs, knocking them over, and tying them up despite their huge advantage in numbers could only be viewed as the work of a magician.

No, not a magician.

A shinigami.

Unlike me, he wasn't bothered by the gender of his opponents. He never held back, all while that music roared around him like madness itself.

The people holding me saw their companions being mowed down, and jumped up. But they were met with the same fate.

The cloaked figure stopped in front of me.

"So now we meet," he said, making a strange, asymmetrical expression. Was he smiling? Was he mocking me? "I didn't plan to come out, but if I didn't settle things quickly, a certain nosy someone was going to get herself mixed up in it."

"........." I couldn't answer.

A few more clowns and a lion attacked, but the cloaked figure dispensed with them without even swaying.

He was moving with the melody and rhythm of the music, like a conductor.

"Music is extremely effective in stirring people's emotions. Much like makeup. But music can create a response in a great number of people simultaneously. It rattles them, robs them of their rational judgment," he explained quietly, like a clergyman.

I could do nothing but stare back at him, reacting exactly as he spoke.

The drugs kept me from standing. But even they hadn't, I was so befuddled I would have toppled over of my own accord.

"Th-this is..." I could hear my own teeth chattering. "This is what I...pretended to be?"

Talk about completely out of my league; talk about nerve.

"Oh, that wasn't your fault," the "real" one nodded. "You'd been brainwashed."

He said it so easily that I couldn't grasp his meaning for a moment.

"I'd what—?"

"There should be at least one moment during your activities with Orihata Aya where your memories become indistinct. That is when Spooky E paralyzed your 'fear,'" he said, as if it was the most natural thing in the world.

"............!"

Leaving me stunned, the "real" one moved past me, heading back into the fray.

A moment later, everyone who had attacked him was lying on the ground, no longer moving. They were all unconscious.

The "real" one came back to me. Not even out of breath. He really...didn't seem human.

"You should probably take that needle out. You can move that much, right?" he said.

I noticed that half the needle was still jammed into my arm.

But the hell with *that*.

"What do you *mean*?"

"Mm?"

"Brainwashed? How?"

The "real" one shrugged beneath the cloak. "The usual fashion."

"But that's—!"

"You know I'm right," he said, calmly.

That was true.

But—

"But...then... then...I..."

I wasn't acting of my own free will?

My feelings were lies?

"I...thought I was in love with Orihata... Was that a lie as well...?" I was stunned, my mind completely blank.

The music thundered on around me.

"What have you ever thought about?" he suddenly asked.

I raised my head, dazed.

He was wavering right and left, probably because of the drugs.

"Have you ever done anything that you are totally sure was of your own free will?"

"..........."

"Adapting yourself to society is essentially being brainwashed to match societal requirements. The only difference from your situation is that the source of it is not clearly defined. There are no humans who have not been brainwashed."

"..............."

"Now the problem: within that context—within your brainwashed, restrained psyche—what do you value the most? Bound tightly by the world, what do you still desire?"

"..............."

(I'm...)

(I want...)

The music grew even louder.

And then it stopped.

(Wh-what was it...?)

Asukai Jin had a pair of binoculars out and was scanning the park below from atop The Ladder. It was almost dark, so he could barely see—but he could make out several people lying on the ground.

"What...?!"

That 'Boogiepop' could not be *this* good, surely?

Then...he was coming *here*.

"What's happening?" Orihata Aya asked. She was tied to a pillar in the center of the roof.

"We can't waste anymore time," Asukai said, his back to her. "I have to deal with you right away."

Even now, Aya's expression failed to change.

"Oh... Then get it over with," she said, peacefully.

"Okay." Asukai turned to head over to her. Suddenly, he stopped in his tracks. "......!"

He was too late.

There was a shadow standing directly behind Orihata Aya.

But...something was strange.

The shadow was shorter than Taniguchi Masaki.

"Who are you...?!" Asukai cried.

Aya turned to look behind her.

Her face stiffened. "N-no......!"

The shadow looked like it had risen directly out of the darkness. Its mouth opened. "Don't be so surprised, Camille-kun. You've been looking for me, haven't you?"

"————————"

"Wh-what?" Asukai looked at Aya, and realized that this figure was hardly her ally. "Th-then who *are* you?"

"You already know who I am," the shadow said quietly.

Asukai's head was spinning.

What in the name of god was going on? He couldn't get a grip on anything.

But...after all he'd done, he wasn't about to let anyone stop him.

"Right!" Asukai whipped out the gun he had hidden in his pocket, the one he'd stolen from Kinukawa Kotoe.

He fired without hesitation.

The shadowy figure dodged it with ease.

But by this time, Asukai had raced to Aya's side. "St-stay still and I won't have to kill you!" Asukai said, one hand around Aya, the other aimed at the shadow.

"Quite the philanthropist, Imaginator," the shadow said.

Asukai frowned. "If you know that name—!"

"Then what? You won't let me live?"

"…………"

"That's unimportant. Go ahead, do what you're going to do," the shadow said unexpectedly.

"What?"

"I mean it. Do whatever you like, see if I care."

"……………?"

"If you even *can*," the shadow said, with a trace of derision.

Asukai glanced sideways at Aya.

Her face was white with fear. She clearly viewed the shadow as an enemy.

(What the hell is he…?!)

He'd never seen anyone like this.

(Even worse: th-there's no "vision" at his chest…!)

This being was beyond the scope of Asukai's power.

(I've never seen him… I've never seen him before…so why? Why do I feel like I already know him?)

It was like he'd met something similar before…but how could he?

"What? Why hesitate now?" The shadow nagged. "Go on, get a move on."

It was as if he were looking forward to some great joke...but underneath, fundamentally, not laughing at all.

"Argh..." Asukai turned his gaze to Aya.

She shook off her fear and looked back at him.

Then closed her eyes. "Eep!"

Asukai reached for the flower on her chest.

But his hand passed right through it.

"————?"

He tried again, not believing his eyes.

But again, his hand passed right through the vision, unable to grab hold of anything.

"Wh-what? Why?" Asukai panicked.

He had done this so many times, so easily, but he couldn't do it with hers...!

"Why can't I touch it?!" he exclaimed.

Aya opened her eyes.

Her expression was tinged with loneliness.

"I thought this might happen," she said, quietly.

"What? What do you mean?"

"You wanted to do something to humans, right? That's why you needed me—but that won't work."

"Why not?!"

"Because I'm not human," she said, her voice filled with deep resignation.

"............!" Asukai's face twitched.

The shadow spoke. "See? Either way, you had already lost." It moved towards him.

"Ah..." Asukai staggered back, away from Aya. "H-how can... that be?"

"The moment you first met this girl, your loss was already decided. I may not be Sun Tzu, but clearly, 'Everything is already decided before the battle even begins.'"

"B-but this is..."

"You and this girl—whatever brought you together, whatever inexplicable, ironic twist of fate that was, I do not know, but you had already lost to it," he declared, his voice as cold as ice.

Asukai tried to remember when and how he had met Orihata Aya—but he couldn't.

"Th-that's just..."

He reeled backwards.

The shadow followed. It passed in front of Orihata Aya, chasing the retreating Asukai.

"If you only look to the future, things like this happen. Imaginator! If you believe yourself to be the only possibility, then some other possibility will arise when you least expect it and sweep your feet out from under you."

But the shadow's eyes were not looking at Asukai Jin, but at something behind him.

"Aaaaah...!" Scrambling backwards, Asukai felt his back come up against something hard.

Seven canisters, with a sinister gleam.

"......!" Asukai's eyes widened.

He reached a hand towards the valve. "In that case..." he screamed, and tried to release the vial of death contained within...

But his hand would not do it.

"Ah!"

It was shaking like a leaf.

He couldn't do it.

"It's impossible, Imaginator," the shadow said, quietly. "Completely impossible. *He* can never break through."

Whoever he was talking to, his voice sounded, for the first time, a little sad.

"All you can do is fall. No other possibility remains before you."

"Ah..."

"Even if snow *does* fall in April, Imaginator, it will only melt in the warmth of spring. It will never accumulate."

"Aaaahh..." Asukai's feet buckled under him.

A huge gust of wind swept across the rooftop.

"——!"

The wind was so strong that even Aya, tied to a pillar, had to fight against it.

The shadow was unaffected, but Asukai was knocked clean off his feet.

He rolled, headed towards the tower's edge.

"Ah...!" His expression was completely vacant, as if he had given up on everything.

The tower was incomplete, and there was no fence for safety. Even as he tumbled over the edge, Asukai reached his hands towards thin air. Even he had no idea who he was reaching for.

"........"

He opened his mouth, but no words came out. A great emptiness opened beneath him.

Wire glinted.

Several strands hurtled through the air, wrapping around the falling form before it was even out of sight.

They took the form's weight and stopped it. It hung suspended in the air...

Unmoving.

"And..." The cloaked figure, which had hurled the wires, tied them to a nearby pipe. That was all—it made no move to lift the form.

".............."

Aya's eyes widened. "Wh-what did you do?"

"Mm?"

"Did he...die? Did you kill him?"

"Oh, let's see... Well, he may have a little whiplash."

"Why did you save him?"

"He was not worth killing," the cloaked figure said.

"..........." Aya was astonished. She couldn't think what else to say.

"Without the Imaginator, how much power does he really have? He has simply returned to his former self. He is no longer my enemy."

"..........."

Aya caught her breath.

The cloaked figure's enemy...

"So..." Aya said, voice trembling. "So you...would not hold back, if there was a clear enemy?"

"Exactly." The cloaked figure briefly put his hand inside the cloak.

When it emerged again, it held a knife.

Aya gulped.

The cloaked figure came towards her.

This time, Aya didn't—*couldn't*—close her eyes. She couldn't close them.

The figure gazed directly into them, pinning her in place. She couldn't even think...

He stood before her now.

He swung the knife.

"............!"

Aya saw the blade catch the last rays of light from the setting sun.

"Ah.........!" She almost screamed...but the sound was drowned out by the snapping sound a moment later.

The knife had sliced through both the chain on her handcuffs and the rope tying her to the pillar.

"Eh?"

Ignoring Aya's confusion, the cloaked figure looked towards the seven canisters.

"I guess I can leave those. In the next couple of days, the Towa Organization is sure to be by to pick them up. Best to leave it to the experts," he said, innocently.

"Wh-why?" Aya asked, looking at her newly freed hands, then at the cloaked figure.

"Mm?"

"A-aren't I your enemy? Why did you help me?"

"How are you my enemy?"

"B-but...I... I'm not human, and..."

"Yes, you mentioned that. But that has nothing to do with anything," the cloaked figure said, decisively.

"Nothing?"

"The reason Asukai Jin was unable to harm you has nothing to do with your physical nature. After all, he had already defeated Spooky E. His corpse is over there. If it came down to physicality, that monster would have posed a far greater problem than you."

"B-but..."

"Asukai Jin seems to have seriously misunderstood his own ability. I do not know exactly what that power was, but it seems to have been something to do with seeing people's hearts. However, the human heart is not complete in and of itself, and it is not so easily understood. The heart is purely a product of communication with others, and is not to be mistaken for the true self, the ego. Asukai Jin failed to grasp this. No matter how much you change a person's heart, it will only be fleeting, and eventually, it will return to its original form."

"............."

"So from the start, I was ignoring Asukai Jin himself. No matter how much he poked at people's hearts, it would never amount to anything significant. Even if he had taken your heart from you,

you would have recovered. You see, you have something protecting you deep within."

"Eh...?"

"And because of that, a one-sided power like Asukai Jin's was unable to affect you."

Aya put her hands to her chest.

She felt like something very warm was resting there.

When she thought about it, it gave her courage. She knew it was there.

But...

"But isn't the Towa Organization your enemies? I—"

"The Towa Organization *itself* is not my enemy. I have no idea what their opinion on the matter might be, but from my point of view, sometimes their agents simply trigger my sensors."

Beneath his cape, he shrugged.

"............" Aya could think of no other arguments. This was beyond her understanding.

"If you have nowhere to go, there is a very strange girl called the Fire Witch near you. Talk to her. I'm sure she can help. She's a lot more sympathetic than I am."

Aya looked up. "B-but..." There was one more thing she had to ask. One final question. "If you were ignoring him...then why did you come here? Why did you save me?"

"Oh." The cloaked figure made a strange, asymmetrical expression, kind of like a smile, but more like a sneer. "That *is* a long story. I'll say just this—it was not my idea to save you. Someone asked me to."

"Wh-who...?"

The cloaked figure looked astonished. "Do you really not know?"

"Eh?" There was another gust of wind.

Aya hurriedly grabbed onto the pillar.

When she looked up again, she was alone on the roof.

Alone with the wind.

"Unhh! God... god damn it!!" I groaned, dragging my paralyzed body through Paisley Park. I couldn't even stand. My head was reeling. It was all I could do to stay conscious.

The "real" one had abandoned me and gone off somewhere. I gritted my teeth in desperation.

"Shit...shit!"

My hand slipped, and my chin slammed into the ground.

"Oww..." Clutching hold of my retreating consciousness, I moved forward again.

And discovered a girl in front of me.

She was on her knees, palms on the ground. On closer inspection, however, she was not actually touching anything, but instead floating just above the earth.

She was very beautiful.

"..............."

I stared at her, dazed.

She had to be a delusion. She was transparent; I could see right through her. For some reason, she was humming. It was a quiet melody, but I got the impression it was a longer, louder piece of music, and only this movement was quiet—like a moment of calm in the center of a storm. It was a very beautiful piece of music.

"And that's it," she whispered. She sounded almost relieved. Her voice was so peaceful."Asukai-sensei was too preoccupied with flaws. I knew that...but it seems flaws are merely a space for something new to be born and can never bring about enough power to break though."

She spoke in such a small voice, yet I could hear her so clearly, it was as if she was whispering directly in my ear.

She looked at me.

"You...are very impressive," she said, as if she knew me.

"............" I didn't answer.

"This is it for me, there is no more... But as long as there are people as strong as you, I'm sure someone will 'break through' one day," she said, smiling. It was an unbelievably bright, hopeful smile. The polar opposite of the "real" one's expression moments before.

Then she crumbled, like she was being crushed by something from above.

"......?!" Shocked, I scrambled over to where she had been.

There was nothing there, except a faint white stain on the ground. As if it had snowed in that one spot.

"............" I was out of it now. All the energy seemed to have been drained completely out of my body. I didn't know why, but I knew that in that moment, things had been decisively concluded. Everything was finished. The whole thing was over.

"............"

I heard footsteps behind me.

Boogiepop returns

VS Imaginator Part 2

VIII

To my eyes, you are filled
with gentle nobility.
I see a king with the power
to grant water, or a friend...
Or even an enemy, coming to
me through you.
Yet at times I know that I no
longer have any enemies.

—Antoine De Saint-Exupéry
(Terre des Hommes)

VIII.

"OH...MY...GOD!" I gaped around me. The situation in Paisley Park by the time my scooter reached it was beyond words.

People were lying on the ground everywhere, all of them in costumes or clown makeup—and all unconscious and tied up.

I know a lot about weird things, and maybe everyone says to "talk to Suema Kazuko" if something weird is going on, but even I had never read about anything as strange as this.

What the hell had *happened* here?

"Uh...umm..." I said, gingerly picking my way forward, following the path of fallen bodies in the hopes of tracking down the source.

"But...could this really be...?"

It was quiet all around me.

Certainly something strange had happened here...but could it already be finished?

Again?

Yet another mess had gone down right next to me and passed me right by?

"Why does this always happen?" I muttered, really meaning it.

I went a little further in and found someone still awake.

"Unh," he groaned.

I ran over to him. He wasn't tied up.

"A-are you okay?"

It was a boy. I hesitated for a second, but then helped him sit up.

And was surprised again.

I knew him.

"Y-you're...Taniguchi-kun?!"

He was the younger brother of a girl I knew.

"Oh...Suema-san," he said, eyes not really managing to focus on me.

"What's going on? Taniguchi-kun, what happened here?" I asked. I was getting a little frustrated, so I shook him.

"P-please, I need your help. There's a girl here somewhere... Help her..." he said, his words slurring.

"Taniguchi-kun?! Hey!!"

"Please..."

His head lolled, and he was out. I slapped and shook him, but he didn't even bat an eye. He was totally under.

"Come *on*!!!" I shouted.

I knew the world wasn't ever fair...but everything around me was pure chaos.

Something had happened—that much was certain.

Taniguchi-kun had asked me to save a girl.

If this were a fairy tale, then he was the prince. It was his job to save the princess and get his kiss.

Why did he have to leave it up to me? Why had he fallen asleep? What was up with all the crazy-looking people in makeup? Would anyone ever explain *any* of this stuff to me? Just what was my role in all of this?

I remembered back to one of Kirima Seiichi's books...

"The problem lies with your own frailty of resolve that forces simple, easy to understand answers and resolutions on others. This is the main reason the Imaginator is overrunning the world. No matter how long you wait, nothing ever begins."

When I read that, I'd thought I understood, but now that I found myself in this very situation, I desperately wanted a simple, easy to understand explanation and a happy ending. I really—

I sighed, took off my coat, and covered Taniguchi-kun with it. I wiped the sweat off his forehead and checked to see if he had a fever. It looked like it was safe to leave him alone.

"But, a girl?" I said. "*Which* girl? Who is she, Taniguchi-kun...?" I wondered aloud to myself.

Suddenly, a strange voice spoke to me. "That girl is at the top of The Ladder—the tall tower to your left."

I couldn't tell if the voice belonged to a boy or a girl.

"Wh-who's there?"

"You must go to The Ladder, and find the girl, Orihata Aya. Bring her to this boy. The man you are looking for, Asukai Jin, is hanging from the roof."

"Wh-what?!" I looked around, but I couldn't figure out where the voice was coming from.

And Orihata Aya? I was *sure* I'd heard that name before.

"Do you know what happened here?"

"Nothing of consequence."

"I'll make up my own mind!" I roared. "I need to know why something this screwed up can happen! What should I do with all the people lying here?"

"Nothing. Soon they will be leading ordinary, tedious lives again. The lives that let the Imaginator hook them..."

"Eh?"

"Forget about them. When they wake, they will know their only choice is to return to the world they left."

I couldn't understand this. My head swam. But even so—why? I felt a strange familiarity with this voice. Even though it should have been the first time I'd ever heard it...

"Your earnest strength is an admirable thing, but beware of causing worry for those around you."

"Wh-who are you?!" I yelled.

From the darkness came a strange feeling, part mocking, part feigned innocence. "You already know who I am."

Then the feeling melted away, leaving me alone.

VS IMAGINATOR PART II - "PARADE" closed.

Boogiepop returns

VS Imaginator Part 2

Epilogue

A GIRL ENTERED THE TOWER that rose out of the darkness. She pulled up the man suspended over the tower's edge, swaying dangerously. A few minutes later, a different girl emerged from the tower.

She moved along the path at a near run to where a boy lay sleeping.

Kneeling down by his side, she stroked his cheek lovingly.

"Unh... Unhhh..." the boy moaned.

A smile of purest joy rose on her face, and she waited quietly for him to wake.

Afterword

VS IMAGINATION, ETC.

(I'm blathering, so please don't take this *too* seriously.)

THERE'S AN OLD EXPRESSION, "Pretty things are dirty; dirty things are pretty." (Really.) When I first heard or read the phrase, I thought, "That's so true," without any actual basis for it. This might be a little challenging for normal people to grasp, but it just might be that the most unforgivable thing is something that really we should all be forgiving, and the most wonderful, widely accepted thing is something we should all be denying. I mean, sometimes I just sit around thinking about stuff like this: *If hatred is a kind of love, a phrase often spouted on awful melodramas, then is not love a form of hate?* And so on. Just a thought, don't really have anything to support the idea.

So I'm a pretty big fan of music, but when people ask me what kind of music I like, I always end up going, "Umm..." because I just like so many different kinds. Yet when I was in school, I was so fatally bad at music class that I wound up loathing it. I couldn't even play the recorder. My fingers wouldn't move. I never learned to read music, either. How those little tadpoles relate to music baffled me. Of course, you all must think I was stupid, but my point is that I hated music for an awfully long time. There was a pressure involved in music at school, a sort of pervasive attitude that "people who understand music are cool and have good taste," which all just made me go, "Forget that," and want to run. I wasn't able to listen to it properly until some ten years after I graduated—quite recently, actually. Now I feel like I was really missing out. Good taste has nothing to do with it; anyone can listen to good music... That whole attitude just pissed me off. I don't know what the goal of musical education was at school, but man, did it ever backfire with me. Story of my life.

When splendid, important people dispense pearls of wisdom like, "Value your imagination," or "Follow your dreams," why does it always make you want to throw up? Always makes me want to say, "Shut up and mind your own business," or "Screw imagination." I see a phrase like, "The power of imagination and positive thinking," and I want to start strapping bombs to people. I am what I am, and I'm not so good at being bright and merry. This causes me no end of trouble. I see everyone being cheery and react like I've come across something incredibly sinister. Sure, I can laugh with everyone, but that creeps me out more than anything. *Sigh*...

But this is a perfect example of why "Dirty things are pretty" is so very true. If you run into something creepy, then you still have to do something, right? But in that case, I've got to make a case for "Pretty things are dirty" just to be fair...and the more I think about it, the more I want to do something like that, which is how I'm living today.

I think everyone is really much, much more simple and uncomplicated. We're all just banging our heads into whatever is right in front of us—but the world seems to be getting along just fine. Banging our heads into things seems to work. Ain't it a shame?

(Are you even trying to write an afterword?)
(Ah, whatever...)

BGM "THE GOOD LIFE"
by NEW POWER GENERATION

Boogiepop

the Boogiepop saga continues...

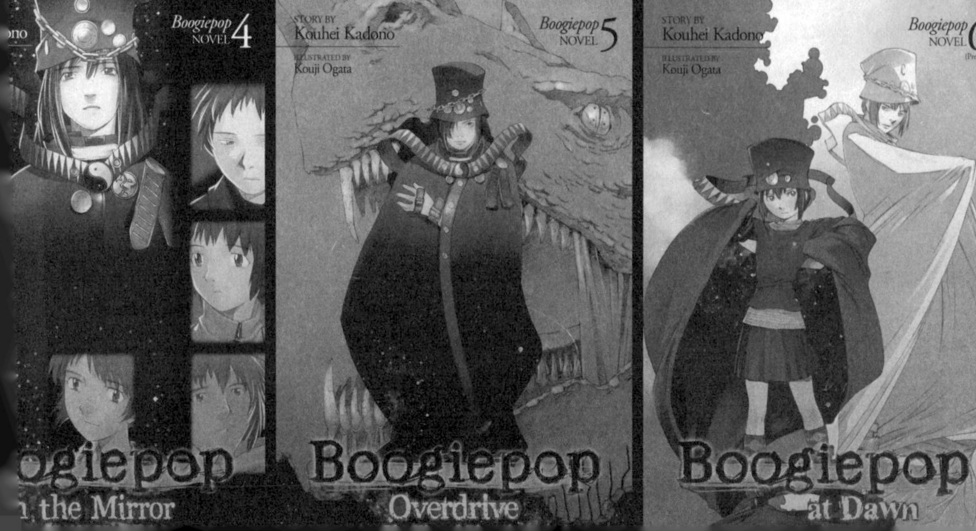